Special
Relationship

Special Relationship

R O B Y N   S I S M A N

A DUTTON BOOK

DUTTON
Published by the Penguin Group
Penguin Books USA Inc., 375 Hudson Street,
New York, New York 10014, U.S.A.
Penguin Books Ltd, 27 Wrights Lane,
London W8 5TZ, England
Penguin Books Australia Ltd, Ringwood,
Victoria, Australia
Penguin Books Canada Ltd, 10 Alcorn Avenue,
Toronto, Ontario, Canada M4V 3B2
Penguin Books (N.Z.) Ltd, 182–190 Wairau Road,
Auckland 10, New Zealand

Penguin Books Ltd, Registered Offices:
Harmondsworth, Middlesex, England

First published by Dutton, an imprint of Dutton Signet, a division of Penguin Books USA Inc.
Distributed in Canada by McClelland & Stewart Inc.

First Printing, August, 1995
10 9 8 7 6 5 4 3 2 1

Lyrics from "I Feel Like I'm Fixin' to Die Rag" by Joe McDonald are reprinted by kind permission of the publisher, Alkatraz Corner Music Co., and by Chrysalis Music Ltd.

Lyrics from "I Wanna Go Back to Dixie" © 1953 by Tom Lehrer are reprinted by kind permission of Thomas A. Lehrer.

 REGISTERED TRADEMARK—MARCA REGISTRADA

LIBRARY OF CONGRESS CATALOGING-IN-PUBLICATION DATA:
Sisman, Robyn.
    Special relationship / Robyn Sisman.
        p.   cm.
    ISBN 0-525-93872-9
    I. Title.
PS3569.I75S67   1995
813'.54—dc20   95-3796
                                                        CIP

Printed in the United States of America
Set in Sabon
Designed by Leonard Telesca

Acknowledgments

My thanks go to Carole Blake and her supremely efficient literary agency, Blake Friedmann; to Caroline Upcher for prompting new lines of thoughts; to my mother for her moral support; and to the following for practical help and information: Sean Magee, George and Marjorie Misiewicz, Lucy Sisman, Mickey Spillane of Magdalen College.

I owe two special debts. One is to Douglas Hawes, for his heartening faith in my writing ability; he has had to wait a long time for any evidence. The other, and greatest, is to my husband, Adam Sisman. Without his encouragement, inspiration, practical support, and constant constructive criticism, this book would not have been started and certainly never finished.

1992

PROLOGUE

It Was Twenty Years Ago Today

*I*t was dark outside. Jordan sat at the kitchen table, kicking the leg the way his mother always told him not to. But she wasn't home. He was alone in the house. The only sound was the scurry of wind in the cottonwood trees. Suddenly the porch door opened. A tall figure stood in the doorway, wearing a uniform. His face was shaded by his army cap, but Jordan knew, with miraculous certainty, that this was his father. Joy flooded through him. His father stepped into the room, his polished shoes eerily silent on the wooden floor. He started to walk toward Jordan, with a tread so slow and measured that it became menacing. The visor still hid his face. Jordan began to feel frightened. "It's me, your son!" he wanted to say, but no sound came from his throat.

Then the man stretched out his hand, and Jordan shrank back in terror. His father was holding a live rattlesnake. Jordan tried to get away from the table, but he couldn't move. The snake came nearer, its flat head weaving, searching. Despite his fear, Jordan felt a desperate curiosity to see his father's face. One more step would bring it into the beam of light from the kitchen lamp. Then Jordan would *know*. Jordan looked up, but under the army cap there was only blackness. He could see the cold glitter of the snake's eyes, inches from his own. The rattle of its tail grew faster, louder. Inside Jordan was screaming, "You can't do this! I'm going to be president of the United States!" His father stepped into the light—

Jordan woke with a shout of terror, his heart stampeding. A low buzzing came from an alarm clock by the bed. He slammed it quiet and sat up, taking in the bland hotel furnishings, the pile of yesterday's ransacked newspapers, his empty suit hanging like a shadow on the closet door. Pale sunlight seeped through blinds closed tight against the snooping lenses of the world's press.

"Jesus!" Jordan blew out a great gust of breath and pushed back his sweat-soaked hair. He wasn't back in Indian Bluffs. He wasn't a small, frightened boy. This was Dallas, Texas. He was forty-six years old and running for president.

Jordan got out of bed and swung his arms, easing the tension in his shoulders. It was months since he had had this nightmare. He knew what had triggered it. The call had come late last night—a voice out of his past, the voice of a girl he had once loved who now threatened to ruin his career.

No, "girl" was wrong. Jordan shook his head in self-reprimand, though there was no one to see him as he sprawled into the hotel armchair. His wife had drilled him thoroughly in the vocabulary of political correctness; besides, "girl" could no longer be an appropriate term for a forty-two-year-old woman with a grown-up son. But when he thought of her, as he had once done fiercely, passionately, a hundred times a day, and did even now, especially after one of the painfully sensual dreams that still haunted him, he always thought of her as a girl. Her responsiveness and vitality, the quick-changing flush and pallor of her skin, the bouncing energy of her long legs, the abandon with which she laughed and cried and made love—once, he remembered, all three at the same time—could surely, without offense, be called girlish.

If it had been anyone other than this particular girl he would by now have talked the matter over with Ginny—coolly, sensibly, point by point, as he discussed everything with his wife nowadays. He would have called an immediate damage-control meeting, no matter how late the hour or how tired they all were after months on the campaign trail. If it had been anyone other than this particular girl, he would have suspected a dirty tricks operation that made pinpricks of all the innuendos and FBI ferretings that he had suffered, and survived, up to now.

But the hours had ticked by while Jordan dozed fitfully, letting his wife sleep on undisturbed in the bedroom next door. Even now, when the first electronic whines from the outer room of the suite that served as his temporary campaign office told him that some eager beaver was stoking the fax machine, Jordan sat calmly sipping his Ozark Mountain Spring Water, remembering.

Bare willow trees, warm beer, bicycles swishing through rain, the peppery smell of the Lower Reading Room, gas fires that lit with a *whump* and ran out of money. He had never been so cold in his life. Or so lost. It was as if he had passed into a looking-glass world that turned all his values upside down and disparaged the very talents that had brought him to Oxford in the first place. His manner was wrong, his jokes were wrong, his ideas were wrong.

Until he met Annie. She was the rightest thing that had ever happened to him.

This wasn't a trick, he was sure of it. He couldn't have mistaken her voice. But *why now?* In 1970 she had disappeared from his life with a thoroughness that a retiring spy might have envied, and eventually he learned to file her away in the mental drawer marked "Oxford," an era in his life that privately, despite the powerful allies he had picked up there, was also labeled "failure." How dare she reenter his life now, of all times, demurely laying this ticking bomb at his feet?

When breakfast came he had no appetite for it; nor for the jubilant congratulations that accompanied the morning's newspapers, which conceded, with varying degrees of enthusiasm, that Jordan Hope's chances were looking good. He played his part successfully enough—he had always been good at that—but with secret anxiety hammering at his heart. As he got ready for his speech, the intoxicating headlines spread over his worktable mocked him. There were only six more days to go, and the whole damned circus was riding on his shoulders. Nobody knew how hard he had worked for this, how long he had planned. Not Shelby, who went way back to Miss Purvis's class in that funny old schoolhouse that had been turned into a museum. Not Rick, who had seen him at his best and his worst and had always kept his mouth shut. Not even Ginny. The thought of Ginny made him twist his fingers viciously in his hair and groan softly. She wanted this as much as he did. She had to, after what she'd sacrificed.

Jordan could pinpoint the exact moment when the mixture of emotions that had raged within him as a boy—tenderness, hate, resentment, yearning, guilt, fear—had coalesced into an adamantine spike of pure ambition. He could remember in hallucinatory detail the brilliant green of the lawn, so different from the yellow scrub of his own backyard. The heavy scent of the roses—imagine having a whole garden just for roses! The dampness of his palm, which he had anxiously wiped on the thigh of his Boys' Nation regulation trousers. The immaculate little triangle of handkerchief that peeked out of the president's breast pocket. Above all, the way those candid, forgiving eyes had seemed to look into his heart and see nothing unworthy of that sunburst smile of approval, almost of complicit acknowledgment. Jordan had truly felt as if the hand of God were pointing straight out of a cloud, like those pictures back in Bible class, in a shaft of light that burned straight into his soul. *This is my beloved son, in whom I am well pleased.*

For the team, it was just a publicity gimmick. Jordan was to be packaged as Kennedy reincarnated—young, energetic, idealistic, with a gorgeous wife. Only no bad stuff. No Marilyn Monroes, you hear? And, please, no Lee Harvey Oswalds, Rick had drawled. But for Jordan that moment almost thirty years ago when he and JFK had clasped hands was sacred. He had a mission to carry on where Kennedy had been stopped dead in his tracks just three months later—but in his own style, on behalf of his own generation.

Now he was so close it hurt. If the people would only give him a chance, he knew that he could do it. He understood their problems. Hell, he had been there himself. Poverty, racism, alcoholism, unemployment, corruption—they had been part of his everyday world from his earliest memories. They had been the spurs that drove him to ever more spectacular heights of achievement. Which was more than could be said for those carping media snobs who portrayed him as some down-home boy getting a mite uppity. He would show them. There were no prizes for losers. Adlai Stevenson, Barry Goldwater, Michael Dukakis, and all the other almost-presidents—what had they been able to achieve without the ultimate mandate of real power? Jordan Hope, president of the United States of America. From Indian Bluffs, Illinois, to Washington, D.C. From clapboard shack to White House. That was what he wanted. That was what he was going to get.

Jordan wasn't sure that he could manage this crisis alone. It would help if he could take somebody into his confidence—but who? Ginny was out. Shelby had always idolized Jordan in his good ol' boy way, without a trace of envy; on the other hand, he had the subtlety of a jackrabbit in the mating season. Besides, he would be shocked. Jordan swept his hands through his hair and shook his head like a swimmer. Rick was much more suited to the role of go-between. At Oxford his parties had been legendary and his first a foregone conclusion. He cruised the political shadows like a shark masquerading as a dolphin. He had pledged his allegiance to Jordan's cause and proved to be a public relations genius. But something made Jordan hesitate.

The intercom crackled. "Five minutes," sang a cheerful voice.

Shit. For a moment Jordan tuned in to the buzz of activity coming from the outer room of his suite: phones, faxes, TVs, urgent voices shouting across each other. "Who's got the schedule?" "Milwaukee wants to know, can we confirm Thursday?" "I'm saying no to Jay Leno and the saxophone show, okay?" "Two points ahead in, wait for it, *New Hampshire*!" They were a great team. He loved every one of them. He couldn't let them down.

Five minutes. For a scary second he couldn't even remember what town he was in. For months he'd been carrying a whole raft of speeches in his head. Detroit meant Japanese car imports and gun laws. Florida meant pensions and immigration. Kentucky was GATT, God, and horses. What the heck was Dallas? Up until now he hadn't put a foot wrong. The hand of God was on him. Like Elijah, when he opened his mouth to speak the right words just poured out.

She must have used every ounce of ingenuity to get hold of him. Even his mother had trouble getting through. Letters were opened, faxes scanned. All conversations were taped, all messages filed, every call-back telephone number logged in the computer. As well as screening out the weirdos—there had already been over a hundred assassination threats—a record had to be kept of promises made, funds pledged, deals done. It was also, he knew, the team's way of keeping tabs on him.

Time to go, Jordan.

Time. It was a rarity to get even five minutes alone. How was he going to slip his leash for several hours? What would it be like to see Annie again?

"We have nothing to fear except fear itself." This had been Jordan's mantra since the day he had gotten his college scholarship, and it had served him well. He repeated it now as he put on the pressed dark jacket and sober tie that had been chosen for his forthcoming speech, just as yesterday's jeans and corduroy jacket had been judged appropriate for California. He flashed himself his heart-throb smile in the closet mirror while the surface of his mind automatically reshuffled the familiar phrases. Change. Hope. The economy. The deficit. Maybe his Stetson joke, if the mood was right. Dallas meant oil, banking, the aerospace industry. Dallas meant Neiman Marcus and the Cowboys. Dallas meant Kennedy.

But while the autocue played in his head, the wheels of memory whirled and clicked on another loop. Oxford. The summer of 1970. Moonlight on the Cherwell, the throbbing rhythm of the Doors, and Annie silky and warm under his hands.

Annie. Of course it had been her voice, that actressy huskiness softening the crystalline consonants. Typically she had come straight to the point. The curious thing was that, amid the flood of disbelief and despair that engulfed him, Jordan had also felt an unmistakable surge of elation.

Jordan, I have a son. He thinks you're his father, and he's coming to find you.

1

Picture This

Tom rested his arms on the broad stone windowsill and leaned into the misty air, chilly and sharp with wood smoke. He was actually here. He had made it. For a moment he listened to the echoing offbeat chiming of many bells. Soon he would learn to distinguish the deep note that boomed from Sir Christopher Wren's gatehouse tower at the entrance to the college—*his* college—marking the quarter hours for anyone in central Oxford, from scurrying shoppers in the tinselly malls of St. Ebbe's to the most reclusive don toiling in a corner of Duke Humfrey. Now it was lost in a pleasing jumble, evoking a collage of hazy images in Tom's mind: medieval monks, Jude the Obscure, Sebastian Flyte with his teddy bear. Taking a final look at his view—a typical first year's allotment of lead roofs, twisting stone pinnacles, and a triangle of gray sky—he pulled the casement window closed and turned to survey the eccentrically shaped room under the eaves that was to be his home for the next year.

His father had looked askance at the stained pseudo-Persian carpet and the worn leather chairs leaking stuffing at the elbows. Tom hoped that he hadn't noticed that someone had carved "Oxbridge Sucks" into one of the desks. Dad could be incredibly high-minded. Possibly he would have been more hearty in his approval of the modern residential block, but its boxy uniformity held no charm for Tom. There was more to life than showers that worked. Here he could feel the aura of history, of young lives lived to the full, even, perhaps, a very faint echo of Evelyn Waugh's county families baying for broken glass.

Or had he already fallen under the spell of Aldworth's tall stories? Aldworth was to be Tom's scout, an elderly man with burgundy cheeks and badger-striped hair and the burr of rural Oxfordshire still strong in his speech. He had chanced upon Tom and his father taking a breather on Tom's trunk in the middle of one of the court-yards and offered to show them the way. Any egalitarian squeam-ishness Tom might have had about servants evaporated when Aldworth gave Tom's baggage a glance of magnificent disdain and, like the family butler in some horror movie, led them to Tom's room, pausing ceremonially at each landing as Tom and his father breathlessly manhandled his trunk up the sharply angled stone stairs. At the sight of a whiskey bottle that Tom's father unexpect-edly produced as a roomwarming present, Aldworth graciously ac-cepted a generous measure in a mug and set out to live up to his reputation as a Character. Tom heard about the young gentleman who had thrown his bed into Mercury pond, the young gentle-man who used to take Aldworth to the races, having provided him with a hundred-pound betting stake, and the young gentleman who had been sent down after being found with not one but two young ladies in his room. "*And* one of them of royal blood. But that would be going back a good bit now. Nobody cares what the undergrad-uates get up to nowadays, young gentlemen and females higgledy-piggledy all over the college."

When Tom's father, with an amused lift of his eyebrow, said he'd better be getting back to London—"and don't forget to ring your mother tonight"—Aldworth accompanied him, leaving Tom with the clutter of trunks and suitcases, cardboard boxes, squash rac-quets, lamps, and coats that now confronted him. Not all the stuff was his, of course. Tom would be sharing this room with Brian, a tall guy in a baseball cap who had dumped his baggage before going off to have tea with his parents. He had looked okay, though his belongings were a good deal flashier than Tom's. He had brought an elegant black halogen reading lamp and a set of matching olive suitcases that easily outclassed the paint-stained light and wooden-ribbed trunk that Tom had wrested from the cobwebbed corners of his parents' attic.

Tom dragged the trunk into his bedroom, an unheated cubicle

with an iron bedstead, a chest of drawers, and a basin scarred with lime scale. Brian had its identical twin next door. Tom opened the trunk and stared gloomily at the jumble of his belongings. Inside the lid his mother's name was written in large, neat capitals, which had later been elaborated into a swirling, psychedelic design bright with stylized flowers and eye motifs. She had done it herself, he supposed. It was funny to think of his mother being young, though she had been a student here herself, back when everyone had to wear gowns and all the colleges were single sex.

Tom yanked out his shiny new kettle, Walkman, tapes, umpteen books, and dumped them on the floor. In a nest of socks he found his Prague poster and unrolled it carefully. He had already decided to hang it above the little Victorian mantelpiece next door. Here were his photos, and he sat back on the heels of his sneakers and riffled through them. There was a brilliant one of Rebecca, grinning at him through a tangle of dark hair. He couldn't help smiling back. His "older woman," he called her— six months older, anyway, and already in her second year at Sussex—a wonderful and mysterious being whom he had met just a few weeks ago. He hoped she wasn't going to fall for some Sussex stud. Then there was Mum and Dad, his sisters, him under the arch of the Brandenburg Gate, and all his other photos from last year. The trip to Eastern Europe had been his reward for getting into Christ Church, even if it was his second attempt. Maybe he'd find a more intelligent audience here than he had encountered at home, where his sister Cassie had dogged his footsteps, melodramatically intoning "It is an ancient brother and he stoppeth one in three." She was studying the Romantics at school.

He was just finishing when he heard a knock on the door. Shouting "Come in!" he lifted out the last wad of underpants and T-shirts. Clothes were easy. Apart from one decent jacket and shirt, he had operated on the brilliantly simple principle of packing nothing that would ever need ironing.

Aldworth appeared in the doorway. "Dinner in Hall at seven-thirty. And if you want to get rid of that, there's a storage room down the bottom. Give you a hand with it, shall I?"

"Great." Tom flipped the trunk shut, not bothering to fasten it, and he and the old man took hold of the worn handles at each end. "Have you always been at the House?" he asked as they maneuvered through the door, somewhat self-conscious at using the college's nickname for the first time.

"Fifty years, man and boy. Apart from the war. I was in the desert, mending tanks. And bloomin' hot and thirsty work it was too. Still, we had them on the run in the end."

Tom tried to work out how old that made Aldworth. Even if he'd started at Christ Church when he was fifteen, he must be practically seventy now. Christ. They said scouts were a dying breed. From the way Aldworth was puffing away, Tom just hoped he wasn't going to expire on the spot.

"I suppose the college has changed a lot in your time."

"It has. We've had the young ladies now six years. And the new block, of course. Nice little cottages they knocked down—and for what? Load of bloomin' egg boxes. The last duel in the history of the university was fought there. Young gentleman shot his friend over a female." Aldworth sighed heavily, as if the decline in the ritual slaughter of undergraduates were a matter for regret. Perhaps it was this that made him relax his hold on the trunk, for as they neared the top of the final landing Tom felt the whole weight of the empty trunk hanging from his hand, before the old leather strap snapped and the trunk catapulted end over end down the steps, socking Aldworth on the way.

Tom clattered down anxiously to him. "Are you all right?"

Aldworth pointedly brushed down the sleeve of his jacket and then chuckled. "Take more than that to do for me."

Together they retrieved the battered trunk and stowed it in the storeroom. Tom waited politely while Aldworth locked it again with maddening solemnity. Then, apologizing again, Tom took the stairs two at a time back to his room. He was just in time to witness the protracted good-byes between Brian and his parents, a jovial golf-club sort of man in a blazer and his hair-and-teeth wife. Brian withstood the usual parentspeak about work, late nights, and the existence of launderettes before closing the door with a mighty exhalation of breath.

"Parents." He hurled himself into one of the armchairs. Tom nodded in solidarity.

Over the next half hour, the two of them fenced around the ground rules of cohabitation. The Prague poster could stay as long as Brian was allowed to put Paul Merson on the other wall. (Bloody hell, Tom thought, an Arsenal fan.) They would use Brian's brand-new bicycle helmet, which he wouldn't be seen dead in, as the communal kitty for buying coffee and tea. They would both try out for rowing and the college football team. They would have a tremendous party as soon as they knew enough people.

They sealed their agreement with Tom's whiskey, and he went into his bedroom to get changed while Brian put up his picture. Off with the jeans and checked workshirt; tonight the jacket and decent shirt would get their first airing. Through the open door he could hear voices. Aldworth was back again, engaged with Brian in a competitive discussion of cup finals. Tom wandered back in to the living room, shirttails trailing, and eavesdropped on a blow-by-blow account of England's legendary defeat of West Germany in 1966, which Aldworth claimed to have witnessed in person. "We had them bang to rights," the old man said gleefully, "just like in the war." Catching sight of Tom, he gave him a wink. "I've put your young lady on the mantelpiece," he said incomprehensibly. With a last word to Brian about the college team, he took himself off again.

"Crazy old tortoise," Tom said. "What was he on about?"

"Dunno. Something about a photo falling out of your trunk. It's up there."

Crazy or no, there was a photo on the mantelpiece. Tom picked it up, frowning. It wasn't one of his. For a start, it was obviously old. The color had faded. Nobody produced photos like this anymore—small and square, with a white margin all the way around. Even more mystifying, it was not a picture of a girl by herself, as Aldworth had implied. There were two people in the photo, a laughing couple about Tom's age sitting on the grass with their arms around each other, squinting into the sun. The man had tousled coppery hair and a big cheesy grin. Cuddling into his chest, spilling golden hair across his shirtfront, was a girl in a white dress. Behind them was the corner of a red-brick building. With a shock Tom realized that the girl was his mother. The man he had never seen before.

"It *is* yours, then, is it?" Brian asked curiously.

"I suppose so." Tom flapped it casually, and as he did so he noticed that there was something written on the back. He took the photo into the privacy of his bedroom. There was something about it that was oddly unsettling. His mother looked so—well, so unlike his mother, or anyone's mother. Young and wild. And incredibly happy.

The writing was bold and loopy, set at a diagonal across the blank back of the photograph. Tom read, "For Annie, my two-times girl. Love always. J."

For a long while Tom sat on his bed, gazing into the faces and rereading the corny message, though neither needed much interpretation. Here was a young couple wildly, obviously in love. Abruptly he shoved the photo in with the others in his rickety bedside table. He banged the drawer shut. Tucking in his shirt, he moved over to the basin to wash the grime of unpacking off his hands. As the water filled the basin, he looked absently into the mirror above it. His hair needed smoothing down. He flicked the drops of water from his hands, then stopped dead. He could feel his heart begin to pound. The trickle of water was suddenly loud in his ears.

The photo. Aldworth had confused him by saying it was a picture of Tom's girlfriend. Now he knew why. Aldworth had thought that the man in the photograph was *him*. The reason was staring him in the mirror. He and the man could have been brothers.

2

It's Alright, Ma
(I'm Only Bleeding)

"*Benedictus benedicat. Per Jesum Christum dominum nostrum. Amen.*"

From the dais a bulky figure in black said grace with the casual disdain of a judge passing sentence, then turned his back with a flourish of scarlet lining. Tonight was the first official dinner of Michaelmas term. As the dons clustered around High Table, nodding and bobbing in their academic gowns of crimson and blue and lilac, they resembled a particularly prize collection of endangered fowl. Below them the undergraduates settled themselves noisily like so many common crows.

Tom forced himself to concentrate on details. Squat, shaded lamps punctuated the polished length of two dozen or more refectory tables, lighting up the faces of his companions and sending a golden glow into the Great Hall. Wood paneling rose to a height of some thirty or forty feet, broken by vast fireplaces and soaring Gothic windows. Then stone took over, culminating in the spectacularly carved and studded hammerbeam ceiling. Christ Church was not tops academically, nor were its history results the best in the university, but on his tour round Oxford Tom had fallen in love with it. This was the hall where Charles I had assembled his parliament during the Civil War, where Dean Liddell had entertained the young mathematics lecturer who was to immortalize his daughter in *Alice's Adventures in Wonderland*. Portraits by Gainsborough, Reynolds, Millais, Orpen, Sutherland, and lesser artists cluttered the walls in what was a very grand version indeed of family snapshots on a kitchen bulletin board. Tom recognized one or two—Anthony Eden, Gladstone, was it?—but of the dozens of faces that loomed out of the shadows most were just that. Faces. A stray line from Shakespeare wormed its way into his mind. "There's no art to find the mind's construction in the face." Faces could tell you things. Perhaps it didn't take an Old Master to do the trick. Perhaps even an old snapshot would do.

A plate of soup was put before him, and automatically he began to eat. He wasn't hungry, but Brian had just assumed they would go in to supper together and Tom hadn't been able to think of a reason not to. The reason was there, though, sticking into his brain like a thorn. *Love always. J.*

Conversations ebbed and flowed around him. A group of men opposite had clearly been at school together. They were boisterously swapping stories of somebody called Charlie, a figure of legendary rebelliousness. Next to Tom two women students seemed to be having some impenetrable feminist discussion. He had been abroad for so long that he was out of touch. "I agree that she shouldn't have to bake cookies," one was saying, "but then why does she feel she has to highlight her hair?" He tuned back in to Brian's story of his summer as a camp counselor in Maine, a tangled account of water-skiing feats and forbidden encounters with female campers. Tom nodded and exclaimed at what seemed appropriate points. He felt completely removed from the scene, as if his head were encased in a glass bubble.

Loads of people looked like each other, he thought. How often had he mistaken a complete stranger for a friend, if only for a brief moment or at a distance? It would be madness to read anything into the fact some man in some crummy old photo looked rather like him. Except that it wasn't just "some man"; it was someone whom his mother had known. Had known damn well, in fact. *Annie, my two-times girl.* Whatever that meant.

There was something else too, the thing he privately called the Quarrel, though he had never discussed it with another living person. For as long as he could remember, it had descended on the family without warning, like a black cloud. Conversations missed a beat, stories faltered. There were whispers in the hall, warning frowns across the dinner table. It had something to do with a fight between his mother and her family before he was born. To Tom,

Grandma and Grandpa meant Dad's parents. For years he had spent a part of every summer at their house near Cuckmere Haven, roaming the cliffs and learning to sail.

But on his mother's side there was a black hole that had simply sucked in the sort of anecdotes and recollections that were common currency in most families. He didn't even know exactly how old his mother was. Her coyness about her age was a family joke. Whenever they traveled as a family, she was guardian of the passports and never allowed anyone to see what she called the Hammer Horror of the Photobooth. Her father had died before Tom was born. The last time he had asked about her mother—his grandmother—she had said flatly, "I don't know where she is and I don't care."

A hand removed Tom's soup bowl and replaced it with a plate of sole with baby vegetables. In response to Brian's questions, Tom embarked upon his party piece about the drunken soldiers he had encountered in Slovenia. At home he was accused of embellishing this story with new and ever more death-defying details each time he told it, but tonight he wasn't doing it justice. He couldn't concentrate.

Odd memories kept floating into his head. His little sister's bossy voice as she took a visitor through the family photograph album. "And here's me again when I was a little baby. Wasn't I sweet? There are hardly any of Tom because Mummy and Daddy were too poor to have a camera." And Cassie, the family drama queen, wailing "How come Tom gets the gorgeous curls and the rest of us have this mousy *string*? It's not fair."

He remembered his tenth birthday, the best ever. Dad had taken him and five chosen friends to see *Raiders of the Lost Ark* the very week it opened. A ride into town on the top of a double-decker, hamburgers and fries for lunch, popcorn during the film and ice cream after, and larking about on the way home. In the evening his friends' parents came to collect them, lingering interminably, talking of nothing. Somebody's mother, flushed and laughing, burst out: "I feel such an idiot—thinking you were the nanny, I mean. It's only that you look so young compared to the rest of us. You must have been a child bride." What Tom remembered particularly was the look his mother had given him—a split-second glance of such electric intensity that he could still feel the bubbly texture of the wallpaper under his fingertips. At the time he could not fathom that look. It was simply catalogued with the many other inexplicably charged moments of childhood. Now he could decode it effortlessly. It was panic.

Tom was beginning to feel very peculiar. The heat of closely packed bodies had raised the temperature to an unpleasant level. His stomach was churning the way it did before an exam. He looked around for the jug of water, but it was out of reach. He refilled his glass from a bottle of wine in front of him and swigged it down. Across the table another story of the infamous Charlie was reaching its rowdy climax. Over the roar of a hundred different conversations he heard the exuberant voice: "Drunk? I tell you, Charlie wouldn't have recognized his own father—" Tom felt sweat break out across his back. Muttering something to Brian, he climbed over the bench and ran out of the hall.

Cold air swept up the broad stone stairway to meet him. Idiotic fragments ran through his head. *When did you last see your father? Honor thy father and thy mother. It's a wise child that knows his own father.* He made himself count the steps down . . . thirteen, fourteen, fifteen. The clatter of plates and cutlery faded. At the turn of the landing he slumped against the newel post, cooling his cheek on the stone.

Who *was* that man, the mysterious "J"? Ridiculously, Tom at once felt jealous of him and furious with his mother. He was frightened too, as if a private terror that had stalked him for years had finally stepped out of the darkness.

At home he had a shoebox crammed with postcards from all over the world, each with a one-line message. *Wellington trounced Napoleon here. Ate a live shrimp today! The boy in this painting reminds me of you.* They were invariably signed "All my love, Dad." He had never missed, even if it was a short trip. The best thing was that they were always addressed to him alone—not the family, not his sisters. It was a special thing between him and his father, man to man. Father to son.

Impossible to question this bond. Impossible not to.

Tom walked slowly back toward his rooms through the frosty night. He paused at the bank of phones at the foot of his staircase. Why not? He had promised, after all.

She answered at the first ring, sounding brisk and busy. She was grilling steaks, she said, "but I'm taking them out *this minute,* so we can talk. It's lovely to hear from you, darling. You must have a thousand more exciting things to do." Hearing the warmth in her voice, picturing her wandering about the kitchen with a wooden spoon in her hand and no shoes on, Tom felt a sudden rush of love.

"Is Dad all right?" he asked.

"Of course he is. He's right here, reading about the cricket. Do you want a word?"

"No, I just—Mum, who's 'J'?"

"Jay who?"

"No, the letter *J*. I found something in that old trunk of yours, signed 'J.' "

There was the smallest of pauses before she asked, "What sort of something?"

"A photo."

"Of who?"

"That's what I'm asking you." Let her squirm a bit, Tom thought. If there was a mystery about this man, he wanted to know.

"I don't know, Tom," she said impatiently. "Are we playing Twenty Questions? What makes you think I know him anyway?"

Him, she said. Tom hadn't said whether it was a man or a woman. She must know perfectly well who "J" was.

"Because you're in the photo too. Looking rather friendly with old 'J.' "

"It could be anybody. There was a boy I went out with in Malta once called Jonathan. Is there anything else written on it?"

" 'For Annie, my two-times girl. Love always. J.' "

Tom heard a catch of breath. Was it a gasp or a sigh?

"That sounds like him. Very romantic and very dull. And an awfully long time ago. Now, Tom: football boots. I don't know how you and your father managed to forget them, but they're still here, under the hall table. Shall I post them?"

And that was that. They talked inconsequentially until his money ran out, and Tom put down the phone feeling outmaneuvered. Back in his room, he took the photo out and looked at it again. Maybe the man didn't really look that much like him. It was just that they had similar hair. He couldn't even see the color of the eyes.

Jonathan, a boy she had known in Malta. He supposed this was plausible. What, after all, did Tom know about his mother's life before he was born? She never talked much about herself, probably because no one ever asked. Putting together the little he did know —only child, a succession of boarding schools, problems with her mother, an adored father who had died—it struck Tom that hers might not have been an ideal childhood. Perhaps that was why she was so particularly brilliant at planning special treats. He thought of the Easter egg hunts, the surprise outings to the zoo, on the river, to a restaurant, the longed-for gifts that appeared with a fanfare just as one had abandoned all hope. She *seemed* happy. Tom felt a clutch at his heart. He didn't want anything to change.

Damn Aldworth. Why did the old idiot have to let go of the trunk? Why couldn't he have left the photograph where it lay? It must have been in the lining or perhaps one of those fancy little elasticized pockets. There was probably no mystery, except in his own head.

That night, in his cold, narrow bed, Tom turned back and forth on the squeaky springs. There went the bells again, marking the passing of each quarter of an hour, jangling and clashing like the thoughts in his head. He was still awake when Brian came in, well after midnight, swearing at the furniture. Tom counted six more quarters and at last fell asleep.

3

Tracks of My Tears

*A*nnie held her front door open with a slim, Ferragamo-shod foot, running a mental check. Note to cleaner—check. Chicken out of freezer—check. Bag, keys, daily planner, briefcase, spare panty hose for tonight's party—check. Wallet? For heaven's sake, she wasn't a complete moron. Annie banged the door shut, hard enough to make the Georgian fanlight quiver, and at that precise moment remembered the football boots. With a growl of exasperation she unlocked the door again, retrieved the boots from the kitchen table where she had placed them ready in a plastic shopping bag, and started again. As she was double-locking the door, she caught sight of her bus sailing down the hill toward her and sprinted for the bus stop, bags banging at her legs. She took her place in the queue behind a man in an elegant camel coat who appeared to be carrying nothing but his travel pass. How did men manage it? The only woman she knew who passed serenely through life carrying nothing more than a shoulder bag the size of a piece of toast was Rose. But then she went everywhere by limousine.

Annie found a seat and unzipped her briefcase. She took out a plastic folder and slid out a bundle of typescript. If she got paid for the hours of reading she put in every day commuting to and from work, she would be a rich woman. Today it was an outline for a book on arms dealing, by one of her writers who had become a successful television newsmagazine host. Though prodigiously talented, he had the attention span of a setter puppy, and she feared that some new cause would claim his enthusiasm before the ink on the contract was dry. On the other hand, his last book had been a bestseller. It had also been, she reminded herself, a sizzling account of a royal scandal. Somehow armament sales to the Gulf didn't have the same allure.

The word *scandal* set up reverberations in Annie's head. Her concentration slipped. As the gray London buildings slid by, her hands tightened unconsciously around the plastic parcel of football boots. How could she have been so stupid as to leave that old photo in her trunk? The image of Tom blundering around Oxford with a photograph of her and Jordan made her want to sob out loud with anxiety. For years she had successfully impersonated a typical, middle-class professional woman. She had worked hard, checked her children's homework, and kept the freezer stocked and the front hedge clipped, just like a grown-up person. She had made every effort to bolt the door on the past, constructing a version of events so close to the truth, so fiercely defended, that she had begun to believe it impregnable. If memory and desire could not be so easily silenced, that was her problem. But for Tom it was different. He was an open-hearted boy, guileless and uncomplicated. As a baby he had been a charmer, chuckling at her with such innocent delight that even on her most suicidal days he had lifted her spirits. In his teenage years the reign of loutish pimpledom had been mercifully brief. He would breeze through life happily enough—drawing friends to him, finding doors of opportunity swinging open as if to a magic password—as long as nothing damaged the core of his identity. But he was still young enough to be stampeded into doing something stupid.

Had he believed her story about the photograph? Like the best lies, it was partly true. When she was sixteen, a boy named Jonathan had invited her to a tennis dance. Her mother had insisted on putting Annie's hair up into an elaborate arrangement stiff with hair lacquer, which drew Jonathan's wondering gaze. She had no idea how to behave with boys and veered between tongue-tied shyness and arch ripostes. On the dot of eleven he had brought her home, thanking her with a chill formality that could still curl her toes with mortification. But Tom was not to know that. She could only hope it would not strike him that the background was not very Mediterranean, for she remembered that photo. She remembered every detail of that day, and of the previous night, and of each moment she had spent with Jordan. Whenever she saw his picture in the papers—

wholly familiar, yet unreal—she wondered whether he remembered too.

As the bus neared her usual stop, Annie guiltily gathered up the unread script and stowed it away. Everything would be all right, she told herself. Tom was a happy-go-lucky boy with all the temptations of Oxford at his feet. Surely an old photograph would not be enough to distract him.

Annie took her usual route through the alleyways that joined Charing Cross Road to St. Martin's Lane and led into Covent Garden. Smith & Robertson was one of a dwindling number of literary agencies still left in the old heartland of London publishing. Positioned halfway between the covered market and the Strand, its offices occupied the top three floors of a sturdy Victorian building that old Mr. Smith had had the foresight to buy outright. There was no elevator and the decor was strictly 1950s grunge. Pigeons warbled maddeningly on the window ledges and occasionally one fell down a disused chimney in a shower of soot. Some people liked to complain about the area—too many tourists and tramps and overpriced boutiques, not enough ordinary shops where you could get milk or shampoo. Annie adored it. Where else could you buy a nineteenth-century edition of Gibbon and a Madonna-style bustier, eat ten different types of cuisine, take tap-dancing lessons and bump into Maggie Smith or Pavarotti on a rehearsal break—all within a half-mile radius? Besides, running up and down three flights of stairs kept her in shape. At the office door Annie tapped in the code on the electronic entry box and let herself in.

The reception area was still empty. Annie liked to get to work early, before the phones started, and nowadays only hired secretaries who were prepared to do the same. Sally was her latest, an Australian raised on a cattle farm, whom no crisis or bizarre request could ruffle. Her personal reading material did not stretch beyond gossip magazines, but it was typical that she took Annie's request to post the football boots without a blink.

"Jack's in," Sally said. "He wants to see you at nine-thirty."

"Oh," Annie said flatly.

"And"—Sally smiled broadly—"the GWH has delivered his last chunk."

Annie whirled round. "He has? Why didn't you say? Where is it? Did you read it? Is it good?"

Sally held up a hand like a traffic cop. "It's on your desk. And I didn't even peek. Would I spoil it for you?"

Annie strode into her office, half out of her coat, and hurried round to the other side of her desk. As always, her mail was in three piles. On top of the priority pile was a blue folder with a note pinned to it: "Any good?—Sebastian." Annie smiled. Sebastian Winter, her Great White Hope. What a nincompoop he was.

Two years ago she had suggested that he should try his hand at fiction. At thirty, he already had a column in a prestigious newspaper and three nonfiction books to his name, but Annie had a hunch that he just might have the talent for a blockbuster. After a long silence, he had come up with a plot that put a wholly original spin on the Nazi thriller—an idea so powerful and so different that she had felt the pricklings of excitement which come an agent's way only once or twice in a lifetime. Over the months she had coaxed, cajoled, threatened, flattered, and finally shamed him into producing the first hundred pages. Last July they had landed on her desk, accompanied by a diffident note in which Annie could read his terror of failure. In jitters herself, she had stayed up late that night, reading with rising jubilation. If she knew anything about anything, this was going to be a bestseller. She had called him at once. It was well after midnight, but she had long ago learned that there was no such thing as an inconvenient moment for telling an author good news. The next day they had met for lunch at Orso's and downed two bottles of champagne, hysterical with mutual congratulation. It was only as Annie was making her way tipsily back to the office that acid reality curdled the *crostini da basilica* in her stomach. She had better make a success of this—a spectacular mega-success, in fact—or she might as well start looking for another career.

Over the summer news of the book leaked out to publishers. By September she was besieged by requests for an early look at the manuscript. It was just at the time when editors were slinking back from their holidays in Umbria or the Dordogne, hungry to boost their reputations with a splashy buy. Annie took another gamble and, while interest in London was raging, offered the unfinished script at auction. The auction stretched to four days and was finally concluded at a figure exactly twice what Annie had dared hope. Just as she had planned, the British companies had leaked the script to their American partners, and now they too were hot for it. Where New York led, Europe and Japan would follow. Maybe even Hollywood. With the right director it would make a sensational film. Earlier this month Annie attended the Frankfurt Book Fair, as usual. She had been showered with invitations to dinners and exclusive parties and tête-à-tête drinks. On her last night, a gravel-voiced American publisher of legendary ego made her a preemptive bid of a quarter of a million dollars in the back of a taxi. Annie refused. The fair wasn't the place to sell this particular project. She would wait until she had the full script and sell it in New York herself.

And now here it was, nestled innocently in its baby-blue folder. Annie's fingers itched to take it out and start reading, but she was due to see Jack shortly and he didn't like to be kept waiting. Besides, this deserved her absolute concentration. For the next twenty minutes she worked methodically through her mail. At the bottom of the pile was one letter that hadn't been opened, a handwritten airmail envelope marked "Personal" and "Please Forward." Curious, Annie flipped it over and read the return address. Lee Spago, Sheridan Road, Chicago. It meant nothing to her. She placed the envelope in the middle of her desk, where she couldn't miss it later, and then took the linoleum-covered stairs up to the next floor.

At the landing she ducked into the ladies' room. If Jack had changed his mind about the partnership, she ought at least to look the part. She examined herself critically in the mirror. Black skirt, black panty hose, silver-buttoned tartan jacket nipped in at the waist over a cream Lycra T-shirt. Thick tiger-striped hair blunt-cut to within an inch of her shoulders, assessing blue eyes, this morning's lipstick still in place. Good enough for Jack.

Nodding to Tabitha Twitchit, Annie's private name for Jack's fluttering secretary, she knocked on his door and went in. Memories assailed her, for she did not come in here much anymore. The crowded shelves, the elegant pedestal table piled with new books and magazines, the brass reading lamp, even the square green glass paperweight recalled the man whose portrait now hung above the mantelpiece. Bow-tied, gray-haired, with an ironic twist to his mouth, old Mr. Robertson had been her boss, her mentor, finally her friend. It was her tutor, Miss Kirk, of all unlikely people, who had recommended Annie for the job, explaining her delicate situation. If in business Mr. Robertson had displayed all the canniness— sometimes the sheer pig-headedness—of a native Scotsman, in private he had been kind beyond expectation. In recent years he had taken things easy, popping in only occasionally after a good lunch at the Garrick, but there had never been any question of Jack's taking over his office until Mr. Robertson had died, quite suddenly and peacefully, in his sleep.

That was nearly six months ago, but to Annie it still didn't look right to see Jack behind the familiar old partner's desk. To be fair, Jack had put in a decent apprenticeship as an editor in various publishing houses, and he could put on a show of boyish charm that went down well with the older, female writers. But Annie continued to see the bumptious schoolboy who used to fiddle with her papers and ogle her legs when he came to visit his father. She couldn't detect any backbone of real authority underneath a skimpy cloak of management jargon—not that it bothered her. Mr. Robertson had long ago given her a free hand to manage her own affairs. She figured that as long as she was making money—and she was—Jack would leave her alone.

"With you in a moment, Annie," Jack said, gesturing with a characteristic unfurling of his fingers toward the chair where faithful Tabitha spent hours encoding the letters and eternal memos that he dictated with the speed of a dripping ketchup bottle. Jack regarded the word processor as a mystical, exclusively female tool, on a par with the spinning wheel. To Annie, who composed her own complicated letters straight onto the PC and trained her secretaries to draft the routine ones, his old-fashioned methods seemed a shocking waste of resources.

After a good minute or more, Jack finished annotating the document he was working on, put down his pen, and pushed back his ridiculously boyish forelock of dark hair.

"I've had a rather worrying letter," he began, "which I thought I should share with you." He moistened the tip of a finger and leafed one by one through a pile of papers in front of him. At length he drew out what he wanted, and Annie recognized the letterhead of one of the major publishing groups.

"Apparently you did not see fit to offer them Coburg's new book on Eastern Europe. Could you fill me in on that?"

Annie, who had come prepared to battle for her partnership, was momentarily at a loss. "There was a good auction," she said defensively. "Four bidders, I think, and an advance of forty or forty-five thousand. Not bad for a heavyweight political book that's bound to have a lot of competition."

"I think you're missing the point—if I may say so." Jack gave her his more-in-sorrow-than-in-anger smile. "The point is, why didn't you offer it to a powerful group that already has some of our best authors on their list?"

Annie sighed. "I suppose Madame Guillotine is complaining," she said, using the industry's nickname for the group's publisher, a woman notorious for her staff purges. "The reason I didn't offer it to them is that I couldn't think of an appropriate editor. Celia does schlock and showbiz, Simon likes his nonfiction with a more wacky edge to it, Sarah's drowning in a sea of admin. Bill would have been perfect, but she fired him last month."

"You forgot Martin."

"The Boy Wonder? You know, Jack, I sometimes wonder if his reputation isn't just PR. Whenever I offer him anything, all I get is a five-page report telling me what's wrong with the script and how brilliantly he'll edit it. I suppose I wouldn't mind that if he actually published effectively. But of the last two books I sold him, one came out nine months late and the other had half its photo captions the wrong way around and no proper index. And whenever you ring him up, he is never, but never, in the office. I'm not saying Martin isn't bright, but—well, let's just say efficiency is not his middle name."

Jack took his time carefully placing his fingertips together. "That doesn't seem to be the general view. Just between you and me," he added confidentially, "Martin's name has already come up more than once in connection with the Nibbies."

Annie looked at him blankly for a moment, then burst out laughing. The Nibbies were annual awards conferred by one of the trade magazines on writers, editors, designers, distributors, publicists, and anyone else they could think of. It was a bit of fun that pierced the winter gloom every February, and Annie enjoyed the circus atmosphere of the awards ceremony, but it wasn't exactly the Nobel Prize. Even Jack, she was sure, didn't give a fig who won what. Any more, she suddenly realized, than he cared who had bought Coburg's book.

"What's this all about, Jack?" she asked directly. "I came up here to discuss the partnership. Let's not waste time bickering about an auction that, in my view, was entirely successful."

"In *your* view," Jack repeated, with a quiet venom that startled her. "That's what it always comes down to, doesn't it? Annie Hamilton's view is that we need a television specialist—and, lo, my father appoints one. Annie Hamilton's view is that the office should be computerized. Bingo! Thousands of pounds' worth of equipment appears overnight. Annie Hamilton's view is that one of the world's major international publishers is not good enough for her author, and I'm the one"—Jack brandished the letter—"who takes the flak."

Wow, thought Annie. But it was her fault for laughing at him.

"I'm sorry about the letter, Jack," she said soothingly. "I'd be happy to answer it myself. I'll even show you my reply, if you like. But we did need a television expert—and Elizabeth's already done brilliantly, as you know. And the computerization was years overdue. Your father only did what I suggested because he trusted me to know what I was talking about."

"And I don't, is that what you're saying?" With a furious shove Jack pushed himself away from the desk and stood up.

"Of course not—"

But Jack was now thoroughly angry. Bracing his hands against the desk, he leaned across it and addressed her in a strangled shout. "Smith & Robertson is my firm now, whether you like it or not. I decide how and with whom we do business. The way you're always chattering with the staff, sorting out their problems, setting up new systems, arranging foreign trips without a by-your-leave—I sometimes think you forget that. It was all very well in my father's day, running helpfully up and down in your miniskirt doing whatever job he wanted, but we're a modern business now and we should be following modern business practices."

In her miniskirt? Up to now Annie hadn't been too bothered by Jack's display of adolescent temper. Tantrum management was a vital skill when you had teenage children. But this remark was so outrageous that she felt her mouth fall open. In a sudden flash she remembered the humiliating scene that had taken place in this very room, years ago, at some Christmas party. Was that what this was all about? Surely Jack wasn't going to use his newly inherited position to make her pay for that?

Regaining control of himself, Jack sat down. "I've said I'll consider the partnership, and I will—when I judge that you have understood the financial and management controls necessary in a modern business. To take a current example, we can't have everyone running off to New York every five minutes. You know perfectly well that I have for some time been planning an American trip in

December. Yet I gather that you have unilaterally decided to go yourself shortly. That's a quite unnecessary duplication, and I have decided to postpone your trip until next year."

"But what about Sebastian? I've got the whole script now. You know the Americans are desperate to buy it. We need to strike while the iron is hot."

"I shall handle the sale of Sebastian Winter myself," Jack said pompously.

Annie gasped. "But he's *my* author."

"You see, there you go again, Annie." Jack stabbed a finger at her. "Winter is not my author or your author. He is a Smith & Robertson property, which we shall exploit as effectively as we can."

"But I've always sold American rights to the big books myself. People will be expecting me."

"Then they'll just have to make do with the head of the agency," said Jack with a smugness that made Annie long to slap his ferrety face.

"But in the past—"

"I've made my decision, and I'm afraid you'll just have to accept it." Jack's mouth tightened into a spiteful line. "Better not go into the past, don't you think?" he said, with a subtle emphasis that made Annie tense with wariness.

"I've been sorting out some of my father's private papers," he continued casually. "Fascinating stuff. Letters from famous authors that I should think are really rather valuable. But also some unfortunate personal stories which are probably better destroyed."

"Like what?" Annie asked steadily.

"Just little human dramas." Jack gave a tight smile. "Past history, nothing that need concern us here, I'm sure. For the time being, I would be grateful if you would draft a reply to this"—he handed her the offending letter—"as from me. This afternoon will do."

Annie stood up and stalked out of the room, leaving the door wide open. Rose was right, she thought. She should have set up her own agency years ago. But it hadn't seemed necessary when old Mr. Robertson was alive. She had an office she liked, colleagues for company, specialist departments for foreign and television rights, and as much freedom as she wanted. It had always seemed too difficult to disentangle her own personal deals from those of the firm.

That wasn't the whole story, though, and she knew it. It was sheer cowardice, the little Miss Mouse syndrome, that had kept her from striking out boldly on her own. Boldness had not rewarded her in the past. Once she had followed her instincts, and they had led to unhappiness and muddle. It had taken years to regain her equilibrium. If she sometimes dreamed of a different life, she had learned to value what was solid and dependable.

Stupid, cowardly, blind—Annie heaped every insult on herself that she could think of. Jack had been waiting in the wings for years. It was obvious that one day he would take over. How could it not have occurred to her that he might abuse his position?

Annie was seething when she got back to her office. The first thing she saw was the strange letter from America. Without premonition she ripped it open.

Dear Annie,

That seems a pretty familiar way to start, so I guess I'd better explain right away that your mother and I have been married twelve years now. Marie always said that you two didn't get along, and up to now I have minded my own business. Marie is very precious to me and I would never upset her.

Annie stiffened in her chair and reread the paragraph in disbelief. *Married?* Annie had not seen or heard from her mother for over twenty years. Memory had warped her mother's image into a monstrous icon that bore no relation to a real woman. It had not occurred to Annie that anyone might want to marry her mother, any more than that someone would propose to Bette Davis if she stepped from the screen of *What Ever Happened to Baby Jane?*

Anyway, just who the hell was "Marie"? The last Annie had heard, her mother was plain Mary Paxford, born Mary Hoggett. An old, familiar rage made her whole body flush with heat. How utterly typical of her mother to have upgraded her name, as she had always tried to refine her family. "No tie, Charles?" she used to say in that poisonous, faultfinding voice as she dolled up for yet another cocktail party, and obediently Annie's father would return to his wardrobe like a dog fetching its toy.

Annie nearly crumpled up the letter there and then. But her eyes had already jumped to the next words. With a sick feeling she read on.

Now she is in the hospital, and they don't give her much more than a month. The thing is, she has started talking about you. I think there is something on her mind that she wants to settle. It's a lot to ask, but if you could come see her I truly believe it would help. If it is a question of money, I have plenty. Let me know if I can take care of your ticket and hotel—though we have a nice condominium by the lake where you would be welcome.

Please think about it at least. I have made a lot of mistakes in my life, and I know there are some you can never fix. Whatever happened in the past, Marie needs you now.

Yours respectfully,
Lee Spago

Well, the part about the money made sense, Annie thought viciously. It wouldn't be like her mother to pick anyone poor. She slapped the letter facedown on the desk. There was a postscript on the back.

P.S. I hope this letter reaches you. I got your business address from an article Marie clipped in the New York Times. *I found it in her jewelry box.*

Annie remembered that article. One of her authors had been approached to help Margaret Thatcher write her memoirs. In the end, he didn't get the job, but for a few short weeks both he and Annie had received a measure of useful publicity. There had even been a photograph of her.

How strange to think of her mother reading that article. In fact, now that Annie thought about it, it was more than strange. The article must have appeared well over a year ago: which meant that her mother had not only taken the trouble to cut it out; she had also kept it, all this time, in the place where most women keep their very special treasures.

Annie bowed her head and, cradling it in her folded arms, rested it on her desk. Jordan. Tom. Her mother. Would the memories never leave her? Would the lies ever stop? When would it be her turn for happiness? She didn't even notice that she was leaning on Sebastian's precious script, darkening its pale blue folder to navy with her tears.

4

I Heard It Through the Grapevine

*I*t was a perfect autumn day, the sky as fresh and blue as if it had never heard of the ozone layer. Tom decided to walk, having been given detailed directions of the scenic route by Aldworth. It took him up Catte Street, past the Pitt Rivers Museum, and into the University Parks. On this quiet Sunday morning—only the second of the term—there were few people about, a sprinkling of old ladies with their dogs and mothers with prams, enjoying the bright bursts of autumn crocuses and the way the sun set the copper beeches on fire. Just as the duck pond came into sight, Tom took the little brick-walled path that led to the bottom of Norham Gardens.

Lady Margaret Hall had not escaped the brutalist additions of the 1970s, but its central quadrangle, rosy-bricked with a clock tower and cupola, had a cozy domestic charm appropriate for a college built to house women. Tom followed the gravel path around the square of green, peering furtively into the windows. One side of the quad was taken up by a library, traditionally divided into bays, empty at this hour. On the other side were student rooms, most with their curtains still drawn, though Tom could hear the thump of music and caught sight of one man shrugging himself into his sweater.

Which had been his mother's room? he wondered.

Opposite the library was an archway linking two buildings. Tom passed through it into the gardens. Though not as grand as those of the older, originally male colleges, they were surprisingly extensive, sweeping down to the Cherwell. He took the willow-shaded path along the river, past the boathouse and grass tennis courts, then turned off to explore a small garden, hedged with yew, where gray stubs of lavender encroached on mossy paths and windblown chrysanthemums shrouded the broad, shallow steps of old brick.

"Good morning, young man. I take it you are not a member of the college."

Startled, Tom turned to find a bulldog of a woman, stoutly encased in tweed, outlined in one of the arched entrances to the garden. She was wearing gardening gloves and carrying a pair of pruning shears. Before Tom could answer, she went on, in the same well-spoken boom, "Otherwise, you would no doubt be aware that this is the Fellows' Garden and out of bounds to junior members."

"I'm—I'm terribly sorry," Tom stammered politely. "I was just having a look around. My mother was an undergraduate here."

"Indeed?" The woman stood her ground for a moment, legs well braced, then stripped off a glove and advanced toward him. "That puts a different complexion on the matter. I am Miss Reeves, dean of the college. How do you do?"

Tom shook her hand. "Tom Hamilton. I've just come up to Christ Church."

"Oh, well done," said the Dean heartily. "I approve of continuity in the university. The great-granddaughter of one of our founder members has just come up to the college. Charming girl. Could have had her pick of any of the colleges—but, no, LMH or nothing, she said. Most gratifying. We're not as popular as we used to be when we were a women's-only college." Grunting, she bent down to lop off a cluster of rose hips with the shears. "I was against integration, of course, but what chance has a lone voice against the baying of the herd for progress?" She allowed Tom no chance to respond to this rhetorical question but shot him a penetrating glance. "So, young Mr. Tom Hamilton, who was your mother? Daresay I might remember her. I'm quite a fixture here."

"Paxford was her maiden name. Ann Paxford."

The dean's lumpen features softened into an unexpectedly sweet smile that gave Tom a glimpse of the young girl she had once been. "Good heavens, Annie Paxford. Read English, had rooms in Deneke and—was it Wordsworth? Very quiet at first, just seeing how the land lay, you know, but then she quite blossomed, found herself some friends. There was one particular girl, a real 'live wire,' as they say. Rose something. Carlton? Kennedy?"

"Rose Cassidy? She's my godmother."

"Is she? Splendid. And what has become of her?"

"She's something very grand in New York, editor of *The Magazine*. You must have read about her—she's always in the gossip columns."

"But do I read them?" the dean asked dryly. "I am afraid one becomes shamefully insular. And your mother, what does she do with herself?"

"She's a literary agent, with Smith & Robertson."

"Good for her. It is dispiriting when our old girls simply turn bovine with domesticity and motherhood. And your mother was clever. I believe Miss Kirk had hopes of a first." *Snip* went the shears, and another thorny plume fell to the ground as Miss Reeves added, "We were all very disappointed when she didn't stay to take her degree."

Tom tried to hide his astonishment, but the old lady was sharp. "Didn't tell you, eh? I expect she had her reasons. Difficult home life, as I recall. We do our best, but we never really know what goes on inside their pretty little heads."

Tom rummaged in his back pocket. "I've got an old photograph of her. Would you like to see it?"

The dean, farsighted with age, held the photo at arm's length. "Well, well, Annie Paxford." She shook her head, smiling. "To think that she has a grown-up son. And who is the young man with her? He looks familiar."

"I don't—I can't remember. Why, do you recognize him?"

Miss Reeves gave a barking laugh. "If I were to try to keep track of all the boyfriends that come and go in this college I'd have my work cut out." She handed back the photo. "They've filled in that flower bed now. Pity. We used to have splendid black tulips in the spring, but one simply can't get the gardeners these days."

Tom was confused. "Do you mean to say that the photo was taken *here*?" he asked.

"Yes, by the archway where you probably came in. The girls like to sunbathe there in the summer; that slope catches the sun beautifully."

Tom stood for a moment, digesting this. The dean looked on kindly, but with a gathering frown that threatened awkward questions if he didn't leave quickly. "Well, thanks," he said, waving the picture. "I'll just have a look, if you don't mind, on my way out. I'm sorry to have trespassed."

The dean held out her hand. "Not at all. A pleasure to have met Annie Paxford's son."

As he turned to go, Tom remembered something. "You mentioned another lady, Miss somebody. Is she a tutor here?"

"Miss Kirk? She retired a good many years ago. I'm afraid there has been something of a decline, although she still dines occasionally."

"Is she still in Oxford? Perhaps she wouldn't mind if I dropped in on her one day."

"What a kind thought. Honeysuckle Cottage, Wytham. It's a charming little village. Though you may find her somewhat . . . frail. There's a pub, I believe, the White Hart." She flourished the shears encouragingly. "You could make it a real outing."

Tom thanked her again and headed back the way he had come. He wondered what reminiscences his mother might have about the old battle-ax. But the thought of his mother brought the old anxiety flooding back. At the porchway into the quad, he checked the photograph again. The dean was right. The flower bed might have gone, but here was the same ornamental stone urn, the same strip of gravel, the same crisscross shutters over the ground-floor window.

So why had his mother told him that the photo was taken in Malta?

5

She's Not There

*L*eaving the untidy sprawl of Wolvercote behind him, Tom raced his bicycle over the humpback bridge by the Trout, passed the flat reaches of Port Meadow, and arrived at a string of vine-clad cottages hugging the twisting road. The village of Wytham was indeed charming, dominated by a spectacular medieval abbey. As in most English villages, the pub was conveniently placed next to the church and easy to find. The White Hart was paneled inside, whitewashed on the outside, with rustic benches and tables in the sun and a dovecote loud with cooing. It was already crowded and, judging from the accents around him, firmly established on the tourist map, but the long ride up Woodstock Road had taken its toll of Tom's calf muscles, and it was with considerable relief that he leaned his bike against the low stone wall, bought himself a pint, and took it into the garden. Brian had muttered something about a picnic on the college lawn today, but it was just too bad if he missed it. After LMH, Tom had gone straight back to college to pick up his bicycle. Never put off till tomorrow what you can do today, as his mother always said. Well, he would take her advice.

For the moment, however, beer and sunshine made a seductive combination. After downing his pint thirstily, Tom went indoors to line up for sausages and beans and another half, and settled himself in a little rose-covered bower vacated by a family of enthusiastic Germans. It was astonishingly warm for the time of year, and the bees were buzzing around the roses as if a whole lifetime lay ahead of them, instead of a few short days before the autumn chill froze them dead. It must be odd, Tom thought, to live your life with no premonition of what was to come.

Having asked directions from the publican, Tom walked a few yards back the way he had come and onto a rough track until he reached a white picket fence with a gate marked HONEYSUCKLE COTTAGE. The front garden had an untended look, without a twig of honeysuckle to be seen, just daisy-studded grass and a few blowsy hollyhocks. There was a sagging trellis around the door and a brass knocker shaped like a sleeping cat. He let it drop noisily and waited. Eventually he heard a faint shuffling, so slow and erratic that he began to fear that his journey would be wasted, that he would be met by the blank gaze of senility. But when the door at last opened, he found himself looking into a pair of faded blue eyes in which intelligence still glimmered. Miss Kirk was tiny, her face as wizened as a monkey's under a frizz of gray hair, kept tidy with a fine net. She cut an elegant figure in her dark skirt and pink silk blouse caught at the throat with a cameo brooch, though Tom noticed a splash of food on the sleeve. A shawl of muted colors was draped across her shoulders, and she breathed audibly, leaning on a brass-headed stick.

"Good afternoon," she said politely enough, but with an upward inflection of inquiry. It must be an anxious business, Tom realized, living alone in a world of con men, muggers, and rapists. Carefully he offered his credentials, conscious that he too, in his own way, was here under false pretenses. But the old lady seemed delighted.

"How very kind. Come in, come in. I always enjoy hearing of my old pupils. May I offer you a cup of coffee? Or perhaps lemonade might be more fitting for such a splendid day."

Picturing the slow and painful arrangements this might entail, Tom convinced her that his pub lunch had left him wholly satisfied. Besides, a peculiar smell, which he eventually identified as cat, made him feel queasy about the state of her kitchen. Tap-tapping with her stick, she led him into one of the most extraordinary rooms he had ever seen.

It was a typical cottage parlor—beamed ceiling, diamond-paned casement windows, stone fireplace—but transformed into an Aladdin's cave crammed with antique treasures. Through a gap in the heavy curtains, sunlight gleamed on delicate Georgian side tables, a pigeonhole desk inlaid with ivory, a long case clock, bronze busts, a Regency chaise longue with yellow silk bolsters, leather-bound books scrolled with gold. In fact, books were everywhere, spilling out of the shelves that lined one wall and filled the fireplace alcoves, piled on tables and windowsills, balanced on chair arms and rising like giant anthills from the jeweled Persian carpets on the floor. Above the fireplace hung a striking print of the expulsion from Eden, a beautiful naked Eve and a protective Adam quailing at the sight of the corrupt world that awaited them. Everything was of an austere classical elegance; there was nothing feminine about the room. A wing chair flanking the fire marked itself out as her familiar workstation: kidney-shaped writing board to balance on her lap, tartan rug for her knees, scatter of cushions for her back. The only incongruous element was a modern cart holding a kettle and assorted tins, a large bottle of ink standing on a pad of blotting paper, and a sheaf of papers covered in handwriting as tiny as a doll's. On the lower shelf of the cart a vast ginger cat lay splayed in sleep.

Tom picked his way around the teetering plinths of books to the magnificent carved chair that she indicated, its polished arms ending in lions' heads, and removed a bulging file from the seat. It was, he noticed, marked "God."

"It is untidy," Miss Kirk agreed crisply to Tom's unspoken thoughts as she settled herself in her chair. She spoke a beautiful, precise English of the sort Tom had only ever heard from the BBC radio archives. "Hodge does *not* approve, do you pusskins?" She ran a fragile hand over the cat's pale, spreading stomach. "But I need my books about me. I am too old to be leaping up and down like a Jack-in-the-box. My work is nearly complete, but I must keep at it, you know, before I am 'called.' "

"You're writing a book?" Tom hazarded a guess.

"*The* book, dear boy, *the* book. My magnum opus. The definitive concordance to the works of Milton. Oh, yes," she said, as if Tom had voiced some objection, "there have been attempts at it. American scholars, with their computers and research students." Her tone was dismissive. "I have no aids but my memory and my brain. And the good Lord to guide me. Tell me," she asked with an almost coquettish turn of the head, "do you read Milton?"

"Er, I'm afraid Pepys is more my line."

"Pepys!" she cried enthusiastically. "Nothing to be ashamed of there. A most lovable man, though not perhaps of scrupulous morals.

"Certainly I remember Ann Paxford," she continued without a

pause. "Nineteen sixty-eight is a year I could hardly forget. That was the last time the old syllabus was taught, before it was decided that young minds were too impatient and too sensitive to endure the rigors of proper study. The whole of the Michaelmas and Hilary terms were spent in preparation for the preliminary examinations. *Beowulf*—complete, and in the original, naturally; Latin—*The Aeneid*; Old English and morphology; and of course Milton." She clasped a hand to her thin chest. "The sublime Milton. He was always my particular love. *Paradise Lost*, 'Lycidas,' *Areopagitica*, *Comus* . . ." Her eyes closed for a moment and her lips moved, as if recalling some fragment of verse.

She reopened them with a snap. "It gave one a grounding, don't you see?" she said fervently. "What is one to make of literature without the basics of language and classical allusion? They tell me that critical theory has supplanted a study of the text, that it is no longer thought necessary to read literature.

"But *this* is where the precious life-blood of the master spirit resides." She patted a pile of books at her knee—all, Tom saw, volumes of Milton. "The blind can be very perceptive. The poor man had to keep all his verse in his head, you know, waiting for someone to come and write it down for him. Like a cow waiting to be milked, he said."

A silence fell. Miss Kirk leaned forward courteously. "Who did you say you were, dear boy?"

"Tom Hamilton. Ann Paxford's son." She was like a doll, Tom thought, a macabre clockwork doll whose essential mechanism had received some fatal injury. Parts still moved, but in a grotesque and unpredictable way.

"Yes, of course, forgive me. One gets so tired these days. Do tell me about her. Is she well? Does she flourish?"

Tom told her about his mother's job, realizing as he spoke how little he knew, had never bothered to ask. Miss Kirk questioned him about his sisters and the likelihood of their coming up to LMH one day. Nil, in Tom's opinion, though he was too polite to say so. All the while, something niggled in his brain. He would pinpoint it later if he could, but for the moment he needed to keep her talking.

"You must have been disappointed when she gave up her studies," he prompted.

"It was a blow. I enjoyed teaching your mother. She had an instinctive response to the sounds and rhythms of language. I did hope that, with proper study and guidance in her final year, she might do very well indeed. But alas—"

Her eyes strayed to the picture above the fireplace, and she began to quote, in a passionate low warble. " 'These two / Imparadised in one another's arms, / The happier Eden, shall enjoy their fill / Of bliss on bliss.' " Then, eerily, still on a note of reverie, Miss Kirk continued, "Annie Paxford. I wonder what happened to her."

Tom's hands tightened over the lions' faces on his chair, willing her to continue. Somewhere in her memory, he was sure, was a piece of information he wanted, though if the condition of her brain was anything like that of her room, he had little hope that she could lay her hands on it even if she wanted to. A snowstorm of dust, spotlit by the sun, floated down onto files and papers and piles of indexers' slips that would surely, one day soon, prove to be no more than an indecipherable muddle, fit only for carting away in black plastic sacks.

Miss Kirk spoke again, in the disengaged drone of a medium. "I tracked her down, you know. Oh, yes, I found her in that filthy little hole. But it was too late. I did what I could, a word in the right place. It was my Christian duty."

"Where?" Tom demanded, abandoning any pretense of polite chatter. "Why did she leave Oxford? Tell me. Please."

But the old lady was deaf to his questions, following her own mazy track. "No doubt it was easier for our generation. We had no distractions from our academic calling. All our young men were killed in the Great War. Young men like you. All gone." She looked at Tom reproachfully. "No one visits anymore, you know. One might as well be dead." Her voice deepened again as she declaimed, " 'Oh, dark, dark, dark, amid the blaze of noon.' "

With an air of finality she closed her eyes and leaned into her chair's familiar embrace. She was silent for some long seconds. In the shadowy room the clock ticked loudly. The seconds stretched into one minute, two minutes. The old lady's face slackened, and she began to snore gently. She was asleep.

Tom didn't know what to do. It would be rude to leave but worse to stay until she awoke. Besides, he was unlikely to get more from her pitifully scrambled brain. Eventually he rose carefully from his chair and tiptoed his way round the furniture. At the door he looked back and saw, with a thrill of horror, that her eyes were open, fixed on him with the wide, vacant gaze of a sleepwalker. She gave him a smile, as if inviting him to share a delightful joke.

"She left because of you, dear boy, didn't she?"

Then her lizard lids fell, and she slumped into instant, slack-jawed sleep.

It was on his way back along the towpath, his mind floating free, that something the old lady had said hit Tom so hard that he nearly wobbled into the river. "Nineteen sixty-eight is a year I could hardly forget." So his mother had gone to Oxford in 1968. He had now discovered that she had left at the end of her second year, which would have been the summer of 1970.

One thing Tom did know was his own birthday. It was the seventeenth of March, 1971.

In Jericho Tom passed a corner newsstand and remembered that Brian had asked him to bring back a Sunday paper—any of the qualities, he wasn't bothered. Tom's eyes slid listlessly over the headlines. On the masthead of the *Sunday Times* the word "Oxford" caught his eye. He paid for the paper, stuffed it into his bicycle basket, and rode home.

6

Daydream

A truth universally acknowledged by women's magazines is that
the departure from home of her children plunges every mother
into soul-searing depression. Bunkum, balderdash, and baloney,
thought Annie, as she wriggled deeper into her warm nest of pillows.
Tosh, tripe, poppycock, piffle, and pure applesauce. With Tom in
Oxford, and Cassie and Emma staying with friends following last
night's party, the house exuded a deep Sunday morning calm that
was as palpable and relaxing as a blanket. It was not so much the
actual noise the children made, now that they were slouching toward
adulthood; it was the continual expectation, day in and day out, of
some epic eruption that was so wearing.

Edward, thank God, had never been the erupting type. An invet-
erate early riser who complained that breakfasting in bed got
scratchy crumbs in his pajamas, he would be downstairs tranquilly
working through his legal papers and a fearsomely strong pot of tea.
Annie luxuriated in the knowledge that some batsqueak communi-
cation perfected over the years would shortly impel him up the stairs
with a tray of coffee, freshly squeezed orange juice, a croissant
flanked by an indecent amount of unsalted butter and apricot jam,
and a slab of newspapers. Today there would be no Sunday lunch
to cook, no squabbles to resolve, nobody to ferry to a party, swimming pool, football game, or film. She was nobody's mother and
nobody's employee. Just for one day she would not worry about
Tom or her job or the letter from Chicago, which she had hidden

in her underwear drawer, knowing that Edward would say she should go. Today was hers.

Still languorous with sleep, she hadn't the energy even to turn her head toward the bedside clock, but she could tell that the morning was well advanced. Sun blazed through the yellow chintz curtains, and a warm breeze sent them fluttering like circus pennants. She could sense an energy in the air outside that promised a delicious Indian summer day. Later they might walk across Hampstead Heath and have lunch in a pub garden. They could even try to get a court and play tennis. Or if Edward was busy, she might deadhead the roses and give the lavender a good haircut. Or . . . or what?

Annie felt a spurt of unfocused longing. What had she done on this kind of day when she was young? Sleep, said a cynical voice. Her children's capacity for sleep was astounding, and Annie knew that she had once been the same, though she could not recapture that teenage sense of limitless time. But as she stretched out on her back, feeling her body still lithe and responsive, another answer whispered to her. Make love. That's how people used to spend their mornings—and their nights and afternoons—when she was young. Then it had all seemed so innocent, so natural, so all-embracing, as if sex conferred some kind of universal benediction on the planet.

Nowadays it was easy to poke fun at sixties philosophy—the rhetoric of peace and love, handing out flowers, the earnestly argued views that everyone was bisexual and that rock music could shatter barriers of class and color. With hindsight one could see how women had allowed men to abuse them in the name of sexual liberation. Mysticism had become tainted with materialism. Few rock musicians had survived their fortieth birthdays with their bodies or their brains intact. But there had been a joy, a sense of expectation, that was shockingly absent among today's knowing, anxious teenagers. Did nobody know how to have fun anymore?

"Breakfast is served." Like a shimmering Jeeves, Edward appeared at the bedroom door carrying a loaded tray. Compared to most men she had known, and certainly to Tom, who sounded like a cavalry regiment on the stairs, Edward moved like a cat. He had the lean, wiry frame of the sort of Englishman she used to see in the old wartime films shown every Saturday in the army film club, typically dispatching an opponent's croquet ball into the shrubbery or giving a jubilant thumbs-up through the windshield of a Spitfire.

Often there would be a brash Yank who blundered through English etiquette, calling the gardener "Mr." or wolfing a week's rations at a sitting. Sometimes he got the girl; other times he heroically sacrificed his life for his Limey chum. Those Saturday afternoons, sitting with her father in a darkened Nissen hut, cocooned in a world of adventure and romance, had been some of the happiest moments of her childhood.

Edward put the tray on the bed and dropped a slithering mass of newspapers beside her. Annie studied him as he went over to pull the curtains open. Clothes always looked good on him, even today's old sweater and pale cotton trousers that had shrunk above his ankle bones.

"Good sleep?" he asked.

"Heaven." Annie sat up and stretched her arms wide. For a moment her cream silk pajamas pulled open across her breasts. Edward was fiddling with the window catch, his back to her. "Isn't it bliss to be alone, just the two of us? Or am I a shockingly unnatural mother?"

"Definitely a case for the Social Services," Edward said absently, still busy at the window.

Annie pulled the crisp tail off her croissant and munched it thoughtfully. "Have you got a lot to do today?"

"I've a meeting this week with the Union of Democratic Mineworkers, poor buggers. There's a fair amount of homework to do if I'm to be of any use to them." He left the window and leaned on the brass rail at the foot of the bed, considering his wife. "Why? Was there something special you wanted to do?"

"Not really. I just feel like doing something frivolous, like—oh, I don't know, having a lazy lunch in Julie's Wine Bar or watching some wonderful old Truffaut film. Just *being*, for a change, instead of always doing."

"Julie's Wine Bar! That's a blast from the past. We can go out for lunch, if you like," Edward said amiably. "But the parking's impossible round Julie's, and I've got a colleague phoning at three. He's giving me some advice with the case, and it would be rude if I wasn't here. What about that Thai place you like in Islington?"

Annie shrugged. "Never mind. I've got hundreds of things I should be doing too. I just thought it might be fun to forget the real world and do something spontaneous for a change."

Edward came around and sat next to her on the edge of the bed, steadying the tray with one hand. He put his other arm around Annie and drew her head to his. "What a disappointment I am to you," he said. "I'd love to whisk you off to some romantic paradise. How about if I make you a special little alfresco lunch later and whisk you into the garden instead? We could have some champagne, if you like."

Annie put her arm around his warm, familiar body and hugged him fiercely. "You're never a disappointment. You're my favorite husband, and the work you're doing is important." Tilting her head up, she gave him a kiss and rubbed her hand against his stubbly cheek. "It's all right. Really. Now bug off. I'm going to have a lovely wallow in the soft porn that passes for today's journalism."

"Oh, yes, I meant to tell you," Edward said, pausing in the doorway, "there's a piece that may amuse you about your old friend Hope."

"Amuse me?" Annie queried sharply, her heart beginning to thud. "In what way?"

Edward raised his eyebrows. "And I thought I was the star cross-examiner. It's just some story about Hope when he was at Oxford. Looked like a lot of nonsense to me. I didn't read it. But you might know some of the people quoted."

"He wasn't *my* friend anyway," Annie said. "You know me and politics. It was Rose who was always having earnest discussions with him about the means of production or positive discrimination."

"Mmm. It's funny to think of Rose as a feminist revolutionary. Nowadays I suppose she'd only be interested in trying to get him into some beefcake pose on the cover of her magazine."

Annie giggled and threw a bit of *Observer* at him, which Edward neatly sidestepped. "We can't all be as lofty as you, Mr. Lawyer-with-a-social-conscience."

When Edward had gone, the smile faded from Annie's face. She listened to his light padding down the stairs and waited tensely for the thunk of the study door as it closed safely behind him. Then she put the breakfast tray aside, threw back the duvet, and sat up cross-legged. Urgently she started sifting through the mass of newspapers, discarding each unwanted section onto the floor. Fashion, Books, Appointments, Comics, Magazines. *Please don't let me be in it,* she begged. Style, Review, Travel, Business. Ever since the story of Jordan's draft dodging had become an election issue, the media searchlight had been trained on Oxford. Annie had spent half her life disengaging from her past and keeping her profile at snail height. But when journalists were in a feeding frenzy, who knew where and when they might attack?

The picture caught her eye first—a grainy blowup of Jordan, center stage in a group of Rhodes scholars. Fresh-faced in their dinner jackets and gleaming Beatles haircuts, they were as adorable as choirboys. She'd never seen the photo before and couldn't help lingering, just for a moment, over the details of Jordan's broad shoulders and blazing smile. This was just as she had seen him for the very last time, right down to the tuxedo. On the next page there was another picture, an informal little snapshot of him in his Afghan coat, so familiar that a wave of memories washed over her. The angry, staccato chanting. The red nostrils and rolling eyeballs of terrified horses. The pub she had never been able to find again.

A YANK AT OXFORD ran the headline. Annie saw that no fewer than twelve people had researched the piece. She reached for her orange juice, poured its contents down her dry throat in a single slug, and settled down to read every word.

7

Love Child

*T*he south end of Kingsway is dominated by Bush House, home of the BBC World Service. From above its yellow stone porch a statue of two men grasping a flaming torch leans perilously into the Aldwych traffic. At their feet the plaque reads: TO THE FRIEND-SHIP OF ENGLISH-SPEAKING PEOPLES. You can't miss it, a policeman had told Tom. Stand under the statue, look right, and St. Catherine's House will be staring you in the face.

Tom crossed the road to the gray building with its ugly sixties frontage. Could this really be the Public Search Room? Dog-eared census posters and hand-drawn arrows indicating the entrance were taped onto the blank windows, projecting a crushing image of bank-rupt state bureaucracy. Inside, however, it was surprisingly efficient. A color-coded plan at the entrance explained the layout. It was not so much a room as a warren of rooms, each crowded with gunmetal bookcases holding leather-bound ledgers, two foot by one, stiffened with a brass spine. Red for birth, green for marriage, black for death. There was an Inquiries desk, a counter where one could apply for copies of certificates, and a collection point. Between each pair of bookshelves an extended wooden lectern provided a place to prop open the heavy ledgers. Tom had been expecting something like the British Library. This was much scruffier, but also more relaxed, with an air of bustling, companionable activity. Teenagers swarmed in the births section; older people seemed more attracted by the deaths. Several couples were working in tandem, one calling out names and dates while the other heaved books in and out of the shelves. Here were the personal records of every man, woman, and child born in England and Wales since 1837, wide open to public scrutiny, waiting to yield up their secrets.

In the births section Tom found the volume for January, February, and March 1971, E–K, and hauled it out by its black strap. He carried it to a space on the nearest lectern and propped the ledger open. His heart quickened as he reached "H" and looked for his name. Hamid, Hamilford, Hamilton. HAMILTON, Thomas Stanley. There he was, in black and white, sandwiched between Sylvia Mamie and Tracey Monique. Mother's maiden name, Paxford.

Thank God for that. At least there was one fixed point in the spiral of doubt that had begun to engulf him. His birth had been registered in Chelsea. That sounded right. His mother had often mentioned the little flat in Battersea Park Road, where she had been forced to carry Tom and his pram up and down two flights of stairs and the landlord banged on his ceiling with a broom handle whenever the baby cried. "We would have been out on the street if you hadn't been such a good little thing."

There was a final column of numbers: 0372 06 J74. A notice explained how to obtain a copy of a birth certificate by quoting this reference. A sample taped to the wall showed Tom that the information offered in a full certificate was extensive. Name, place of birth, and occupation of father; maiden name of mother or surname at marriage if different from maiden name. He took one of the forms but didn't fill it in yet. There was something else he wanted to check.

He wandered deeper into the network of rooms, noting the gold-blocked spines: Consular Births, Service Department Births, Overseas Marriages, War Deaths. Two vast black tomes caught his eye, and he was moved to see that they listed the dead from World War I, divided into Officers and Other Ranks—as if it mattered after you were dead. Passing through a linoleum-covered corridor, he came to a room that was wall-to-wall green. Marriages.

Half an hour later he was hot, frustrated, and his arms were aching from the weight of the ledgers. No wonder the regulars came in their shirtsleeves. Starting from the date of his birth, he had worked backward for five years, looking in both the E–K and P–S sections for every quarter. A lot of men called Hamilton had gotten married, including two called Edward Hamilton, but none of them had married Ann Paxford. Only one female Paxford had married, but she was called Marissa and came from Pontypridd.

But Tom had seen pictures of the wedding, his mother long-haired and laughing with flowers in her hair, his father in a suit with hilariously wide lapels and a rather dashing silk scarf round his neck. His godmother, Rose, had been there too, exotic in a caftan and headband. Tom was sure that it had taken place in London, a small, informal register office wedding. Neither of his parents was religious.

He decided to work forward instead. 1972—nothing. 1973—nothing. January–March 1974—nothing. Tom thought of all those doomed Catholics trapped by marriage in the novels of Graham Greene and Evelyn Waugh, of poor Mr. Rochester with his wife cackling in the attic. Could it possibly be that his father had already been married, to a woman who wouldn't divorce him? He heaved down the next volume. He would just keep looking, even if it meant going right up to 1992.

But he never got that far. There it was: HAMILTON, Edward C., married Paxford, Chelsea, 16 June 1974. Tom considered for a moment, then checked the spine to make sure of the date, then double-checked in the P–S volume. PAXFORD, Ann M., married Hamilton, Chelsea, 16 June 1974. No doubt about it. He had been alive for over three years before his parents got married.

Tom suddenly craved fresh air. He retraced his steps past the Births and out into the cold. Mean little crosscurrents of wind sent litter skittering about his feet, and he started walking.

So his parents weren't married when he was born. Was that the big secret? Tom opened his mind to the idea, taking stock of his emotions. It didn't seem too terrible. Hadn't he read a statistic recently that a third of all children nowadays were conceived out of wedlock? There was even, perhaps, something rather buccaneering about being illegitimate. For a moment he felt quite buoyant. Then he remembered the photograph, and his mother's reaction to it, and all the doubts and anxieties about his parentage that they had set off. It was one thing to be illegitimate. But exactly whose illegitimate son was he?

As he trudged along High Holborn, hands thrust deep into the pockets of his football jacket, another inconsistency struck him. If he had been born when his mother was still Ann Paxford, how come his birth had been registered under the name of Hamilton? Tom quickened his step around the block and reentered St. Catherine's House.

Back to Births, January to March 1971, but this time the P–S volume. Here he was again. PAXFORD, Thomas Stanley. Ignoring the sign telling him not to remove more than one volume at a time, he got out E–K to cross-check the details. They were identical except for the reference number.

Tom joined the line at the Inquiries desk, where a large lady in a floral dress was patiently answering questions. When his turn came he showed her the two entries he had copied out.

"This is the same person," he explained. "Paxford is the name of the mother and Hamilton the father. I was just wondering, is it normal to register somebody under both names?"

"It's probably a case of reregistration. Let's have a look." She picked up the eyeglasses that dangled from a cord around her neck and peered through them at the page in Tom's notebook.

"Yes, you see, the reference numbers are different. Do you know when this person was born?"

Tom felt himself flush under her assessing gaze. "March 1971, I think." *I think.* What an idiot he was. Why should she suspect, or care, that he was inquiring about himself?

"Well, look at the reference number in the Paxford entry—0371. That means the birth was registered in March 1971 under that name. That would be the compulsory registration within six weeks of birth. But this column, in the Hamilton entry, has a different code—J74. That means June 1974. So for some reason this person was reregistered three years after his birth."

"Why would that be?"

The woman took off her glasses. Her eyes flicked down the line. "That I couldn't say. We're only trained to explain the registration system. You'd have to look at the documentation to understand why."

"Supposing—well, supposing the parents weren't married when the baby was born, but then they got married three years later. Would that explain it?"

"That's one possible reason."

The woman was not going to make this easy for him. Tom tried to work out what other explanation there might be. She had mentioned documentation. "So would both birth certificates say the same thing? I mean, assuming the mother is definitely the mother, would both certificates show the same father?"

"Not necessarily."

"Why not?"

"Sometimes the person registering a birth leaves the space for the father's name blank. They may not know who the father is, or they may choose not to name him, or he may refuse to be named. You can't put just anyone's name down, you know," she added reprovingly. "The man has to agree that he is the father."

"Do you mean to say that the first certificate, the 1971 one, might have no name for the father or a different one from the Hamilton one?"

"There could be no name, certainly. And it is possible that the names would be different, though it's not very common. As I said, you have to get the man's permission to put his name down, and if you then want to register a different father's name you would have to persuade the registrar that the second man was the real father, and explain why his name hadn't been given in the first place."

Tom became conscious of the line shifting impatiently behind him. "So even if the second man, er, Hamilton, agreed that he wanted to be named as the father, it wouldn't just automatically happen?"

The woman's eyebrows rose in disapproval. "Certainly not. He could legally adopt the child, of course, but he couldn't register himself as the birth father."

Adopt. Christ!

Tom wrenched his mind back on to the track. "So if I wanted to check that the two entries married up, I could apply for copies of both certificates."

"Wouldn't do you much good. The most recent registration supersedes all previous registrations. Either way you would get the 1974 document."

"Even if I gave the reference number of the 1971 entry?"

"That's right."

"So what you're saying is that I can't look at the 1971 certificate."

"That's right."

"Not ever? Not anywhere?"

"Not here, anyway. If you apply on one of the pink forms, you will be sent the reregistration details, whichever reference you give."

"So—" So nothing. Dead end. Impasse. Tom stared into the woman's doggy brown eyes.

"Look," she said finally, "you can write to this address, if you like, and explain why you want to see the earlier certificate. They might show it to you. But you need a very good reason."

Tom took the piece of paper from her and moved away from the crowded desk. In a quiet corner he read the printed slip, which gave a Merseyside address for the Office of Population Censuses and Surveys. Tom folded the slip and put it in his jeans pocket. What now? Bang in front of him a bookcase of yellow-backed ledgers caught his eye. ADOPTIONS FROM 1927 said the label.

No harm in making sure. He did the job thoroughly, checking every year from 1971 to the present. But there were no Thomas Stanleys, whether of the Paxford or the Hamilton variety.

Tom left the building and walked up Kingsway until he came to a café tucked away behind the archway leading into Sicilian Avenue. It was still only half-past eleven, and apart from the cheerful Israeli owner he had the place to himself. He ordered a cappuccino and carried it to a corner table. For a while he just stared into the speckled froth, trying to make sense of the facts he had discovered. Then he drew out his notebook and pencil and a bundle of papers from his backpack. The whole point of education was to train your mind to assess facts logically and draw a conclusion. So what exactly did he know?

One, he was illegitimate. Two, there was no accessible documentation that proved who his father was. Three, his mother had lied to him consistently. The photograph he had found hadn't been taken in Malta but in the gardens of LMH sometime between 1968 and 1970. Nor, he now knew, was it a picture of some half-forgotten teenage admirer called Jonathan. Tom unfolded the News Review section from yesterday's *Sunday Times* and smoothed it out on the table. Again he felt a jolt of familiarity as he studied the confident young face. How carelessly he had joined in the laughter as Hugh, a tall Wykehamist with flowing locks and a braying laugh, had read out extracts from the Jordan Hope profile. The scene that had taken place in the Christ Church gardens—was it really only yesterday? —replayed in his mind with a retrospective irony that made him squirm.

On his return from Wytham, he had only just padlocked his bike and was walking across the quad to his rooms, preoccupied by his thoughts, when he heard someone shouting his name. Brian and a group of other first-years were sprawled on the grass in the sun, surrounded by the remains of a picnic. "Eat, drink, and be merry"

—Brian gestured expansively—"for tomorrow ye may have to write an essay." It showed how drunk they all were that everyone laughed as if Brian had just coined an aphorism of exquisite Wildean wit.

Suddenly, getting drunk seemed the perfect thing to do. Tom dumped the hefty newspaper on the grass and Brian divided it up among the group. As in the miracle of the loaves and fishes, there was a section for everyone. Tom poured himself a glass of chardonnay, drained it thirstily, and refilled it. He lay down on his back, balancing the drink on his stomach and lazily watching cottonball clouds chase one another across the sky. He was thinking about Miss Kirk—her frail body confined to that bizarre room, her brain locked in perpetual, pointless motion like an old rat in a familiar maze—when one of the guys suddenly let out a howl of laughter. It was Hugh, who had already taken on the role of class comic.

"Listen to this, chaps," he said, brandishing the paper. " 'A Yank at Oxford'—the rise of Jordan Hope, from his humble beginnings as a mere Rhodes scholar to potential president of the Yoo-nited States." He started to read aloud a profile of the presidential candidate, Jordan Hope, imitating the clipped voice-over from old film newsreels.

" 'As the USS *United States* slipped its New York berth, bound for Southampton, Jordan Hope marveled at the sight of Manhattan slipping away. Leaning on the rail alongside him were some of America's most favored sons, Rhodes scholars bound for Oxford, England.' " A raucous cheer went up, and Tom raised his glass in a mock toast.

" 'Hope, a small-time boy from the wrong side of the tracks, knew this was a special moment in his life; a romantic departure from the country of his birth and the start of an adventure in'— God, I don't believe this—'in "swinging" Britain, land of the *Beatles*'!" Howls and groans greeted this masterpiece of painting-by-numbers prose, interspersed with cries for "More!" Hugh was a good mimic. Encouraged by his audience, he read out highlights in a range of voices, from schmaltzy American soap opera—" 'The moment I met Jordan I knew that someday he was gonna be president,' said fellow Rhodes scholar Donald Custard Flugelbaum"—to drawling Blanche du Bois Southern. " 'Merrilee Meriwether, a former Miss Mississippi, invited Hope to his first British antiwar march. "Y'all, I want to go. I've never been to a demonstration." And Jordan said, "Gosh, can I come too?" ' "

By the time Hugh reached the last, finely delivered line—"It was the start of his climb to the White House"—his audience was hysterical. Tom felt quite sick with drink and sun and laughter. Gradually the mood of hilarity quietened and the afternoon began to cool. People started to drift away, muttering about strong coffee and overdue essays.

Tom was helping Brian gather up the scattered newspaper when he caught sight of the picture accompanying the article. All subtlety deserted him. "Just remembered something," he said, grabbing the paper and running. The first place he came to was the cathedral. Evensong was not for another half hour, and it was empty. Tom tucked himself away in the side chapel, pulled out the photo of his mother and "Jonathan," and compared it to the newspaper photos. There was no doubt about it. It was the same man.

That night, wild fantasies chased around his head like a jumble of Hollywood film trailers. In one Tom sold the photo of Hope and his mother to a hard-faced tabloid hack for a million pounds and disappeared to a new life in Australia. In another, evading the Secret Service with the panache of 007, he confronted Hope on the tarmac as he ran down the steps of his campaign plane. Another had Tom's mother sobbing at his feet begging for his forgiveness. When he finally did get to sleep he had a terrifying nightmare in which he dreamed he had killed his father.

It was barely light when Tom woke. He walked round to the twenty-four-hour automatic teller machine in High Street and took out his limit of fifty pounds. On the way back he stopped to buy a handful of chocolate bars and a newspaper. A middle-aged, phonily coiffed Hope—unrecognizable from his Oxford self except for the cocky smile—had once again made the front page. Tom packed everything he needed into his backpack. It didn't amount to much. Then he left a note to Brian outside his door, weighted down by an empty wine bottle, and drove down to London.

And here he was. Tom drained his coffee. He wished there were someone to talk to. He thought of his two oldest friends, one at Cambridge, one studying law at the City University here in London, virtually around the corner. There was Rebecca, in Sussex. But what exactly was he going to say? Hi, guys, I've just found out I'm illegitimate and I think my father might be the next president of the United States. Just thinking the words made Tom wonder again if he weren't going mad. But why had his mother made such a mystery of everything? Why had she never mentioned the fact that she had once known Jordan Hope?

As the catalogue of his mother's lies and evasions mounted up, so did Tom's anger. It was his life. He wasn't a child anymore. He deserved to know the truth.

8

Get Off of My Cloud

"Right, I've got that," Annie said, scribbling furiously. "Presumably those royalties would apply to European sales too?"

Pen poised, she listened intently to the voice on the other end of the phone. "Good. Now, what about the movie escalator? Remember, you'd probably be getting a second bite at the paperback and a tie-in cover . . . *Fifty?*" Very gently Annie laid the receiver down on a soft pile of papers. She reached for her pocket calculator and, swiveling her chair out of earshot of the phone, stabbed out a calculation. Eighty thousand, it said. The receiver was squawking. Annie picked it up quietly, frowned, listened, waited some more, and finally laughed. "Hard bargain? Me?" she said. "Come on, Mike, this is the Freddie Forsyth *de nos jours,* and you know it. A hundred thousand ought to do it."

As soon as she put down the phone Annie shot her arms into the air like a Wimbledon champion. The scribbles in front of her represented a major new deal for Sebastian Winter's next novel. His publishers had now read the last section of the first book, which they already had under contract. Evidently they liked it. They were so confident of having a winner on their hands that they wanted to make sure that he couldn't be lured away to another stable. By offering a temptingly large sum for another book, they had bound him to them with chains of gold and tied up his time for at least two years. If she said so herself, Annie had just done a terrific deal. She spared a moment to offer up a prayer to a fellow agent who had taught Annie the art of the silence. When you don't like an offer,

Julia Barnes used to say, just go dead on them. Nine times out of ten, the other party will crack. Once they start blustering, you know you've got them cold.

Annie checked her watch. Noon. In half an hour she was meeting Sebastian. They had set up the meeting in order to discuss some minor changes to his book, but this new offer would be a perfect opening for the other proposition that had been buzzing around her head all week.

She looked around her funny, familiar cubbyhole of an office. Packed into her shelves were just some of the books she had worked on. There had been failures, of course, and plenty of promising books that had nevertheless sunk without trace. But others needed an entire shelf to encompass the history of their success: translations into every language from Czech to Korean to Urdu, book-club and large-print editions, paperbacks, educational abridgments, comic strips, even tapes and videos. Framed photographs of authors, book posters, and prize certificates crowded the walls, and some of the postcards and cartoons stuck to her bulletin board went back ten years and more. The geraniums on the windowsill had unfurled their green leaves, blossomed, and dropped their petals in a drift of pink and white, year in and year out. Soon it would be time to take them home again, to overwinter in her tiny conservatory. Whether she would be bringing them back next March, as usual, was another question.

None of her contemporaries had stayed with the same company for the whole of their working life, as she had done. Everyone moved. That was the way to get on. But for Annie the company had been her family and her home when she had no other. She could still remember the precise figure of her starting salary as a filing clerk: £937.80. It had been a particularly miserable December during the miners' strike when she joined the firm. The three-day week meant that she had to wear her overcoat and fingerless gloves and work by the light of a hissing camping lamp. The office manager, horrified to hear that Annie had no Christmas plans, had invited her to spend the day at her flat with her eighty-five-year-old mother. The mother turned out to have a wooden leg, which provided an embarrassing source of fascination to two-year-old Tom. They had drunk sweet sherry and worn paper hats, and stood up for the queen's speech.

Eventually Annie had become Mr. Robertson's secretary. Then

he had started deploying her in other departments. Step by step, she had achieved her current position. Whatever that was. With Jack in charge, she no longer knew where she stood. Ever since their meeting last week Jack had been remote and nitpicky, checking up on minor details and burdening her with unnecessary administration. Annie suspected that his ambitious wife had been nagging him to exercise his authority. She thought that he probably would agree to a partnership in the end. Even he would see that it was in his interest. But she dreaded the grudging negotiating process. Besides, in the last week the vista of a much larger and more frightening ambition had opened before her: the Annie Hamilton Literary Agency.

She knew exactly how to do it. It would be a two-pronged attack. Sebastian Winter, potentially her most lucrative author, was one prong. The other was the grand old man of English letters, Trelawny Grey. His recent books had proved too oblique and whimsical to be very successful commercially, but the string of novels he had written from the 1930s into the 1970s had made him a household name. He had retired to Ireland with his severe Swedish "housekeeper" and a brace of Burmese cats. Annie had once been deputized to go over to Tipperary and coax his latest book from him—"He likes clever blondes," Mr. Robertson had said. Fortunately Annie had always loved his books and knew them inside out. She had weathered a cantankerous grilling about his work, a roisterous trip to the races, and a four-hour whiskey marathon in a Dublin bar. "I like your Annie," Grey had written to Mr. Robertson afterward, adding cryptically "She reminds me of Salsabil, the only filly to win the Irish Derby this century." Thereafter Grey had insisted that no one but she—not even his editor—be allowed to tamper with even a semicolon of his prose. For years Grey had been threatening to write his memoirs. If the book was ever completed, it would be a sensational literary event, for his youth had been politically adventurous and sexually exotic. But just having his name on her list would be enough. With both Winter and Grey in the bag, surely other authors would follow.

Sebastian Winter's new deal would bankroll the setting up of her own agency and give her breathing space to build her list. But she had to grab it now. The minute Jack found out about the offer, the new book would become the property of Smith & Robertson. Not tomorrow or next week or next month but today, in ten minutes' time, she had an opportunity to take a decisive step in her life. Here was her chance to be her own boss, financially independent, free to choose the course of the rest of her life. The prize lay before her; all she had to do was step forward and pick it up. Yet fear of the unknown and a guilty sense of disloyalty held her like the bars of a cage.

The sudden buzz of her phone made her jump. Annie just had time to hear Sally begin, "I'm sorry, Annie, but your son—" when Tom walked into her office and slammed the door behind him. He looked so pale and unhappy that Annie dropped the phone at once and ran around her desk to him.

"What's happened?" she cried, fearing some terrible accident to Edward or the girls. She put her arms around him, but Tom stiffened and turned his head away, as he used to do as a sulky child.

"What is it?" she asked again, tightening her hold protectively. "Tom, don't frighten me like this. What's the matter?"

"What's the matter?" he said, stepping out of her embrace. "Oh, nothing much," he spat out bitterly. "I'd just be grateful if you would enlighten me on the small matter of who my father is."

Annie gasped and took a step backward. "Your *what?*"

"Come on, Mum, you heard." He stared hard into her face. Annie was shocked by the bruised look about his eyes.

"I don't understand what this is about," she said, "Your father is who he has always been. Edward, Daddy, Dad. Your father."

"Then why didn't you marry him until I was *three years old?*"

"Who told you that?" Annie whispered.

"Nobody told me. I looked it up in the Public Search Office—as anyone else could. Half the world could know I'm illegitimate. It's only me that has to be kept in the dark."

Tom's voice wavered, and he turned to hide the hurt in his face. Above the rim of his T-shirt Annie could see the delicate, boyish furrow at the back of his neck. Her heart went out to him even as her brain raced like a fox before the hounds. This moment had haunted her for twenty years, but she was still unprepared for its sudden, savage arrival. "Tom—darling," she pleaded, "I know it's been a shock, but there were reasons. Do stop glowering and sit down for a minute." She gestured toward a chair.

Tom thumped his backpack on the floor. "For God's sake, I'm not one of your bloody clients," he said angrily.

Annie suddenly remembered Sebastian. Was he already sitting in the restaurant, waiting for her? Sebastian Winter, her ticket to freedom. Without thinking, she checked her watch with a quick flick of her wrist. The gesture infuriated Tom.

"Stop looking at your watch!" he shouted. "What sort of a mother are you? You lie to me about my birth. You lie to me about my father. You lie to me about that photograph of 'Jonathan' in Malta. God, you must think I'm stupid not to recognize a man who's got his picture in every newspaper in the world."

"What do you mean?" asked Annie. "And keep your voice down," she added angrily. "Why we have to discuss this in my office rather than somewhere private I don't know. As it happens I do have an appointment. You might at least give me half a minute to cancel it and make other arrangements." Annie moved toward the door. She could get Sally to call the restaurant. A moment alone might calm Tom down and give her time to think.

Tom reached out and grabbed her arm, hard enough to hurt. "I don't give a damn about your stupid appointments," he said. "I want to know about Jordan Hope. Some people think that I look like him. Is he my father?"

"Don't be ridiculous." Annie yanked her arm out of his grip.

"Then why did you make up that lie about the photograph? Hope is front-page news. How come you never bothered to mention that you even knew him?"

"I should have thought that was obvious." Annie realized that she was shouting too and tried to control her voice. "The press has been hounding everybody who even went to the same Oxford party as Jordan. You might like to wake up to a gaggle of prurient newsmen on your doorstep, but I don't fancy it."

"So you did know him?"

"He was a friend of Rose's. They were both interested in politics. I used to see him around."

"What about all that 'two-times girl' stuff? 'Love always, J.' "

"For heaven's sake, Tom, he was an American," Annie said. "A big, gee-whizz American who wanted to be president even then. He was always hugging people and signing books or photos for them. That's how politicians work."

"So you never went out with him?"

"We might have turned up at the same party. I don't remember."

"You don't remember?" Tom was nearly crying with frustration.

"When are you going to start telling me the truth? You'd better be careful, Mother. I've been doing some checking up. That photograph was taken in the LMH gardens. I've been to the very spot. I know all about how you didn't take your degree, how disappointed Miss Kirk was, and Miss Reeves—they send their best wishes, by the way."

Annie felt panic overwhelm her. The walls she had built around her past were crumbling on every side. "How dare you go around prying and spying into my private life?"

Tom's face twisted as he tried to squeeze the tears back into his eyes. "How else can I find out the truth?" he asked. "Can't you see, it matters to me what happened back then. It matters to me who my father is. Do you want me to check with Jordan Hope and see what he says?"

Annie rounded on him like a tigress. "Don't you dare contact Jordan. Grow up, Tom. Do you realize the damage you could do to him if you even suggested he had an illegitimate son? And all because you've built up some utterly absurd fantasy based on an old snapshot."

Tom's face closed against her. He picked up his backpack by the strap and moved toward the door. Annie took a deep breath, fighting to regain a tone of reason. "Tom. Edward is your father. We fell in love, then we . . . parted. That was a mistake, and we put it right. I can explain—we'll both explain. But not here. Why don't you go home—please. I'll come as soon as I can. We can all talk this evening."

Tom didn't even look at her. He opened the door and walked into the corridor, where Sally watched nervously from her glassed-in cubicle. Annie followed him. "Tom . . . ?"

He carried on, quickening his pace. Annie ran after him. At the angle of the corridor she nearly bumped into Jack by a bank of filing cabinets. As Annie brushed past she caught a glimpse of his face, inscrutable as a mask. Now they were at the stairs. Tom, sure-footed in his sneakers, bounced down them ahead of her.

"Wait!" Annie yelled. "Where are you going?"

Annie caught only two words from his angry, muffled shout: "My father."

"*No,*" she screamed. "Tom, if you upset Edward I'll never forgive you."

Tom whirled around on the landing below and looked up at her with a face she hardly recognized.

"Who said anything about Edward?" he asked coldly.

Annie moved toward him, but it was too late. She heard his urgent tread continuing down the stairs, the jingle of his backpack buckle and the thud of the heavy front door. He was gone.

9

Bridge Over Troubled Water

*F*rom its niche above the shelves of cookbooks, the Victorian clock struck eleven. Annie sat alone in her kitchen, elbows propped on the scrubbed pine table, staring into the fruit bowl. She was wearing one of Edward's old shirts over her T-shirt and leggings, clutching the too-long cuffs tightly in her fists. Hair tumbled from a knot on the crown of her head, roughly secured with a tortoiseshell clip. On the principle of the watched pot, she kept her back to the telephone, which had remained obstinately silent all evening. At the sound of a footstep in the hall, Annie looked up eagerly. But it was only Edward.

"Come to bed," he said. "There's nothing you can do now. It won't do you any good to be tired on top of everything else."

Annie raked her fingers into her hair and clenched them tight, until her scalp ached. "Where is he?" she asked fiercely.

"Probably crashing on somebody's floor," said Edward. "He's a sensible boy. He got himself through Eastern Europe. He'll manage a night on his own, wherever he is."

"I handled it all so badly, Edward." Annie turned to him a face pale and dark-eyed with strain. "I shouted at him. I told him to mind his own business. I did the exact opposite of everything I should have done—everything we planned to do if he ever found out. But after all this time, I thought we were safe. I still can't believe he just went and looked up those records himself."

"Stop blaming yourself. We always knew this might happen.

Tom needs time to think about it. He'll come to us when he's ready."

"But what's he doing?" she growled. "Why can't he at least call? How can you be so bloody calm?"

"Because I know our son."

"You wouldn't have this afternoon," she said bitterly. "I couldn't even tell you some of the horrible things he said. And this ridiculous bee in his bonnet he's got about Jordan Hope."

"Yes," Edward frowned for a moment. "That does seem perverse. It's not as if you even knew him particularly well."

"I told you about the photograph, didn't I?" Annie snapped. "Tom's had a shock, and he's gone off the deep end. Didn't you used to imagine that you were adopted or swapped at birth in the hospital?"

"When I was about seven or eight," Edward said dubiously.

"God, I used to long for my real mother to come and reclaim me. I imagined her just like Mother in *The Railway Children*—brave and loving, with a kind face and sensible clothes and homemade cakes in the oven. And that was without any lies or mystery about my birth. Tom's entitled to indulge in a few wild fantasies, I suppose." Annie rocked impatiently in her chair. "I just wish he'd come home."

Edward came around behind her and squeezed her shoulders. "Leave it alone, darling. It's late. He'd be here by now if he were coming."

Annie pressed her cheek against his hand. "You go on up. I'd only thrash about in the bed and drive you crazy. I might have a whiskey. That always makes me sleepy."

Edward sighed and let her go. "Don't be too long. You know I can never sleep properly when you're not there."

When he had left, Annie poured herself a small whiskey and filled up the tumbler with water. Drink in hand, she wandered restlessly around the room, pausing to look at the postcards and invitations propped up on the china cabinet shelf, pulling the dead leaves off her plants, straightening the chairs around the table. She loved this room. She had colorwashed the walls herself, long before the "distressed" look had become fashionable, experimenting to reproduce the kind of pure color she'd grown up with in the Mediterranean. She'd designed everything too, from the shape of the arch above the stove to the slate-topped worktops made specially high so that she didn't get a backache. In the mornings sunshine filled the room; at night the lamp that she and Edward had bought years ago in the Paris flea market gave it an intimate, friendly glow. This is where she liked to work in the evenings, laying out her scripts on the big table or reading in the cushion-filled wicker chair by the window.

She and Edward had committed their last penny to buying this house and had invested years of their life in fixing it up. Midway in an elegant Georgian terrace, separated from the road by a phalanx of magnificent horse chestnut trees, it exuded a calm English confidence. It was the only place Annie had lived that felt truly hers. After her own haphazard childhood, she had been determined that her own children should never be in any doubt where "home" was.

Annie's thoughts circled back to Tom. Her stomach lurched as she tried to envisage where he might be or what he might be doing. It was perfectly possible for him to have flown two thousand miles across the Atlantic by now. Nobody could be more supportive than Edward, but there were certain things he couldn't fully appreciate. Suddenly Annie was struck by a thought of such blinding obviousness that she choked on her whiskey. America! It was too late for anything to be happening in stuffy old London, maybe. But it was barely cocktail time in New York. Annie grabbed the phone and punched in a familiar pattern of digits.

"Rose Cassidy's office," said a sugary voice. "How may I help you?"

"Is Rose there?"

"I'm sorry, she's in a conference right now. May I have her call you?"

Annie nearly groaned aloud. "Is it an important meeting? I mean, could you interrupt it? I need to speak to her very urgently."

There was a pause, then the same singsong inflection. "Whom may I say is calling?"

Annie spelled out her name letter by letter, rolling her eyes in frustration. Why did American "assistants" always sound as if they'd had their personalities surgically removed, like graduates of some Stepford Wife training school?

Annie was treated to a few bars of Vivaldi's "Winter," then there was a series of clicks and, miraculously, Rose came on the line. "Darling, I rushed straight out of my meeting. You've never said 'urgent' before. What's happened?"

At the sound of Rose's voice, pukka English with a subtle American slur, Annie's eyes brimmed with tears. She took a deep breath, wondering where to begin. The problems that had been crowding in on her seemed overwhelming, insoluble. "Oh, Rose." She moaned. "My whole life is falling apart. I don't know what to do."

"Hang on a minute," Rose said briskly. "This sounds serious." Annie waited, hunting for a tissue in a drawer of the oak china cabinet. Rose came back on the line. "All done. Now, tell me everything."

Many yards of newsprint had been devoted to profiles of Rose Cassidy. Annie had seen her described as a genius and a witch; as dictatorial, calculating, capricious, and snobbish; as Queen of the Brit Pack and even—in one notorious American headline—"Killer WASP." But Annie had no secrets from Rose. Too much had happened between them. She poured out her story and, with it, every emotion, good and bad. Rose grasped instantly the implications of Tom's disappearance.

"My God, Annie, you really think he might get in touch with Jordan?"

"I don't know" was Annie's anguished reply. "He seems completely obsessed by this father thing. I had to ring Edward and warn him, in case Tom burst in on him as well. But he never turned up at Edward's chambers, and he hasn't come home either. By nine o'clock I couldn't stand it any longer. I drove up to Oxford like a lunatic and found out that his roommate hadn't seen him since last night. But he showed me a note from Tom. Can you believe it, Rose? Tom told him that his father was seriously ill in the hospital and he'd be away from Oxford for *several days*. The roommate was stunned to see me, as you can imagine. I had to pretend I'd come up to get some of Tom's clothes for him."

"His passport!" Rose said excitedly. "Did you think of looking for that?"

"Of course I did. It's not in his room at Christ Church, and I can't find it here either."

"Annie," breathed Rose, "this is seriously terrible. The election's next *week*. Everyone with half a brain wants Jordan to win. I hate to think what might hit the fan if Tom turned up claiming to be his illegitimate son."

"Don't." Annie groaned. Tethered by the long telephone wire, she paced around the kitchen in her bare feet. "But what can I do?

I can't exactly call up Jordan and explain. I suppose it's preposterous to think that Tom could even get to him. But he's in a dangerous mood—all wired up and unstable, like a package of dynamite. He might have gone to stay with a friend, which is what Edward thinks. But he might be throwing himself off Beachy Head. He might be getting on a plane. Wherever he is, he's unhappy and mixed up, and I'm terrified he could just explode and start talking. God knows whether Jack overheard us shouting in the office today. He was only yards away. As if I haven't got enough trouble with Jack as it is. . . . Rose? Are you still there?"

"I'm thinking. Go on. What's all this about Jack?"

Annie explained. "But that's brilliant! Tell the bozo to stuff his partnership, and do your own thing. This isn't a problem, Annie—it's your big chance."

Annie snorted. "You sound like some ghastly Victorian sampler. 'Man's extremity is God's opportunity.' You don't understand. I'd have to do it now, like tomorrow, before Jack gets his mitts on Sebastian. I can't possibly think about that with Tom on the loose. Besides, I—well, there's a chance I might have to leave the country for a few days."

"Whatever for?"

Annie fiddled with the curly telephone wire. "It's my mother," she confessed. "Apparently she's dying and wants to see me."

Rose was astounded. "But you've always hated the old dragon. I felt like carving her up myself once."

"I know, I know. I've tried not to think about it. I've tried to say 'Go on then, die, you old bitch.' But I can't. She's dying, Rose. She wants to see me. I suppose I'm curious, if nothing else."

Rose was silent—disapproving or sympathetic, Annie couldn't tell. "I probably won't go." Annie sighed. "Not with Tom and everything else. Anyway, she could be dead already. I got the letter about her over a week ago, and—"

Rose interrupted, sounding incredibly portentous. "On the contrary, you positively must go."

"I must?"

" '*Eppur si muove,*' " Rose said enigmatically.

"Rose, stop being mysterious. What are you talking about?"

"It's what Galileo said about the earth moving around the sun, dummy. Annie"—Rose lowered her voice to a conspirator's whisper—"I have just had a truly awesome brainwave. It would solve everything—Jordan, mother, job, the lot. Listen. Here's what you do."

After thirty seconds Annie burst out, "I can't!" After a minute she protested, "I couldn't possibly." At the end of three minutes she sagged against the wall, completely silenced. Maybe Rose was a witch after all.

"Admit," Rose said smugly, "it does have a kind of fearful symmetry to it."

"Fearful is the word. I don't think I'm brave enough."

"Rubbish. Is this the Annie Paxford who brought Oxford to its knees with her incandescent Rosalind?"

"But that was—"

". . . who smoked joints through Helen Gardner's Shakespeare lectures?"

"Only once," Annie protested.

"The Annie Paxford," Rose continued remorselessly, "who jumped fully clothed into the river at the Eights Week Ball and danced the rest of the night away wearing only a rugby shirt?"

"No, it isn't," Annie said sadly. "It's boring old Mrs. Hamilton, aged forty-two and a quarter, with her career on the line, a dying mother, and a missing son."

"Don't be feeble. I didn't like to tell you, but while we've been talking I've had to leave John Updike and Stephen Spender kicking their heels next door, with only Cindy and some iced water for company. Imagine, two literary lions with their tails positively twitching. If I can risk alienating those two for you, *darling* Annie, you could at least consider my fiendishly cunning master plan. I'm volunteering to do the tricky bit, after all."

"But—"

"Got to go now. I'll call you back when I've got the information. Don't worry. Everything will be fine."

Rose smacked a kiss down the phone, and the line went dead. Annie hung up. She felt buffeted, wiped out, drained—and starving. She rummaged in the pantry until she found half a chocolate cookie at the bottom of a package. Munching hungrily, she pushed open the double doors from the kitchen and went into the back living room that led out to the garden. She lay down in the dark on the big, comfortable chesterfield and wrapped herself up in a worn quilt that was always kept folded over one arm of the chair.

Now she knew how Rose managed to get celebrities to do impossible things. Hadn't there been a sensational cover showing a naked movie star astride a rearing stallion? And a portrait of the Princess of Wales in the style of Gainsborough? She had probably already lined up Ginny Hope for a full-color, center-spread makeover.

Still, the Rose treatment was kind of exhilarating, once you got used to it. No doubt people felt much the same about shooting the rapids or bungee jumping. Annie thought her way carefully through Rose's outrageous plan, combing it for flaws. There weren't any. Unless you counted one or two tiny deceptions.

Annie tried to imagine what it would be like to see Jordan again. How would he play it? Embarrassed, businesslike, angry? Would he try to smother her in professional charm like one of his prospective voters? A smile tugged at her mouth. Let him try.

She yawned. It was all such a long time ago. What were those lines she used to quote to herself when it was all over?

> Shake hands forever, cancel all our vows
> And when we meet at any time again,
> Be it not seen in either of our brows
> That we one jot of former love retain.

Well, maybe. But one thing you found out as you got older was that the important things didn't change. Perhaps Rose was right. Somewhere inside sensible Mrs. Hamilton, Annie Paxford still lurked—a secretive nineteen-year-old with her head stuffed full of literature and a passion to prize life open like an oyster.

Annie yawned again. A glorious drowsiness invaded her body. She loosened her hair and dropped the clip on the floor. As her eyes closed, the years curled back and floated away like the pages of a burning book.

Oxford
1969–70

10

Wild Honey

Michaelmas Term 1969

Annie leaned out of the train window, watching the stoutly rain-coated figure recede to a square of navy blue and fluttering white. She returned a final wave, drew in her head, and pulled the window shut. Alone at last. Squatting on the floor of the corridor, she rummaged in her Greek bag and extracted a pack striped in purple and azure blue. With two forefingers she flipped her heavy, honey-colored hair over her shoulders, letting it trail down her back. Then she lit a cigarette in relief and celebration. Soon she would be back at Oxford, in a world she loved and understood, where she could do her own thing, without muddle and fights.

Aunt Betty meant well. For ten years her Kensington apartment had been Annie's staging post between boarding school and wherever home then happened to be. Annie knew every creaky floorboard and the proper position of each piece of Staffordshire pottery. She had long ago lost her terror of the clanking cage of the elevator, which rose and descended at a dowager's pace, and learned the knack of making the lavatory chain work the first time. From this apartment she and her aunt had sallied forth to Fortnum's for lunch and Gorringe's for school uniforms, to museums and art galleries, walks in Kensington Gardens and the occasional "suitable" film. When she was old enough to be allowed out on her own, she had spent hours wandering down the King's Road or foraging through stalls in Portobello Market. Sometimes she met school friends whose parents lived in London. They would doll themselves up in high heels, pale lipstick, and thick mascara, and talk their way into X-rated films like *Tom Jones*. Once they had taken the train to Surrey and walked for miles to stand outside the high walls of George Harrison's house, fantasizing about how he might invite them in to meet the other Beatles. Later they had discovered that the Fab Four had been meditating with the Maharishi at the time.

Annie enjoyed her aunt's schoolgirlish zeal for treats, usually edible ones involving a great deal of cream. But three days with Aunt Betty, when Annie desperately needed to sort out her thoughts, was long enough. Aunt Betty was an unworldly spinster of fifty-something, married to her secretarial job at the BBC. The guiding principles of her life were doing her duty, being kind to animals, and wearing wool next to the skin. Her idea of excitement was watching *The Forsyte Saga* on Sunday nights. She was not the sort of person one could talk to about sex.

Annie took a last, determined drag of her cigarette. Her aunt disapproved of smoking. After a period of polite abstention, the cigarette tasted of burning garbage dumps and made Annie's head spin. So what? She was free, female, and nineteen. She was officially an adult. She could do as she liked. She blew out the smoke with a loud sigh, wishing she could as easily expel the memory of that ghastly last day in Malta.

Annie swayed down the corridor, nearly tripping over her fashionably long purple scarf, and slid open the door of the second-class compartment where she had bagged a corner seat with her coat. An elderly couple sitting by the door drew back their legs, as if the terrifying word "student" were branded across her forehead. Annie glanced at her other traveling companions: a bossy-looking woman who reminded Annie of her old piano teacher and a furtive man with a gingery halo of hair, reading T. S. Eliot. A postgraduate student, Annie diagnosed, the quintessential Oxford gnome who haunted the upper reading room of the Bodleian by day and spent the evening crouched over cocoa in some damp rented room off the Cowley Road. Annie shook out her hair to form a curtain between her and the rest of the compartment, turning to look out the window. Grimy London terraces gave way to privet-screened suburban homes and finally to the open countryside. England looked misty and melancholic, just as it should. Ponies huddled in the corners of fields, ears back, tails clamped tight against the October wind.

Leaves of amber and bronze sagged under the weight of rain. Annie felt restless, excited, and nervous all at once.

Over the long vacation she had relived every moment of last term's consuming romance. She had first seen him last April. *As You Like It* was to be put on in the sixth week of the summer term in St. Hilda's meadow. In the term's first week, the cast had gathered for a read-through in a bleak college seminar room furnished with molded plastic chairs. Annie was to play Rosalind. It was her first big part at Oxford, and she was nervous. The director was an intense second-year student with John Lennon glasses and a corduroy cap, bent on making theatrical history. This was to be a landmark production, he proclaimed, making a break with the trendy, modern-dress approach to Shakespeare that had become such a cliché. No Peter Brook or Charles Marowitz for him, thank you very much. This *As You Like It* would be as Shakespeare himself would have liked it. It would emphasize the roots of the play in masque and romance. It would be pastoral, poetic, and perfect. The verse would be beautifully spoken and the songs sung properly—to the strains of a lute, if obtainable. He was in discussion with a local farmer about borrowing a sheep for the shepherd scenes. Instead of the traditional strawberries and wine, mead and syllabub would be served during intermission. In the final act, Hymen, god of marriage, would waft magically across the Cherwell, a coup de théâtre to be effected by means of a punt and underwater ropes.

In the middle of this visionary speech, a tall, dark-haired student had strolled in, casually apologetic. Seating himself at the front, he had stretched out long legs encased in tight, bright-red trousers tucked piratelike into black boots. From the row behind, Annie studied his profile—sloping forehead and narrow, disdainful nose—as he listened to the remainder of the speech. He appeared quite unruffled by the director's grandiose expectations. Annie knew at once that he must be monstrously arrogant. He would make a perfect Jaques.

As it turned out, she was right. There was an amused detachment about Edward Hamilton that suited the part of Shakespeare's self-dramatizing cynic. He was in his second year at Trinity, reading law. His natural theatricality expressed itself in black shirts and a succession of outrageous waistcoats. As Jaques he was to wear a long black cloak and broad-brimmed hat, with which he made much dramatic play. Along with the rest of the cast, Annie teased him about his clothes and the stuffiness of his chosen career. But she was intrigued. There was a calmness about him that was attractive.

One gloriously hot afternoon they were rehearsing in St. Hilda's meadow. Hymen had smuggled a bottle of Pimm's past the director and Annie was feeling giggly. Egged on by the rest of the cast, she tried to put Edward off his "All the world's a stage" speech by acting it out behind the director's back, hamming up each part from the mewling, puking baby to the old codger "sans teeth, sans eyes" et cetera. Edward never blinked an eyelash. At the end of his scene he beckoned Annie over to the river's edge, looking serious. Annie followed, half nervous and half defiant. Surely he could take a joke. As she approached his eyes narrowed with concentration.

"Is that a new dress?" he asked.

As a matter of fact, it was. Annie thought she looked rather wonderful in it. She looked down, brushing the skirt dismissively. "What, this old thing?"

"Good." He picked her up and then dropped her, squealing and kicking, into the river. The cast applauded.

After that Annie was aware of a certain frisson of complicity between them, but they had few scenes together and were never alone. Anyway, there was no shortage of men asking her out, a fact she made no special effort to conceal. She wondered if Edward had a girlfriend and discovered that the very idea made her feel savage. On the night of the dress rehearsal, she was waiting to go on, dressed in her Ganymede outfit of breeches, boots, shirt, and jerkin. A pall of gloom hung over the cast. The weather had turned cold. Touchstone still hadn't learned his lines. The lights kept shorting out. In the darkness and confusion someone had stepped on the lute. Annie could already feel the sarcastic bite of the reviews.

She was waiting in the dark, hunched with cold and anxiety, when Edward suddenly appeared beside her, opened his cloak, and enfolded her in it. For a moment Annie was shocked into stillness, then she slid her arm around his warm body. They stood in the shadows, still as statues, not speaking, hardly breathing.

Afterward she found him waiting for her outside the changing tent. He took her to the Bear and bought her a schooner of sherry, looking at her with those grave, gray eyes as if every idiotic thing she said and every nervous gesture she made were a miracle. When last orders were called, she watched him carry their glasses to the bar, boots scuffing across the bare floorboards, eyes half closed against the smoke twisting up from his cigarette. She saw the way his body moved as he fished for coins in the back pocket of his tight jeans. As if he could feel her eyes on him, he turned around and gave her a slow-burn look across the crowded room. At closing time he walked her back to Lady Margaret Hall, a distance of about half a mile, but they stopped to kiss so often that it took an hour. When at last Edward let her go, Annie stumbled through the brightly lit corridors to her room, her lips on fire, her cheeks sore from his rough stubble.

It was Annie's first intoxicating taste of an Oxford summer term. Suddenly the Cherwell, which had been the wintertime preserve of ducks and willows, sprouted punts full of exhibitionist young men in striped blazers and barefoot girls in hats. Trees she had never even noticed exploded into blossom, of every shade from palest vanilla to raspberry pink. By day the lanes were loud with bicycle bells and the anguished protestations of third-year students that they would never be ready for finals. At night the Beach Boys and the Stones and Pink Floyd blared out of open casement windows. The air smelled of wisteria and roses and newly mown grass. There were tea parties, tennis parties, garden parties, beer-cellar parties, river-barge parties, Edwardian parties, Twenties parties. Annie fell headlong in love with Oxford and summer and Edward all at once.

The day after the dress rehearsal, Annie went to lunch with Edward at Trinity. The sun had reappeared, and they carried their plates of salmon mayonnaise and bowls of strawberries and cream onto the lawn. Edward's roommate, Anthony, brought over a bottle of cold white wine. An ex-Etonian with a Roman nose, he looked Annie over with frank admiration, stamping his foot like a stallion. "What a heavenly girl. Can I have one?" After lunch they wandered down to Christ Church Meadow, idling along the broad elm-shaded path to the Isis to watch the boat races. By chance it was the day that Trinity bumped Oriel out of third place. The college boathouse was raucous with celebration. Everyone seemed to know Edward and to think it quite natural that he and Annie belonged together.

The few remaining weeks of the term passed in a blur of new enchantments. Annie had to work at night. The days were too exciting. They bicycled out to the Perch and the White Hart for drinks, returning in the late midsummer twilight. They held hands through *Un Homme et une Femme* and sighed over Terence Stamp and Julie Christie in *Far from the Madding Crowd*. One rainy afternoon they played darts for champagne stakes with Edward's friends, consuming three bottles in the Trinity beer cellar. In the evenings Edward took her for a curry at the Taj Mahal or cannelloni at La Cantina.

Every night there was the adrenaline rush of another performance—making up, horseplay in the changing tent, and that shivery moment in the second half when darkness stole across the meadow and Shakespeare's verse, even indifferently recited, worked its magic. On the third night a gust of wind caught the punt sideways, depositing Hymen in the undergrowth five feet from his target. Instead of gliding ethereally on stage, he spoke his lines invisibly from a hawthorn thicket, to the sounds of his costume ripping and muffled hiccups of laughter from the other players.

Fortunately the reviewers had already pronounced. If no one hailed it as a landmark production, the seats were filled almost every night. One morning Rose burst into Annie's room to show her the *Cherwell* review, which rated the production workmanlike but called Annie's Rosalind "enchanting." It was enough to guarantee an all-night cast party, awash with booze and sentiment, in the director's rooms in the Iffley Road. Annie flirted with most of the men and danced with all of them. She hugged everybody and drank everything in sight. She wished that the party could go on forever and ever, and called Edward an old bore when he tried to take her home. Only when the director passed out and had to be put to bed did Annie concede that it was time to go.

It was already light when they crossed Magdalen Bridge. A thin layer of mist hovered above the river. Before them High Street curved gracefully away, looking much as it must have two hundred years ago. Oxford was utterly still, apart from the electric whine of a milk van and the chatter of the dawn chorus. Edward and Annie walked up the middle of the empty road, hip to hip in an easy rhythm, their arms around each other. Annie still felt full of energy. She wanted to do something. But Edward was silent, his thoughts apparently far away. She punched him in the ribs.

"Say something."

He stopped and turned to look at her, dropping his arms to his sides. "Okay," he said slowly. He took her face in her hands. "Come back with me. I want to make love to you."

"Edward . . ."

"Anthony's gone to London for a party," Edward urged. "He won't be back until tonight." He moved his hands to the sensitive skin under her hair, then down her back, pulling her hard against him. He pressed his forehead against hers, staring into her eyes. She felt their eyelashes brush. "I love you, Annie. Come back with me. Please."

Annie leaned into him, smiling. "All right."

His attic bedroom was high and secret. Annie lay tangled with Edward in the narrow bed, eyes shut, mind floating. How was it possible for her body to feel like this—at once as tight as a drum and as limp as a ragdoll's? The sweep of skin and muscle down Edward's back was delicious. Her fingers found two little hollows at the bottom of his spine and tickled them gently. Edward moaned. He must like that. She did it again. On the inside of her eyelids she could see zigzag patterns from the sunlight that glimmered through the curtains. "Busy old fool, unruly sun—" how did that poem go? Was it the same one that went on "License my roving hands and let them go / Before, behind, between, above, below"? Edward must have read it. His hands were warm and inquisitive. Annie did a bit of exploring herself. Heavens, how extraordinary!—she had always imagined that it would stick straight out, not *up* like this. At Edward's persuasive touch on the inside of her knee Annie stretched her legs out languorously, sinking deeper into a narcotic trance. In a distant corner of her brain a voice was saying, *My God, I'm really going to do it. Please don't let him realize this is my first time.* But it didn't really matter. Nothing mattered except the amazing sensations in her body and Edward's breath urgent on her neck.

Annie crossed her legs as the train shuddered through a culvert and out into the flat plain around Didcot. They must have passed through Reading without her noticing. The piano woman had gone, and ginger hair was eyeing her interestedly over *The Four Quartets*. She gave him a cool stare, noting his nerdy suede shoes and baggy trousers. He must be nearly thirty! A creature like this could be her fate if she followed her mother's advice and waited until she was a hundred and twelve for Mr. Right to appear. All the beautiful men like Edward Hamilton would have been snapped up.

On her last night in Malta she had gone with her parents, as usual, to the club for her farewell treat, driving the long way around to see the castle at sunset. At the bar of the officers' mess there was the usual heavy gallantry about her father's "harem." "Hard to tell which is the mother and which the daughter, what?" The colonel teased Annie about the number of suitors awaiting her in Oxford and congratulated her on returning to "civilization." Each expatriate community she had lived in was the same—Aden, Cyprus, Malta. Everyone acted as if they were perilously marooned among a remote tribe of cannibals. They were scathing about the locals and talked of "ukay" as of some lost paradise. Annie believed most of them wouldn't last five minutes in rainy Guildford, with no clubhouse or tennis courts or the much-reviled "girls" who did all the work. Privately, she saved up a few choice phrases for Rose, who loved her to "do" Malta.

But publicly she smiled and charmed, and in due course they had moved on to the dining room to eat prawn cocktail, well-done beef with Yorkshire pudding, followed by baked apples and custard. Afterward there had been more banter at the bar. As usual her mother had collected a circle of eager admirers and drank too many brandies. But she had seemed in a good mood. Annie had no inkling of what was to come.

Her father drove them back to the villa through the darkening countryside. Annie wound down her window and relaxed in the backseat, enjoying the warm wind on her face. Tomorrow she would be leaving.

"This young man of yours," her mother suddenly began.

Annie stiffened. "I've told you, Mummy, his name's Edward."

"This 'Edward,' then," she said, enunciating carefully as if it were some outlandish name, "I hope you aren't sleeping with him."

Annie said nothing. *I'm nineteen,* she thought. *It's none of your business.*

Her mother twisted around from the front seat to peer at Annie. Her earrings glinted in the headlights of a passing car.

"Well?" she insisted.

Annie stared at the blond nimbus of her mother's bouffant hair.

In the lengthening silence her father cleared his throat. "Mary dear, I don't think we really—"

"Shut up, Charles. Anyway, it's no good her pretending she isn't, because I found some contraceptive pills in her room this afternoon."

"You were snooping!" Annie was shocked. What if her mother had read Edward's letters too? The idea made her feel sick.

"I do not call it snooping to be concerned about my daughter. Are you sleeping with him or aren't you?"

"Yes, I am. And I'm not ashamed of it."

"I knew it," shrieked her mother, clasping her temples. "You stupid, stupid girl. Don't you know anything about men? This Edward, he's just using you for sex."

"He's not! Edward loves me. And—and I love him," she added defiantly.

"My darling child." Her mother threw out a dismissive arm, bracelets jangling. "You're barely nineteen. What could you possibly know about love? You wait. You'll get back to your precious Oxford and find he doesn't even give you the time of day—let alone a proposal of marriage."

Annie gasped. "Marriage! I don't want to marry him," she said scornfully.

"The way you're carrying on you may have to," her mother said grimly. "I've read about all this student nonsense—pop concerts and sit-ins and not wearing bras—but I never thought you would lower yourself to that kind of behavior."

"It's not like that," Annie protested. "You're just jealous because I'm having a good time. People in your day didn't have sex before marriage because they didn't dare to. It wasn't anything to do with morality."

"Well, actually—" began her father.

"Stop the car, Charles!" her mother shouted. "I will not be spoken to like this."

Far from slowing down, Annie's father gunned the car forward. "You're drunk," he stated coldly. "If you ever thought before you spoke, you would realize that what you're saying is both cruel and unfair."

"At least I do speak," her mother retaliated. "All you ever do is read the bloody paper and play chess with yourself."

"And why do you think that is?"

Annie put her hands over her ears. "Shut up, both of you," she begged, tears squeezing under her eyelids.

She felt the car turning into the villa gates and was out of the door even before it stopped. She ran inside and up to her room, slamming the door. Bicker, bicker, bicker. Why did they do it? Even on her last night they couldn't stop themselves.

When she was a little girl, she used to get right down under the bedclothes and pour out her heart to an imaginary sister, a twin rather improbably named Rita. The great thing about Rita was her total fearlessness. She thought up brilliant things for Annie to say to people who were nasty to her, and she made up fantastic stories, usually about running away, of which Annie was always the heroine. But Rita had faded away when Annie went to boarding school. The real brothers and sisters she had longed for never appeared. When it came to dealing with her parents, she was on her own.

She undressed, put on her nightshirt, and locked herself in the bathroom. She washed her face in cold water, rubbed Vaseline into her eyelashes, and swallowed one of her pills. The next time she took one she would be in England, where Edward was.

As she went back down the hall she could hear a familiar pattern of sounds downstairs: her mother's voice loud and petulant, heels tapping on marble as she crossed and recrossed the room, and the conciliatory murmur of her father's replies. Were they talking about her? She paused by the balustrade, listening.

". . . do as they bloody well like?" Her mother's voice rose to a crescendo. "Thank God I never let you persuade me to have any more. Nine months of feeling sick and fat and ugly, and then all that terrible pain. And for what?"

There was the chink of bottle against glass and the gurgle of liquid. "So that my own daughter can tell me to leave her alone so she can 'do her own thing.' "

There was a pause. Her father's reply was inaudible.

"Oh, yes, throw my past in my face."

Annie heard the rustle of a newspaper.

"That's right, Charles, ignore me. Bury your head in the paper. Go off and cure some bloody patient. Just don't expect me to help when she gets herself into a mess. Thank God it's her last night."

"I imagine she feels the same way."

"And don't expect me to get up to see her off. I'm taking a sleeping pill."

This time, even as she was sidling back to her room, Annie heard her father's weary reply. "Take as many as you like."

In the morning she found him at the kitchen table in front of yesterday's *Times*. His face looked thin and gray. He had missed a patch of stubble under his jaw. Annie went over to him and put her hands on his shoulders. She breathed on the bald spot on the top of his head and made as if to polish it with her sleeve: an old joke. He reached up to pat her hand.

"Ready to go, monkey?"

They bumped along the potholed airport road, between rows of scrubby oleanders. A young man on foot, seeing their British army license plates, shook a fist at them. Right on, Annie cheered silently. The British were in retreat everywhere from their old empire—and about time too.

"You mustn't mind what your mother says," her father began hesitantly. "Life hasn't been quite as she expected. Always living abroad. Moving on every few years."

"She hates me." To her horror, Annie felt her eyes fill with tears. "My own mother. That's why she never had any more children, isn't it?"

Her father negotiated carefully around a mule, almost invisible beneath a load of firewood.

"Isn't it?" Annie sniffed, rummaging for a tissue. He handed her his handkerchief.

"What was so awful about me?" Annie blew her nose loudly. "I adored her when I was little. I remember hanging on to her knees and begging her not to leave me with Yasmin or Concepcion or whoever it was. Just sometimes she stayed home with me. She'd put on the radio and try to teach me to dance—jitterbug, she called it. Such a funny word—like a beetle. She loved that music. It made her happy.

"But she was always on her way out somewhere. And then you sent me away. I used to keep her photo on my chest of drawers—even at that awful first school where we were only allowed to have one personal item showing. The other girls said how lucky I was to live abroad and have such a glamorous-looking mother. But I always wondered—I think—she just wanted to get rid of me."

Her father pulled up at the low airport building and switched off the engine. In the distance the Mediterranean looked choppy. The windsock strained at its pole. It would be a rocky takeoff.

"It's not you who's disappointed her," he said finally, staring ahead. "It's me.

"When we first met, your mother seemed to, well, admire me. She was a very young nurse just down from Lancashire, and I'm afraid she thought of me as an experienced older man who was going to sweep her into a glamorous new life. The National Health was only just beginning then. Doctors were still thought of as rather grand. Big houses in the country, pillars of the community, perhaps a knighthood one day. And I'd been to university and not done too badly in the war." He grimaced diffidently. "All that nonsense.

"The fact was, I hadn't even qualified yet. I soon saw that she would never be happy while I struggled my way up to becoming a surgeon. So I found myself a medical officer's job instead. It meant more money, travel abroad, all sorts of perks. Rather dull work, of course, but I didn't mind that if Mary was happy."

But she isn't. The unspoken words hung awkwardly between them. Annie didn't know how to respond. She had never heard her father say so much.

"Heigh-ho." He tapped the steering wheel, breaking the mood. "What about those suitcases, then?"

They checked Annie in, then sat on high stools at the bar and ordered coffee. It came in little glasses, thick and syrupy.

"So—why did you marry her?" Annie asked abruptly.

Her father stared back in surprise. "I loved her. I worshipped her." He laughed almost joyously. "She was like a firework lighting up the sky. Everyone was after her—all the doctors, and half the patients too. But . . . well, she chose me."

He set his glass on the aluminum-topped bar with a click. "Say not the struggle naught availeth. You stick with your young man, if you think he's worth it."

"Yes," Annie said thoughtfully.

"No need to be in too much of a hurry, eh?"

"No."

"That's the ticket."

Annie's face softened with affection as she remembered her last sight of him as she crossed the tarmac to the plane, an upright, emphatically English figure in checked shirt and glossy brogues.

The train squeaked to a halt. Jolted out of her reverie, Annie looked up to see a little graveyard checkered with afternoon shadows and tumbled about with leaves. She exchanged a smug, conspiratorial look with ginger hair. This was a familiar trick of the Oxford train, designed to confound outsiders who hustled to collect their bags as the train slowed and were then left stranded among their luggage in the corridor. She could still recall the anxiety that had gripped her, at exactly this spot, twelve months ago. "I'm afraid there's been a mistake," she had imagined them saying at Lady Margaret Hall, with that chilly Oxford courtesy, perusing a leather-bound ledger. "Paxford, did you say? We have no record of that name here." She had actually brought with her the telegram offering her a place at the college, in anticipation of such a scene. The memory of her insecurity made her blush now, but the early days had not been easy. No one had told her that LMH was the "posh" college, attracting shriekingly well-bred girls with double-barreled names and high-caste Indians in saris. Annie's achievement in getting into Oxford had been unusual enough, at her school, to merit a half-day off and a new line on the wooden scroll of honor in the assembly hall, and she had come up—one always went "up" to Oxford—knowing no one.

She found soon enough that her unusual background did not mean she was more stupid than others. It took even less time to discover that, in this university of twenty-odd male colleges and only five female, she was socially in high demand. Fresh from a girls' boarding school, Annie had said yes to every man who asked her out, until a few evenings of crippling boredom and gauche gropes had made her more discriminating. By the end of the first term she had begun to make friends within the college and had landed a nonspeaking part in an Oriel production of *Twelfth Night*. By the second term—Hilary, they called it—she had dumped Aunt Betty's idea of a suitable college wardrobe at the thrift shop, exchanging her Jaeger skirts and "nice" dresses for groovier gear. Her minuscule Oxford University Diary, printed on India paper and furnished with a tiny wooden pencil, into which she had dutifully copied the times of lectures and worthy-sounding society meetings, filled up with parties, lunches, films, auditions. Annie had never dreamed that anyone could have so much fun.

Oxford was, she had found, a place of secret pleasures, closely guarded. The best pubs were invariably hidden in courtyards and down unpromising alleyways; the most breathtaking buildings behind walls black with car fumes. A chance turning in the monastic gloom of a Gothic archway could lead equally well to enchanting cloistered gardens or the fellows' parking lot. There was an entirely new language to master too. The head of a college might be a dean, provost, warden, rector, president, master, or principal. Exams, depending on their nature and timing, might be called collections, prelims, mods, or schools, and when you took them you had to dress entirely in black and white, known as "subfusc." New College was "New," University College "Univ," Brasenose College "BNC," St. Edmund Hall "Teddy Hall." "Matriculation" was the Latin ceremony that formally admitted students to membership of the university. If you were going *on* the river, that meant punting on the

Cherwell—from the "Oxford" end of the boat, naturally. Going *down to* the river meant rowing, or watching the boat races, on the Thames, which in Oxford was called the Isis.

Like all first-years, Annie had initially found this new vocabulary strange, even pretentious. Now she wouldn't think twice about referring to one of the world's greatest libraries as "the Bod." She was a cool second-year, with friends and a lover waiting. Annie stretched out her legs, admiring the boots that she had bought from a new shop called Biba. They were ravishing pink suede, tightly laced to follow the curve of her calves from ankle to knee. She was sure Edward would like them. Even Rose might concede that they were groovy.

Everyone knew Rose Cassidy. It was impossible not to. She had distinguished herself in her very first term by being dragged away from a demonstration outside the Union debating club, hair-first, by the police, then lodging a complaint for excessive violence. She argued with her tutors, played Frank Zappa at top volume, and smoked French cigarettes. Dressed almost exclusively in purple, with lots of jangly silver jewelry, her dark hair long and loose with bangs cut dramatically just above her extraordinary green eyes, she looked quite unlike the other LMH girls. Although Annie had overheard disparaging remarks about Rose—too bossy, too outspoken, too politically extreme—she had rather admired her from afar. But their rooms were in different buildings. It wasn't until their second term that they had become friends.

All first-years majoring in English were bound together by their terror of prelims, an exam designed to get all the really boring bits over with in one huge gulp of mindless learning. As well as literature tutorials, which they attended in pairs, there were classes in the history of the English language, in which they all struggled together to grasp the significance of sound changes and the Great Vowel Shift. It was dreary work. One gloomy February day, in the middle of such a class, Rose had pushed up her bangs in a characteristic gesture and exclaimed in exasperation, "This is all bullshit, isn't it?" The teacher, an Irish woman not much older than her students, froze in front of the blackboard. The rest of the class had sat in stunned, well-bred silence, broken by Annie's quip, "The Great Bowel Shift." Even the teacher had laughed.

After that, Rose had taken Annie up. Annie's room was near their tutor's quarters, and Rose often banged on the door to borrow An-

nie's college gown when she was late for tutorials and couldn't be
bothered to get her own. On the rare occasions when they both ate
in Hall, they sat together. Last summer, they had played tennis before breakfast a few times, until the novelty wore off. Rose seemed
to find Annie's life abroad glamorous, and Annie let her think so.
For her part, she loved to hear about Rose's large, noisy family, the
bizarre patients who frequented her parents' psychiatric consulting
rooms, and the succession of lame ducks, refugees, and revolution-
aries who inhabited the basement flat of their London house. When
the time came to choose where she wanted to live the following year,
Annie was flattered to be recruited for what Rose called "my" corridor. Whatever happened with Edward, life with Rose would not
be dull.

Suddenly the train lurched into movement. In a couple of minutes
it would be drawing into the station whose rusting Victorian iron-
work and crumbling wooden structure testified to Oxford's carefully
cultivated air of shabbiness. Stuffing *Lord of the Rings* into her bag,
Annie pulled down her suitcase from the overhead shelf and dragged
it through the compartment door into the corridor. It was heavy
with books, for there had been little else to do but read during the
interminable long vacation. She couldn't possibly lug it from the bus
stop to LMH; she would have to fork out five shillings for a taxi.

Her spirits rose as she counted the landmarks out the taxi window. Behind this grimy wall was Worcester, where a shy boy called
Colin had taught her to ice-skate when the lake froze over last winter. Here was the Playhouse, where she and Rose had once hung out
in the coffee bar hoping to be spotted. Instead they had found an
all-male posse of egomaniacs admiring one another's bone structure.
At the top of Beaumont Street, where the taxi turned into the extravagantly wide avenue of St. Giles, Annie was reassured to see that
no amount of scrubbing had been able to obliterate the famous graf-
fito on the walls of the Taylorian building: "Matriculation makes
you blind." Almost next door was the pub where she had often met
Edward, the Eagle and Child, known to initiates as the Bird and
Babe—and to a few would-be wits as the Fowl and Fetus.

At St. Giles' Church, the taxi forked right into North Oxford,
the far-reaching Victorian suburb colonized by dons almost a century ago, when they were at last allowed to marry. Annie felt a
squeeze of excitement as they turned into a gloomy street lined with
monstrous houses of neo-Gothic patterned brickwork, each gabled

and crenelated like an ogre's castle. This was Norham Gardens, at the bottom of which lay Lady Margaret Hall. She leaned forward as her taxi rounded the final curve. There at last was its undistinguished but friendly red-brick facade, shaded by lime trees and cluttered with the usual ramshackle array of bicycles.

Annie paid the cabdriver and stepped through the arched gateway, checking the blackboard for any phone messages; there were none. Leaving her suitcase, she went down the steps into the porter's lodge to look in her pigeonhole. As always at the beginning of term, it was stuffed with flyers. A Chinese restaurant was offering a free bottle of Mateus rosé with every meal for two during the next two weeks. The Oxford Revolutionary Socialist Students were staging a demonstration next week. "We will make your parties go with a bang!" promised a pop group called Climax Far.

Annie discarded them impatiently and riffled through a pile of college circulars, identifiable by the LMH crest on the envelopes. From Edward there was nothing.

"You've been somewhere warm," said the porter brightly. "Good vacation, was it?"

"Great," Annie lied. She felt bitterly disappointed. She looked through her mail again, wondering if her mother could be right. Had last term just been a casual interlude for Edward, easily forgotten over the long summer months?

After retrieving her suitcase, she crunched along the gravel path around the quad and pushed open the door to Wordsworth, the pretty nineteenth-century building where she had chosen to live this year. As she climbed the stone staircase, she could hear laughter and doors banging. Someone's record player was blasting out a song about revolution.

Her new room was at the far end of the corridor. Outside it she could see her old school trunk, which she had left in storage over vacation. But there was something else as well. Annie dropped her suitcase and ran down the hall.

Propped against her door was a bunch of tightly furled, dark-red roses, encased in cellophane and tied with a huge bow. A small, stiff envelope was attached, addressed to Miss Ann Paxford.

Annie drew out a card and read: *Welcome back, darling. Dinner tomorrow at seven? Can't wait. All my love, Edward.*

11

Keep on Runnin'

Jordan rested his elbows on the parapet of the little humpbacked bridge by the Trout Inn, catching his breath. He was out of condition after a long summer back home and too much of his mother's home-fried cooking. This run from his new place off Walton Street—"digs," they said here—took him across Port Meadow to the Trout, then back down the other side of the river. It was a distance of only five or six miles, but hard going over the waterlogged ground. The English thought he was crazy, of course. Mackintoshed dog-walkers tended to avert their gaze from his University of Illinois sweatshirt and fraying cut-off jeans, as if he were practicing a bizarre foreign ritual. But he needed an escape valve for the energy that drove him to fill every waking hour. Today, after Mrs. Dickson's letter, he wanted to run until he dropped, until sheer physical exhaustion numbed his emotions and his heartbeat hammered thought into silence.

In the gray October twilight the river looked like lead. The ruins of Godstow Abbey seemed to float above the cow-cropped grass. Jordan could almost imagine that he saw a ghostly shrouded figure at one of the broken Gothic arches. A desolate wail pierced the silence, startling him with its piteous appeal until he remembered where he was. Not a child, not a ghost: only a peacock, one of the ornamental features that made the Trout such a popular pub. Jordan shook his head as if to clear it, crossed the bridge, and opened the gate onto the towpath. Then he was running again, past dark copses and tilting willows, past staring piebald cows and stumpy ponies already showing the fuzzy outlines of their winter coats. He could hear his breath and the slap of his sneakers on the mud. In time with them the words beat in his head: *dead, dead, dead.* Eldridge was dead. He had been flown home from Saigon in a body bag. Mrs. Dickson had copied out the letter for Jordan from the captain of Eldridge's company. Eldridge had been shot down on a reconnaissance mission. He had been a fine soldier. The officer, who had nominated him for a citation, was very sorry.

Jordan vaulted a stile between two pastures and pounded on, the past scrolling out of his memory like a reel of film. He could picture the exact moment when he had first seen Eldridge. Jordan was nine years old. He had been kept home that day because of an outbreak of mumps at school. He was pleased, because it meant his mother had to take him with her to the fancy college where she worked as the dean's secretary. "Up the hill," they called it. Indian Bluffs itself, a straggle of sagging clapboard homes punctuated by the schoolhouse, the inn, and the church, was known simply as "the village." Ever since the river trade had moved down the Mississippi to the next town, with its superior wharf, most residents who were not farmers or bums worked for the exclusive private college set high on the bluffs overlooking the river. Jordan loved going up there. With its white-steepled chapel and ivy-covered dormitories, tennis courts, and landscaped gardens, it was like a fairy-tale playground. The students were godlike beings, the men in pressed flannels and two-tone saddle shoes, the girls deliciously perfumed and draped in cashmere, hugging their books. Sometimes Jordan earned a few nickels as a ball boy. Once he had been given a quarter just to deliver a note to a girl on the other side of the lawn. Mostly, though, he obeyed his mother's fierce instruction to stay out of sight and out of trouble. It had cost her every dime she had, and late nights struggling with the assignments, to complete her correspondence course and land this job. She could not afford to lose it.

The day he met Eldridge, Jordan had gone into the wild land behind the chapel. He had a favorite spot, high on the bluffs, overlooking the great brown river. If he lay on his stomach along the grassy cliff top, his nose just over the edge, he could look a thousand feet straight down to the derelict roof of the old mill where they used to make lime from stone quarried from the bluffs. Farther along were crumbling warehouses and a tall chimney, all that remained of the distillery that had burned down long before he was born. Behind them, hugging the shore, was the barred line of the old railroad track, soon to be dismantled to make way for a new highway. Each of these had its own fascination, but what Jordan liked best was watching the river. Here it was almost a mile wide. It was always different, sometimes as smooth and empty as a brand-new road, sometimes frothing white as powerful currents swept around the tree-tangled islands where Jordan went in spring to look for turtle eggs. You never knew what kind of boat you might see: fishing boats drifting along the shore, patrol launches with their flags fluttering importantly, paddle steamers churning past carrying tourists. The most exciting were the huge, flat barges carrying logs from the North or bringing cotton up from the South, and the police launches cruising for bodies. Everyone in Indian Bluffs learned to respect the river. It was not a place for pleasure boats or swimming. One fierce winter, when the river froze, a party of students from "up the hill" had gone skating on it and drowned. You couldn't see the town from here; that's why Jordan liked it. There was just the river, and beyond it the Missouri flatlands stretching south to the horizon.

It was one of those summer afternoons when the mosquitoes drew blood and the air was like steam. Jordan was looking for Indian arrowheads. Instead, he found the biggest snake he had ever seen, lying quite still in thick, black coils in the sun. He had been staring at it for some time when an awed voice behind him said, "He's a big one." Jordan turned to see a skinny-legged colored boy in shorts. Together they admired the magnificent and fearful beast.

"I reckon he's dead," Jordan said eventually.

"Let's poke him and see," suggested the boy, looking around for a stick. Jordan wasn't too sure about this. He didn't like snakes, even though his mother had told him that the black ones were harmless, unlike the rattlesnakes that infested the caves in the bluffs and had to be regularly killed. In town it was rumored that Hutch Carson kept a sack of live rattlesnakes under his bed. No one knew why, but Jordan could well believe it. He always checked the ground when he walked by Hutch's porch, just in case.

The snake wasn't dead. Jordan let the other boy do the prodding. The snake unwound to an awesome length and slid away while the boys watched. Afterward, bonded by this adventure, they shook hands solemnly and exchanged names. Then they had a contest to see who could throw a stone farthest into the Mississippi. Eldridge won every time.

"You can come to my house and see my cowboy outfit, if you want," Jordan offered. "There's a shortcut through the woods."

His new friend hesitated and then explained that his mother, who worked in the kitchens, had told him not to go far. She always had to leave work right on time, Eldridge said, so that they were home before dark.

"Scaredy-cat," Jordan jeered.

"I ain't scared of the dark," Eldridge shot back. "Negroes have to get out of the county by nightfall. It's the law."

Jordan couldn't make sense of this, but that night over dinner he asked his mother what Eldridge had meant. She loved explaining things to Jordan, getting down the atlas or the encyclopedia, or drawing pictures and diagrams for him while the dishes soaked in the sink. She read the *St. Louis Post-Dispatch* every day; there was always a story that fired her up, like the Rosenberg execution or the McCarthy hearings. Tonight she tried to explain about segregation. A law had been passed the previous year, 1954, outlawing segregation, but there was a lot of resistance, particularly in the South. Had Jordan never wondered why there were no colored children at his school? Why did he think that the colored men going to the fields in the back of pickup trucks, or helping out in the grocery store, or maneuvering barges down the river, went home to the next county at night? That's why her friend Minnie, who worked as a cleaner up the hill, could visit with them only on weekends, never for dinner. "A lot of white folks don't want to mix with Negroes or have them living next door," she concluded.

"Why not?"

"They're frightened of them, I guess."

Jordan considered this. Eldridge hadn't seemed very frightening. "Are you frightened of them?" he asked his mother.

She laughed. "I'm a lot more frightened of Hutch when he's all liquored up. I had to take a shotgun to him once, when he came sniffing around after your father died." She took Jordan's hand. "Honey, you play with Eldridge all you want. He's welcome in our house. Don't pay any mind to what other people say."

Jordan didn't. And once Eldridge had passed the initiation test of being held head-down over the disused well in the woods, he was accepted by Shelby and the gang too. They played touch football and Capture the Flag and shot baskets against Shelby's dad's garage doors. They fooled around in skiffs down by the old wharf. Eldridge was smart, with a quick, mocking humor that at first threw Jordan off balance but then formed a special link between them. When Jordan discovered that Eldridge loved reading, as he did, Jordan lent him books. Sometimes they would go off along the river, just the two of them, acting out adventures from *Tom Sawyer*. In the summer, when school was out, Jordan's mother used to let him stay overnight at the Dicksons'. After a huge dinner of fried chicken, cornbread, mashed potatoes, and gravy, the boys would set out a timber and cane bedframe on the porch, talking and watching the fireflies, until they fell asleep.

Things got more complicated as the boys got older. Jordan went off to high school across the river, in St. Louis, and then to college. Eldridge finished school early and took a series of low-skilled jobs. The civil-rights movement brought them together again; they spent hours in passionate, sometimes fierce discussion. When the draft was instituted, there was no student deferral for Eldridge as there had been for Jordan. He had come back from his first Vietnam tour physically tough but mentally distant. The last time they had met, Jordan was about to take up his Rhodes scholarship and Eldridge, now a sergeant, to return to Vietnam. Jordan had gone over to his house to say good-bye, but there had been no chance to talk. Now there never would be. At twenty-two, Eldridge's life was over.

It began to drizzle. Jordan slicked back his hair and wiped the moisture from his eyes. Before him were the blurred outlines of Oxford's spires against a watery sky, gray on gray. Sometimes the mystery and exotic beauty of Oxford overwhelmed him with delight, but not today. This endless, terrible war bit into his soul. He loved his country and was ashamed of it. Every day he gave thanks that he was not in Vietnam yet felt guilty nevertheless. They all did. The Americans stuck together in Oxford, not just for the familiar companionship or because the Brits were so snooty, but out of a compulsive need to examine and probe and pick at this perpetual sore. They had all grown up as patriots, believing in America the beautiful and pledging daily allegiance to the flag, hands on hearts. The growing awareness that this was a bad war that bombed civilians and propped up a corrupt government was bewildering and hurtful. Inside, most of them were a mess. It was the war that had turned Bruce into a recluse; that drove Rick to play dangerous games with drugs and sex; that made Eliot retreat into the patrician haughtiness of his Boston Brahmin family.

Jordan had supported the war at first. JFK himself had initiated the first moves to protect South Vietnam from the aggression of the communist North. It had seemed as noble a cause as fighting the Nazis. The accidental napalming by the United States of twenty of its own servicemen, four years back, had brought home the barbarity of America's war technology. Reports of gruesome civilian massacres had become commonplace. When Shelby had come home on leave last year, Jordan had been shaken by his account of the fear, the drugs, the racism, the degradation, the shame, and the cynicism. Afterward he had read everything about the war that he could lay his hands on. Intellectually he was now convinced that this was a bad, brutal, pointless war, conducted under the false colors of ideology and patriotism. He wanted no part in it. But from a personal angle, the situation looked different. For every American who ducked the draft, as Jordan had, another American died, as Eldridge had.

At Medley's Boatyard, Jordan crossed the river and stumbled over the railway bridge. His sweatshirt was soaked; his mud-spattered legs ached. He was panting as he crossed the final bridge over the canal and trudged up Walton Well, past Lucy's Eagle Ironworks into Jericho, once the workingman's part of Oxford, where Jude the Obscure had lived and died. He reached a three-story Victorian house and pushed open the squeaky gate.

Hearing the door slam, Eliot shouted out from the kitchen to ask Jordan what time he was leaving tonight. Getting no answer, Eliot appeared in the hall at his usual elegant lope, a steaming cup in his hand, and took stock of Jordan's arrested stance halfway up the stairs.

"Don't tell me you forgot," Eliot chided, eyebrows raised under a thatch of black hair. "Rick's party? In *Magdalen*? With the *viscount*?" His ironic emphasis made Jordan smile. They both knew Rick's little weaknesses. Magdalen, pronounced "maudlin," was probably the most seductively beautiful of all the Oxford colleges. Bordering the river, it had its own elm-shaded deer park, an ancient stone pulpit where Newman had preached, and a fifteenth-century bell tower from which choristers sang at dawn on the first of May each year. Its grounds covered more than a hundred acres; its buildings were of golden stone, arranged around precise quadrangles of emerald grass. Joseph Addison had given his name to the riverside walk where rare lilies grew in spring. C. S. Lewis and Tolkien had read their work to each other here; Edward Gibbon and Oscar Wilde had been undergraduates. Magdalen admirably fulfilled Rick's social pretensions and his taste for theatricality. His party had been billed as a reunion of old friends after the long vacation. It would also give Rick an opportunity to show off the magnificent suite of rooms he was sharing this year with a titled undergraduate of fabled degeneracy.

Of course Jordan would be going. Everyone knew he never missed a party. Rick had a genius for attracting interesting and influential people. Only something as devastating as Eldridge's death could have driven it from Jordan's mind.

"I remember," he said lightly. "You want a ride?" Last summer Jordan had squandered a chunk of his Rhodes allowance on the smallest, cheapest convertible he had ever seen, a soft-topped Morris Minor the size and shape of a small elephant. His compatriots bellyached about the legroom but rarely passed up the chance to keep out of the cold and rain.

"Thanks. And let's try to get, you know—" Eliot pointed a finger upward, indicating the room where their other housemate, Bruce, sat for hours closeted with Leonard Cohen and a dwindling stock of cannabis. Bruce should have gone back to the States last summer, in answer to the draft. Instead he had bummed around Europe and North Africa, ignoring the summons. Now he was an official draft dodger. Ignominy and a five-year prison sentence awaited him if he ever went home. Both Eliot and Jordan had been shocked by Bruce's bloated appearance and depressed mental state. They had an unspoken agreement to get Bruce out of the house as much as possible.

"I'll see what I can do," Jordan promised.

Upstairs he lit the water heater and fed a shilling into the meter for the gas fire in his bedroom. After a meager bath that made him homesick for real showers, he toweled his hair roughly and dressed for the party, adding an old sweater on top to keep warm. He switched on the goo, goosenecked lamp on the rickety table that served as his desk and sat down. A sheet of writing paper lay in front of him. *Dear Mrs. Dickson,* it read. That was all.

What could he say to comfort her? It didn't seem enough that Eldridge had been his friend or that he had triggered Jordan's earliest awareness of social injustice—not that his nine-year-old self had thought in terms any more sophisticated than a schoolboy cry of "It's not fair." Besides, a calculating part of his mind that Jordan could not silence whispered that Mrs. Dickson would be pleased by anything he wrote. He was a Rhodes scholar, one of America's elite, studying at the world-famous Oxford University. His letter would be passed around to the neighbors and kept with other treasured documents in the family Bible. He must choose his words carefully.

Half an hour later, with a growl of frustration, Jordan scrunched up yet another piece of paper and threw it into the wastepaper basket to join its predecessors. There was no way of hiding from Mrs. Dickson—or himself—the brutal truth that he had avoided the summons to war and Eldridge had not. Eldridge had gone to boot camp while Jordan was still in college. Later Jordan had benefited from the rule that graduate students could defer the draft. When that had been revoked in July 1968, he had protected himself once again by joining the Reserve Officers' Training Corps. This committed him to the army but deferred active service, buying him time, which he had privately sworn to commit to the antiwar movement. This had seemed an inspired solution; today it looked like a shabby compromise. How could expressions of affection for Eldridge, or of sympathy with Eldridge's mother, be worth anything while Jordan spent his days dipping into Hobbes and Locke in the hush of ancient vaulted libraries or talking over a beer in the Turf Tavern—or going to parties?

The problem spun around his brain, tying his conscience in knots. He could not get the picture of that body bag out of his mind. How had Eldridge died? Had he been shot or burned or blown up? Jordan was assailed with vile images of spongy, moldering flesh that corrupted his memories of Eldridge's springy hair, his slow smile, his loose-limbed body full of strength and energy. Eventually Jordan tossed down his pen and gave up the struggle. He replaced his heavy sweater with a dark jacket, combed back his hair, and methodically filled his pockets with wallet, keys, his tiny University Diary, and its miniature pencil for jotting down useful names and numbers. Experience of frosty undergraduettes to the contrary, he still dreamed of finding a beautiful, intelligent girl willing to find in him a romantic prospect. Sometimes he yearned for a distraction from conscientious study and from all the Vietnam discussions and activism that swallowed his time and made him question his own motives. Was that too much to ask?

In the hallway Jordan caught sight of himself in the full-length mirror, a tall, broad-shouldered guy with no glaring deformities. Maybe this would be his lucky night.

12

Eight Miles High

Rose lay submerged in sandalwood bubble bath contemplating her red-polished toenails. Perhaps tonight would be her lucky night. There were bound to be some useful men at Rick's party—men with power and contacts, not least Rick himself. Men were gloriously simple. They would do anything for you if you handled them right. And she wanted a favor.

Rick Goodman was a New Yorker, a Rhodes scholar. He was older than the usual undergraduate and infinitely more sophisticated. When he wasn't giving parties, he wrote a gossip column for *Cherwell*. Last year Rose had been the subject of one of his scurrilous "Ox Vox" pieces when she was "gated" after attending an all-night vigil for Jan Palach in one of the men's colleges. Outraged at the antiquated university rule that forbade her to leave LMH for two whole weeks, she had organized a constant stream of visitors to her room. Someone—well, Rose herself actually—had daubed "Free Cassidy Now!" on the college walls. Her plight had been taken up by "Ox Vox" under the headline "Red Rose." She had been interviewed by Rick in her bedroom. It had been the sensation of the week, but to her fury she had still not managed to prize open the door to Oxford journalism. Men wrote everything, even the fashion and makeup pages. Anyone female was automatically allocated the backroom drudgery. Rose was sick of her role as little helper, typing up other people's listless copy. She wanted Rick to get her a proper job.

From the bath cubicle she could hear girls doing the usual girlish stuff—getting ready for dinner in Hall, moaning about essays, swapping stories about their holidays. Rose stirred impatiently in the cooling water and pulled the plug. None of them seemed to see further than the next essay crisis, the next tea party, the next boyfriend. Even Annie was not immune to such bourgeois distractions.

Rose Cassidy had been brought up in London ("the Smoke") competing with two older brothers and a younger sister in a chilly Victorian house with dog-pee carpets and antiapartheid stickers in the windows. Her parents were both psychiatrists and left-wing activists. "Cause" was their middle name. Once they had spawned the great Cassidy tribe, they were too busy saving the world to take much notice of their children, beyond insisting on a sound education. Rose had been sent to one of London's best schools for girls, where she had always been among the top two or three in her class—though that had not stopped her from carving "Fuck the public school system" on the headmistress's door. Many of her friends had elected to go to the newer universities, Sussex or Warwick, scorning the elitism of Oxford and Cambridge, but Rose had been determined to follow her elder brother to Oxford. An Oxford degree still carried more *cachet*. Even so, she had been shocked to discover how provincial and conservative the place was. As soon as she got her first—anything less than a first-class degree was unthinkable— she would be straight back to London and the real world.

After gathering up her belongings, Rose unlocked the cubicle door and ran across the corridor to Annie's room. She found her sprawled bare-legged on the floor unpacking her trunk, wearing an outsize T-shirt. She smiled dreamily at Rose through her Joni Mitchell hair.

"Buck up and get changed, or I'm not taking you," Rose said.

Annie unfolded her legs and stood up. "I like your gownless evening strap," she said, nodding at the damp towel wrapped tight above Rose's breasts. "Whose party is it anyway—one of your boyfriends'?"

Rose made a face. "What a horrible word. It's being given by an American, a real smoothie. You must tell him how brilliant I am. I want him to persuade *Cherwell* to let me write something for them, maybe a piece about the demo."

"What demo?" Annie asked, taking off her clothes and rummaging in her closet.

Rose was shocked. "The demonstration. Vietnam, remember?

Even in Malta they must have heard about the Moratorium. In the States it's going to be like this incredible, massive protest strike against the war. Millions of people are going to stay home from work. In Washington they're going to march on the White House and read out the names of the dead. Only the Americans, of course," she added disapprovingly, hitching up her towel. "Nobody cares about a few hundred thousand slitty-eyed peasants. Anyway, next Sunday we're going to march to Grosvenor Square with a petition. We're hoping to get Vanessa Redgrave to deliver it."

"It sounds amazing."

"It will be. Everybody's going. You should come."

Annie hesitated. Rose read her mind effortlessly. "You want to spend a cozy day with Mr. Red Roses," she said accusingly. "You could keep a Biafran family for a week on what they cost."

"You're just jealous," Annie retaliated calmly, taking a white button-up skirt out of her closet.

Rose felt stung for a moment. Then she laughed. "I don't give anyone a chance to send me red roses. Fuck 'em and chuck 'em, that's my motto." She watched Annie button up her skirt, then undo the bottom two and slide her knee forward to see how much leg showed. "One more," Rose commanded.

"Really? You don't think it's too . . ."

"Of course it is. That's the whole point." Rose shook her head. "Isn't it funny, how we're so different? Like chalk and cheese."

"Yin and yang," Annie countered.

"Kama and sutra." Rose joined in the game.

"Jekyll and Hyde."

"Rowan and Martin."

"Pride and Prejudice."

"Sense and Sensibility. And I get to be Sensibility," Rose added.

"Pearls and swine." Annie gave a piggy snort. "Now get out so I can concentrate on my eyeliner."

Back in her room, Rose put *Surrealistic Pillow* on her record player, then covered herself in skin cream. While she waited for it to sink in, she lit a Gauloise and practiced narrowing her eyes seductively as she inhaled, then blowing the smoke down her nose, like Jeanne Moreau. Her eyes watered.

"Plastic fantastic lov-errr . . ." she sang to herself into the mirror. She modeled herself on Grace Slick: creamy skin, dramatic green eyes beneath dark bangs, silver rings crammed onto her fingers, short, tight dresses. If you were small, you had to do something to get noticed.

She stubbed out the cigarette in her Chairman Mao ashtray and started to pull on her purple panty hose. The thought of Annie's long, tanned legs made her wonder if it had been such a good idea to invite her along. But the two of them did make a wonderful picture, one statuesque and blond, one petite and dark. They were bound to cause a stir.

Jordan stood in the doorway, surveying the scene. The party glittered, as Eliot had predicted. Black candles in ornate candelabra cast a dramatic light on wood-paneled walls and frayed brocade curtains. White-coated college servants proffered champagne cocktails on silver salvers. Under the ripple of conversation Fats Waller sang about his very good friend the milkman. The company was a daring mix of dons, students, theatrical types, journalists, bearded lefties from the London School of Economics, and a pack of the viscount's aristocratic cronies with London dollybirds in tow. Over it all presided Rick, a charismatic guru in black Nehru jacket and white collarless shirt buttoned to the neck. Only his snapping brown eyes betrayed his excitement as he pointed out his prize catches to Jordan: several heavyweight dons, including two heads of college; the theater director, who was having a wildly successful season at the playhouse; a notoriously radical ex-president of the Union club; a snake-hipped character in purple velvet trousers whose underground magazine had been the subject of a scandalous obscenity trial. In a far corner brooded the pocket-size son of a famous novelist, cocky in snakeskin boots and patterned shirt.

Jordan stood in awe of Rick's social panache, as he did of Rick's Choate/Yale education, his summers in the Hamptons, his winters in Aspen, even the dubious glamour of his multiple stepmothers.

"I'm impressed," he admitted.

"We try." Rick looked satisfied. "Did you bring Bruce?"

Jordan and Eliot exchanged glances.

"He said none of his clothes fit him anymore."

"Shit." Rick reached up to put his arms around his friends. For a moment they stood together, three young Americans, heads bowed as if in grim silent prayer.

Then Rick straightened. "The show must go on. Eliot, come and be witty. I've been telling my roommate's sister *all* about you." He waved a hand at Jordan. "I know you can take care of yourself. Enjoy."

Though Jordan didn't much like champagne, he took a glass for camouflage and cruised the party. He flirted mildly with the third wife of a famously uxorious philosopher and was rewarded by an invitation to Sunday lunch later in the term. Taking pity on a lonely looking Nigerian, he made a date with him for a drink in the King's Arms. A likably bumptious Conservative candidate called Jeffrey introduced himself as Britain's youngest MP-in-waiting and promised to show Jordan around the House of Commons when he got there.

Jordan had one unsettling encounter, with a bow-tied senior member of the college, to whom he had made some polite remark about Magdalen's rich historical associations.

"Ah, yes, history," the don enthused. "Very important for you Americans. I understand that in your country you believe that the Second World War started in 1941." He chuckled mischievously.

Jordan gave a stiff smile. He had discovered that the English, particularly the older generation, were obsessed by the war, constantly harking back to rationing and Dunkirk. It seemed to rile them that they had not managed to win it single-handedly.

"Well, 1941 *is* when the war started for us," he said mildly.

"Better late than never, eh?" old Bowtie suggested with a malicious twinkle.

"I think so," Jordan said evenly. "I guess the Russians would have defeated Germany in the end, but without the Americans the map of Europe might look very different today."

The old man frowned at this, then changed tack. "Bloodthirsty lot, aren't you? First Korea, now Vietnam. Still," he nodded at Jordan's champagne glass, "I suppose you wouldn't know about that, all tucked up and cozy at Oxford. Must be a cushy billet, being a Rhodes scholar, what with your fares paid and a salary and all that."

What was it with these dons? Sometimes the most frosty turned out to be extraordinarily generous with their time and knowledge; others seemed riddled with spite.

"Yup, it's almost as good as being a don," Jordan agreed blandly. "Except we miss out on the free port." Before politeness failed him utterly, he reached forward and shook the other man's hand. "It's been a real pleasure."

Jordan moved quickly away, angry with himself for losing his cool, stung by the man's words. He looked around, wondering whether to try to break into one of the knots of men that signaled the presence of a pretty girl. The party was heating up. Fats Waller had been succeeded by the Stones and T Rex, and dancing had started in the next room. The older contingent were collecting their coats, off to dine elsewhere. Jordan's gaze rested idly on Rick's roommate, the viscount, who was leaning on the mantelpiece, staring hungrily at a waiflike girl with kohl-rimmed eyes. She looked stoned. While Jordan watched, the man reached over, put his hand down the girl's dress, and squeezed one of her breasts. Jordan could see his knuckles moving under the thin material. Involuntarily he remembered Eldridge, for whom there would be no more fleshly pleasures, to give or to receive. Suddenly he felt sickened by the noise and the smoke and the press of warm bodies.

He looked around for Rick, wondering if it was too early to go home. Finally he caught sight of him, talking to a dark-haired girl whom Jordan was sure he'd seen demonstrating outside the Union last summer. He gave her a big smile, just in case, and mimed his intention to leave. Rick just shrugged. By the time Jordan had retrieved his coat and scarf, Rick was holding the hand of a tall girl with her back to him. Great legs, he noticed, and a sheet of blond hair to her waist. For a moment Jordan was tempted. But his mood had soured. He was eager to be alone with his thoughts.

"But don't you see, that kind of materialism is just another manifestation of the sick society?"

Rose was trying to persuade the president of St John's that he should sell all the college property and distribute the proceeds to the needy of the Third World, when she felt a warm hand caress her back.

"How's my favorite little Marxist?" asked Rick, drawing her away from the affronted-looking don.

Little yourself, Rose thought with a flicker of irritation. Rick's dark, knowing eyes were only a few inches above her own. She always felt he was laughing at her. But at least he had sought her out. She flashed him one of her best smiles.

"About *Cherwell,*" he drawled. "I hear they need some help on the advertising side. I'll see what I can do for you."

Advertising! Rose bit her lip with disappointment. How could she get Rick to take her seriously? He seemed to have lost interest in her already and was signaling to someone over her shoulder.

"Someone I know?" she asked, determined not to be ignored.

"Just one of my compatriots—Jordan Hope, the man most likely to."

From across the room a tall man with a suntan and that sheen of health all Americans seemed to possess gave her a blazing smile.

"Wow," murmured Rose. "Is he for real?"

Rick frowned. It was the first time Rose had ever seen him at a loss for words.

"Good question," he said at last. "On the boat coming over I got seasick—vilely, abominably seasick. Jordan used to come and read poetry to me. I couldn't believe it—this hick from the boondocks, reading Dylan Thomas!"

"But is he worth knowing? Is he interesting?"

Rick made a seesaw gesture with his palm. "As long as you stay off politics. He once lectured me for so long on the economic and social significance of the watermelon crop that I almost prayed for us to hit an iceberg."

Jordan Hope. Rose stored the name in her mind, while her eyes moved on. Suddenly she clutched Rick's arm. "I don't believe it! Isn't that Don Jago over there?"

"Probably. You want to meet him? Foxy lady he's got there."

Rose clicked her tongue. "That's no lady—that's my best friend."

Annie had been dancing with an Australian called John, or possibly Don or Ron—it was too noisy to hear anything. It didn't matter. He was a good dancer, and she had drunk enough champagne cocktails to send her floating. The strobelight twirled. "Let's Spend the Night Together" throbbed through the floorboards. She smiled into the middle distance, shook out her long hair, and undulated her body to the beat. It would have been even better if Edward were here, but a party was a party. At least Rose had saved her from a dull evening of solitary unpacking.

When the track ended, the Australian grabbed Annie's hand and pulled her toward the drinks table, shouting, "Drink! Drink! I'm gasping." In the light she saw that he was quite old, late twenties probably. He poured two glasses of wine and handed her one with a sly wink.

"I've got some grass you might like to try. Interested?"

Annie had never actually taken any drugs, though it seemed un-cool to say so. Before she could reply she heard a familiar voice saying, "I am."

There was Rose, pushing up her bangs the way she did when she was excited about something. "Aren't you Don Jago?"

"I could be. Depends who I'm talking to." He bared his teeth, slid an arm around Annie, and pushed her toward the man following in Rose's wake. "Hey, Ricky baby, have you met this fabulous creature?"

Rick clasped Annie's hand in both of his and gave her a piercing look of concentrated charm. "Annie," he said solemnly, "hello and good-bye." He withdrew his hands with a slow, regretful stroke across her palm that made her shiver. "Do me a favor, guys," he added coolly. "If you want to smoke dope, go outside."

"Great!" said Don. "We can get high and look at the moon."

"Only if you've got X-ray vision." Rose laughed. "It's pouring. What do you say, Annie?"

Annie looked at her friend. Rose was fizzing like a firework. This mad Australian she had picked up must be some kind of star.

"Why not?" she said.

The staircase was littered with people leaning against the banis-ters or sprawled on the steps, nursing their glasses and tapping ash down the stairwell. Don led the way down to the shelter of the long colonnaded porch. After checking to make sure that no one was looking, he drew a little packet from his jacket. Annie watched care-fully. Although everyone talked about pot parties, she had never seen anyone roll a joint.

Don lit the twisted end, took the first drag, and then passed the joint to Rose. When it was her turn, Annie copied their way of sucking in the smoke with a hiss, then slowly exhaling. She waited for her brain to melt or some mystic revelation to appear. Nothing happened. Feeling relieved, she leaned back against a pillar, taking her turn with the circulating joint. Above the whisper of rain, she could hear "Marrakesh Express." Don told them all about the ob-scenity trial. The worst bit, he said, had been the compulsory prison haircut. England was ruled by a bunch of blinkered, geriatric old farts. Still, London was the scene; he was never going back to Australia.

"You know the difference between Australia and yogurt?" he asked.

"Yogurt has a live culture," Rose answered, blowing smoke down her nose.

"Yah. Spoilsport." He pinched her knee. "Listen, chicks, I'm freezing my balls off here. Why don't we go back to your place, get warm, have some fun?"

"College, you mean?" Rose asked dubiously.

Don jumped up excitedly, as if he had seen a vision. "Wow, yeah, a whole college full of beautiful pink-and-white girls. I can start with you two and gradually work my way through. Let's split!"

Annie giggled. He was rather attractive, despite being so old. Perhaps the joint was having some effect after all. She felt pleasantly dopey; the stuffy, conventional world of home was slipping blissfully away. Besides, she had a feeling that Rose wanted something from him.

"You can drive us home, if you like," she heard herself say.

As they went back in to collect their coats, they heard a strange grunting noise from the trees behind them.

"Jesus! What was that?" Don asked, clutching both girls to him.

"Rutting deer," Annie said distinctly. For some reason they all found this hilarious.

In the High Street, Don stopped beside a mini car painted in a psychedelic pattern of hearts and flowers and exploding suns. "Here it is, the 'pash' wagon."

Annie climbed into the back, wondering how many girls Don had transported to the heights of passion on its sheepskin-covered seats and embroidered cushions. Strips of Indian tasseled silk hung above the windows. The car had a strange, musky smell.

They shot into the road with a squeal of tires.

"Which way, lovelies?" Don shouted. Annie could tell that he was drunk, but who cared? So was she. She lay back across the seat with her feet braced against the far window, feeling her head spin.

"Red light!" Rose yelled.

A horn honked furiously. The car braked and lurched off again. Something rolled thunderously along the ledge behind Annie's head, and she reached up to grab a bottle of vodka. She could hear Rose in the front seat, swearing at Don.

"Was that really a red light?" he asked in amazement. "I thought it was some wonderful, phantasmagoric great *strawberry* in the sky." He made an expansive gesture, and the car wobbled again.

He started singing, drumming out the beat on the steering wheel. Annie and Rose joined in, as they zoomed up St. Giles.

"And it's one, two, three, what are we fighting for?
Don't ask me, I don't give a damn
Next stop is Vietnam
And it's five, six, seven, open up the pearly gates
Ain't no time to wonder why
Whoopee! We're all going to die."

"Not Woodstock Road," Annie shouted as the car wavered at a fork in the road. "The other way!"

"Woodstock! That's beautiful!" Don gave an ecstatic shiver. "I wish I'd been there. All those people wandering hand in hand, just like the Garden of Eden. Can you imagine how mind-blowing it must have been, lying on the grass, listening to music and making love? That's what the future will be like. No one's going to get married and imprison themselves in boring little boxes. We'll all live in communes, surrounded by fields and animals, with barefoot children running free in the sunshine."

What sunshine? wondered Annie.

"Monogamy's dead, that's for sure," Rose agreed. "It's so bourgeois. What a drag to be stuck with the same person all the time."

"What if you love them?" Annie asked from the back, but no one heard her.

The gates were just closing when the car screeched to a halt outside LMH.

"Oh, no," Don complained, jumping out. "I only just got here. Couldn't you hide me in the closet—or in your bed? I promise to be good."

Rose stroked a consoling hand down the sleeve of his velvet jacket. "Another time, maybe." She shot him a sparkling look from under her lashes. "If you asked me to write something for your magazine, I could come up to London and . . . discuss it with you."

"You're a little witch." He grinned, patting her bottom. "You want to watch out for her," he said to Annie. "She'll lead you astray."

He took out a felt-tipped pen, pushed up Rose's sleeve, and wrote his telephone number on her bare arm. Then he sighed and kissed each of them enthusiastically on the lips. "You're both gorgeous, and I love you. See you, girls."

Annie and Rose watched him prance back to the car in his high-heeled boots.

"Bet you he has a water bed." Annie giggled.

"He's got a magazine," Rose answered repressively. "You must learn to concentrate on the essentials."

"Oh, but I do." Arching her eyebrows at Rose, Annie pulled something from under her coat and flourished it.

Rose yelped with laughter. "Annie!"

"Don't 'Annie' me." She handed Rose the bottle and threw an affectionate arm around her shoulders. "Come on, let's finish his vodka."

Jordan ran to the car, jumping over puddles, and drove slowly home, thinking about Eldridge. Even now it was not too late to change his mind. One phone call to the States, and his name would go back into the draft pool. Maybe this was one time when he should let the great diceman in the sky roll for him. But he wanted his life. He did not want to die. The Morris's windshield wipers clacked back and forth. Yes, no. Yes, no.

Jordan stopped in Walton Street and picked up a couple of chicken curries and some popadams. The house was dark and silent. Alarm washed over him. With the warm, aromatic bags still in his arms, he took the stairs two at a time and knocked on Bruce's door. There was no answer. He turned the handle, releasing a gust of stale smoke and rancid body odor.

"Bruce?" he called anxiously.

There was the squeak of springs and a tired voice. "For Christ's sakes, Jord, I keep telling you guys, I am not going to kill myself." Bruce sniffed loudly. "Do I smell curry?"

They ate in the kitchen, straight from the tinfoil cartons, with the oven door open to warm the room. Jordan tried to turn Rick's party into a string of anecdotes, while implying that Bruce had not missed much. Afterward Bruce said he felt like a walk. He didn't care about the rain. He liked it. Jordan watched him shamble off, unwashed hair hanging down the back of his plaid lumberjack shirt. There was no point in saying that he would be soaked to the skin in minutes.

He took a cup of instant coffee up to his room and switched on the light. His eyes went straight to the white square of writing paper. *Dear Mrs. Dickson* . . . Jordan hung up his jacket, pulled off his tie, and sat down heavily, banging the teetery desk. A pile of books collapsed. Carefully he restacked Jouvenel's *Sovereignty* on top of Beloff's *Europe and the Europeans* and Theodore H. White's *The Making of the President*. Amid the clutter on his desk was a cube with a photograph on every facet. This one had been a going-away present from his mother. Jordan picked it up and rotated it idly. His whole life, it seemed, was contained in this little box. Here was a little boy, posing on the porch steps one Halloween in his pirate's outfit; and here, an absurdly clean-cut sixteen-year-old, shaking hands with President Kennedy in the Rose Garden of the White House. Here was a picture of Miss Purvis, his teacher from the two-room schoolhouse in Indian Bluffs, who had encouraged Jordan to believe that he could achieve anything he wanted. Here was a picture of his mother, triumphantly holding up a fistful of dollar bills after a day at the racetrack. The final photograph was a black-and-white studio portrait of his father, handsome and serious in his army uniform—the father he had never known.

It was not World War II that killed Jordan's father but a car accident just weeks before Jordan was born. Jordan couldn't have been much more than three years old the first time his mother had shown him his father's presidential citation for war service. Every year thereafter, on the anniversary of his father's death, she had made a point of bringing out the citation and talking to Jordan about the man she had admired and loved. Jordan sometimes dreamed of his father. In the dreams his father was always dressed like this, in uniform, and always seemed on the verge of imparting a momentous secret. For hours after Jordan woke, he would feel infused with a nameless, bittersweet emotion composed of loss and longing.

How would his father judge him now? Was it nobler to fight in a bad war—or against it? While his coffee grew cold, Jordan stared into the clear, light eyes, searching for some message. At last he picked up his pen and started to write, hesitantly at first, then with ease, almost with pleasure, as he took control. He would mail the letter at once, tonight, slotting it into the red postbox at the corner of the street before he could change his mind. He would make Mrs. Dickson guardian of his conscience; whatever he wrote now would commit him forever.

The words flowed on. Eldridge was vivid in his mind, alive and whole. He was the key to everything.

13

Satisfaction

"So where are we going?" Annie asked as they passed through the LMH porch, arms wrapped tightly about each other. It was early evening, just twenty-four hours after Rick Goodman's party.

"Dudley's, I thought," Edward said.

Annie looked at him in surprise. "Dudley's" was the colloquial name for the Lamb and Flag, a country pub run by a canny father-and-son team known as Old Dudley and Young Dudley. Its cheap food and lively atmosphere meant it was always packed with undergraduates. The only trouble was, it was at least ten miles from Oxford, in the village of Kingston Bagpuize. Annie's heart sank at the idea of getting a ride from someone. She wanted Edward to herself.

"And just how are you proposing we get there?" she asked.

"I thought a car would be convenient." He pointed theatrically to a bright blue sports car parked at a rakish angle under the street lamp. "Ta-dah!

"Present from Dad for my twenty-first," he explained, watching her face. "I wanted it to be a surprise."

Annie circled around it. "Edward, you lucky thing. It's fabulous. Can we have the top down?"

He looked at her as if she'd said something marvelous. "You'll freeze."

Annie gave him a sexy, sideways look from behind her hair. "No, I won't. Not after what we've been doing."

Edward unsnapped the roof fastenings, pushed back the hood,

and held the passenger door open for Annie. She slid down in the low-slung seat until she was practically horizontal, aware of Edward's gaze as her coat fell open, exposing her legs and a tiny fringe of skirt high on her thighs. As he came around the other side to get in, she smiled lazily at him and dropped one hand provocatively onto the knob of the gear lever.

"Don't do that." Edward groaned, climbing in. He leaned over to pull Annie into a lingering kiss, sliding his hand under her coat.

"God, I've missed you," he said at last in a voice furry with lust. "Are you absolutely, totally, one hundred percent sure you want to go to dinner?"

"Yes." She laughed, then raised her eyebrows mischievously. "There's always later."

Edward sighed good-humoredly and started the car. He raced through Oxford with a lot of showy revving and gear-changing, then sped up Hinksey Hill.

"What do you think of her?" he shouted.

Annie just smiled, shutting her eyes against the cold wind, listening to the trees whoosh past. She thought she had never been so happy.

Edward had come at seven as promised, looking more beautiful than ever. At first they had been slightly self-conscious, making small talk. Edward had been on a walking holiday through the Sierra Nevada in Spain. He had brought her a hand-painted coffee mug as a present and also a small leather-bound edition of Elizabeth Barrett Browning's *Sonnets from the Portuguese*, which he had inscribed to her in his spiky hand. Annie thought this was desperately romantic. Their awkwardness with each other dropped away. Soon they were kissing. Then Edward had gotten up to lock her door and had made love to her on her narrow college bed. Nothing had changed. If anything, it was better, more natural and intimate than before. Afterward they lay pressed together, Annie's leg thrown across his body, talking quietly. At length they had got up and dressed slowly, smiling at each other as they did up buttons and zippers. This is how it will be, Annie had thought, a whole year of loving each other and being together.

She found she was smiling and opened her eyes to look over at Edward. He looked wonderfully serious as he drove, his hair tangling behind him, the collar of his leather jacket turned up. A bubble of happiness rose within her until she thought she would burst. She started to belt out a Rolling Stones song, head back, hands clapping out the beat, until Edward joined in exuberantly.

She arrived at the restaurant with her cheeks glowing, so pleased with herself and the world that when Young Dudley recognized her from last summer, she kissed him. He found them a place at the end of one of the long candlelit trestle tables. "I know what I want already," she confided. "Chicken casserole, honey and brandy ice cream, and lots of lovely wine."

The restaurant was warm and noisy and jumping with life. Annie looked happily around the familiar barnlike room, with its brick walls and crisscross roof timbers. Their wine came almost at once. Edward lit two cigarettes and passed her one.

"So what play are we going to try out for this term?" Annie asked him. "Wouldn't it be great if we could get parts together, like Beatrice and Benedick, or Eliza and Professor Higgins?"

Edward sighed regretfully. "I'd love to, but I can't. Not this year. It takes up too much time."

Annie laughed incredulously. "But finals aren't until June!"

"You make it sound like the year 2000. I've got to get a good degree if I want to get into a decent chambers and make it as a barrister."

Annie drank her wine. She felt sharply disappointed. "Well, I think it's very dull of you." She pouted. "I hope you're not expecting me to sit around mopping your brow and making you cups of coffee."

"Don't be silly."

"I've seen it happen. There are some girls at LMH who met some boy in their very first term and afterward spent their entire time cooking them instant curry in the pantry. It's true," she protested when Edward laughed at her disdainful tone. "I've knocked on their doors to borrow milk or something, and there they are in armchairs by the fire, with a drying rack of men's socks and horrible gray underwear between them. They might as well be married." She shook back her hair. "Monogamy is so *bourgeois*," she pronounced.

Edward raised his eyebrows, amused. "Who said that?"

"I did." Annie bristled.

While they ate, Edward told her more about his vacation. After the Sierra Nevada, he had gone down to the sea to a village called Cadaques, which sounded very cool, full of hippies and jazz bars.

"And beautiful girls?" Annie asked.

"Crawling with them. But none as pretty as you." Edward took her hand and kissed it. "Anyway, I had to come home early to be an usher at my cousin's wedding. Talk about a family palaver! Cakes and flowers and bridesmaids' dresses—and the bride swanning up the aisle in white, three months pregnant."

"Oh, dear." Annie giggled.

"Yeah." Edward rolled his eyes. "My ma was very tight-lipped about it all."

"And what about your cousin?"

Edward shrugged. "It was okay once we took him into the vestry and poured a hip flask of whiskey down him. Poor bugger, he's only a year older than me. Still, he'd been going out with the girl for years. I suppose one has to do the honorable thing."

Annie began to tell Edward about last night's party. Feeling jealous of the beautiful girls in Spain, she set out to impress him, describing all the cool people who had been there and quoting Don's funny stories.

"You mean you went off with him?" Edward looked hurt.

"Nothing happened. I was with Rose. Anyway he was old—even older than you," she teased. "And he did have the most amazing grass. It was just fun," she added defiantly.

"Ah, Rose," Edward said suspiciously.

One afternoon last term, Rose had come punting with them. It had not been a success. Rose and Edward had done everything they could to present themselves to each other in the worst possible light. What should have been an idle afternoon turned into a heated argument about whether students could legitimately claim solidarity with workers. Of course, Rose had insisted. Idealistic claptrap, Edward had argued, citing the Paris *événements* of '68. Annie had ended up exasperated with them both.

"Well, I like Rose," she said now. "I'm going on a demo with her next week. We're going to march to the American embassy." Until that moment Annie hadn't made up her mind.

"Since when have you been interested in Vietnam?"

"It's important." Annie flushed. "A supposedly civilized Western nation is perpetrating a terrible crime against humanity. They're bombing civilians and burning little children to death and devastating the landscape. If enough people stand up against it, we might actually stop it. Isn't that worth doing?"

"What's going to end that war is the realization that it can't be won, plus Nixon's desire to get himself reelected in three years' time."

"How can you be so cynical?" Annie asked hotly. "Even if you're right, shouldn't we do everything we can to shorten the war? For every person who makes a protest, a life could be saved. Hundreds of thousands of people could be killed in three years. It's an oppression of a poor nation by a rich one. It should be stopped. If you can't be bothered to go because of your stupid work, that doesn't mean I can't."

Edward sat back. His mouth tightened. "You've turned into a proper little Lady Margaret Hall revolutionary."

Annie was stung. "You think it's a waste of time, do you?"

"No. I think you must do as you choose. Not accept what Rose or anyone else tells you to."

"Including you."

"Including me," Edward agreed. But he looked annoyed.

Perhaps in an attempt to restore their good humor, he ordered two Rusty Nails, a Dudley's specialty that was half whisky and half Drambuie. The drink scorched down Annie's throat but did not improve her mood. She was still smarting when they went outside. Edward put his arm around her.

"So what shall we sing on the way back?"

"Nothing. It's too cold. I don't want the top down again."

They drove home in silence. Annie had eaten and drunk too much. She felt sick as the car wound around the corners. She shut her eyes, pretending to be asleep.

The car slowed as they approached Oxford. "Wake up, little Suzie," Edward sang in her ear when he stopped at a traffic light. "Back to my place?" he asked lightly.

"Not tonight, Edward. I haven't even finished my unpacking, and I've got collections on Monday. As you say, work is very important," she added pointedly.

He drove her back without comment, but the atmosphere inside the car was charged. As LMH came into sight, Edward put his hand on her knee.

"Don't change," he begged. "I love you the way you are."

"Everyone changes," Annie answered, feeling depressed. If he thought she had changed, did that mean he didn't love her anymore?

As soon as Edward stopped the car, Annie clicked open her door. "Thanks for a super dinner," she said stiffly, starting to climb out.

Edward reached out to grasp her elbow. "What about lunch to-morrow? The King's Arms at one?"

Annie turned to him with a rush of relief. "Okay." She smiled.

The first thing she saw when she switched on the light in her room was her bouquet of roses. Annie felt her heart twist. She did love Edward. Perhaps she would just have to accept that things could not be the same as last term. She bent down to sniff the flow-ers but could smell nothing. The petals were already browning at the edges.

14

Something in the Air

Annie sat with her face turned to the watery sun, hugging her knees with excitement. Perched high on a plinth with the giant paw of one of Landseer's bronze lions at her back, she had a clear view across the swarming northern half of Trafalgar Square. Immediately below her was a crude platform of planks and scaffolding for the speakers and other dignitaries. If she tipped her head back, she could just see a foreshortened Nelson at the top of his column, today wearing a U.S. Marine's cap on top of his admiral's hat.

Ten of them had traveled down to London in a rattletrap van. Annie had grumbled when Rose had woken her up at seven to a damp, gray dawn, but things improved once they had stopped for breakfast somewhere outside Henley. Afterward one of the girls got out her guitar. Sprawled in the back on cushions, Annie had sung along with the others. They had started quietly with protest stuff like "We Shall Overcome" and "Where Have All the Flowers Gone?" By the time they reached London, they were yelling, "We all live in a yellow submarine," banging out the rhythm on the metal sides of the van. They had left the van near Hyde Park, where the march was due to end, and walked arm in arm through the quiet Sunday morning streets, which gradually filled as they approached Trafalgar Square.

When they arrived, the crowd was already sizable. Now it seemed impossible that the square could accommodate the people who still converged on it from all directions. Some burst from the tube in rowdy student groups, carrying signs that proclaimed the distance they had traveled: Durham, Brighton, Leicester, even Berlin and Amsterdam. Others were disgorged from the buses, vans, and cars that crept into the square in a slow line of traffic and drew up in front of the formal pillared facade of the National Gallery. Couples ambled from the side streets, amorously entwined, as if this was a normal sunny Sunday, making Annie wish for a moment that Edward had come too. On the steps of the church of St. Martin's-in-the-Fields six tramps sat in a row, passing a cider bottle back and forth, waiting as if for a play to begin. High above the crowds, lining roofs and pediments and windowsills, hunched several hundred displaced and disgruntled pigeons. There would be no peanuts from the tourists today.

Vietnamese flags poked defiantly out of the crowd. There were hundreds of placards with angry slogans: "Better Red than Dead," "Hands off Vietnam." Annie even saw a "Wanted" poster with a photograph of Nixon's furrowed, jowly face. A group of students, presumably Americans, carried a U.S. flag daubed with a black cross. She could hear their hoarse chant, "Hell, no, we won't go." Around the edges of the square, dark-blue clumps betrayed the presence of the police in discreet, watchful huddles, the silver stars on their helmets glinting in the sunlight.

Rose gave a deep sigh of satisfaction, as if she had personally conjured the crowd out of the ether. "Far out. There must be at least eight thousand people—maybe ten."

Annie put her rolled-up demo leaflet to her eye, like Nelson's telescope. She squinted at the multicolored sea of denim and tweed, embroidered coats and military jackets, headbands and hats. "How on earth can you tell?"

Rose pulled on her Gauloise, blowing the smoke out through her nostrils in a way Annie had tried to copy but that always left her out of breath. "It's in the blood. Not for nothing am I named after Rosa Luxemburg. I've told you, my parents are demo freaks—ban the bomb, antiapartheid, Labor rallies. I was only ten when they took me on the Aldermaston March."

When Annie was ten, her parents had put her on the P & O liner back to England and boarding school. How much more exciting to share the warmth and solidarity of a crowd like this one, perhaps carried high on her father's shoulders. "What was it like?"

"Spam sandwiches and blisters from my school shoes." Rose scowled. "I sometimes think that what would really please my parents is if I wound up dead in a canal like old Rosa, martyr to some noble socialist cause."

"Don't be silly." Annie gave Rose a friendly nudge. "My mother dreams of marrying me off to somebody terribly rich and pompous, giving candlelit dinners so she can flirt and give her awful tinkly laugh. You know, a stockbroker or an advertising executive or a—" Annie paused, trying to think of something truly terrible.

"—chartered accountant," supplied Rose in a doom-laden voice.

"Yeuch!" They groaned, clutching each other in horror. Annie remembered uncomfortably that Edward was going to be a lawyer.

"I'm never going to be a parent," Rose swore fiercely.

"God, no." Annie agreed. "At least, not until I'm too old for anything else."

"Shh!" Rose put a hand on Annie's knee. "It's her!"

The speeches were nearly over. First had been a man in a dog collar, next a trade-union leader in corduroy cap, then a bearded American who turned out to be a draft dodger. Now the last speaker, a woman. After a long pause, there was a ripple of excitement from the crowd.

"Look!" cried Rose. "There she is."

Annie scrambled to her knees and balanced herself against Rose, feeling the sharp edge of the stone bite through her jeans. A tall woman was climbing on to the speakers' platform. She wore a man's long overcoat with a black band around one arm.

The crowd fell silent as the unmistakable voice began a passionate denunciation of America's misbegotten and brutal war on the Vietnamese people. As she listened Annie unfurled the leaflet she had been fooling around with earlier. She felt ashamed of her levity as she scanned the grim statistics—40,000 Americans killed, billions of dollars wasted on killing machines, more bombs dropped than in the whole of World War II, hundreds of square miles of Vietnamese jungle devastated by Agent Orange. The pictures were the worst, even these fuzzy copies. A man winced at the gun pressed to his head, frozen in the split second before the bullet entered his brain. A woman holding her dead baby, dark with blood, opened her mouth in a scream of anguished denial. Annie had seen such pictures before, on television and in the newspapers, but for the first time they entered her heart. This was real. She was involved. She could do something about it. It was an incredible feeling to be part of this vast crowd, to march with them, shout, make a fuss. Perhaps it was good that Edward was not here after all.

The speaker was now reading aloud the letter of protest to the American ambassador, which was the focus of this demonstration. She raised her fist in a kind of Black Power salute, and the crowd began to sway and rumble, ready to start the march. A girl on the lion opposite Annie's stood up on its broad back and pulled her poncho over her head. She had nothing on underneath. "Peace and love!" she shouted, arms stretched wide, bare breasts bobbing. Annie and Rose whooped their appreciation, laughing as a pair of policemen hustled the girl away, wrapped in one of their jackets— as if nakedness were a crime.

"Quick," Rose called, sliding down to the ground. "If we go round this way, we can be near the front." They linked arms, pushing and dodging through the crowd until they found themselves moving steadily up Charing Cross Road in a controlled stream. Annie strode out in her boots, an Indian scarf tied warriorlike about her head, chanting, "Peace now!" She could feel the energy from the thousands of people flooding through her. Quite suddenly a door swung open in Annie's mind. *I've cracked Wordsworth,* she thought with elation. "Bliss was it in that dawn to be alive / But to be young was very heaven!" The exhilaration she was feeling, this extraordinary combination of intellectual purpose and thrilling human solidarity—that's what Wordsworth must have felt about the French Revolution. How simple it all was! She resolved to tackle *The Prelude* again.

At Tottenham Court Road tube station, the crowd turned left into Oxford Street, bunching up quite suddenly and frighteningly as people fought to keep their place. Annie was swept away from Rose like a piece of flotsam and pushed into a steel barrier, so hard that she cried out. By the time she had found her feet, Rose had disappeared. Annie jumped into the air, hoping for a glance of Rose's crazy hat, but it was no good. She had lost her. She moved up along the outside of the crowd, squeezing past the bright windows of the Oxford Street shops. But as she neared the front, the crowd closed tight about her, changing direction once again. The pressure tightened until Annie could see nothing but the bright-blue Chairman Mao jacket of the man in front of her. Her elation was gone. She felt shaken. Something had gone wrong.

An aggrieved murmur rose to an angry buzz as the word was passed back. "They won't let us in. . . . Fascist traitors. They won't let us in!" Annie weaseled her way forward. Her heart began to race as she realized what was happening. The police were trying to stop them getting from Oxford Street into Grosvenor Square. They were spread out in a cordon right across North Audley Street, arms linked, maybe fifty of them and—Jesus!—horses. Annie had felt anxious about horses ever since she had been flung onto the sand by a nasty seaside pony and broken her collarbone. These were no ponies, but great slabs of muscled flesh, with iron soup plates for feet and massive hindquarters swiveling unpredictably at eye level. For a moment the crowd was stopped, seething and shouting but not yet advancing. A rhythmic chanting started up, growing louder and faster as it passed down the crowd. "Let us through. Let us through. *Let us through!*" People stamped their feet in time and banged their protest signs on the road. Annie could feel the pressure building up behind her as more and more of the thousands of demonstrators moved inexorably forward, oblivious of the problem. The press of bodies was stifling. She heard a girl's voice screaming "Let me out!" But it was too late.

There was a sudden, explosive bang. One of the horses reared into the air, then plunged down again, whirling and snorting. Somebody must have thrown a firecracker. After that everything happened very fast. First, the nasal boom of a megaphone, urgent but unintelligible. Then two more loud bangs and the high whinny of a horse. The chanting dissolved into a sustained baying roar. Without warning the crowd surged forward, and Annie was swept with it, slipping, lurching, grabbing hold of people to keep her balance. In front of her a man tripped over the pole of the Red flag he was carrying and crashed to the ground. In seconds the bright folds were trampled. No one helped him up; it was impossible to stop. Through a gap in the crowd Annie caught a split-second glimpse of Rose running, her mouth open and her eyes wide. She looked scared. Then the bodies closed in again, jostling and shouting.

With a cry of triumph they burst out of the tunnel of North Audley Street into the open space of Grosvenor Square. It was huge—a garden the size of two cricket fields, with trees and statues and a fountain, enclosed by dignified old buildings. Annie filled her lungs with fresh air and ran faster, trying to escape from the crowd at her heels. But almost at once she was brought to a halt. Breathless and disoriented, she found herself pummeled by the crowd into a ragged line no more than fifty paces from the American embassy.

It was a huge building, stretching right across one end of the square, a modern statement in pale stone and plate glass. With its high metal palisade and protective moat, it had the air of a fortress. People said that there was a secret underground link in its vast basement, so that key personnel could be whisked to safety in the event of a nuclear attack. High above the entrance was set an enormous golden eagle with a wingspan of perhaps thirty feet. Below the eagle hung a limp Stars and Stripes. Underneath the American flag, hundreds of English policemen formed a slash of dark blue across the embassy's broad, polished steps. The police did not look friendly.

A police officer walked into the no-man's-land between demonstrators and police and raised a megaphone to his mouth. "In the interest of your own safety, please clear the square," he enunciated in booming, suburban vowels. The crowd giggled. He repeated the instruction.

"Go home, fatty!" a voice shouted back. The laughter swelled. Annie could feel the crowd flexing its collective muscle. She looked behind her at the thousands of people milling around the square, snapping branches off the trees and hedges for makeshift weapons. They must outnumber the police by ten to one. The pack instinct was strong.

A figure burst out of the crowd and hurled something into the air. Red paint spilled out in an arc, splashing like blood across the rump of a police horse. The can landed on the embassy's pristine steps, just short of the police line, and clanked down to the bottom, spilling more paint as it went. Two policemen sprinted from nowhere and brought the figure down in a flying tackle. Then they yanked him up and dragged him, shoes scraping across the asphalt, toward a police van—except, Annie suddenly saw, it wasn't a he but a she, a girl, with blood pouring down her face.

The crowd roared its disapproval. One of the policemen had lost his helmet struggling with the paint thrower. A figure darted into no-man's-land and scooped it up and then tossed the trophy into the crowd. Delighted, they threw it back and forth with whoops and squeals, like bridesmaids catching a wedding bouquet. More paint cans sailed through the air and smashed on the ground. The megaphone man stepped forward again and was met with a barrage of stones. Retreating fast, arms raised defensively, he slipped in a pool of paint and fell. The crowd surged forward hungrily. "Let's get the pigs," growled a voice behind Annie. Then the front section of the crowd ran forward, yelling, pointing their placards and branches like battering rams. They were going to charge the police line! Policemen thundered forward to intercept them. They met in an ugly, scrabbling fight.

Annie saw a policeman gasp with pain as the edge of a sign jabbed him in the stomach. His companions fell on the attacker, kicking him as he slumped to the ground. Somehow he wriggled out of their grasp, leaving his sweater behind. One policeman raced after him and thwacked him across the back with his truncheon. Stones rained down on demonstrators and police alike. More police on horseback cantered onto the scene. A girl screamed. The megaphone boomed again. *"Clear the square."*

Stop it! Annie pleaded silently, digging her nails into her palms. She turned to look for a way out, but the crowd was now in pandemonium, some trying to get into the fight, others desperate to get away. Annie was pushed nearer and nearer to the fighting and the horses, as if she were in the grasp of a huge wave. A firecracker exploded almost under her feet. She heard a squeal. A horse reared terrifyingly over her, then plunged back to the ground, its hooves slicing within inches of her face. She could smell its warm breath and see the tiny red veins pulsing in its nostrils. Panicking, she ducked under its neck and ran. There were steps in front of her and a smooth wall. Somehow she scrambled up it. The next thing she knew she was crouched, panting, on top of one of the pillars that flanked the embassy steps. It was, she realized, just about the most dangerous place she could have chosen. Immediately behind her was the police cordon, arms linked, heads cocked defensively downward to ward off the rain of makeshift missiles. On the steps below, more police were fighting off the demonstrators. Annie was marooned between them, in the firing line. Beyond them, the police horses were now charging at the crowd, scattering them to the far corners of the square. Annie was completely cut off.

Through the din Annie heard a man's voice shouting, "Jump!" She looked around wildly. She couldn't jump. It was too far. She would hit the steps, crack her head, break a leg. She tried to see who was shouting at her, but there were only police, a tangle of arms and legs and flying missiles.

"C'mon. Over here. *Jump!*" urged the voice. Fighting panic,

Annie crawled to the other edge of the pillar and peered down. She had a blurred impression of long hair swept back from a man's anxious face, a tan jacket, arms stretched forward. It was a hell of a way down. She would never manage it. As she hesitated, stones thunked around her feet. Something hit her stingingly on the temple. Annie took a deep breath and jumped.

15

Hello, I Love You, Won't You Tell Me Your Name?

Annie felt the wind lift her hair, then the slam of her body into hard muscle. She had an impression of strong arms at her waist and soft material against her cheek as her feet slid to the ground. Before she could say anything, a hand grabbed hers and raced her across the empty ground, into the skirmishing crowd.

Head down, she barged through the crush of yelling, fighting bodies. The ground was littered with debris. Annie stumbled over broken branches and stones, paint cans and the splintered remains of placards, even a discarded man's shoe. The noise was horrible: megaphones, police whistles, the scrabble of horses' hooves, and over it all the din of a furious, frustrated crowd. At one point Annie's hair snagged painfully on somebody's coat button, but the hand clasped about hers dragged her forward. Her eyes watered as she felt the hairs torn out of her scalp. Two ambulancemen carrying a stretcher shouted for people to clear the way. Annie caught a glimpse of a white-faced policeman lying still. Without his helmet, he didn't look any older than she was.

Suddenly the crowd thinned. Annie slid to a halt as she felt the hand around hers tighten warningly. Angled across the road, blocking the way, were two police vans. A group of officers were standing outside, some murmuring into their walkie-talkies, others interrogating mulish-looking demonstrators.

"Shit," breathed her companion.

Behind the vans Annie could see an empty street with a huddle of spectators at the far end. Beyond them, a line of trees marked the boundary of Hyde Park—and freedom. They were so close she could have wept. She turned to look at the ugly crowd behind her and quailed at the thought of fighting her way back through it.

The hand tightened on hers again. "Okay," he said. "We're going to walk between those trucks—nice and easy. If anyone looks at you, smile as if he's your long-lost brother."

Smile, indeed. He doesn't want much, Annie thought. Then they were moving casually forward, a couple out for a Sunday stroll. As they reached the vans, one policeman looked up from his notebook and frowned at Annie. She beamed back at him. He shot an uncertain look at his colleagues, but they were busy. His eyes darted back to Annie, mesmerized by her fixed grin. Just as they reached the narrow gap between the vans, there was an alarmed shout.

Annie felt herself yanked forward. "Go!" yelled her companion. Annie stretched out her long legs and ran. There was a blur of iron railings, then the knot of gaping spectators at the end of the street came into focus. Their shocked faces and staid Sunday clothes made her want to laugh. There was even a dachshund wearing a coat. In unspoken agreement, Annie and her companion pushed through the crowd and ran straight across Park Lane, leaping the central barrier, until they reached the quiet green expanse of Hyde Park. Then he swung her around to face him and let her hand drop.

"Are you all right?" he asked.

"Yes." She laughed in amazement. "No." She ran a hand over her head, feeling the loose tumble of her hair. "I've lost my scarf."

"Then I guess," he said slowly, "I'll just have to go back and get it."

Hearing the teasing note in his voice, Annie looked at him properly for the first time. He was tall—she had to tip her head back to see into his face—with thick chestnut hair, streaked to gold by the sun, that waved to his shoulders like a lion's mane. His blue eyes slanted in amusement. Underneath his afghan coat he was wearing jeans and a plaid shirt with little buttons on the collar tips. Annie remembered the odd way he spoke, and her brain suddenly clicked back into gear.

"You're American," she said.

"Yes, ma'am," he agreed, and held out his hand. "Jordan Hope, from Indian Bluffs, Illinois."

She shook it, smiling at his formality. "Annie Paxford. You were fantastic. If it wasn't for you, I'd probably still be clinging to that pillar, like Patience on a monument."

Jordan just grinned at her, rocking on his toes with his fists pushed deep into his coat pockets. Was he waiting for her to say good-bye? Maybe he had friends to get back to. Annie suddenly remembered Rose and looked back anxiously toward Grosvenor Square. Jordan gave a startled exclamation and put out a hand to her chin, turning her cheek toward him.

"You've cut your head." He frowned.

Annie rubbed at the stickiness on her temple. "Something hit me. It doesn't hurt."

But he had already taken a handkerchief from his pocket. "Here, let me fix that." He smoothed her hair away and dabbed at her face gently. He smelled of leather and shaving cream.

"There. Good as new. That was a pretty wild scene back there. Just as well your policemen don't carry guns."

"Unlike yours. They shoot students, don't they?" Annie tried to sound composed. Now that the danger was past, she felt an odd exhilaration that left her breathless and jittery. She could still hear the distant roar of the demonstration.

"Well, I'm not going back there. No way," Jordan said. "I think we deserve a rest. There's a great little pub not too far away—if I can find it. What do you say to a Bloody Mary?"

"I don't think I've ever had one," she said happily.

Jordan clapped a hand to his heart and staggered as if he had been shot. Annie burst out laughing, startling a pair of disapproving Mayfair matrons in headscarves.

Jordan shook his head at her. "The trouble with you English," he drawled extravagantly, "is that you just ain't educated."

"I'm at Oxford," Annie replied haughtily.

"You're kidding."

"Certainly not. Do I look frightfully dim?"

"You look fabulous," he said frankly. "All I mean is, I'm at Oxford too." His smile broadened. "I knew I'd seen you before. You were in that Shakespeare play in the garden."

"*As You Like It?*" Annie was amazed. "And did you like it?"

"I liked you."

"Oh." Annie scuffed the leaves at her feet.

Together they strolled south across the park, toward Knightsbridge. Sunshine warmed their faces and made the trees flame into color. Londoners were out in force, taking their pleasure with an urban lack of reserve. Jordan and Annie pointed out to each other a dedicated sun-worshipper stripped to the waist lying on the grass and an old woman with her life's belongings tied onto a shopping cart, feeding pigeons from a plastic bag. There were lovers everywhere. As they walked they talked of Oxford. Annie learned that he was at Corpus, doing a graduate degree in PPE—philosophy, politics, and economics. Jordan seemed to find the whole place beautiful but weird, a sort of cross between *Tom Brown's Schooldays* and *Alice in Wonderland*. He told her about the two college tortoises, one called Corpus and the other Christi, and of the ceremonial race held between them each year; and how until 1963 it was a rule of the college that no living woman could be named at High Table. "I guess it was open season on the dead ones," he commented dryly. One of his tutors liked to sit cross-legged on the floor trying to convert Jordan to Marxism. Another had offered to dedicate his next book to Jordan if Jordan went to bed with him.

Annie giggled. "What did you say?"

"I said I wasn't sleepy. Yeah, he laughed too, but it makes me mad the way these guys don't take their subject seriously. They treat politics like some intellectual game. It's not. Politics is about everyday stuff, like jobs and homes and having enough to eat. Fooling around with ideas in isolation is exactly what leads to craziness like Vietnam."

They reached Rotten Row, waited for a rider in tweeds and black velvet cap to canter past, and crunched through the yellow sand.

"This way," Jordan urged, leading her across Knightsbridge and into a quiet side street.

"The trouble is," Annie explained seriously, "all these tutors and politicians and generals—and parents, of course—are *old*. They think everything's the way it was in the Second World War. They can't understand that the world is different now, that we don't care about all those stuffy things like class and money and religion and —oh, I don't know, marriage and proper jobs and singing 'God Save the Queen.' "

"Wow." Jordan grinned at her. "That's quite a list."

"But don't you agree?"

"Sure. Though I don't think that dropping out is the answer either. You can't expect a better world to materialize out of thin air. You have to do something to create it."

"What about today—the demonstration? That was doing something." When Jordan didn't answer, Annie stopped and turned to face him. He looked sober and distracted.

"Well, wasn't it?" she insisted.

Under her earnest gaze his expression softened. "Yes," he reassured her, "it was doing something."

The sounds of the traffic died away. They could hear the echo of their own footsteps as they walked through a calm square. Then they entered a cobbled mews lined with garages.

"Eureka!" Jordan cried as they turned a corner. At the end of the mews was a whitewashed pub garlanded with ivy. Jordan led the way up the steps and held open the door for Annie. It was dark and warm inside. Immediately in front of her was a bar, with cozy, crowded rooms adjoining. Almost at once Jordan found them a table next to a crackling log fire. Annie pulled off her coat and sat down, while Jordan ordered the drinks. The barman had a large handlebar mustache and wore a white jacket like a ship's steward. Annie watched as he began to mix ingredients in a cocktail shaker with military precision. The drinks arrived, frothy and tomato-colored, in outsize wineglasses. Annie took a sip of hers. It was delicious.

Jordan sat down opposite her. "Have you got plans for this afternoon?" he asked.

"Not really," Annie lied. She was due back at the van by four. But she was not going to pass up the chance of spending a day with this intriguing man. Edward didn't own her, after all.

"Good." Jordan smiled. "It's a beautiful day. I thought we might take a walk in the park, maybe catch a movie later. I'm heading back to Oxford tonight. I could give you a ride, if you want."

"You have a car?"

"You know us Americans. We don't move without our cars, our cameras, our Bermuda shorts, and a refrigerator as big as a bus."

Annie heard the barbed undertone. "Don't you like the English?"

"Yes, I do—at least I probably would if I could get to know them. I'm sorry if that sounded impolite. Just sometimes I get tired of fighting the same old American stereotype: too rich, too loud, too stupid. And with 'frightfully amusing' names."

"I think Jordan's a great name," Annie said truthfully. "If it makes you feel any better, there's a girl in my college called Arabella Farquharson Tennant. Anyway, there's no need to apologize to me. I've lived abroad most of my life. I don't belong either—especially at LMH."

"Lady Margaret Hall? Why, what's wrong with it?"

"Nothing. I love it. I mean that thing about it being the *ladies'* college. You must know the old joke."

"No, I don't." Jordan leaned toward her, elbows on the table, eyes alight. "Tell me."

Annie hid her face in her hands. "Oh, God, now I won't be able to remember it." She swept back her hair, took a slug of her Bloody Mary, and licked the froth from her lips. "Let's see. . . . There are five girls having tea together, each from a different college. Suddenly one of them spots a divine-looking man crossing the quad, and they all rush to the window to have a look."

She stopped in confusion, flushing under his concentrated gaze.

"Yeah?" Jordan prompted.

"So the girl from St. Hugh's says, 'What does he play?' The girl from Somerville asks, 'What's he studying?' The LMH girl says, 'Who are his people?' The St. Hilda's girl says, 'I want him.' And the St. Anne's girl," she finished triumphantly, "says, 'He's mine.'"

Jordan rocked back in his chair with a big, easy laugh that made the people around them look up and smile. Annie, feeling incredibly witty, drained her glass with a flourish.

"That's terrific," Jordan said. "I must write it down."

Annie thought he was joking until he drew out a tiny notebook from his inside pocket. She felt almost embarrassed as he committed her silly little story to paper.

"I know you think I'm crazy," Jordan said in a resigned tone, "and you wouldn't be the first. It's a habit. I like being able to remember."

Annie watched him write. "You're left-handed," she remarked.

"Is that bad too?" He looked up at her teasingly.

"It's a sign of extreme intelligence," Annie replied, "meaning that I'm left-handed as well. In fact," she confided, "I'm a left-handed Leo, which is the best thing of all. Not that I believe in astrology really, but Leo has all the best things, like fire and gold and power and—"

"And having a birthday in the summer."

"How did you know?"

"Because, smartypants,"—he tapped the back of her hand with his finger—"I'm a left-handed Leo too."

They grinned at each other, as if they'd made a secret pact.

After one more drink they left the pub and crossed back into the park. A mellow, golden light shimmered through the trees. Annie laughed aloud at the beauty of it all.

"Isn't it lovely?" She threw out her arms and twirled around, her coat flying open.

"It certainly is," he said, watching her.

"Race you to that tree," she challenged, and set off across the grass.

Jordan overtook her easily, clowning around. Panting with laughter, they leaned back against the broad beech trunk.

"This morning seems like a hundred years ago," Annie said. "It's so awful that we never even delivered the petition. Do you think they'll have another demonstration?"

"I hope so. I sure hope something happens before next summer, anyway."

"Why next summer?"

Jordan reached over and gently pulled a leaf from her hair. He took a breath. "Last week I decided to put my name back in the draft pool. Yesterday I got a letter. I've been rated 1-A. Unless something happens by the time I leave Oxford in June"—he pointed two fingers at her like a gun, making a joke of it—'Look out, Viet Cong, here I come.' "

Annie looked at him in horror. "I don't believe you. They can't make you go. You're a student."

"Oh, but they can. That's what it's all about. I'm twenty-three, Annie. Some boys didn't even make it to nineteen."

Images of the war flooded into Annie's head—a weary Marine smoking a cigarette against a backdrop of skeletal trees cobwebbed with black, blindfolded prisoners roped together, Vietnamese women crouching over their babies while American bombs rained down. A year from now Jordan could be in Vietnam. He could be dead. He could have killed someone. And from what he said, this was his own choice. It was the bravest thing she had ever heard. She held on to his arm as they walked on, feeling its reassuring muscle, while he told her about his friend Eldridge and the crisis of conscience that had precipitated his decision.

They reached the Serpentine. Annie watched people going about the ordinary business of enjoying themselves—reading newspapers on sunny benches, scattering bread for the ducks, throwing sticks for their dogs. Two schoolboys in gray flannel shorts and sagging knee socks had got into difficulties with their model boat. Jordan left her for a moment to help them retrieve it, showing them how to maneuver it so it didn't capsize. Annie watched him squatting by the water, chatting easily, the boys utterly captivated. He looked up, caught her glance, and winked. Annie turned away, hugging her coat around her. It just could not be right for someone like Jordan to risk his life for that criminal, stupid war.

"Couldn't you just stay here—or go to Canada?" she asked when he rejoined her.

Jordan shook his head. "That's not the kind of revolutionary I want to be," he said simply. "I don't think this war is right. It's not consistent with the democratic principles of America. But I can't just run away. We need to get back to our roots, to that *real* revolutionary spirit that drove America to independence in the first place —the preservation of 'life, liberty, and the pursuit of happiness.' " He smiled sadly at her. "I don't want to kill anyone. I want to change things."

They walked on in silence, crunching through the dying leaves. The days were getting shorter now. There was already a chill in the air. In the Bayswater Road, a few hopeful artists and traders had laid out their wares against the park railings.

"There's quite a decent cinema up here, at Notting Hill Gate," Annie said. "We could see what's on. What's the matter?"

For Jordan had stopped suddenly, as if struck with an idea. He marched Annie back the way they had come, hands on her shoulders, then swung her to face a tiny makeshift stall. It was crowded with beads, embroidered belts and headbands, silver jewelry, packs of incense sticks—and silk scarves.

"Choose one," Jordan said.

"I couldn't!"

"Sure you could. What about this one?" He leaned forward to pick one out. She felt his chin graze her hair. Just for a second she let herself lean back against his chest. He felt big and solid—a man, not a boy. Then Jordan moved away and held the scarf up to her face. "See, it matches your eyes."

Eventually they settled on one in turquoise and indigo paisley. Annie wound it around her neck, watching Jordan count out the money. She touched his elbow.

"Thank you very much. It's beautiful."

He just laughed and jingled his change. "Come on, let's go see a movie. I don't care what it is as long as we can sit down. That was one hell of a walk you took me on."

"*I* took you—" Annie protested.

At the Gate Cinema they joined the queue for *Easy Rider* and listened to a street singer mangling Beatles songs. Jordan put half a crown into his hat, to Annie's disgust.

"That's far too much. He can't even sing."

"Me neither." Jordan shrugged. "He's got to live, like everyone else."

When they came out of the theater, it was dark. They wandered around looking for somewhere to eat and eventually found a little restaurant with bare wooden tables and candles stuck into Chianti bottles. There were sepia photographs on the wall; Françoise Hardy sang softly on a record player.

"I think I'll just have a salad," Annie said, looking at the prices. She had only about seven and six in her pocket.

Jordan's eyebrows flew up. "You're not going to tell me you're on a diet. That I won't believe. Come on, I'm going to have steak and French fries, the whole shebang. Let me treat you."

"But I'm making you spend all your money."

"What the heck else is it for? Listen, Annie, they give us a salary as Rhodes scholars. It's worth about five times your student grant. That's how come I have a car. At home I had to work summers and wait tables to get through college, but here I'm rich." He spread his hands, drawling extravagantly "As we all say down South, I'm living high on the hog."

Annie gave in. They ordered their food and a carafe of red wine. Then she leaned forward into the candlelight. "Wasn't that film fabulous?"

"I guess. The music was good. I liked the guy playing the hobo. Otherwise, it seemed pretty dumb to me, just riding motorcycles and smoking joints. Just smelling dope gives me a sneezing fit."

"Well, I loved it." Annie took a sip of her wine. "It's my dream to go to America."

His eyes slanted in amusement. "Anywhere in particular?"

"Everywhere. It all sounds amazing. New York, San Francisco, Woodstock, the Grand Canyon, Big Sur." Annie intoned the names like a chant, making Jordan laugh. "Memphis, Tennessee," she went on. "Phoenix, Arizona. Route 66." She leaned across the table and stretched her eyes wide. "Badlands," she whispered.

"And what about Indian Bluffs?"

"Is that an invitation?"

"You bet. My mom would love you."

"And your father?"

While they ate Jordan told her about his family and his little town on the huge brown river, about the steamy summers and the winters when he and his friends had built snow forts and attacked one another with snowballs.

"And what about you?" he asked. "Do you have brothers and sisters?"

"No."

"Kind of lonely, isn't it?"

"Yes," she said, surprised. She had never admitted it so easily before.

She found herself telling him all about her odd peripatetic life, her exile to boarding school, even her bickering parents. The restaurant filled up and emptied again as they found more things to tell each other, discuss, argue over. Annie felt she had known him for weeks, not hours.

In the end, the waiter pointedly brought their bill. They realized it was late. Reluctantly they left the restaurant and took a taxi back to Jordan's car, a snub-nosed Morris Minor with jaunty red upholstery. It was chilly. Jordan flicked the switch that controlled the heater. Soon Annie could feel warm air blowing up her legs and lulling her into comforting drowsiness. She watched as the ugly old factories and harsh street lamps at the edge of London gave way to dark fields.

"If you don't have to go to Vietnam, what will you do?"

Jordan glanced at her. "Law school maybe, then some kind of public service. There are so many things that need to be done, especially where I come from."

"You mean politics?" Annie said in amazement. She pictured Nixon's brutal face, Harold Wilson with his pipe and horrid belted mackintosh, looking shifty. They didn't fit at all with her heroic image of Jordan.

He laughed. "You say that as if I wanted to boil little babies in oil. There are good politicians, you know."

"Yes, and you shoot them, don't you?" Annie responded tartly. "Kennedy, Bobby Kennedy, Martin Luther King—even Abraham Lincoln."

"I guess I'd sooner be shot because I'd achieved something than be blown to pieces in Vietnam before I had a chance to do anything. Anyway, it's good to have a goal. Don't you have ambitions?"

"Of course." But when Annie thought of them, they seemed vague and frivolous in comparison—holidays in Greece; her own apartment in some groovy corner of London; a car to drive whenever and wherever she liked; perhaps a year in Nepal; a stab at drama school; lovers, parties, fun.

"I suppose you want to be president," she said, more aggressively than she intended.

"Why not?" he said mildly. "Somebody has to be. Wouldn't you rather it was me than some racist bigot like George Wallace?"

A fragment of a Tom Lehrer song floated into Annie's head. Without pausing to think, she started singing.

> "I wanna talk with Southern gentlemen
> And put my white sheet on again,
> I ain't seen one good lynchin' in years."

Jordan shouted with laughter. "You're crazy, Annie Paxford, you know that? Are all Oxford girls like you?"

"You should know," she said provocatively.

"Should I? I've only met one girl at Oxford I really liked."

"Really?" Annie felt faintly piqued. "And who was that?"

"You," he said calmly.

Annie relaxed deeper into her seat as the dark road twisted through sleepy villages, watching Jordan's hands on the steering wheel. When at length they drove into Oxford, the clock at Carfax said half-past one. The college gates had closed long ago. She would have to climb in.

Outside LMH Jordan stopped the car and snapped off its lights. The heater died into silence. They sat in the dark, listening to the tick of the cooling engine.

"So," Jordan turned to her, "when do I get to see you again?"

Annie bent her head, hiding behind her hair.

"Jordan," she began.

"Mmm?"

"I have to tell you something."

He tensed, then flopped back into his seat with a sigh. "I know," he said flatly. "You're very sorry but you already have a boyfriend. He's brilliant, and handsome as hell—and probably English—and you don't want to hurt him. Et cetera."

Annie looked at him in surprise. "How did you know?"

Jordan let his head drop onto the backrest with something between a laugh and a groan. "How did I know?" he asked himself. "I know because there are about forty guys to every girl in Oxford, which means that anything in skirts is already attached. I know because nine out of ten Oxford girls are either Marion-the-Librarian types or act like the queen; whereas you"—he cocked his head at her—"are pretty and smart and funny and just the kind of girl I only ever seem to see on some other guy's arm. I know because nothing has gone right for me ever since I arrived in Oxford, so why should it change now?"

"I'm sorry, Jordan."

"Me too, believe me. Though I guess I wouldn't like you so much if you cheated on your boyfriend. Still"—he propped his elbow on the back of Annie's seat and smiled down at her wolfishly—"I'll give you one more chance."

Annie twisted her hands in her lap. "I can't . . . We could just be friends," she offered at last, raising her head to meet his eyes.

Jordan looked at her searchingly. Annie's heart began to thump. "Could we?" he asked.

Annie dropped her eyes and fumbled for her bag. "I'd better go."

"I'll come and help you." Jordan clicked open his door. "I haven't broken into a women's dorm since the panty raid in my freshman year. This will be something to tell my grandchildren."

It was cold and windy outside, full of night noises. Annie shivered, then felt Jordan put his arm casually across her shoulders. She left it there.

"This is the best way," Annie whispered, taking him down a narrow path flanked by a high brick wall. "If you can help me over this, there's a girl on the ground floor who will let me in."

"I can see you're an expert."

Annie could hear the smile in his voice. She thought how much she liked his accent—the slow trickle of words with an upward inflection at the end, as if everything were a question, but not a very urgent one. She stopped at a certain point in the wall where a broken brick provided a foothold. "Here."

"Hey," Jordan pulled her gently around to face him. "Thanks for today. I had a great time."

Annie steadied her hands against his chest. "Me too," she said, feeling miserable. "I'm sorry."

"Yeah. Well, if you change your mind, you know where to find me."

For a moment she thought he was going to kiss her. She decided she would let him—just once. Instead he gave her an encouraging shake. "Up you go."

Annie set her foot in the wall. Jordan lifted her high, as if she weighed nothing. In a moment she was sitting astride the wall. She looked down. A faint light from the street lamps shone on his handsome, already familiar face. All she had to do, she told herself, was jump back down into his arms. She hesitated.

"Jordan, you're not really going to Vietnam, are you?"

When at last he replied, his tone was weary. "Oh, no. I'll get out of it somehow."

They stared at each other for a long moment. Then he patted her leg. "Now get inside where it's warm. Scoot!"

Annie swung over the wall and dropped to the ground. She waited for the crunch of his slow tread back to the car. Not until she heard the Morris fire into life did she move, making her way through the trees to the curtained windows.

16

Walk On By

June sunshine streamed into the lofty room, glowing on its elaborate Gothic paneling and the spines of thousands of books. For almost the first time in his two years at Oxford, Jordan was positively hot. His tutor must be melting underneath his heavy gown and the same pea-green tweed suit he had worn all term. But the casement windows were resolutely closed against the seductive assault of birdsong and mellow bells and the clack of croquet being played in Chapel Quad below. A fly buzzed impatiently, searching for a way out. Jordan knew just how it felt.

He took a breath and turned the page of his essay. It was beginning to sound turgid, even to his own ears. He glanced at his tutor. Cecil Quelch, reader in Russian and Slavonic history, rested in his usual fireside chair, eyes closed, tortoise neck extended, chin balanced on fingertips pressed precisely together. He looked like a gargoyle popped off a college parapet. Sunlight cruelly highlighted the liver spots on his bald head and a trail of toast crumbs down the front of his gown. He seemed very absorbed indeed in Jordan's views on the Russian Revolution. Unless he was asleep.

Jordan and the imprisoned fly droned on in a monotonous duet until Jordan at last reached the conclusion of his essay and fell silent. His tutor gave a melancholy sigh.

"Interesting." Opening his eyes, Quelch nodded briskly seven or eight times in succession. "You perhaps overstate the *inevitability* of

Lenin's rise to power. History is a great deal more accidental than we think. What, after all, if the archduke's chauffeur had not taken the wrong turn in the backstreets of Sarajevo? No assassination, no war. No war, no revolution." He cocked his head, as if assessing Jordan's ability to appreciate this piece of donnish whimsy.

"And of course you will hedge your bets. The revolution was a good thing in that it overthrew a corrupt aristocracy; a bad thing in that it got people killed. Naive twaddle." He sniffed. "Read your Cicero, my dear fellow. *Salus populi suprema est lex*. However, you're sound on the economics. Your grasp of political imperatives is not unpromising. What shall we say: alpha beta? Next term we shall be able to tackle—"

Jordan interrupted gently. "Sir, if you remember, I won't be here next term. I'm going back to the States."

Quelch gaped like a fish. "Bless my soul, so you are. What a pity. Another year, and I believe we might have made something of you. Ah, well." He raised his arm in a gesture of helplessness and allowed it to fall theatrically onto the worn arm of his chair. "It's been a pleasure, Mr. ah—"

"Hope."

"To be sure. A glass of sherry, Mr. Hope, to cheer you on your way?"

"Thank you, but I have an appointment."

Jordan stood up. He folded his essay and pushed it into the back pocket of his jeans, then bent to retrieve his belongings from behind the chaise longue. There were a couple of books to return to the college library, the camera that went everywhere with him, his saxophone in its hard black case. He had a rehearsal for a gig in thirty minutes in Queen's College, and he wanted to walk the long way around through the meadow and maybe take a couple of pictures. It could be his last chance.

He straightened up to find his tutor peering over his half-moon glasses in extravagant alarm, a hand pressed to his heart.

"Great heavens, what is that contraption?"

Two could play at this game. Jordan decided to have some fun. "This?" He dangled his saxophone by the strap and looked his tutor solemnly in the eye.

"This, sir, is an 007 automatic double-action repeating machine gun." He smiled engagingly. "You know us Americans, we just don't feel comfortable without a real good gun at our sides."

Reaching out, he shook the astonished tutor by the hand. "Good-bye, sir, and thank you. It's been an education."

Jordan clattered down the staircase and out into the fresh air. He felt like turning cartwheels or giving old Quelch a blast of Charlie Parker. He felt like goosing the girl in the short dress who was bending provocatively over her croquet mallet. But he didn't. This was England. It had been his choice to take special tutorials with Quelch, outside his own college. Quelch was *the* man on modern Soviet history. No one had warned Jordan that Quelch had become unreachable behind his barricade of self-parody and intellectual gamesmanship. Jordan had been made to find out for himself. That was the Oxford way.

Jordan sighed. Another failure. He stood watching the croquet players, thinking that it would be fun to join their game. He took a last look at the graceful buildings beyond them. Pembroke was not one of the grand colleges, but it had its own charm. Samuel Johnson had played draughts in a summerhouse once situated on this very lawn. William Fulbright had been a Rhodes scholar here some forty years ago. One of the first things Jordan had done on arriving in Oxford was to send the senator a postcard of Pembroke, on which he had written: "I'm here!" He winced at the memory.

Turning into the cool entrance archway, Jordan stopped to say good-bye to his friend the porter, then emerged into the bustle of St. Aldate's. In front of him a bus was loading up a trail of dispirited-looking tourists. Jordan could guess the itinerary. Oxford in the morning, Blenheim and Warwick Castle in the afternoon, a play at Stratford in the evening. Throw in Bath and London, and that was England done. What would they make of it? There was a trash can on the lamppost next to him—what the British prissily called a litter bin. Jordan reached for his essay, "Power and the Economy in Revolutionary Russia 1917–20," and stuffed it in. Seeing a gap in the traffic, he ran across the road and into Christ Church Meadow.

It was a day of soft, delicious beauty. The roses in the war memorial garden were in full bloom. A faint breeze rustled the elms in Broad Walk and wafted the sweet, tickly smell of cow parsley from the meadow proper, where cattle still grazed. "Schools weather," they called it. Except that Jordan wasn't doing schools. He felt a perverse pang of envy for the undergraduates scribbling away in the vast examination rooms. It was a tremendous ordeal, a blitz of written papers morning and afternoon for a week, covering three, sometimes four years of study. But at least they would leave Oxford with a degree. They would have something to frame and hang on the wall. Something to show their children.

Jordan paused to take a picture of the poplar-shaded walk that led down to the Isis, then turned the other way, toward Merton. He could have completed his postgraduate degree in two years, he chided himself. He could easily have extended his Rhodes scholarship for a third year and taken his B.Phil. Bachelor of Philosophy (Oxon): It sounded fine. But the sense of time drifting away in this dreamy, elusive place filled him with anxiety, especially since the threat of the draft had at last been lifted.

Last November Nixon had instituted a lottery system whereby all potential draftees were randomly issued with a number. Low numbers were bad news; high ones virtually guaranteed that one would not be drafted until the war was over. There seemed no question now that Nixon would yield to overwhelming public pressure and honor his election pledge to end the war. Last December Jordan had received his lottery number. It was a high one, in the three hundreds. That day he had gone into the Corpus Chapel and thanked God for his deliverance. He took it as a vindication of his belief that he had never been meant to fight.

But from then on Jordan's impatience with Oxford had sharpened. This year he would be twenty-four years old. He needed to get started on his career. Last winter, without telling anyone—"hedging his bets," as Quelch would say—he had applied to Harvard Law School and been accepted. A part of him yearned to get back to a regular campus with a regular syllabus, grades he could understand, targets he could achieve to mark his progress. Hamburgers, for crying out loud, Frisbee games, cold beer, people who didn't look affronted when he said "Hi" to them. And yet . . .

Jordan turned into Dead Man's Walk, following the line of the medieval city wall. The sun reflected hot off the stone. Bees buzzed in the cascading wisteria. Here, in the heart of this swarming city, it was as peaceful and unpopulated as Gloucestershire. Jordan found that he had slowed to a stroll, then to a standstill by one of the temptingly placed benches. He shook himself and walked on. Maybe that was what was wrong with Oxford—the weather, either enervatingly gray or bewitchingly beautiful. Maybe that's why no one seemed wholly serious, as if lacking the energy to see anything through.

His generation was living through one of the most stirring periods in Western history. Prague—Paris—Vietnam; the police in Chicago, the colonels in Greece; assassination and terrorism everywhere. You'd never know it here. Jordan had read a poll in *Cherwell* claiming that 10 percent of the Oxford faculty were Marxist-Leninist, Trotskyist, or some other kind of communist. The percentage of self-styled "Communist" students must be double or triple that. But what were they *doing*, apart from grouching about Harold Wilson, or handing out incomprehensible socialist propaganda to the Oxford car-factory workers? Jordan bet that 90 percent of the student body had never seen the inside of a factory. *Cherwell* itself seemed less interested in the poll than in its "Seduce a queer peer in Christ Church" competition.

Last May Day a group of students had drowned out the traditional choristers' singing from Magdalen Tower by playing the "Internationale" over loudspeakers from an adjacent room. When apprehended, they were found drunk as skunks, knee deep in bottles of Bollinger. While students in the States and elsewhere in Europe were actually being killed in violent protests, Oxford didn't even have a proper student union. "The Union," so called, was really a political club, and an archaic and elitist one at that. Sure, it drew an impressive caliber of guest speaker. But Jordan and the other Americans had been dumbstruck to find that its members wore formal dress and hadn't even admitted women until 1963!

He stepped up his pace. If Oxford was the home of lost causes, it was no place for him. He would shake its decadent dust from his good old U.S. of A. sneakers. Nevertheless, he was aware that he had missed something. What, after all, had he achieved here? He had traveled, joined a jazz band, learned to play rugby, failed to grasp the rules of cricket. He had read a lot of books and opened his mind to new ideas. He had made a couple of good friends and had collected the names of hundreds of people who could one day be useful to him. But deep in his soul, he was disappointed in himself. He wished he had shone at something. When he left Oxford, he wanted to be missed. He wished he had met more English people. He wished he had met more girls.

He had been more successful than many Americans in that department, given that there were no mixers or any dating structure he could recognize. At least he had been invited for tea in a couple of women's colleges. For a few short weeks last year he had shared his bed with a good-time girl from the Oxford and County secretarial college—known locally as the Ox and Cow. But the one girl who had really fired his soul—and his body—was unavailable.

Annie Paxford was unlike any other girl he had ever met. Her brand of Englishness seemed unique—a matter of spiky humor and challenging intelligence without the chilliness or adolescent bumptiousness of other English girls. She was open, inviting, with a sense of fun that he envied. Also—and this was the most arousing thing of all—he knew she had liked him too.

He had thought of her often and seen her twice: once speeding by in a sports car with her hair flying—with another man, of course; and once in a New College production of *The Importance of Being Earnest*. He had been invited by a St. Hugh's girl who thought he needed educating. Their relationship was strictly platonic. She wore granny glasses and droopy flowered dresses and had a forehead as wide as Nebraska. She claimed to be a lesbian anyway. But she had seemed annoyed by Jordan's fascination with the blond girl playing Gwendolen, giving him a whispered lecture on the oppression of women in male society when all he wanted to do was admire Annie's breasts. That evening Jordan had actually started a letter to Annie, ostensibly congratulating her on her performance, but the words eluded him. It was not about words. It was about feeling, mystery, excitement. But she already had a boyfriend. He was going home. And anyway—had anyone ever made it to president with a foreign wife?

Jordan reached the iron gates that led out of the meadow into Rose Lane. Here was the famous noticeboard, rotting with age, that had made him laugh out loud when he first read it.

CHRIST CHURCH MEADOW

The Meadow Keepers and Constables are hereby instructed to prevent the entrance into the Meadow of all beggars, all persons in ragged or very dirty clothes, persons of improper character or who are not decent in appearance and behaviour; and to prevent indecent, rude or disorderly conduct of every description.

To allow no handcarts, wheelbarrows, bathchairs or per-ambulators (unless they have previous permission from the Very Reverend the Dean): no hawkers or persons carrying parcels or bundles so as to obstruct the walks.

To prevent the flying of kites, throwing stones, throwing balls, bowling hoops, shooting arrows, firing guns or pistols or playing games attended with danger or inconvenience to passers-by: also fishing in the waters, catching birds, or bird-nesting.

To prevent all persons cutting names on, breaking or injuring the seats, shrubs, plants, trees or turf.

To prevent the fastening of boats or rafts to the iron palisading or river wall, and to prevent encroachments of every kind by the river-side.

Jordan decided to take a picture of the notice. His mother would enjoy it. As he did so, a straggle of Magdalen College School boys in grass-stained cricket flannels filed past him, nudging each other and giggling. A Yank, they signaled to each other, taking in his shoes, his camera, and the white T-shirt showing at his unbuttoned collar. Jordan grinned back.

"Good game?" he called.

"It was only batting practice, you know," piped a patronizing voice.

"Can't win 'em all." Jordan smiled at his own foolishness.

They trotted past, proper little English gentlemen in the making. Jordan wondered whether, in twenty or thirty years' time, he might find himself confronting one of them across some international conference table. If so, he thought he would have the edge.

He snapped his camera back into its case and loped after them, crossing the High Street and turning back toward Queen's. Across the road, outside the Examination Schools, a crowd of undergraduates awaited the release of their friends. Standing slightly apart, with her back to him, was a girl with long blond hair. Jordan caught his breath and stopped short. It was Annie.

The roar of the traffic between them faded. Time slowed. Jordan heard the blood pounding in his ears. He could feel the hot sun on his head. He stepped to the edge of the pavement. As if she had heard a voice calling her, Annie began to turn slowly in his direction. Her head twisted. He saw the curve of her cheek, the gleaming slither of hair down her back. Jordan already had his hand half raised, when he became aware of a gathering noise, a rustling and chattering like the approach of migrating birds. To his dismay, Annie turned away again. Jordan looked to see why.

A crowd of undergraduates in their black and white "subfusce" uniforms was pouring out of the building entrance, giddy and raucous with relief. Girls clutched each other, covering their eyes at the memory of their imperfect answers. Boys stumbled down the stairs, shouting like football fans, pulling at their white bow ties. Annie moved forward, scanning the crowd, and Jordan now saw that she had a bottle of champagne in one hand and two glasses held loosely by their stems in the other.

Suddenly her face lit up. She waved the glasses high in the air. A man with dark hair ran lightly down the steps toward her, pulling the white carnation out of his buttonhole. He presented it to Annie in a gesture so tender and self-mocking that Jordan bit his lip. Annie laughed and held her arms wide, signaling "No hands!" The man bent to fix the flower behind her ear, then kissed her possessively on the lips.

At that moment a rowdy group swept across the road and engulfed Jordan, blocking his view. Schools over, they were deliriously in love with the whole world. They offered Jordan a swig of their champagne and he accepted, infected by their mood. He clapped the men on the shoulders. One of the girls kissed him. Then they moved on. By the time Jordan looked back, Annie was standing among a large, laughing circle of friends, clinking glasses. The strange man had his arm around her. She looked happy.

Jordan felt a savage sense of loss. He wished he could have said good-bye, that he could have let her know how he felt, that he could leave her something to remember him by.

Hitching his saxophone back onto his shoulder, he ran up the steps of Queen's and into the lodge, blind in the sudden dark.

17

Where Do You Go to,
My Lovely?

Annie lay naked in Edward's bed, her back to him, eyes open. Through the doorway she could see plates of chicken bones and strawberry stalks on the sitting-room floor—the remains of their celebration lunch. An empty wine bottle lay on its side among a muddle of album sleeves and discarded clothes. It all looked terribly sordid. Without meaning to, she sighed heavily.

Edward stirred beside her. She could feel his breath on her back as he nuzzled close.

"I'm sorry, darling," he mumbled. "I was too quick for you."

Annie didn't move. "It doesn't matter."

"Yes, it does. I can tell." She felt his hand on the curve of her waist. "It's just that I've been cramming my brain with so many dates and cases and precedents that I can't get rid of them. You know how uptight I've been about Schools. But it's all over now, thank God."

All over now. What dreary words, Annie thought.

"Hey." Edward rocked her gently. "Come here."

After a second or two Annie turned toward him, hearing the bedsprings grate. She settled her head in the hollow of his shoulder.

"I thought you'd fallen asleep," she said. "You must be exhausted."

He squeezed her to him. "You're the most important thing in the world to me—much more important than exams or sleeping or anything else. I admit I could do with one mammoth sleep to get me back on form. But I want this last week together to be special.

I want to take you on the river, and out to Dudley's, and to do the things I've been dreaming of all term. I want to go to parties and get drunk and dance with you all night."

"It's all right for you," Annie grumbled. "I've still got two essays to write."

"Stop being sensible. Nobody does any work in their second year. Besides, we need to get into training for next week."

For a moment Annie wondered what he was talking about. Then she remembered the Magdalen Commem and how thrilled she had been when Edward had asked if she wanted to go. The commemoration balls operated on some kind of rota system, so that each college held one every few years. But the word was that this year's Magdalen Commem was going to be out of sight—the most fabulous ever and the most fabulously expensive. Top of the bill were the Doors, who would be playing in a huge dancing tent to be erected in front of New Buildings. There would be five or six support groups, a jazz band, and a discothèque in the Hall. The cost of the ticket included dinner with wine and a champagne breakfast. There were to be Dodgems in St. Swithun's Quad, fireworks over the river at midnight, madrigals sung in the cloisters at dawn. Rumors seeped out of extraordinary precautions against gate-crashers—of some kind of hand-stamp that would show up only in ultraviolet light, and special bouncers imported from London who would be posted along the river and even at the entrances to the city sewers. The Magdalen Commem was the talk of the term. Everyone wanted to go, though many undergraduates were just too poor. Two tickets cost a colossal eleven guineas. You could fly to Athens for that.

Annie had dug into her father's legacy to buy an amazing dress from Annabelinda. She knew that when she got to the ball, she would have a fantastic time. It would be incredible to see Jim Morrison in the flesh. But right now she wasn't in the mood to think about it.

Edward put his mouth to her ear. "How would you like," he whispered, "to have dinner beforehand at the Elizabeth?"

"Edward! You'll go broke." The Elizabeth was the grandest restaurant in Oxford. Only dons and rich parents went there. It cost at least two pounds a head.

"So what?" he said recklessly. "Soon I'll be stuck in an office all day—chambers, anyway—with a load of geriatrics. I want to have fun before the prison walls close in." He pumped his arm into the air, singing "Born to be wi-i-ild" until Annie giggled and dug him in the ribs.

"Stop it! You sound like a wolf howling at the moon."

"I'll have you know there's a very fine blues singer called Howlin' Wolf," Edward replied with dignity. He rolled eagerly on top of her. "So how about it, darlin'?" he said in mock Cockney. "Fancy an evening out at the Elizabeth?"

Annie put her hands to his chest, holding him at bay. She looked at him seriously. "It would be lovely—if you're sure. But, Edward, I may not be around the whole time."

Edward frowned. "Why not?"

"These essays for a start. In fact"—she struggled to get up—"I really should go to the library in the Radcliffe Camera and put in a few hours."

"You can't go now." Edward sat back on his heels among the rumpled bedding, watching in dismay as Annie swung out of bed and started to put on her clothes.

"I might as well. You know you're longing to go to this college celebration with all the other lawyers tonight. I'd only be a terrible drag while you make in jokes about torts and party-wall disputes."

"You're never a drag."

"This way I can do my work while you catch up on your sleep."

"But when will I see you?"

Annie couldn't keep the impatience out of her voice. "I don't know. Soon." She hesitated, then added casually, "I won't be around tomorrow anyway and possibly not Friday either. God, my hair!" she rushed on. "Can I borrow your brush?"

"What do you mean, you won't be around? Where are you going? I thought you said you had to work."

Annie pulled her striped T-shirt dress over her head. "I do. But there are other things in my life. I don't belong to you, you know."

"Of course you don't belong to me. I don't belong to you either. It doesn't mean we have to have secrets." With an angry gesture, Edward reached for his cigarettes. He lit one moodily, hunched on the edge of the bed. "I hate it when you're like this."

Annie stared into Edward's mirror, silently brushing, hating herself too. At length she put down the brush and walked over to Edward.

"Can I have a puff?"

He passed her the cigarette without looking up. She took a drag and handed it back. Then she dropped her arms loosely onto Edward's bare shoulders.

"The thing is, Eddie, there's something I have to do, but I can't tell you what it is. It's not my secret to tell. I don't want to spoil your celebrations. Just give me a couple of days, and everything will be back to normal."

Edward grunted and leaned away from her embrace to stub out the cigarette in the bottom of a coffee mug. Then he got up and started pulling clothes out of his drawers. Annie watched from the doorway as he slid on his jeans and a white Indian-style shirt, then pushed past her, barefoot, to his sitting room. She followed him in, thinking how beautiful he was. She loved his long slim legs and his aloof profile.

She cleared her throat. "So . . . I'll come round on Friday evening, if I'm back. Okay?"

"Yeah. Whatever."

Edward was crouched by the record player, flicking through his albums. Annie hesitated, half wanting to go back to bed and make it up with him, waiting to see if he would look at her. When he didn't, she turned and let herself out of his room. As she clumped down the stairs she heard the record come on. It was Otis Redding singing "Dock of the Bay." She felt like crying.

When she reached Trinity gates, she remembered that she'd left her bicycle outside Schools. She couldn't be bothered to get it now. And she had no intention of working in the Radcliffe Camera. She was going back to LMH to make sure everything was okay for tomorrow. She turned left into the Broad Street, deciding to walk through the University Parks.

The air was absolutely still and oppressively hot. The freshness of the morning had gone. Her skin itched and her head ached. In the late-afternoon glare, Oxford had a tawdry, hang-dog air. The buildings looked dirty. Even the stone heads outside the Sheldonian Theatre—the emperors—looked miserable. Nothing could more clearly have signaled the end of term than the windows of Blackwell's bookshop, full of tourist maps and student guides to "abroad"—Greece, Kathmandu, America. Annie stopped to stare at a photograph of the Statue of Liberty on one of the book jackets. She knew one reason for her depression. It was that American, Jordan Hope.

Today, when she was celebrating with Edward outside Schools, she had suddenly caught sight of Jordan on the other side of the road and felt her heart leap. He was quite unmistakable, almost a full head taller than anyone else, with that clean American look, smiling his wonderful smile. He looked on top of the world, surrounded by a great group of laughing people. Then she had seen a girl kiss him and felt a spasm of such terrible jealousy that she'd had to hide her face in Edward's shoulder. Annie shook herself and walked on. It was ridiculous to feel so intensely about a man she hardly knew. Eight months ago she had spent a day alone with him. That was it. She hadn't seen him since—though she had looked for him often enough. She had not forgotten the magic of that day, the excitement of meeting someone so different, so exuberant, so . . . sexy, she whispered to herself, feeling guilty.

Reaching the entrance into the Parks, Annie paused to take off her sandals. The sky was a strange color, almost white. There was a distant *thwack* and a ripple of clapping. Shading her eyes, she made out the bleached figures of cricket players. Edward played cricket.

Annie struck out across the grass toward LMH, feeling it dry and prickly under her feet. Why had she not taken her chance with Jordan? It wasn't just her feeling for Edward or a sense of fair play. The very things that seemed most romantic about Jordan—his Americanness, his political passion, his ambition, the threat of the draft—also warned her off. Well, it was too late now. By asking around, Annie had discovered that Rhodes scholarships lasted for two years. That meant Jordan would be going home this term. It was just as well, she told herself. She had already hurt Edward enough by being so secretive. Thinking of what she had to do tomorrow, Annie's misery deepened.

She might never have noticed that anything was wrong with Rose if they hadn't been tutorial partners this term. It had started off by being quite fun, and rather revealing. Although Rose liked to project a devil-may-care image, Annie had discovered that she was actually very serious about her studies and intended to get a first. Her essays were invariably well researched, well written, and on time. So it was surprising when, two weeks ago, Annie had gone as usual to collect Rose on the way to Miss Kirk's tutorial and found her still in bed, saying she was too ill to go. Annie had conveyed Rose's apologies to Miss Kirk. Afterward she had gone back to bring Rose a cup of tea and was extremely annoyed to find that she had gone out. Later, when she asked Rose for an explanation, Rose was irritatingly offhand: She was bored with her studies, Oxford was an elitist anachronism out of touch with the real world. It was all a waste of time.

Rose's behavior became increasingly strange. Often she would still be in bed at midday, with the curtains drawn and her room stale with smoke. Sometimes she had the electric heater on, even though the temperature outside was soaring. Annie began to suspect that Rose had been dumped by some man. She sensed that men didn't always treat Rose well—though who could blame them? When it came to the opposite sex, Rose was like a professional card-player, discarding that one, picking up this one, constantly reshuf-fling the pack. She never talked about love, just of "getting" someone, although she seemed to lose interest as soon as they were got. Annie had once spent an entire evening cheering up some poor boy from Balliol whom she'd found waiting pathetically outside Rose's room, unable to believe that he had been stood up. If Rose had at last met her match, it might be no bad thing. Nevertheless, Annie couldn't help watching out for her friend. She had started bringing Rose cups of coffee to coax her out of bed in the morning and had offered to bring her books from the library or food from Hall.

Yesterday Rose had casually mentioned that she was going to miss their tutorial again. Annie had lost her temper, complaining that it wasn't fair to make her invent yet another excuse. But late last night, hearing music from her room, she had knocked on Rose's door to apologize. Rose was lying flat on the floor in the flickering light of a candle stuck onto a saucer, listening to "Nashville Sky-line." She had raised her head.

"Oh, it's you. Come in."

As Annie dropped cross-legged on the floor next to her, Rose spoke solemnly to the ceiling.

"I have had a revelation. Lying here, listening to this music, I have realized that the sixties are really and truly over." She propped herself up on an elbow to look at Annie. "Can you imagine, a whole album without a single protest song? Just drippy ballads about lo-o-o-ve and the simple country life. Dylan's given up the fight. It's all over—peace and love and a better world. The sixties haven't been the beginning of something new, just a romantic little hiccup in his-tory. My prediction is that the world is going to get meaner and greedier and slicker." She flung herself back onto the carpet. "In ten years' time we'll all be working in advertising."

"I won't." Annie shook back her hair. "You're just depressed. I wish you'd tell me why."

"Depressed," Rose enunciated thoughtfully. "Our parents banned us from using that word. According to them, depression is a serious clinical condition, which we were not entitled to suffer until we'd made at least one suicide attempt."

Annie was shocked. Rose had always seemed so keen to give the impression that the Cassidys were one great big happy family. She put her hand on Rose's ankle and waggled it gently. "I'm sorry I was annoyed with you earlier. It's only that Miss Kirk keeps ticking me off for not bringing you to tutes. I don't mind, I just wish I knew what was wrong. I do think it would do you good to get out of your room, even if you haven't done your essay. Why don't you at least come with me on Thursday and—"

"Stop sounding like the God Squad," Rose snapped, sitting up to scowl at Annie. "Once and for all, I am not coming to our stupid tutorial. I'm not even going to be in Oxford." She pushed her bangs up furiously with the palm of her hand. "If you must know, I'll be in London. In a clinic." She gave Annie a defiant stare. Then her face crumpled. "Having an abortion."

They had stayed up until dawn, talking. Annie had insisted on going with her to the clinic. She was appalled at the idea of anyone going through such an ordeal alone. She couldn't get that horrifying scene in *Alfie* out of her head where Vivien Merchant, alone and in agony, had expelled her aborted fetus into a tin bucket. Of course, abortion was legal now. There were anesthetics and clean sheets and proper hygiene. But the whole idea made Annie squeamish.

Perhaps Rose felt the same way. It was hard to tell. She agreed to Annie's company, but would say very little else except that being pregnant was "ghastly," and that the father was "irrelevant." Annie had no idea who it was or what he felt about the baby—if he even knew about it. This made her faintly uneasy. If she became pregnant, she would tell Edward—wouldn't she?

The thought of Edward reminded her of their unsatisfactory parting. But there was no help for it. Rose was Annie's friend. Rose needed her. For the next couple of days, Rose must come first. Besides, she knew that Edward would forgive her, attributing any moodiness to the loss of her father.

Annie's father had died quite suddenly, of a heart attack. It was the last day of the previous term. Carrying her suitcase through the lodge to her taxi, Annie had seen her name on the blackboard and had gone to look in her pigeonhole for the telephone message. *Phone your mother urgently.* By the time she had reached Malta, her father's body was in the hospital mortuary. The funeral had taken place the next day. Infusing her shock and grief was a terrible anger that her father had not waited just twenty-four hours so that she could have seen him one last time. Logic said that it would have made no difference. Her father had died almost instantly. But Annie felt an illogical, desperate regret that she had not had the chance to see him, even in death. People said that the bodies of the dead looked shockingly empty and alien. Annie knew this must be true, but she still wished that she could have seen for herself. She could not rid herself of the fantasy that her father was still alive and would appear around the next corner, smiling his diffident smile, saying, "All right, monkey?"

The sky had been steadily darkening. As Annie neared the path that led out of the Parks to LMH, she heard a rush of wind in the beech trees. A fat drop of rain landed on her arm, then another and another. She began to run, wincing at the sharp stones underfoot. From far away came a long growl of thunder. Annie could not suppress the superstitious thought that the gods were angry.

18

With a Little Help from My Friends

Rose stood in front of her open wardrobe, naked apart from a scrupulously clean pair of underpants. Exactly what did one wear to an abortion? Should she dress like a bishop's wife to quell comment or like the tart without a heart they would be expecting? Forget respectable, she decided. There was no need to add hypocrisy to her other vices.

She reached for a long, wraparound skirt in bright cotton paisley, then rummaged in her chest of drawers for something to go with it. A tight black T-shirt—that would do. She pulled it on, then wound the skirt about her waist and tightened the sash viciously. According to a book she had sneaked a look at in the public library—a horrorama of photographs and disgusting cross sections —the "thing" was only about the size of a kidney bean. But Rose could feel it—she knew she could—low in her belly, smugly swelling by the minute. She loathed the sensation, as she loathed the way her whole body had suddenly gone into overdrive. *Lie down,* it urged, flooding her with a horrible, unfamiliar lassitude. *Let's pump up those breasts!* it ordered, like a gung-ho gym teacher, as if she were going to start breast-feeding tomorrow. Rose curled her hand into a fist and punched herself hard in the abdomen. "Get out!" she whispered to the incubus within her. "Go away. I don't want you."

How did anyone stand this for nine whole months? Ever since that electrifying moment when the doctor had told her that the test was positive, the streets of Oxford seemed to have sprouted pregnant women. Rose saw them behind serving counters, hauling shopping onto buses, even working in the Bodleian Library, as if their monstrous, swollen condition were perfectly normal. Their stoicism stunned her. All Rose wanted to do was lie down, nibbling water biscuits to mask the perpetual faintly metallic taste in her mouth. She didn't even like alcohol anymore.

And all because of a missed pill and a few minutes of sex—be honest, Cassidy, a few *seconds*. Rose shoved her feet into shoes and pulled open the curtains. Last night's thunderstorm had cleared the air. A disgustingly perky blackbird was hopping across the sparkly grass, looking for worms. The sky was pearly blue. It was going to be another beautiful day. Everyone would be enjoying it except her. She leaned her forehead against the cool glass of the window and closed her eyes against a prickle of self-pity.

She had never meant to go that far. She had run into him in First Week, at a fizzle of a party in St. Hilda's. It had always faintly nettled her the way he regarded her as a useful organizer, a political sparring partner, never as a woman. When she saw him lolling against the wall, paper cup in hand, oozing that easy American charm, she had set out deliberately to alter his perception. Somehow the conversation had gotten around to Jimi Hendrix. They were both fans. The next thing she knew, they had skipped out of the party and were sitting in his room listening to *Electric Ladyland*. He had a bottle of whiskey and some good grass. They got completely wasted; later Rose suspected that he had slipped something into her drink. She couldn't remember much, although one memory mercilessly persisted—of herself, dressed only in panty hose and his tie, strumming along with Jimi on a tennis racquet. It had seemed funny at the time. Then suddenly—wham!—he was on top of her doing his electric woodpecker impersonation. You couldn't call it lovemaking. The whole thing was fast, impersonal, brutal. Rose was still trying to catch up with him when he gave a loud moan and slumped on top of her, as if he had been shot in the back. Almost immediately he started snoring.

Rose had lain still on the hairy carpet, her head cricked against a sofa leg, feeling the warm trickle between her legs. He was very heavy, but she didn't dare move him. She didn't feel like looking him in the eye just yet. After a while she started to get cold, and rather depressed. She felt bruised and used. Eventually she rolled the inert body off her. Even zonked out, he looked wickedly sexy: not a bad conquest to notch up. She tiptoed about the room retrieving her scattered clothes and walked back to college, uncomfortable in soggy underpants. She ran a bath, not caring if the noise woke anyone up. She lay in the cooling water, recasting the evening's events. It had been a wild time with a wild man. She had really turned him on, but sadly not vice versa. What was it her Yorkshire grandmother used to say? "All mouth and no trousers." That was a good line.

Rose usually slept naked, but she had an old flannel nightie that she sometimes wore if she was cold or ill. That night she put it on and climbed into her narrow bed, pulling the blankets tight around her body. Outside some damned owl or something was hooting away. Perhaps it was the mating season. She didn't know and didn't care. She was clean and warm and sleepy. She was alone. Everything was cool.

Except it had all turned out to be extremely uncool. The truth had smitten her, bizarrely enough, in the middle of a tutorial on John Donne. Miss Kirk was talking in her prim way about Donne's having "anticipated the marriage ceremony." It was obvious from his poems that Donne was terrifically sexy. He had made his boss's niece pregnant, then married her secretly. His wife had died, aged thirty-three, after giving birth to their *twelfth* child. Rose was pondering the lifesaving benefits of contraception when the word *pregnant* lit a firework in her brain. The odd symptoms she had noticed only subliminally—nausea, tiredness, the pain in her breasts when she turned over in bed, the way she was no longer interested in sex—crystallized into an immediate, awful certainty. She tried to remember the date of her last period. For the rest of the tutorial she had sat in a trance, hands hidden in the folds of her gown, counting days on her fingers.

She couldn't bear to confess her stupidity to anyone she knew, including the college doctor. There had been an article about abortion in *Cherwell* not too long ago. Rose looked it up and found the telephone number of a clinic in London. The next day she went up for a test. A week later she returned to London for the result. The doctor was a supercilious Scottish cow. "Abortion is a very serious matter, Miss Cassidy. You can't just walk in and ask for one like a bar of soap." Two doctors needed to sign a certificate saying that Rose was physically or mentally unfit to complete the pregnancy. Rose had been dragged through her family background, financial circumstances, feelings about the pregnancy. She even had a lecture on adoption. Rose held her ground. She wanted the thing out. Now.

Finally she was referred to a Harley Street clinic. There were more questions, tests, forms, examinations. She never wanted to see a pair of rubber gloves again.

Now the waiting was over. By this afternoon she would be herself, single again. The moment she had longed for had arrived. And she was petrified.

Rose banged her head against the window, trying not to think of sharp instruments in tender, private places, of fat, prying fingers, of the anesthetic that would dull her will and suck out her spirit until she was just a slab of flesh to be prized open and sliced. Anesthetics could go wrong. She had read that sometimes the patient heard every word in the operating room and felt every agonizing pain without being able to move a muscle. "Don't be silly," her mother used to say briskly when Rose had nightmares before school injections. "In the Third World you'd be dying without them." Right now Rose didn't care about the Third World. When it came to doctors and hospitals, she was a first-class coward.

A door slammed. Rose opened her eyes with a start. She could hear the shuffle of slippers in the corridor, the flush of a toilet. The college was beginning to stir. From the window she could see two first-years scampering down the gravel path to the tennis courts, racquets swinging. She looked at her watch: past eight already. Annie would be collecting her any minute, and she hadn't even done her packing.

Rose had been determined to go through the abortion on her own. It was her mistake, and she would have to rectify it. There was no point in turning to her family. Her parents were too busy saving lost souls to bother with her. It would be different if she were a homeless teenager or a drug addict. As for her brothers, of course they would have helped if she had asked, but asking them would mean losing face. All her life it had been a point of honor with Rose to be as clever and as tough as the boys. When her brothers joked about paternity suits and buns in ovens, she had joined in their cavalier, masculine talk. It was unthinkable to be on the receiving end of their pity.

Nevertheless, the experience of being pregnant had been strangely disturbing. As the day of the abortion neared, Rose had begun to suffer bouts of real panic. It had occurred to her to confide in Annie, but she didn't know how to do it. Once Annie's insistent, gentle, maddening questioning had broken through her stubbornness, the relief was overwhelming. Annie had not judged her or laughed at her. She was just sympathetic and practical. Though Rose had still not managed to say so, it made all the difference to know that Annie would be coming too.

Rose was still frowning over the contents of her bag when there was a knock on her door and Annie entered, wearing her mauve Laura Ashley dress. On her shoulder was the inevitable overstuffed Greek bag. She looked ridiculously pretty and healthy, as if she were going to a garden party. Trapped in her own alien, treacherous body, Rose felt a spurt of envy.

"Tell me what I've forgotten." Rose waved toward her bed. "It somehow doesn't look like enough."

Annie dumped her bag on a chair and considered the collection of items Rose had laid out. A nightgown, neatly folded. A spare pair of underpants. A new box of sanitary napkins for the bleeding afterward. Rose watched Annie's face grow sober.

"Gruesome, isn't it?"

Annie caught her hand. "Oh, Rose. It's not wicked, you know, or immoral. You mustn't think that. It's not a baby yet, just a tiny little, um—"

"Yeah, yeah, I know—thing," Rose answered flatly. It seemed impossible to explain to Annie that she didn't give a damn about the baby—it was the operation she was worried about.

"Okay." Annie put a forefinger to her temple like a gun. "Think, Paxford. . . . Soap and towel," she said after a moment. "You might want a bath. Slippers and dressing gown. And your mouth will feel like an armpit after the anesthetic. Mine did when I had my appendix out. Where's your toothbrush?"

Rose handed her things, watching Annie pack them neatly away. Then Annie stooped over her own bag. "I've brought you some treats," she said.

First she held up a little bottle. "Chanel No. 5, only half full—sorry about that—to make you feel nice." Next she drew out a book whose tattered jacket showed the haunted face of a girl against the backdrop of a Roman bridge. "One slushy novel, slightly foxed. Total garbage. I loved every minute of it. And finally—" She flourished a chocolate bar.

"My favorite!" Rose made a grab for it. "Do you know, I'm not supposed to eat or drink for twelve whole hours before the—the grisly deed. I'm starving."

"Afterward," Annie said firmly, packing it away. "The anesthetic will make you sick otherwise."

She zipped up Rose's bag and picked it up. "Ready? We'd better go, or we'll miss the train."

In the doorway Rose paused to take a last look at her familiar things: her Che Guevara poster and the Indian bedspread she'd hung on the wall, her psychedelic tea tray set out with glasses and sherry and a tin of Chocolate Olivers, Oxford's fanciest biscuit. The next time she saw this room, everything would be over. *If* she saw it . . .

From outside the room came Annie's voice. "What is it? Have you forgotten something?"

Rose stepped into the corridor, pulled the door shut, and locked it. "Too late now."

Annie and Rose traveled to London in silence, intimidated by the presence in their compartment of two middle-aged women in silk print dresses, nose to nose in a discussion of wedding hats. Annie was reading *Tom Jones*, making notes in her cramped, left-handed way. Rose held Annie's novel on her lap, but her eyes kept skittering across the print. She could already predict that the man with the cynical twist to his mouth would turn out not to be a murderer after all. On the final page he would claim the ninny-brained heroine with a fierce, possessive kiss on her heart-shaped face. True love. Yuk. No one ever said what happened afterward—whether Jane Eyre itched to tell Mr. Rochester that he had spilled food down his frock coat yet again, or whether Elizabeth Bennett threatened to ban Darcy from her bed if he invited Lady Catherine de Bourgh for Christmas. Rose did not want to be married; she wanted to be famous. In only five years' time she would be as old as Keats was when he *died*. She would not, not, *not* be boxed in by domestic trivialities, even if it meant being carved up by some cold-eyed surgeon.

Fear washed over her again. She sucked in her stomach as tight as it would go, feeling the "thing" lodged within her. Looking out at the flash of sun on the Thames, she saw only the chill glitter of instruments. At least the days of coat hangers and death by septicemia were over, she told herself. This would be a Rolls-Royce of abortions—120 guineas' worth. Rose had hated asking him, but there was no one else. He seemed as embarrassed as she was by the memory of the Jimi Hendrix night. He hadn't even challenged her statement that the baby was his, just asked what she needed and given her the money, glad to be rid of her. Rose had taken it in silence, feeling cheap. It was like hush money.

From Paddington they took the tube to Baker Street and emerged into the hot, acrid air of central London. Annie insisted on carrying Rose's bag. "I'm not an invalid," Rose protested, but she was grateful. Annie stopped by a newspaper seller who shouted directions over the rumble of buses. They passed a long queue of wilting tourists outside Madame Tussaud's and then crossed Marylebone Road. There was a big church with an ornate clock. Rose wished she believed in God.

Halfway down Harley Street, Annie stopped outside a black door with a brass doorbell. Rose felt sick.

"You ring," she said to Annie.

A woman in a lime-colored suit and silvery hair teased back from a broad hairband opened the door. She led the way down a marble-floored hallway, high heels echoing, into an ultramodern reception area. There were pop-art prints on the wall and a glass coffee table scattered with magazines. Two long-legged girls who looked like models were giggling together on a leather sofa. Rose suddenly felt scruffy and schoolgirlish. She curled her bitten nails into her palms.

Indicating two chairs, the woman sat herself on the other side of a futuristically curved desk and picked up a pen. She gave a professional smile. "Which of you is Mrs. Cassidy?"

"Me. *Miss* Cassidy," Rose added defiantly.

The woman's smile remained in place. "We find it easier to call all our ladies 'Mrs.' Now, we'll just sort out the paperwork and then pop you upstairs to see Doctor."

"She can come too, can't she?" Rose nodded at Annie.

The woman frowned.

"Please," Annie said, "I won't be any trouble. I'll go away when you say."

Rose laid a hand on Annie's arm. "I *need* her." It sounded melodramatic. But it was true.

The woman shrugged. "Just for a bit then, to settle you in."

It was all eerily businesslike. Rose handed over the forms with all her medical history and wrote the biggest check in her life. She was given a form that seemed to entitle the doctor to perform any further surgery on her he thought necessary. Rose read only halfway and signed it.

A nurse came down to collect them and led them up the broad,

curving staircase to the next landing. Here the character of the building changed. Heavy swing doors opened onto a polished expanse of
pale linoleum. Carts and wheelchairs were ranged along one side,
beneath reproductions of famous paintings. The other was lined
with a series of cubicles screened by flowered curtains. At the far
end was another pair of ʹswing doors. Bright lights gleamed ominously through two frosted panes set at eye level. Rose flared her
nostrils at the sweet hospital smell.

The nurse showed them into one of the cubicles and told Rose
to undress, put on the folded gown, and get into bed.

"Not like that, you idiot." Annie giggled. "The ties go at the
back." She fiddled for a bit, then patted Rose on the shoulder.
"There you go. And very kinky too."

"Huh," Rose said grumpily, climbing into the high bed. She
bounced nervously on the mattress, eyeing the pristine walls and van
Gogh's sunflowers. "At least it's not a dump," she conceded.
"Thank God for rich Americans."

At that moment the nurse came back, pushing a cart piled with
alarming-looking objects. On top was an enamel bowl and a syringe.
The nurse whisked the curtains shut behind her.

"Right," she said brightly, "visiting time over."

Rose's heart accelerated. This was it.

Annie slid off the bed and touched Rose's hand. "Will you be all
right?"

Rose nodded. But her face must have given her away, for Annie
suddenly bent down and hugged her fiercely.

Without meaning to, Rose whispered the words that were in her
head. "I'm frightened."

Annie held her shoulders. "It will be fine," she said with calm
authority. "I absolutely promise." She walked over to the curtain,
looked back to blow Rose a kiss, and ducked out of sight.

The nurse picked something off her cart and gave it an experimental buzz.

"What's that?" Rose asked suspiciously.

"We need to shave you first, don't we?"

Rose lay staring at the ceiling, her gown pulled up around her
waist, legs splayed. She felt hot with humiliation. Never again, she
vowed.

The nurse took the blood pressure, checked through her notes,
and then swabbed a little patch of skin on Rose's arm and reached

for the syringe. "This is the premed," she explained. "It will help to make you feel more relaxed."

Rose looked away as the needle went in. Almost immediately she felt the drug take hold, flooding through her body. For a moment she fought the loss of control, then subsided beneath a tide of lazy well-being. The feeling was not altogether unpleasant. It was a little bit like being stoned.

The next thing she knew, a West Indian man was pushing her bed down the corridor and into the bright room at the end. Rose had an impression of white walls and shiny metal. The doctor's face surged into view. He had purple cheeks and smelled of mints and cigar smoke. He touched her arm.

"Mrs. Cassidy, is it?"

Rose nodded. Who the hell did he think she was? She hoped he knew which operation he was supposed to be performing.

"Splendid. Do you think you can open and close your fist a few times for me?"

Rose tried it. Miraculously her muscles obeyed.

"Good girl. Now, just a little prick to put you to sleep. I want you to count to ten for me. Can you manage that?"

Of course I can, you moron, Rose thought. She saw the flash of a syringe in his hand and felt a sting in the crook of her elbow. Aloud she said, "One, two, three, f—"

Downstairs in the reception area, the models had gone, leaving an ashtray full of pink-tipped cigarette butts. Annie flipped the pages of *Punch,* seeing instead Rose's pale face, remembering her casual words, "Thank God for rich Americans." Which particular American? she wondered.

"Your friend won't be able to see you for at least an hour," the receptionist said finally. "Why don't you enjoy this lovely sunshine? Regent's Park is just across the road."

Annie practically ran into the park, clearing her lungs of exhaust fumes from Marylebone Road. She walked up the broad path between gaudy municipal flower beds, so different from Oxford gardens. The scene was like a Victorian painting, full of incident. There were office workers eating sandwiches on the grass, old men on benches with their newspapers, solitary women feeding buns to the birds, children everywhere. She even saw a proper old-fashioned nursemaid, pushing a pram that looked like a miniature carriage.

She walked as far as the zoo, where a couple of deerlike creatures stood dejectedly in their dirt allotment. Farther on she could see Lord Snowdon's famous new aviary poking into the sky, but it was time to go back. Rose might need her. As she turned, a shiny red ball rolled into her path. Annie stopped, looking around to see whose it was. From a couple of feet away a small boy stared solemnly into her face. Annie picked up the ball and held it out to him, smiling. He put his thumb in his mouth. She stepped closer. She could see the fresh perfection of his skin, the lustrous lashes fringing clear, shining eyes. He still wouldn't budge. Annie rolled the ball gently to his feet. He bent his fat knees, lifted the ball with a grunt, and carried it off like a trophy to his mother.

Annie walked back slowly, her thoughts returning to Rose, hoping she was all right. Though she knew that Rose would never ask, Annie couldn't help wondering if Rose's baby had been a boy or a girl.

19

Band of Gold

The Elizabeth boasted not only the best cuisine of any Oxford restaurant but also the most spectacular view. Situated in a small, oak-paneled room above Alice's Shop, where the old sheep had sold Alice an egg in *Through the Looking-Glass*, it looked due east across St. Aldate's to Christ Church. Edward had booked them a window table. While they ate they watched high pennants of cloud flush apricot and pink in the sunset. When dusk approached, a sudden spotlight magically illuminated the soaring Gothic pinnacles of Christ Church Cathedral.

Annie ran her spoon round and round the earthenware dish in front of her and swallowed the last mouthful of crème brulée with a regretful sigh.

"That was the most delicious dessert I have ever eaten," she pronounced. "In fact, the most delicious dinner. I hope all these buttons can take the strain."

Annie gestured at her dress, a shimmer of white taffeta with a row of tiny buttons from the deep V-neckline to below her waist. There were more buttons on the long sleeves, beginning almost at her elbows and extending down to tight cuffs, which ended in points low on her wrists. She wore no jewelry, just a white velvet ribbon fastened around her throat. Her hair fell loose, apart from two slim gold plaits that held it away from her face.

"You look like a medieval princess," said Edward, smiling at her over his wineglass.

"And you look like Byron." Annie leaned forward and kissed him on the lips, unfazed by the presence of the other diners. Edward did look ravishingly romantic, she thought. Under his dinner jacket he wore a ruffled white shirt with a bottle-green velvet bow tie and matching cummerbund. Dinner jackets could make men look like either smug Tory MPs or dissolute dandies. Annie was pleased to discover that Edward fell into the latter category.

There was only one other couple dressed, as they were, for a Commem. Everyone else was old. Full term was over now, and most undergraduates had gone home the previous weekend. For days the streets of Oxford had afforded the painful sight of overdressed mothers beaming at their insouciant offspring from a respectful distance and fathers grumpily loading cardboard boxes into car trunks. LMH was unnervingly quiet. The libraries were empty. Every day there were more tourists and fewer students. It was this valedictory, slightly wistful air about the very end of Trinity Term that the Commems were designed to counteract in as noisy and hedonistic a fashion as possible.

Annie had mended her fences with Edward on her return from London. The whole Rose affair was over so quickly she needn't have been so secretive. Annie had imagined days of looking after Rose, perhaps even escorting her home to her parents. But as soon as the operation was over, Rose had bounced back to normal with almost shocking swiftness. She had insisted on going straight back to Oxford on the evening of her abortion, her only concessions being to allow Annie to pay for a taxi from the station and bring her supper in bed. She seemed to regard the whole episode as a humiliating failure, a blot on her breezy reputation. If Annie didn't wholly understand her reaction, she was pleased to see her friend back in good spirits. Tomorrow night Rose was going to the Keble Ball with a group of friends. Next week she would be flying to Boston for a coast-to-coast trip across America by Greyhound bus.

Edward had hardly let Annie out of his sight. Now that his finals were over, the realization had struck that he was leaving Oxford for good. Together they revisited all their favorite places, as if Edward had to put his stamp on them before he left. He had been in a strange mood, veering between exuberance and nostalgia. Although he had never questioned her further about her mysterious disappearance, Annie would catch him looking at her thoughtfully, as if making up his mind about something. He was doing it now. She hoped that he wasn't going to go all sentimental on her. Tonight she just wanted him to be wild and witty and dance with her until dawn.

But all he said was "Coffee? Brandy?"

"Both," she said extravagantly. "Tonight I'm not going to say no to anything."

Edward gave her a smile she couldn't quite interpret. "Good."

As they sipped their brandies, the waiter set up a glass coffee-maker in the middle of the table and lit a spirit lamp underneath. Annie watched dreamily while the water heated and began to bubble up through the coffee.

"I'm glad we finally made it here," Edward said in a melancholy way.

"Me too. It was a sumptuous dinner. Thank you."

"I wish I wasn't leaving."

"You'll be back again next month if you get a viva," Annie said cheerfully. She knew that Edward was hoping for a first, in which case he would probably be called back for an oral examination to determine which class of degree he merited.

"Yes, but you won't be here. And next year I'll be stuck in London."

Annie laughed. "You sound as if it's Outer Mongolia. London's only an hour away on the train. You can come up for weekends."

"It's not the same. In fact—"

Some emotional undertone in his voice made her suddenly alert. Annie saw that Edward was looking at her solemnly while he reached into his jacket pocket. All at once Annie knew what was coming. Every nerve in her body protested: *No! Not now!*

Edward placed a small, square jewelers' box in front of her. Annie stared at it, searching for words. Then she looked at Edward. His face was quite impassive. He had looked like this when she had escorted him to his first finals exam. She picked up the box. In the front panel was a small metal button, which she pressed. The lid flipped up. Fixed in a bed of pale velvet was a gold ring with a dark-blue stone. There could be no mistaking what kind of ring it was: not a present; an engagement ring.

The silence between them seemed to go on forever. Annie became aware of the clank of heavy silverware and a burst of laughter from another table.

"We can exchange it if you don't like it," Edward said.

"It's lovely," Annie said, her eyes welling with tears. "Just what I would like if—if I wanted to get married." She touched the blue stone gently with one finger, then pressed the lid down slowly. The box snapped shut with a click.

"But I don't," she whispered. "I mean, it's too soon."

"We don't have to do it right now," Edward said defensively. "Just . . . one day."

Annie shook her head. "It doesn't feel right. I've got another year here. You're the first proper boyfriend I've ever had. I'm not even twenty yet."

"I know." Edward made a despairing gesture. "I'm too young to get married too," he said almost angrily. "I never thought I'd want to. But I can't bear to lose you. Every time I think I know you, you . . . evade me. It's that damned upbringing of yours." His voice softened as he reached for her hand. "Don't you love me?"

"I think so." She squeezed his hand. "But *marriage* . . ." Her voice trailed away. Like any other girl, she had sometimes day-dreamed about a candlelit proposal by a handsome man in romantic surroundings. But it had always been something immeasurably distant, in the realms of pleasant, foolish fantasy. The reality was uncomfortable. Although she was ashamed of herself for feeling this way, Annie felt angry with Edward for laying such a heavy trip on her just now, before the ball that was intended to be so much fun.

"So it's no then," Edward said flatly.

Annie stared miserably at the tablecloth. "It is for now, if you don't mind. I'm sorry." She wiped her nose surreptitiously on her napkin.

With a sudden, swooping gesture, Edward reached across for the box and pocketed it. "No sweat. Forget it." He tried to smile. "I may try again one day; I may not. Who knows?" He raised his hand and summoned the waiter with an imperious gesture.

"Two more brandies, and a large cigar for me, please."

Annie didn't think she could manage another brandy, but she said nothing. Two more balloon glasses arrived with an inch of deep amber liquid at the bottom. Edward swigged almost all of his in jittery gulps. The waiter brought a large, polished box and displayed its contents to Edward, who selected an important-looking cigar. Deferentially, the waiter sliced off one end with some kind of implement Annie had never seen before and lit the cigar for Edward with a long match. Edward took an experimental puff and coolly blew out the smoke, head turned to admire the view. Annie's eyes lingered on his haughty profile. He looked self-contained and unreachable. She feared she had hurt him horribly.

"Nothing like a real Havana." Edward lounged back in his chair, giving Annie a narrow-eyed smile. "Rolled on the thighs of luscious Cuban virgins, you know."

"Do you still want to go to the ball?" Annie asked gently. "I won't mind if you don't. Honestly."

"Of course we're going to the ball." Edward's eyes glittered. "I may not be allowed to marry you, but I can at least dance with you, can't I?"

"Of course. I'm really looking forward to it."

Edward nodded curtly and continued to puff away at his cigar. Annie thought it looked rather hard work.

"So, how's your ma?" he asked conversationally.

"All right. Now that the initial shock is over and she knows she's got a decent pension to live on, I think she's quite enjoying herself. She's on a sort of royal tour of her friends, supposedly to decide which part of the country to settle in. But I don't think she can face setting up on her own yet. And of course, now that she's finally back in England, she does nothing but complain about everything."

They continued to make small talk about their families and holidays. Annie was heading for the Greek islands with some friends from the cast of *The Importance of Being Earnest*. Edward was going to Mallorca with his parents in August. By the time he asked for the bill, they were talking normally. Only a certain tightness in his face, and the amount he was drinking, betrayed Edward's emotional turmoil. He signed a check with a flourish.

They walked across the meadow, hand in hand, without speaking, enjoying the great sweep of trees and shadowed grass. The sky had paled to opal. There was a white semicircle of moon on the horizon. As they approached Rose Lane, they could hear the thump of music from the ball.

Suddenly Edward threw back his head and laughed theatrically. He was drunk, Annie realized.

"You're quite right, my darling—as always." He threw an arm around her, staggering slightly. "Marriage is a *terrible* idea. I was just thinking about Harry—remember, my cousin who had to get married last summer? He wanted to be a songwriter. You know what he's doing now? Selling vacuum cleaners on commission. Every night he goes home to a squalid little flat in Fulham that smells of baby sick. So thank you." Edward planted a wet kiss on her cheek. "You have saved me from a ghastly fate."

They had now reached the far side of the meadow. Just here a branch of the Cherwell divided from the main river to enclose St. Hilda's Meadow, where Edward had pushed her into the water almost exactly a year ago. Before Annie realized what he was doing, Edward had taken the jewelers' box out of his pocket and was moving toward the river with the curious, tight run of a slow cricket bowler.

"Edward. No!" Annie shouted.

But it was too late. Suddenly he stopped, leaned back, and sent the box arching through the air. Annie heard a small splash and the grumbling of disturbed ducks. Edward brushed off his palms and walked back to her, looking pleased with himself. He grabbed her hand. "Come on," he said, dragging her down the lane at a run. "We're going to have *fun*!"

Despite everything, Annie felt a thrill of excitement as they walked through the archway into Magdalen. There was a tremendous burst of music and laughter and the hurdy-gurdy sound of the Dodgems. While Edward showed their tickets to a posse of ball officers and received a fistful of vouchers and a program of events in return, Annie peeked into the first quad. Chinese lanterns had been strung around the high walls, giving out a fairy-tale glow. Right in front of them two men in harlequin costumes and masks were juggling with phosphorescent balls. In the middle of the quad a Twenties band in striped blazers was playing "Has Anybody Seen My Girl?" There were high banks of flowers everywhere. Couples in dinner jackets and long dresses streamed past, swinging champagne bottles by the neck. Over the rooftops the sky was stained with the flashing colors of a giant strobelight. Annie tugged impatiently at Edward's hand.

"Come on, let's dance."

Annie thought she was rather good at the Charleston, and Edward was brilliant at it. She hoped that the bouncy music might restore his confidence and good humor. He certainly threw himself into it, laughing when he bumped into the other dancers. He sang along to the music and smiled, but not at her. When they left the dance floor the first thing he said was "Let's go get our free wine."

They walked under a tower and through into the cloisters, where tables and chairs had been set out on the lawn and a string quartet played. Under one of the covered walkways they found a trestle table covered in bottles. Edward traded in the appropriate voucher and poured them a glass each. They sat in one of the stone arches for a while, watching the spectacle, until the pounding dance beat drew them upstairs to the dining hall. Here it was all heat and sweat and flailing hair. Heliotrope lights swirled over the linenfold paneling and across the impassive portraits of Elizabeth I and Cardinal Wolsey. In the center of the packed bodies a peroxide blonde in bare feet and a short chain-mail dress, with apparently nothing underneath, had all the males goggling, including Edward. Men were so simple, Annie thought. All they wanted was for you to say yes to everything and take off as many clothes as possible. She tossed her hair and spun around, giving herself to the music.

They danced to Mungo Jerry and Smokey Robinson, Creedence Clearwater and Procul Harum, until it was too hot to breathe. Edward retrieved their wine bottle from a high ledge and led the way back outside. It was quite dark now. The cool air felt marvelous. They slipped through a narrow passage and into the last, and largest, open quadrangle, where a huge canopy striped red and white like a circus tent had been set up in front of New Buildings. It was here, Annie remembered, that she had smoked her very first joint. It seemed a lifetime ago. She wondered what the deer were making of the extraordinary noise.

Inside the tent, a group called Audience was playing the sort of druggy music you couldn't dance to.

"When are the Doors coming on?" Annie asked.

Edward consulted the program, then looked at his watch. "They should be on now. Punctuality probably isn't their strong point. Let's see if we can find the Dodgems."

They pushed their way back through the jostling crowds until the clank and crash drew them into Longwall Quad. Here they joined the queue for a bumper car. While they waited, Edward drank steadily and kept topping off Annie's glass. Her head was beginning to feel numb. When they finally got into the car, Edward drove like a maniac, crashing into everybody.

"I thought 'Dodgems' meant we were supposed to dodge the other cars, not hit them," Annie complained. Edward just laughed and spun the wheel. Annie was beginning to feel sick. Every few seconds another car banged into them from some unexpected direction, making her head snap. Suddenly she half rose in her seat.

"I feel sick," she shouted into Edward's ear. "I have to get off."

As soon as they were near enough to the edge, she jumped out of the car and ran into the darkness, a hand clamped to her mouth. There was a herbaceous border at the edge of the quad. Annie made it just in time to retch behind a large shrub. Tears of effort and shame squeezed under her closed eyelids as she heaved up the Elizabeth's legendary haute cuisine. *De haut en bas,* she thought inanely.

She felt a hand stroke her back. "Poor baby," Edward said. These were the first tender words he had spoken to her since they had left the restaurant.

At last the nausea subsided. Annie stood up, trembling slightly. Edward handed her a paper napkin, and she wiped her mouth. "How disgusting," she said. "I'm sorry."

Edward took her arm. "It doesn't matter. You need to lie down. Hang on." He reached into his breast pocket. "They've allocated us a room somewhere. Let's see if we can find it."

Eventually they found themselves in a small college bedroom. Stripped of all personal belongings, it had a depressing air. Annie washed out her mouth at the basin, then bathed her face in cold water. Now that she had actually been sick, she felt almost as good as new. Waiting for the water to dry on her skin, she checked herself in the mirror. She looked quite normal—pretty, even. She tucked a strand of hair back into her braid and turned to Edward. He had taken off his jacket and was lying zonked out on the bed, not looking too good himself.

He opened one eye and shut it again. "Come here," he commanded, stretching out his arm.

Annie hesitated, then went over and let him pull her down beside him. He gave her a squishy kiss. "That's better," he murmured, stroking his hand over her body. He knew what she liked. Soon she began to respond. She was just wondering whether they should lock the door, when Edward rolled onto his back with a sigh and settled her head on his shoulder.

"Isn't this nice?" He yawned.

Annie lay there silently, wondering what he was up to. Was this a punishment? She could hear distant whoops and the cacophony of the different bands. It seemed terrible to miss out on all the fun. Then another, much closer noise intruded. Edward was snoring.

"Edward?" Annie shook him. He felt like a giant lump of dough. He groaned protestingly and settled his head deeper into the pillow.

Annie slipped out of his embrace and got off the bed, watching him. He was definitely asleep. She picked up his arm and lowered it again. It was as heavy as lead. By the look of him, he would not wake until well after the ball was over. There was a sudden crackle from outside. Annie went to the window. Bright green stars were falling out of the sky. She opened the window and leaned out. Another firework streaked up through the darkness and exploded into scarlet and gold lilies. She turned from the window, making up her mind. First she took off Edward's shoes and covered him as well as she could with the bedspread. Then she filled the plastic cup with water and put it next to the bed. Edward was bound to wake up with a dry mouth and a hideous hangover. As her hand hovered over the light switch an idea occurred to her, and she fished the ball vouchers out of Edward's jacket. With one last look at his sleeping figure, she switched off the light and closed the door quietly.

In no time she was outside again, hurrying down to the crowded riverbank to watch the fireworks. It was the most spectacular display she had ever seen, not a simple matter of rockets and pinwheels, but multiple explosions of stars that drew shrieks and sighs of pleasure, cascading fountains that gushed one out of another, pillars of flame that lit up the sky and left a smoky trail. At the very end a fixed display on the other side of the Cherwell spelled out the words MAGDALEN COMMEMORATION BALL 1970 in letters three feet high.

When the crowd began to disperse into couples and groups, Annie felt faintly self-conscious about being on her own. But it was all so beautiful, with the river and the lights and the music. Everyone was happy, or drunk—or both. It was a relief to be on her own, free of Edward's reproachful presence. She thought it was just as well that they were both leaving the next day. They needed some space. For the moment it was fantastic just wandering at will, observing the other people, slipping among them like a ghost. Underneath the kitchen walls, she came to a table laden with bowls of strawberries. They looked delicious.

"Got your voucher?" a voice asked.

Annie held out her sheaf of vouchers and let him take one. She strolled on toward the big tent, spooning fruit into her mouth. At the entrance was a group of disheveled men, swaying gently.

"Have the Doors been on yet?" she asked.

"There's been a hiccup backstage," one said and then hiccupped loudly himself. His companions clutched each other, finding this excruciatingly witty.

"Eh oop, trouble at t'mill," quipped the first clown, setting his friends off again. Then he squinted down his nose at Annie and said in his normal voice, "I say, do you want to dance?"

"No, thanks." She laughed.

She strolled back through the cloisters and into the first quad, where a steel band was now playing. In one corner of the quadrangle was a stone pulpit with a canopy over it. Annie sat on the curving stone staircase and finished her strawberries. She was turning to go back, when an intriguing little archway caught her eye. She set down her strawberry bowl and walked down to it. A network of festive white lights stretched over the vaulted ceiling like a spider's web. The tink-tonk noise of the steel band receded and was replaced by a lazier, more seductive rhythm. She could hear the slow, upward slide of some instrument that was exhilarating and melancholy at the same time. Her nerve endings tingled. The music drew her like an enchantment.

Annie stepped through the arch and caught her breath at the scene. She was in a small, triangular courtyard, enclosed by high monastic walls on one side and a chapel with stained-glass windows on the other. On a swath of perfect grass, couples sat or lay as if in a delicious trance. In the far corner, lit only by an Edwardian standard lamp with a tasseled shade, a jazz band was playing. The black pianist was singing "Is you is or is you ain't my baby?" in a low, heartbreaking voice.

It was with no surprise at all that Annie saw that the saxophone player was Jordan Hope.

20

Love Me Two Times, Girl

Annie stepped on to the lawn, feeling as if she were in a play and had just heard her cue. When she was a few feet from the band, she sank down onto the soft grass, her eyes on Jordan. He was wearing a white jacket and a black bow tie. Golden sparks flashed from his saxophone. Behind him Magdalen Tower rose out of the shadows like a fairy-tale castle. Annie wasn't sure if he had noticed her until he took the saxophone from his mouth. An incredulous smile spread over his face, revealing almost every one of those perfect American teeth. Annie leaned back on her hands, slid off her shoes, and wriggled her toes in the velvet lawn.

The music he was playing was unfamiliar and bewitching. This band had none of the frenzied peacocking of pop groups. It was spontaneous and intimate. They all seemed to be enjoying themselves. She liked the way they gave one another a chance at a solo and consulted between songs, communicating in a secret language of raised eyebrows and casual gestures. In one such break, Jordan whispered something to the pianist, unlooped his saxophone from around his neck, and walked out of the pool of light, over to Annie.

"Hi," he said, squatting beside her.

"Hello." She felt herself beaming back helplessly and tried to sound cool. "Shouldn't you be playing?"

"I'm sitting this one out." He lowered himself to the ground and clasped his hands around his knees. "My friend the piano player is going to sing something for you."

"For me!"

The pianist was rippling up and down the notes in an introductory way. Suddenly he swung into a lilting rhythm and started singing "When somebody thinks you're wonderful . . ."

Annie hid her face in her hands. They both laughed.

Jordan plucked a blade of grass from the turf and started to chew it. "What are you doing here by yourself?"

"My partner passed out."

"Uh-oh."

"What about you? Haven't you brought someone?"

Jordan held up a disclaiming hand. "Hey, I'm working."

For a while they watched the band in silence. Annie couldn't stop smiling. "You never told me you played the saxophone."

"You never asked. Listen, I'll be through at two. Maybe we could talk, have a drink, check out the ball—I don't know." He laughed almost shyly.

"I'll wait," Annie said.

At the end of the song he stood up, then turned slowly back to her, as if he had remembered something. His handsome face was serious, regretful.

"I'm going home tomorrow, back to the States."

"It doesn't matter." Only when the words were out of her mouth did Annie realize that this was an odd answer.

When he rejoined the band, Annie understood that Jordan was now playing for her. She felt his awareness of her in the way he stood, bending low over his instrument to coax forth moody sounds as husky as his own voice, or throwing back his head to release a triumphant blast of pure energy. Annie had never realized what a wonderful instrument the saxophone was. Whatever Jordan did, her eyes followed him. A current flowed between them. It was a new and exquisitely exciting form of flirting. The other spectators seemed to realize that there was something going on between the big sax player and the solitary girl in the white dress. Annie could tell from their indulgent glances that they found the situation intriguingly romantic. A beautiful boy with a public-school forelock loped over the grass toward her.

"We thought you needed this," he said, gracefully setting down an almost full bottle of champagne and two glasses in front of her. "We're all pissed as newts anyway."

Annie stared at him, speechless. By the time she had recovered, he was back with his friends. She poured herself some champagne and raised her glass to them. They nodded encouragingly.

Just before two, Jordan announced the last number. Right on cue, the bells in Magdalen Tower pealed out their chimes and struck the hour, drowning out the applause. Jordan stepped forward, scowling humorously at the bells while he waited for them to finish. Then he bent to the microphone and spoke in his slow drawl.

"Everyone in the band tonight is from the United States. I guess you all know that Christopher Columbus discovered America in 1492, which was the year they started building this old tower behind me. If all that bell ringing is Oxford's way of telling us colonials to shut up, well, we can take a hint. Good night, and thanks for being a wonderful audience."

There were enthusiastic whoops amid the applause that followed, and a ripple of laughter. People began to climb to their feet and drift away. Jordan beckoned Annie over. She went shyly, taking the champagne, and let him introduce her to the rest of the band. They were friendly and relaxed, admitting her to their circle. After retrieving the drinks they had stashed around the small stage, they stood around chatting, winding down. Here, in this intimate corner, it was hard to believe there was a whole ball going on around them. Annie sat on the piano stool, watching Jordan unscrew his saxophone, clean it out, and fit the pieces into the case. He arranged for one of the other players to take care of it for him, then picked up the champagne bottle and glasses and turned to Annie.

"Ready?" He smiled. "Let's go find somewhere to talk."

They walked through into the cloisters and found an empty table where they could sit down. Jordan poured their drinks. Annie leaned forward into the candlelight and asked the question that had been in her mind ever since the day she had met Jordan.

"You said you were going back to America. That doesn't mean you've been drafted, does it?"

"No, thank the Lord." Seeing the anxiety in her face, he explained about the lottery system. "It looks as if I'm off the hook," he concluded, "and I owe it to Richard Milhous Nixon, of all people. Still, it's kind of nice to know you were worrying about me."

"Well, I was." Annie flushed. "I read in Cherwell about a Rhodes scholar—a draft dodger—who committed suicide, and I thought of you."

Jordan looked down at the table. "Yeah, that was Bruce. He lived in our house."

"Jordan, no! How awful," Annie whispered.

"He got this letter from his dad saying it would be better for Bruce to be dead than to disgrace his family through cowardice. Can you believe it? What kind of father would say such a thing? That was in April, just about the time Nixon started the attacks on Cambodia. We all knew that Bruce was pretty rocky mentally. I guess the two things together just flipped him over the edge. We tried to keep an eye on him. But we failed."

"What happened?"

"One night he slipped out of the house and went down to the canal. He put some rocks in his pocket and jumped off the bridge. At the inquest they said his body was full of alcohol and drugs. He probably passed out pretty quickly. But, Jesus, what a waste. He had the courage to say no to the war, and he had the courage to take his own life." Jordan gave a harsh laugh, as if admitting something painful. "Bruce was braver than me."

Annie laid her hand impulsively on his sleeve. "Don't say that."

Jordan's face softened. In a sudden, swift gesture, he picked up her hand and kissed it. Annie's body jolted at the touch of his warm lips. Their eyes met.

"What's that for?" she asked.

"For being nice. For thinking about me. For being here on my last night in Oxford." Jordan grinned. "What the hell."

He was flying back to St. Louis the next day. Most of his things had already been packed up and sent home. He had stayed this long only because of his commitment to play at the ball. Annie listened to Jordan's plans for a summer job in Washington and then law school in the fall. First he would go see his mother and maybe take her on a trip over to the Ozarks lakes. As before, Jordan conjured up an exotic and alien world. Annie envied his positive sense of his future, when hers was so cloudy. She didn't even have a home to go to anymore. When she told Jordan about the death of her father, he was sympathetic in a way that was easy to accept. Most people didn't know what to say. Annie had found it was usually easier to avoid the subject.

"Isn't it sad?" Jordan said thoughtfully. "Here you and I are, without fathers, and there's Bruce's father, without a son. People are too alone these days. I tell you, Annie, when I get married I want to have a great big family. I want lots of daughters I can give away at weddings and make sentimental speeches about; sons I can teach to play baseball and take duck shooting. One day, when I've achieved everything I can, I'd like to be one of those white-haired old men who sit rocking on the front porch, telling the same tall stories, and who can count their grandchildren by the dozen."

Jordan radiated so much energy that Annie found it hard to imagine him sitting anywhere for long. Still, he made marriage and family life sound like an adventure, not a trap. Annie felt a pang of envy for the girl he would one day marry.

They talked on, one subject leading to another, as if they would never run out, until they became aware of a commotion around them. People were streaming through the cloisters, all headed in the same direction.

"Listen!" Annie sat up excitedly. "It's the Doors."

"What doors?"

"The Doors, you idiot—the group. They're finally playing. Only three hours late." She laughed happily. "I bet they're stoned out of their tiny minds by now."

Jordan saw the light in her face and jumped to his feet. "Well, come on, what are we waiting for? This could be my last great cultural experience in England."

They began to make their way toward the big tent. Every one of the hundreds of people at the ball had the same idea. Now that the group they had waited for—and paid for—was finally playing, the narrow passageways between the buildings were clogged. People pushed impatiently. Jordan put his arm around Annie, keeping her close. It seemed the most natural thing in the world to put her arm around his waist too. She could feel the breadth of his back and the pressure of his thigh against hers. Above the noise of the crowd rose the scream of an electric guitar. Annie shivered with excitement. Jordan felt the movement and looked down at her with his smiling, seductive eyes. Her stomach somersaulted. He bent his head to her ear.

"Did I tell you that you look sensational in that dress?"

"No." She smiled mischievously into his face.

"Or that you're the prettiest girl at the ball?"

Annie shook her head, eyes sparkling.

Jordan lowered his head farther. "Or that I want to kiss you?"

Annie turned her face into his shoulder, hiding her smile. *Later*, she thought, her body fizzing.

Finally they burst out onto the lawn of New Buildings. Everyone ran toward the music. It was such a warm night that the flaps of the canopy had been raised. Behind the stage loomed a giant screen. Colored lights flashed across it like the rays of the sun in some drug-induced vision, converging on a fiery ball. In front of it, outlined against the lights, was the brooding figure of Jim Morrison, singing "When You're Strange" in his hypnotic wail. The tent was packed. Every last chair was taken. People were standing on the tables, sitting shoulder to shoulder on the dance floor. Some had even shinnied up the tent poles for a better view. Jordan took Annie's hand and threaded his way through the crowd until he found a tiny space and folded himself into it, pulling her down between his knees.

At first they just sat and listened reverently. But at the first screaming guitar slide of "Two Times Girl," the audience exploded. People rose to their feet, clapping their hands over their heads and jumping up and down until the dance floor bounced like a trampoline. They stood on tables, twirling dangerously. They spread out onto the lawn and started dancing. The mood was intoxicating. Jordan tapped Annie's shoulder.

"Come on," he said. "Dance with me."

They pushed their way out onto the lawn and joined the whirling bodies. Annie took off her shoes and leaped into the beat. The lights flashed across their faces, turning them different colors. They could see the tent swaying. A man on one of the punts got so carried away that he jumped into the river, fully dressed, with a jubilant scream. One song rocketed into another. Annie and Jordan showed off shamelessly, laughing at themselves and at each other. Annie felt as if her body were an instrument tuned to perfection.

When the music slowed, Jordan reached out and drew her into his arms. They swayed together across the grass. Annie slid her arms up around his neck and leaned her face into his shirt. He smelled delicious. They danced like that for a long time, learning the feel of each other's body. Then she felt his mouth against her ear.

"I have a dream," he murmured into her ear. "I have a dream about punting a beautiful girl down the river in the moonlight." His arms tightened around her.

There was a punt station under Magdalen Bridge. Normally it

would be closed by now, but the ball organizers had made a special arrangement to lease a few punts for the night. When she saw the crowds of people waiting, Annie almost cried out with disappointment. Jordan steered her to a quiet spot on the riverbank. He took off his jacket and wrapped it around her shoulders. "Wait here."

"But the queue." She pointed. "You'll never get one."

Jordan pivoted on one toe and spread his hands cockily. "Watch me."

Annie didn't need the jacket, but she hugged it to her. It smelled of Jordan. While she waited for him, she gazed across the silken river to a line of trees hung with white lights. This was Addison's Walk, where she had often strolled with Edward. Ruthlessly she closed her mind to him. Edward wasn't here. Jordan was. Tomorrow he would be gone. Once before she and Jordan had been thrown together, and she had resisted. This time it seemed like fate.

Five minutes later a punt glided toward her out of the darkness. She saw the gleam of a white shirt. Jordan was standing at the sloping end of the flat-bottomed boat in bare feet, trousers rolled above his ankles. He had removed his bow tie and loosened his shirt. He swung the long pole through the water and brought the boat to the bank.

"Jordan!" Annie laughed with delight. "How did you do that?"

"Ah-ha."

"You didn't steal it, did you?"

"Of course not. I was raised a Baptist. I know the punt guy. He eats lunch in George's, in the market. Now get in."

Annie took his hand and stepped in carefully. She began to settle herself among the cushions.

"Contacts, you see, Annie." Jordan sighed in a worldly way. "That's what life is all about. Also," he added, "I gave the guy a pound."

"A pound!" Annie shot up in the boat, sending it rocking.

"Jesus!" Jordan dropped to a crouch, trying to keep his balance.

They punted upriver, past Magdalen Grove toward the Parks. Annie stretched out her legs and leaned back luxuriously against the headrest, watching Jordan drop the pole into the water and bend down to propel the boat forward. It was a soothing rhythm—the rumble of wood on wood as the pole slid down the side of the boat, the crunch of gravel as its metal tip hit the riverbed, then the sudden hiss of water as the boat shot forward, fading to a gentle ripple.

They passed one or two other punts; then there was nothing but trees and river and sky. The noise of the ball faded. The darkness deepened. Annie draped her arms over the sides of the boat, trailing her fingertips in the warm water. Behind Jordan's head she could see a million stars and the pale glow of a half-moon. Then she felt leaves brush her hair as the boat nosed toward the bank, under an arching willow tree. Jordan ducked down to avoid the branches.

"The trouble with punting a beautiful girl down the river," he complained, "is that you can see her, but you can't touch her."

He thrust the pole deep into the mud to secure the boat alongside the bank. Annie shifted to one side of the cushions to make room for him.

"Be careful," she said as Jordan stepped over the far headrest and walked down the boat toward her. "The boat's rather wonky."

Jordan slid down beside her. " 'Wonky'?" he said disbelievingly. He pulled her close to him, laughing into her eyes. "What kind of crazy English word is that?"

"Wobbly. Unstable. Liable to capsize." At the first touch of his hands, Annie felt a kind of delirium sweep through her. "Unsteady. Shaky. Prone to collapse. Not—"

"Stop talking," Jordan said and kissed her.

For a long time there was silence, as his lips, then his tongue, explored hers. When at last they drew apart, Jordan let out a long sigh. His eyes wandered over her face in delight and astonishment.

"You know, this is like a miracle. I saw you in the street the other day, and I thought it was for the last time."

"I saw you too," Annie said dreamily, then frowned. "You were kissing a girl."

"I was not!"

"You were. Outside Queen's. A girl in subfusc."

"Oh, her. She was just someone who'd finished her exams. I'd never seen her before. She'd have kissed Joe Stalin if he'd been standing where I was." He smiled exultantly at Annie. "Don't tell me you were jealous?"

"Madly."

"Anyway"—Jordan carefully stroked a strand of her hair from her cheek—"that wasn't kissing. *This* is what I call kissing . . .

"These buttons," he mused after a while, fingering the neckline of her dress. "Are they just for show, or do they do something?" He undid the top one, answering his own question. Annie watched languorously as he unfastened her dress. She was wearing nothing underneath. Her breasts fell into his hands like warm fruit.

Under the touch of his fingers and his lips Annie began to tremble. Jordan peeled her dress down her shoulders and leaned over her. He swept back her hair and put his face to hers.

"Are you sure?" he asked fiercely. She could feel the effort it cost him to ask the question.

"I'm sure." Annie mouthed the words. She had no breath left to make them audible. For answer, she tried to put her arms around Jordan, but they were imprisoned in the folded-back sleeves of her dress.

"Wait," Jordan said. "Let's do this right."

He freed Annie's arms from her sleeves, then slid her dress down her body, hooking off her underpants as he went. Annie gasped as she felt the soft air on her skin. All she wore now was the ribbon around her neck. Jordan put his hand low on her stomach, and they both felt the deep muscles contract.

"Now you," she whispered.

Kneeling in the bottom of the boat, Jordan stripped off his shirt. Then he stood up carefully, catching hold of a willow branch to steady himself. His body was dappled with moonlight. Annie could see smooth curves of muscle and the taut hollow under his rib cage. He loosened his trousers and kicked them off, to stand naked above her. Annie reached out, suddenly wild with impatience, and ran her hand up the inside of his thigh. His skin was hot, as smooth as silk. Jordan let go of the branch and gently fitted his body on top of hers. The sheer weight of him brought tears of desire to her eyes. Water lapped at the boat as it began to rock, cradling the two of them in their willow cave. Annie felt pierced with joy. She heard a low, crooning sound that might have been Jordan's saxophone and realized that it was her own voice. She closed her eyes, thinking *I am going to remember this for the rest of my life.*

1992

21

Honky-Tonk Woman

Rose Cassidy stood at her living-room window, flushed from her shower, wearing the monogrammed robe she had stolen years ago from the George V in Paris. One hand rested on her hip, elbow cocked assertively. In the other was a Styrofoam cup of freshly squeezed orange juice, which she had picked up on her way back from the gym. She sipped impatiently as she looked across Central Park at the skyline of Fifth Avenue. It was a stupendous view, one that normally made her spirits soar. On clear winter mornings, when the bold pinnacles reared up against a fiery sunrise, she felt like mistress of the universe. But today the buildings seemed tawdry and diminished under a blanket of dark cloud. The park was a dripping expanse of stunted trees. Eight floors down Rose could see the jostle of umbrellas and a snarl of yellow cabs along Central Park West. She suddenly remembered the bright-red umbrella inscribed with *"Merde, il pleut,"* which she used to think so dashing in her fashion-magazine days, and felt the faintest twinge of nostalgia for shabby old England.

There was still no message from Chris. Where was the bastard? Last night Rose had left messages on his work number and with his answering service. She had tried his mobile phone dozens of times, crashing down her receiver when she found it switched off. That corn-fed wife of his had promised to make him call back urgently, but it had probably slipped her brain cell. Ten to one Chris was right this minute snoring off a bender, or hustling pillow talk from some ball breaker in the White House Press Corps. Rose rattled her polished nails across the windowpane. Chris was Chris. She would simply have to wait. Exasperating as he might be, he was still her best route to Jordan Hope's inner circle.

Rose herself had been up for over two hours. Her alarm was always set for 5:45, though today she hadn't needed it. She had slept badly, her thoughts whirling around Annie and the thunderbolt she had delivered yesterday afternoon. Thank God Annie had possessed the wit to phone her. Best and oldest friend though she was, Annie was not sophisticated enough to see past her own anxiety about Tom and her absurdly romantic desire to shield Jordan from disaster. British elections were like a children's tea party compared to an American presidential race. Annie would not be able to conceive of the millions of dollars—not to mention careers, ambitions, businesses, and vested interests—staked on a Hope victory; nor of the vindictive rage if, at this late stage, he ruined everything with another sex scandal.

No one must learn about Tom. The damage must be contained. That was Rose's mission. Schemes, alternatives, contingency plans chased each other through her head. And somewhere, in the midst of the crisis, she caught the sweet scent of opportunity.

Rose drained her juice and crossed the expanse of immaculate gray carpet to deposit her cup in the kitchen trash can. Naturally she had a perfectly good kitchen of her own, stocked with the expected gadgets, doubtless including an orange-juice squeezer. There was a frighteningly authentic-looking butcher's block whose virgin surface reproached her every time she slunk past it to get her wheat germ and vitamins out of the giant refrigerator. But it was pointless to stock up on food when she was always out, easier to buy what she wanted when she wanted it. That was the Manhattan way. No one cooked for themselves here, even the minuscule fraction of the population that wasn't permanently on a diet. This was not a city where people stayed in. New Yorkers did not have friends "to supper" in the cozy way they did in London—pasta slopped onto plates straight from the stove and handed casually round the kitchen table, followed by cheese remnants from the fridge and pickings from the fruit bowl. This was partly a question of space but overridingly a matter of style. Manhattan was a stage—the most fabulous, glitzy, intimidating stage in the world, with every player fighting for the spotlight. You didn't so much live here as perform with a capital P.

The evidence that Rose had performed her socks off surrounded her in gratifying profusion. Success was conspicuous in the lofty grandeur of her apartment and its fabulous view, in the Hockneys and Stellas on her walls, in the elegant lines of the Eames reclining chair and Italian floor lamps, in the walk-in closets lined with dress bags full of Chanels and Versaces. The apartment was stylish, precise, severely modernist—the exact opposite of her childhood home with its mismatched furnishings and lurking squalor. In a city that disdained nobodies, Rose was undeniably a somebody.

She took it for granted now. Shrugging off her robe, bare feet padding across the polished parquet and Persian silk rugs, Rose returned to her bedroom to dress. She had laid out her clothes the night before. It had become a habit. She put on the black silk underwear, slid her stockings up smoothly waxed legs, then sat down at the Biedermeier dressing table. Tilting the swivel mirror on her chest of drawers to catch the light, she shaded her eyes and rubbed color into her lips and cheeks. As she leaned close to darken her eyelashes, she caught sight of her furrowed forehead and winced.

Abruptly she stood up. Still in her underwear, she went over to the full-length art deco mirror, taking stock. Her glossy dark hair was cut precisely at earlobe level in a style that was both elegant and gamine. No gray hairs, thanks to her hairdresser. Her neck was holding up pretty well, her green eyes clear. Her body, petite but curvy, was in better shape than when she was twenty. There was nothing wrong with her legs—apart from being about twelve inches too short. She still looked thirtysomething. Didn't she?

Rose felt a clutch of panic. In February she would be forty-three. Middle-aged. Decaying. Heading for menopause and the dreaded o-word: *old.* The aging process for women seemed to progress in quantum leaps. They could go on looking twenty-three until they were thirty-five. Then, almost overnight, they started looking thirty-five and could go on doing so until they were fifty. After that, there was nothing to do but get the telephone number of the best plastic surgeon in town. Or retire from public view. That gave her another, what, ten years?

Rose stepped into her skirt and zipped it snug around her waist, allowing her mind to wander in a familiar groove. Her supremacy in the magazine world would not last forever. The honeymoon between America and the "Briterati" was over. It was important to have an alternative fantasy up one's sleeve. Rose had determined that she would never wait to be eased out. If the crunch came, she would throw the best fuck-you party of all time, then disappear. She had always liked the Suffolk coast, some whitewashed cottage tucked behind a honeysuckle hedge. In summer she would go to concerts at Aldeburgh and learn to sail and tie up her lupins—whatever lupins were. Winters she would spend by a crackling fire, a cat draped across the back of her armchair, catching up on the books she had only pretended to read for so long. Long walks on the beach would take the place of blusher and the StairMaster. She would become a regular at some atmospheric local pub. She would—

A screech from the fax machine cut across her thoughts. Automatically Rose started down the hall toward her study, adrenaline flowing. Could it be Chris? Had Annie found Tom? Maybe John Updike had changed his mind about the "Couples '90s style" piece. The fantasy of the Suffolk cottage evaporated. Who was she kidding? Cat hairs—yuk! Rain—double yuk! Who wanted to sit in the pub listening to conversations about the royal family and dog breeding until some overweight, opinionated publican hustled her out into the rain with an insincere "Mind how you go"? Rose shuddered, smoothing her jacket into place.

She tore the fax out of the machine, but it was only a confirmation of her booking at the Golden Valley Spa over Thanksgiving weekend. It still amazed her the way Americans, otherwise so hardnosed, turned to marshmallow every November and willingly incarcerated themselves with the very families that had driven them crazy the other fifty-one weeks of the year. Rose had crossed Thanksgiving off her social calendar after one memorable experience of nonstop schmaltz and brown food. The whole thing was a frightful waste of good working hours at one of the busiest times of year. Now, while others overdosed on turkey and pumpkin pie, she grew sleek on lemon water and mud baths and ten-hour sleeps, and dreamed up killer ideas for the magazine.

Rose tidied the fax away, picked up the neat piles of last night's work, and began slotting them into her briefcase. Her intercom buzzed twice, the signal that her car had arrived. *Right, Chris,* she thought. *Your time's up.* To think she'd nearly married that scumbag! For a few weeks they had thought they were made for each other—two maverick Brits flaming with talent and ambition, out to conquer America. They had talked and argued and made love with a ferocity that Rose had never experienced before or since. Fortunately they had recovered their sanity in time. Now Chris had cute, compliant Kimmie and a brace of towheaded children with weird American names she could never remember. And Rose had . . . her freedom. Sometimes she thought it would almost be worth being married just to silence the gossip columnists, or to have someone to wake up and say, "Look, it's snowing!" On the other hand, a husband might not let her go out to black-tie dinners five nights a week, or veg out in front of old Hollywood weepies, spooning frozen yogurt straight from the container. Come to think of it, he probably wouldn't let her sleep with other men either.

It was a pity that society had not yet evolved to a point where women could have wives too. What Rose really needed was a male version of Kimmie, someone who would make dental appointments, put clean sheets on the bed when Rose was ill, and otherwise keep a low profile. But the sexes didn't work that way. It would be a long time before Penelope came home from her adventures to find faithful Odysseus by his spinning wheel.

Rose stiffened like a birddog. She sensed an article in this. Dropping her briefcase, she switched on her computer and brought up her "Ideas" file, fingers flying over the keys as she made notes. There was that new Hollywood star whose husband took the kids to school and checked her contracts: That would give it a glamor angle and an excuse for pictures. Maybe she could persuade that classy English woman who wrote about myth and madonnas to write a little commentary, to give the piece a gloss of intellectual credibility. It would need a good headline: "The Little Man" or "Chain Male" or—oh well, it would come to her later. Hurriedly, Rose saved the file and shut down the computer.

Feeling more cheerful, she carried her briefcase into the hall and set it on a chair. She took her Vivienne Westwood raincoat out of the closet and put it on, assessing the effect in the mirror on the back of the door. Stylish but slightly wacky—just right. That was the fine line Rose trod in this rigidly conformist city. She had learned that if you played by most of the rules, you could bend the rest. It was okay to live on the West Side as long as you lived in a "named" building. You could confess to liking alcohol if it was something eccentric, like manzanilla sherry. You could get away with mixing designers, but only if it was done with panache.

Rose picked up her briefcase, scooped a pile of clothes off the hall chair, and slammed the apartment door behind her. She pressed the polished elevator button and did a few pelvic floor exercises while she waited. Although she loved the kitsch grandeur of the Dakota, with its sentry box and moat and Wild West adornments, its elevator system retained the habits of a more leisured age. When the doors opened again onto the lobby, she came out like a bullet from a pistol, firing instructions at the hovering doorman.

"Morning, Carl. Ida says the vacuum cleaner's started growling again—could you be an angel and take a look? Here are my shoes for polishing, and this stuff needs to get over to Louie's pronto." She handed him an armful of clothes without breaking stride. "Tell him I need the green dress back by five tomorrow or I'll be looking for a new cleaners."

Coat billowing behind her, she sailed through the door and across the sidewalk straight into the backseat of her waiting car. The driver shut the door after her and got in behind the wheel.

"Office," Rose said succinctly.

She took her latest gadget out of her briefcase, an electronic notepad that had been a present from Japanese advertising clients. As the car wound its way across Central Park, she tapped in a code and brought up her agenda for the day.

There was that new photographer to see at eleven, then lunch with Mitzi Meyerhof, whom Rose was thinking of appointing as a contributing editor. A former talk-show hostess now married to a phenomenally successful plastic surgeon, Mitzi was a total airhead, but she had great contacts. At three o'clock Rose had a strategy meeting with Walt. After that she had planned to sneak out of the office to see an English girl she secretly wanted to replace Barney as design director. Barney had acquired a fatal habit of thinking he was right about everything. If the entire art department walked out, tough. Walt would forgive her when she told him about the December advertising pages. At five-thirty John was coming to her apartment to blow out her hair ready for tonight's dinner at the Metropolitan—the Temple of Dendur *again*. Really, the place was becoming so popular it might as well be called Club Met.

Rose reached for the car phone and postponed her meeting with the English girl. She had enough problems for one day. Then she pulled out the folder she had been working on last night. The Lagerfeld piece was good—plenty of insider gossip and a sassy style that was just right for *The Magazine*. Steven had sneaked some fabulous backstage pictures at the designers' collections. Together they would make a great story. And yet—wasn't there something a little banal about the copy line? Rose closed her eyes, trying to summon up one particular transparency that had stuck in her memory, a terrific black-and-white shot that caught Karl's sly, sideways smile and the impish thrust of his ponytail against a background blur of half-dressed models. She imagined how it would look fully bled opposite the text. Fabulous—with the right headline. Rose considered for a moment, then crossed out "King Karl" and in bold capitals wrote "Moi?" That was more like it.

A sudden outbreak of honking horns and furious shouts made her look up. A delivery truck had jumped the light on the 50th Street intersection and was now imprisoned in a gridlock of cars. Two cabdrivers with their torsos thrust halfway out their car windows, like latterday jousters, yelled abuse at each other. "You wanna drive a car, get a license!" "What's your problem, fuckhead?"

Rose felt a spurt of pride for her adopted city, like a mother for her wayward child. New York was a cesspool, but it was *her* cesspool, and she loved every unique and fabulous inch of it—from Castle Clinton, where the poor and huddled masses had awaited entry to the promised land, right up to the spooky Cloisters.

She had arrived in the city ten years ago with a thousand pounds, some good magazine contacts, and a frizzed hairstyle she didn't now like to think about. It was August. An editor on *Ms.* magazine whom Rose had met in her *Spare Rib* days offered Rose the use of her place on the edge of Chinatown while she was on vacation. It had seemed a truly sisterly gesture, until Rose discovered that the air conditioner emitted nothing more than a rhythmic clanking and that she would be sharing the apartment with several families of cockroaches. At night, sweating onto the futon with every muscle tensed for the click of insect legs on the wooden floor, she felt like Alec Guinness in his hotbox in *Bridge on the River Kwai*.

New York had been dead. Everybody was on "the Island" or "the Cape." Rose gritted her teeth and spent the month acquainting herself with the city she was determined to conquer. She checked out all the magazines and papers, reading at newsstands until her calves ached or burrowing in the public library. She lived on salad and bagels and lost ten pounds in two weeks. Just before Labor Day, her friend came back from vacation early, lured by a rumor that Walt Kernitz wanted someone to revamp *A La Mode*. It certainly needed it. Rose said nothing, but laid her plans. Walt was famous for starting work at four in the morning. Rose got hold of his number and called him at four-thirty the next day. Ratcheting up her English accent a few social notches, she apologized for disturbing him; she knew he was an early riser, and so was she. She knew about the job and she knew she was the person to do it. She had already prepared a ten-page editorial and business plan. He would regret it if he didn't see her. There had been a long silence, then "Okay, breakfast tomorrow. Is five too early for you?" "Five is perfect." That day Rose had spent her last five hundred pounds on a new outfit, shoes, and a haircut. She had felt a teensy pang, but her old friend already had a job. Rose hadn't. Besides, she knew she'd do it better.

The rest had passed into magazine legend. Walt gave her the job. Rose fired 30 percent of the staff, imported a stable of British talent, wormed her way into high-life parties, cajoled the advertisers. Amid howls of outrage and hopeful predictions of failure, Rose had brought the magazine into profit within six months and eventually established it as the bible of America's well-heeled woman. As a reward Walt had given her the chance to start another magazine for a younger, hipper readership. With supreme confidence she had named it, simply, *The Magazine.* Now it was threatening to outsell its elder sister, and New York had bowed its head in homage to her success—though waiting, Rose knew, to sink its teeth into her ankles at the first opportunity. She wasn't really worried. Annie's phone call had given her an idea.

The car dropped her outside the Kernitz Building. Rose took the elevator to her office. Catching sight of Cindy already at her workstation, Rose checked off her mental list as she strode down the corridor.

"Did you remember to send those flowers to the Plaza?"

"Yes, Miss Cassidy."

"Has anyone called Chris rung?"

"Not yet."

"The Whatsernames have had their baby—you remember the TV star we profiled who set up a birthing pool with a dolphin in her basement? Can you buy it a present in your lunch hour? A hundred dollars max."

"Boy or girl?"

"It's bound to be one or the other," Rose threw over her shoulder as she walked into her office and shut the door.

Hanging up her coat, she worked through her messages and mail, then checked the editorial lineup for the December issue. There was an article about the gravitation of stars to Ireland, provisionally called "The Irishtocracy." Jeremy Irons and Daniel Day-Lewis had places there. So did Ken and Emma, Nicole and Tom, Mick and Jerry of course. Rose gave it a checkmark. An attack on supermodels by that new backlash feminist sounded a lark, but it would have to be toned down or the advertisers would kill her.

The centerpiece of the whole issue was a photo essay on Ginny Hope, including a revolutionary double-page spread of photographs without a single line of text. The pictures spoke for themselves: Ginny as a little girl with gappy teeth and pigtails, Ginny as high-school class president, virginal college girl, peacenik, civil-rights campaigner, bride, children's caseworker, electioneer, and finally—via an astonishing number of hairstyles—potential First Lady.

The article had already cost a ton in researchers, travel, and out-right bribery. Even Walt had warned her about putting all her eggs in one basket. Now Rose wished she hadn't been quite so adamant. All the mags would have a presidential story in the postelection issue. The question was, which president? Until yesterday Rose had been betting on Hope. And now? Rose had flamboyantly nailed her professional colors to Hope's mast. She didn't fancy going down with the ship. *The Magazine* prided itself on being first with the buzz. If Jordan lost, Ginny would be about as hot a topic as the bubble skirt.

Rose's glance roamed around her trophy office, noting the two-way view across and down Madison Avenue, the fresh flowers de-livered daily, the famous slate table that was kept scrupulously empty except when she was working at it, the handmade book-shelves stacked with contemporary novels and social registers, heavyweight political memoirs, and Hollywood biographies. Hang-ing on one wall was the framed cover of the first issue of *The Mag-azine*, which had sold out by noon, and a calculatedly modest selection of de rigueur celeb shots of herself with Jack Nicholson, Mayor Koch, Henry Kissinger, Diane Sawyer. It would hurt to lose all this. On the other hand . . .

The telephone buzzed. It was Cindy, sounding puzzled. "I've got a Robert Maxwell for you? He says he's sure you want to speak with him. I thought—I mean, isn't Robert Maxwell dead?"

Rose couldn't help grinning. This must be Chris's interpretation of "discreet." She could just picture his foxy face. "Put him on," she commanded. Unclipping an earring from her telephone ear, she prepared to charm him into submission.

"Darling," she cried, "how are you? That was a very naughty piece you wrote about La Harrington. I hope you've got your balls well insured. . . . *Is she?* How riveting." Rose's eyes narrowed to crafty green slits as she reached for her notepad and pen. "Of course not," she cooed reproachfully, scribbling fast. "Not beyond these four walls, I promise.

"Listen," she went on briskly, "I need a favor. I've been asked to set up a telephone call to Jordan Hope. It's a purely personal matter—nothing to do with the election—but it's very private and very confidential and extremely urgent. I can't call the campaign office, obviously. You know what it's like with everyone on top of each other, gossiping like mad. 'My Lord, it's that uppity Rose Cassidy from *The Magazine*,' " Rose drawled in a very bad imitation of a Southern accent. " 'Now what in tarnation does she want?' What I need is a middleman, someone really close to Jordan who can contact him right away and will fix the whole thing up without asking questions. And naturally, darling, I thought that of all the people in the entire world you would know who's the best person."

As she listened to his familiar voice, clotted with South London vowels even after a decade in America, Rose's face grew stony.

"I'm not up to anything," she protested. "Honestly, darling, I hardly know what's going on myself, I'm just trying to help someone out. You always used to complain that I didn't need you," she wheedled. "Well, now I do. I admit it."

It was no good. Chris knew her too well. He was firing questions like the bloody Gestapo. Whom was she doing this "favor" for? If this was some cretinous media stunt, she could stuff it. Was there another financial scandal brewing, or was it something more juicy? Was it—ouch!—anything to do with Hope's Oxford days?

Rose's brain whizzed through alternative strategies. She could invent some cover story, but Chris would be sharp enough to spot the flaws. She could promise to tell him the whole story the next time he was in New York—from the downy depths of her double bed, if he liked. But as she had no intention of telling him anything, that would be lying. Rose was well aware of her reputation for dressing facts up or down, depending on the angle of a story. She realized, to her surprise, that she didn't really want to lie. Not to Chris.

A silence fell between them. "All right," Rose conceded, "I do know what it's about. But I can't tell you. I can promise you that it's nothing that you would truly regard as being in the public interest, but that's it. There's no quid pro quo here. Sorry. I only asked because there's no one else I can trust and I'll probably make a mess of it on my own." She sighed. "You've got your rules, and I respect them. So—change of subject—are you coming to my election party? Everyone else is."

But mysteriously she seemed to have pressed the right button. Chris's voice came back at her brisk and businesslike. "I know the bloke you want. Smarmy bugger, but bloody fast on his feet. Hope thinks the sun shines out of his arse. Hang on, I'll give you his private line."

"Who is he?" Rose asked, writing down the number.

"Some sort of glorified PR goon, can't remember his title. Checks the speeches, holds Hope's hand, takes the tricky phone calls—that sort of thing."

"No, what's his *name*, dumbo?" Rose held her pen poised. She had a horrid feeling she knew the answer.

"Christ, didn't I say? That bloody bourbon. Zaps the brain cells. His name's Rick Goodman. You must have seen him on TV."

"Yes, I have," Rose said slowly. She wrote the name down and drew a bold, black box around it, like a funeral card. "I suppose it has to be him . . . I mean, that's terrific, Chris. I really appreciate it. Thank you."

"Always a pleasure, Madame Mystery. Don't worry, I'll tickle your secrets out of you soon enough."

"I can't wait. Love to Kimmie. And, um, Drew and Tyler, of course."

Rose put down the phone. Her smile faded. Rick Goodman. That made things awkward. Or did it? There was a nasty little skeleton in his cupboard that she could rattle if he didn't cooperate.

Rose looked at her watch. Missouri was an hour behind. It would be just nine o'clock. Perfect. She sat quite still for a minute, collecting her thoughts. She had been in touch with Rick once or twice since Hope had won the Democratic nomination and enlisted the help of his old Oxford friend as PR supremo for the campaign. There had been times when Jordan had needed all the media support he could get—and Rose had given it willingly. Rose hesitated, thinking of all the possible consequences of what she was about to do, then straightened her shoulders and tapped in the number.

Rick himself answered at the first ring.

"Rose, how delightful to hear from you," he said with that dangerous, mocking charm. "What can I do for you?"

Trying to sound matter-of-fact, Rose stated her request. A friend of hers needed to get in touch with Jordan personally, as a matter of urgency. Could Rick help?

"What friend?"

"An old friend from England. Nothing political."

"Has he got a name?"

"She." Rose hesitated. "Her name's Annie. Jordan will know who it is."

There was a calculating pause. Then Rick said, "I'm not absolutely sure I like the sound of this."

"I think Jordan will," Rose countered steadily. "I think he will consider it extremely important."

"Really." Rose could almost hear his brain clicking. "Well, it's no big secret," he said at last in a casual tone. "Jordan will be in Dallas tonight. Here's the number. He's a busy man, though. The best time to catch him is between midnight and six."

"Thanks," Rose said coolly. "I'd be happy to return the favor with something on Jordan in *The Magazine* when he wins—as I'm sure he will."

"That's thoughtful of you, Rose, but I think we'd probably want an American on board for that kind of thing."

Rose flushed at the snub. It was true: Brit-bashing was the latest bloodsport. Aloud all she said was "Call me when you need me," and put down the phone.

She let out her breath in relief. She had the number Annie needed. But she still felt uneasy. Rick would move heaven, earth, and probably hell to find out what was going on, and turn it to his advantage—not that she altogether blamed him. She too felt the temptation of holding such a bombshell of a secret in her hands. Imagine, what a scoop! Jordan Hope's illegitimate son! No one knew the inside story as she did—and what a story! Sex and drugs and rock 'n' roll, with Oxford and Vietnam thrown in. Move over, Woodward and Bernstein.

Rose was seized by an irresistible urge. Before she knew it she was sitting at the computer, her fingers itching. She pulled up the list of directories and scooted the cursor up and down until she found "Liabilities." Perfect. No one ever looked in there. She created a new file and gave it the dullest name she could think of, "Storage." If she blocked the file off with a password, no one would ever be able to read it anyway. So what was the password? Operation President—too obvious. No, she had it: "Special Relationship." The double entendre amused her.

Placing her Tiffany bangles on the desk, Rose began to type.

22

I Gotta Get a Message to You

*A*nnie pushed open the heavy front door, shook the raindrops from her umbrella, and climbed the stairs wearily. It was so early that the central heating hadn't come on yet, and the office was cold. But it was empty: That was the main thing. At this hour, she could be sure that no one could observe what she was about to do.

She hoisted her bulging briefcase onto her desk and slumped for a moment into her chair, keeping her coat on against the chill. It was just like the old days, during the miners' strike, when there had been no heat two days a week. But then Harry Robertson had been her boss and she an eager, loyal employee. Now she felt as guilty as a sneak thief.

She took the telltale blue files from her briefcase and fished out the computer disk that contained hours of work done late at night in her tiny study at home. Encoded here were letters to her authors, explaining her new plans; faxes to the American publishers involved in the Sebastian Winter auction; and, most difficult of all to write, her letter of resignation to Jack. She had burned her boats now. Sebastian had leaped at the idea of becoming the first client of the Annie Hamilton Literary Agency. His faith in her was touching, but terrifying too. What if she wasn't as smart as she thought? What if she had miscalculated her ability to sell his novels? If she bungled the auction, she could kiss her career good-bye. No other agency would employ her. The authors who might otherwise follow her to the new agency would politely, regretfully, melt away. Annie jumped up from her desk and pulled off her coat, trying to banish her fears.

She had a fierce need to make this work. Tom's disappearance had made her see what was truly important. It was time to grab hold of her life and dictate its direction.

Switching on her computer, she slotted in the disk and set up the printer. The machines began to hum and click, processing her future. With luck the letters would be signed and in their envelopes, the faxes ready to send, before anyone arrived. But first she had something else to do. With an accelerating heartbeat Annie reached for her daily planner. Her palms filmed with sweat, her fingers fumbled over the pages. For a moment she couldn't find what she was looking for. Panic rose in her throat. No, it was all right. Two pages had stuck together. She pinched them apart. There it was, the telephone number Rose had given her. Annie had copied it down in tiny writing, as if to minimize its significance. But it was everything— her past, perhaps her future. Annie smoothed out the page. Thank God for Rose. At least there was one person she could trust.

Annie frowned at the figures, trying to focus her thoughts. Dallas, Texas. It would be about two in the morning there. Jordan would be asleep, perhaps dreaming of the glorious future that now seemed to be within his grasp. There had been times when she had longed for an excuse to contact him. Here it was, and she could hardly force her hand to the telephone.

"Yeah?" A male voice, not sleepy at all. Alert, expectant, eager for news.

"Jordan?"

"Who is this?"

There it was, that husky twang she remembered. Annie's toes curled.

"It's Annie Paxford."

Silence.

"We met at Oxford years ago. Remember?"

"Of course I remember you, Annie. It's been a hell of a long time. What can I do for you?"

His tone was distinctly cool. He must think she was calling to claim an old friendship with him, now that he had become famous.

"Nothing," she said quickly. "At least, there's something you need to know." Annie cleared her throat. "I have a son. His name is Tom."

"Uh . . . congratulations," Jordan replied, polite but mystified. "When was he born?"

Annie closed her eyes. He thought she'd just had the baby!

"No, you don't understand. He's grown up. Sort of," she added, recalling Tom's recent behavior. *Get to the point.* Her tongue felt swollen and clumsy. "The thing is," she took a breath, "he thinks you're his father."

There was an audible gasp. "He *what?*"

"It's not my fault," Annie protested. "I never told him—that is, I've never mentioned that we . . . knew each other." She rushed on. "Jordan, this is too difficult on the phone. I'd like to explain in person. I happen to be coming to the States this weekend, on business—Chicago and New York, but I could meet you anywhere that fits in with your schedule. Any town you say. Day or night. A bar, hotel, park—it doesn't matter. But I need to see you."

She could feel his resistance in the long silence. "Couldn't this wait until after the election?"

Annie flushed with impatience. "There won't *be* an election—not with the result you want, anyway. Tom's in shock. He's missing. Don't you understand? *He's coming to find you.*"

"Coming *here*—to the States?" Jordan sounded appalled.

"It's possible," Annie backpedaled. "To be honest, I don't know where he is or who he's talking to, but it wouldn't take much to get a rumor into the papers."

"But it isn't true!" He shouted indignantly.

Annie hesitated only for a second. "Of course it isn't," she agreed. "I just wanted to warn you—in case." Her voice softened. "I'm thinking of *you*, Jordan. The election. Your wife."

There was a long pause. Then: "It *is* you," he said unexpectedly. "Annie Paxford. You sound just the same . . . Are you?"

Annie thought of the laugh lines around her eyes, the traces of childbirth on her body, of all that she had been through since they last met. "Hardly," she said tartly. "Are you?"

"I guess not. Listen, Annie, this all sounds crazy to me. I don't understand how you can have gotten me into this mess. Still . . ." She heard the crackle of paper. "Chicago's on my schedule for, let's see, Saturday night. Tell me where you're staying."

Annie gave him the name of her hotel.

"I can't promise anything," he warned.

"I understand."

"Even if I could get away, it would be late—maybe the middle of the night."

"It doesn't matter."

"You're sure this isn't some kind of hoax?"

"Oh, Jordan . . . I haven't changed that much."

"You still say things like 'wonky' and 'actually'?"

"Probably." She could hear the smile in his voice. "You'll find out on Saturday. Good-bye."

Annie carefully put the receiver in place. She felt as if she had just run a race. At least he hadn't said "Annie who?" The printer was beeping at her. It had run out of paper. Automatically Annie rose and went to the stationery closet, feeling a wonderful calmness take control. Rose's master plan was falling into place. Under the cover of an emergency trip to America to visit her dying mother, Annie was going to auction Sebastian Winter from under Jack's nose. She was going to sneak a meeting with her old lover. She was going to lie to Edward. Annie closed her heart to the clamorings of conscience. She deserved her own business. She needed—wanted— to see Jordan. Taking a fresh supply of paper, she squared the sheets with a determined rap on the desk. She had been good long enough. Now she was going to be bad.

23

It's My Life

"*I* don't believe it!"

Tom looked up accusingly from the paper in his hand. He felt winded by disappointment.

Across the small conference table the senior officer met his eyes sympathetically. "I tried to warn you, son. We're only an information service. We're not God."

"But it's completely blank," Tom protested, stabbing a finger at the document. "I've spent three days persuading you to let me see this, and now—" He broke off, not trusting his voice to stay steady. His throat ached with the effort of keeping back tears of frustration.

"Take your time," the older man said gently.

Trying to collect himself, Tom turned away and let his gaze travel round this small room, buried deep in the Office of Population Censuses and Surveys. But there was no comfort to be found in its bare walls and government-issue furnishings. He swallowed painfully and looked back at the treacherous document.

It was his birth certificate, his *real* birth certificate. The one they wouldn't let him see in London. The one he had been so sure would silence his doubts. For this he had driven hundreds of miles north, practically as far as Scotland. For this he had wasted days hanging around the Southport seafront, waiting for the Population Office people to find his file and check his bona fides. For this he had spent wakeful nights on Mrs. Pritchard's slithery sheets. Tom could feel a tide of self-pity welling inside him. Shut up and concentrate, he told himself.

The document in front of him was dated 27 March 1971, ten days after his birth. It had been issued in the name of Thomas Paxford. Okay, so his parents weren't married at the time. He could cope with that. But surely, if Dad was truly his father, his details ought to be here. Three lines were allocated for information about the father. All three spaces were empty. No Edward Hamilton, no Jordan Hope—nothing.

Tom reached into his jacket pocket and pulled out his copy of the later certificate, issued after his parents' marriage in the name of Hamilton. This one had been easy to get. He had picked it up on his very first day in Southport simply by filling in a form and writing a check. Now he unfolded the paper and read again the details under "Father." *Name: Edward Hamilton. Place of birth: Lewes, Sussex. Occupation: lawyer.* There might be other differences between the two documents. He laid them down side by side and began to cross-check.

"We do offer a counseling service," suggested the senior officer, sliding a leaflet across the table. "People often find it helpful."

"What?" Tom said absently. A name at the bottom of the original certificate caught his eye. That was odd. "Is this my copy?" he asked. "Can I take it away?"

"Of course. Found something helpful after all, have you?"

"Well . . . interesting, perhaps." Tom folded the papers and stuffed them back into his pocket. "Thank you," he said, getting to his feet. "I'm sorry if I've been a nuisance."

The man shook his hand. "I've seen worse. Good luck, son. You'll be able to find your own way now."

Tom followed the zigzag corridor out through Reception and hurried across the carpark. Cold air, clammy from the sea, seeped through his thin American football jacket. He ducked into the Morris and fitted the key into the ignition. Now what?

He had come up here on impulse, furious with his mother, burning to find evidence of her deception. He had been so sure of finding a definitive answer in this bizarre repository of documentation that looked like a World War I nursing home. Now he was even worse off than before. *Name of father*—blank! A thought suddenly occurred to him. Did Jordan Hope have any children? He couldn't remember. What would it be like to meet this man and say, "Hello, I'm your son"? It was impossible to imagine. Tom dismissed the thought and started the car. At least he didn't need to spend another night in that grungy bed and breakfast.

He drove back into Southport and parked outside Mrs. Pritchard's house. "You might have given me a bit more notice," she sniffed, wrapping her cardigan tight. Upstairs, Tom collected his few belongings and threw them into his backpack: notebook, sweater, passport for identification purposes, toothbrush, and other stuff he had bought locally. He looked at his watch. Eleven-thirty on—what was it today, Wednesday? He ought to be in midtutorial now, delivering his essay on Metternich. Oxford seemed like another universe. He wasn't ready to go back.

Tom zipped up his bag, slung it over one shoulder, and slammed the door shut on his dismal room with a suddenly lifting heart. He knew what he would do. He would go to Rebecca after all—beautiful, calm Rebecca. He needn't tell her anything; he would just drop in for some tender loving care. Tom studied the road map. Sussex University was just outside Brighton, at least three hundred miles away. He found his way onto the motorway and headed south, holding Rebecca in his mind like the Holy Grail, remembering the warm September evening when they had met.

There was a pub in Hampstead that had become a hangout for kids from the local schools. Every Friday night in the summer months the broad pavement outside would be thronged with groups of hair-tossing girls and lounging boys. Tom had outgrown the scene, but shortly after his return from Europe his sister Cassie had wheedled him into taking her and two girlfriends. As soon as he had bought them drinks—this was his key function, since they were underage—they had dumped him without ceremony, and he had found himself propping up the pub wall, observing the ritual of teenage flirtation with a superior eye. He had noticed Rebecca almost at once, a tall girl with dark, wavy hair, wearing white jeans and a man's chalk-striped waistcoat with nothing underneath. Slim almost to the point of boniness, she had a quality of stillness that was both intriguing and intimidating. It had taken him half an hour to maneuver his way casually to her side and deliver his suave pickup line: "Hello, aren't you at Camden School?" She had looked back at him with amused gray eyes and replied dryly, "South Hampstead, actually, and I left a year ago. But nice try."

Tom had bought her a drink, then persuaded her to have a hamburger with him. While they sat outside, sharing a plate of French fries, Tom had learned that she was in her second year at Sussex, studying biology. She wanted to be a geneticist. Her air of self-possession was explained by the fact that her parents were divorced, and she and her younger brother lived with their father, a political journalist of great brilliance and zero domestic skills. Rebecca had come home from school more than once to find the fridge empty or the gas cut off for nonpayment of bills. In her year out between A-level exams and university, she had worked at a health center in northern Kenya. She played the viola and adored Guns 'n Roses.

Tom went home that night, thinking he might be in love. The next day he cruised around Rebecca's neighborhood in the open-topped Morris until he spotted her and casually offered her a lift. She wasn't deceived, but she liked the attention. In fact, it seemed that she liked him. Over the next few weeks they went to open-air concerts on the heath, wandered around Camden Market, listened to bands at the Town and Country Club. Just before Rebecca went off to Sussex, they had borrowed her mother's remote Welsh cottage for a long weekend, walking miles over the heather-topped hills by day and making love in front of the fire by night. Tom had planned to invite her up to Oxford once he felt secure enough to show her around. He had fantasized about holding a party in some grand, paneled room where he would introduce her to the sophisticated Oxford life. Now all he wanted to do was see her and breathe in her calm air of sanity.

The drive seemed interminable. His car had not been built for modern roads. At anything over fifty-five miles an hour it swayed alarmingly, buffeted by overtaking trucks. Tom had to stop regularly to add coolant and oil and give it a breather. He grew sick of the sight and smell of roadside restaurants. At the circle around London he got caught in commuter traffic, which advanced in ten-yard bursts. It was nearly nine by the time he turned onto the Sussex campus. Stained concrete buildings gleamed depressingly in the harsh flare of the blobby lamps. The ornamental ponds were empty, apart from a sludge of dead leaves. It was hard to believe that this had been the brave-new-world university of the 1960s and, according to Rebecca's dad, a hotbed of revolution.

Tom drove on until he found a couple of students who gave him directions to Rebecca's residence hall. At long last he stopped the car. His eyes felt gritty, his skin stiff. Too tired to get out, he bowed his head onto the steering wheel and whispered, "Rebecca." It was like a prayer.

When he found her room, the door was locked. Tom rattled the door savagely. How could she be out? What could she be doing? He slid his back down the wall and slumped outside her door, furious. He would simply wait—all night if need be—until she returned from whatever irresistible student entertainment might be detaining her. He must have fallen asleep, for the next thing he knew Rebecca was standing over him, eyes shining with delight.

"Tom! Why didn't you tell me you were coming?"

Tom peered blearily up at her. "Where have you been?"

"In the library," she said with a provocative lift of her eyebrows, "having an unbelievably wild time with the reproductive system of invertebrates." She unlocked her door and pushed it open, then reached down a hand to pull Tom up. She wrapped her arms around him. "It's wonderful to see you. I can't believe it."

Tom staggered out of her embrace and collapsed with a monumental sigh into the only comfortable chair in the room. He knew he was behaving boorishly, but something about Rebecca's very cheerfulness irritated him. She obviously had no idea what he had been going through. He pressed a hand to his forehead. "Have you got any coffee?"

Rebecca's smile faltered. "Of course." She switched on the kettle and starting laying out mugs and spoons in her precise way. Tom watched the curve of her back and the swell of her hips under tight jeans as she bent down to reach into a cabinet.

"Oh, come here," he said impatiently. "Stop fiddling about and give me a kiss."

She turned at once and folded herself into his lap. Her lips were warm and soft. Tom gripped her hard, thrusting his tongue deep into her mouth. He could feel her surprise at his roughness, but tightened his hold, desperate to crush all his worries under an avalanche of pure sensation.

He broke off abruptly. "Let's go to bed," he said.

Rebecca pulled away with an incredulous look. "What?"

"Let's go to bed," he repeated. "You haven't got tired of me already, have you?"

Rebecca stood up, her face flushing. "Of course I haven't. But, Tom—you arrive here without any warning, like a bear with a sore head, and after one second expect us to make love. What's going on?"

"I don't want to talk about it." He grabbed at her. "Let's just go to bed."

Rebecca stepped out of reach. "No," she insisted. "Not while I get the feeling you just want to . . . fuck something. Someone. Anyone. Besides, I haven't—I'm not fixed up."

Tom's whole body cramped with exasperation. "That's bloody brilliant, that is. Why not?"

"Because," Rebecca enunciated carefully, "I didn't know you were coming and I hadn't planned on sleeping with anyone else."

Tom couldn't believe how unsympathetic she was being. "Come on, Becca, it won't matter just this once. I'll be careful."

"Tom," Rebecca protested, half laughing, "you sound like a contraception ad. Of course it might matter 'just this once.' "

Tom glowered at her, then jumped furiously to his feet. "Right. I might as well be off then."

"Don't be silly." Rebecca reached out to stroke his arm. "I'd like you to stay. Tell me what's wrong. I can't help if I don't know."

Tom stood his ground, unyielding. Rebecca eyed him thoughtfully.

"This isn't anything to do with your mother, is it? She phoned me this week—to see how I was getting on, she said. She asked if I'd seen you. I thought it was a bit odd."

Tom felt as if he had been plunged into a well of icy water. His mother and Rebecca—*his* girlfriend—colluding behind his back, discussing him, tut-tutting as if he were a child. He felt utterly betrayed.

Throwing off Rebecca's arm, he yanked open the door, then turned to look into her shocked eyes, wanting to hurt her.

"Well, you have seen me now," he said coldly. "You'll be able to make a full report."

Tom bounced the car over the campus traffic bumps and revved onto the main road toward Brighton. He needed a drink. Several drinks. Brighton was supposed to be a wild town. Flooded with a pure, cold energy, he flung the car around bends, king of the road. As he neared an intersection he felt tempted to drive straight across and take his chances. At the last minute he braked. It was just as well. A huge truck thundered by. Its headlights lit up a sign pointing back in the direction Tom had come: GATWICK AIRPORT, 23 MILES.

Tom drove around Brighton until he found somewhere he liked

the look of, a glowing, timbered pub tucked among the back lanes. It turned out to be disappointingly quiet. The few men clumped around their pints looked up when he came in as if he were a novelty. Tom took his drink and a fistful of peanut bags to a corner seat. He was starving. At the next table an elderly man dressed like a racing tout in tweed jacket and flamboyant cravat said good evening. Tom nodded back politely, his thoughts elsewhere.

A plan was forming in his mind. It had first occurred to him days ago, but only as a fantasy. Now it was taking concrete shape. The name he had seen this morning on his birth certificate had opened up an entirely new possibility. He drank his pint quickly and bought another one, the alcohol making him bold. Should he let anyone know what he was doing? No. No one ever told *him* anything. Let them worry. He sat there, wholly absorbed, until the landlord's noisy stacking of chairs and dimming of lights indicated that it was closing time. Tom went out into the street and fumbled at the car door, trying to get the key in the lock.

At his elbow a soft voice said, "You're a nice-looking boy. Want to come back to my flat for a bit of fun?"

It was the man from the pub, smiling in an ingratiating way that made Tom's flesh creep. Tom backed against the car. His horrified reaction must have been plain, for the man's face tightened with spitefulness.

"Just came in for a little thrill, did you, dear? See how the other half lives?" His eyes lingered on Tom, eloquent with longing and disappointment. Tom was uneasily reminded of Rebecca.

"Suit yourself." The man shrugged. He flounced down the hill, cravat fluttering.

Tom leaped into his car and flipped up the catch to lock it. Right, that was it. He was getting out of here. Everything he had tried to do had gone wrong. Rebecca had let him down. His mother had lied to him. He would be thrown out of Oxford for missing tutorials. His father—Tom could hardly bear it—might not even be his father. There was no one left. Except, maybe, a complete stranger who was running for president of the United States.

Tom negotiated his way out of the town, following the signs to Gatwick Airport. For weeks Virgin Atlantic had been advertising standby tickets to America for only ninety-nine pounds. What had he got to lose?

24

Spirit in the Sky

Jordan bounded up the airplane steps. At the top he turned to face the crowd from Billings, Montana, who had followed him out to the airport. Straining hands, grinning mouths, a ripple of red, white, and blue: It was a routine sight that stirred his soul every time. A few steps below him, the new Secret Service man froze into position, scanning the crowd through dark glasses, an attaché case clutched to his chest. Jordan raised a hand to his supporters, extending five fingers in a now-familiar mime. "Five more days!" they chanted back joyously. A fusillade of camera shutters erupted from the tarmac below. Jordan held his pose for a count of ten, then ducked into the plane.

Immediately he pulled off his jacket and tie and started unbuttoning his shirt. It was soaked with sweat. Someone handed him a new one. "Way to go, boy," bawled Shelby, saluting him with a can of beer. Others called out their congratulations as Jordan passed down the aisle, though they were careful not to touch him. Wherever he went, strangers fought to shake Jordan's hand, clap him on the back, pat his arms, his shoulders, even his head. These days his body looked as if he had gone five rounds with a champion boxer.

Bare-chested, Jordan made his way toward the one person whose opinion really counted. He stood over her as he thrust his arms into his clean shirt. The starched sleeves made a noise like ripping paper.

"Go okay?" he asked huskily.

"You know it did." His wife smiled up reassuringly. "You were incredible—*are* incredible. Stop worrying."

"But the polls—"

"The people will decide, not the polls," Ginny interrupted firmly. "Sit down and save your voice." She laid her head back against the seat and closed her eyes.

Jordan watched her for a moment, wanting more, then obeyed. On his wide armrest was a scatter of personal items: bottles, papers, a paperback thriller, a couple of cigars. Jordan unscrewed the lid from a brown bottle and took a gulp, then washed the sticky medicine down with some Ozark Mountain Spring Water. He could feel the pressure in his ears as he swallowed. Soon he would be back in the sky, cocooned in that strange no-man's-land above the clouds where he now seemed to spend half his life. Rapid City was next, then Cheyenne, then on to tonight's rally in Denver. Tomorrow he would crisscross the corn states on his way to another huge rally in Chicago. His mind shied away from the other, more intimate meeting that awaited him there—if he chose to go.

One of the women brought him a folder of the latest clippings. Jordan put on his reading glasses, skimming the passages marked with yellow highlighter. But his mind wouldn't focus. The engines roared, preparing for takeoff. Jordan raised the window shutter and peered out. The media pack that followed them everywhere, cameras and pencils poised to record the tiniest lapse, were still straggling aboard their separate plane. A litter of discarded HOPE banners gusted across the runway. Jordan prayed that it wasn't an omen.

He didn't feel himself: That was the truth. The last couple of nights he had woken, dry-mouthed and disoriented, from wild, piercing dreams. He felt jittery and distracted. He had started to suffer lapses of concentration. Take yesterday. They had touched down in Idaho for an informal lunchtime meeting with a farmers' group. Hot dog in hand, Jordan had worked the crowd, shaking hands, signing autographs, kissing babies, patting dogs, listening to problems, promising to fix them. One of his aides discreetly handed him a napkin to wipe a blob of ketchup from his chin. Jordan signed it.

They all laughed about it afterward, but it was one more thing that made Jordan feel out of control. This morning he had blanked out in the middle of a simple answer about beef imports. It was only for a few seconds, but it shook him, particularly now he understood the reason. *He had been looking for his son.*

Ever since Annie's shattering phone call, Jordan had been obsessed by the thought of his unknown son. He found himself scanning the crowd for a face he might recognize—a face like his own. Every time he stepped onto a stage the subconscious thought was there, that he was performing not just for this particular audience in this particular city, but for his son—a young man who might be proud of his father.

It was a perverse fantasy. Jordan didn't need an advisor to tell him that the emergence of an illegitimate child would kill his chances of the presidency. "Hope is a four-letter word." That was one of his opponents' catchier slogans in what the media had labeled the dirtiest election campaign in America's history. His own guys didn't exactly wear kid gloves, but at least they tried to stick to the issues. The Republicans, on the other hand, had scoured the waterfront for every scuzzy rumor. They had already done their best to portray Oxford as a foul pit of un-American activities, crawling with commies and acidheads. Throw in sex, a foreign mystery woman, and a long-lost love child, and they would think they had died and gone to heaven.

It must not happen. Unconsciously Jordan balled one hand into a fist. He would not—could not—allow the American people to suffer another four years of that corrupt, self-satisfied administration. He wanted to change things, to make them better. It was his God-given mission.

Jordan had learned a lot of things, profound and trivial, since deciding to run. He had learned that the Secret Service agents' briefcases weren't briefcases but bulletproof shields; that to survive the campaign trail you needed an iron stomach and a bladder like a steel trap; that after exhaustion came an energy so exhilarating it was addictive. He had learned not to look at his opponents during television debates but to woo the camera. He had learned that a small meeting in a local diner could have more impact than the glitziest, ritziest rally, and that audiences liked sound bites better than policy. He had learned that he was his own best asset, and the more he gave of himself, the more people liked him. Conversely, he had learned that his biggest liability was his wife.

Jordan looked over at Ginny, asleep, hair falling across her calm, wide brow. He kind of liked her blond. It made her look sexier, though he would never dare tell her so. He had never seen her so angry as when Rick suggested she needed a new image. "Jackie Kennedy was right when she said 'First Lady' sounded like a saddle horse," Ginny had shouted. She was damned if she was going to get all dolled up like an exhibit in the Easter parade. But in the end she had—and for one reason. Because she loved Jordan and believed in him.

He sure wouldn't be here without her. There wasn't a single issue they hadn't debated or a plan of campaign they hadn't discussed. She was an ever-present reminder of the ideals they had cherished back in the days when *liberal* and *radical* weren't dirty words. She told him when he hit a false note and pulled him up when he started believing his own publicity. "Man smart, woman smarter," as the old blues song went. This was the quality that had attracted him to her all those years ago. It had never been sex. For that he had gone elsewhere.

He had met her in his first year at grad school: Ms. Virginia "no cracks please" Lake, valedictorian and summa cum laude from Smith. Mousy in a cute kind of way, she was outspoken, indecently bright, a mover and shaker with a smile that could light up Boston Harbor. Jordan had liked her at once, but that was it. Oxford had thrown him off balance. Harvard marked a new beginning. Jordan's game plan was to study hard and extend his political connections on the East Coast. Romance was not on his agenda.

But Ginny kept popping up—on student committees, in law school debates, in the library. During the summer of 1972 Jordan found himself working with her on the McGovern campaign. Late one night after too many beers, he had revealed the full extent of his political ambitions. Ginny hadn't laughed. The following winter she surprised Jordan by inviting him for Christmas in Minnesota with her folks. Jordan had told everyone that he was too broke to make the trip home that year, though that wasn't the whole story.

The fact was, home had never been the same since his mother had remarried. Hutch Carson had worn her down at last. Jordan never knew whether he would find his stepfather drunkenly abusive, drunkenly charming, or just plain absent, off on one of the "business trips" from which he invariably returned penniless and remorseful. Jordan had tried not to blame his mother. She must have been lonely. Hutch took her out dancing and to restaurants and the race-track. Maybe she thought she could save him. If she regretted her decision, she never admitted it to Jordan. But there were no more late-night talks, no more bursting into each other's bedrooms to brandish the latest headline. That special communion between mother and son was broken.

Ginny's parents lived on the outskirts of Minneapolis-St. Paul in a large neocolonial home picturesquely dusted with snow. Her family was as large and supportive as Jordan's seemed small and beleaguered. Sixteen people sat down to Christmas dinner, ranging from Ginny's grandparents to a rabble of small nephews and nieces. The Lakes were welcoming, argumentative, noisy, and obviously devoted to one another. In their company Ginny relaxed into girlishness. Jordan achieved hero status after fixing a broken toy train for the children. He dried dishes while arguing with Ginny's mother over Nixon's intentions in Vietnam. Ginny's kid brother taught him to play chess. Quite suddenly a new vista opened to Jordan of a life of hard work and political commitment, shared with a like-minded partner and anchored in a secure, loving home. The following summer he and Ginny were married.

At first, everything worked out better than he had dared to hope. After graduation, he and Ginny kept leapfrogging each other with better and better jobs. When Jordan said he wanted to try for governor of Missouri, Ginny supported him, even though it meant passing up a job offer in Washington. Everyone said Jordan was too young, too brash, too inexperienced for governor. He won anyway. That autumn they moved into the governor's mansion in Jefferson City. It was an occasion that still glowed in his memory. He would never be so purely happy again.

It was a gorgeous autumn day. Maples and dogwood flamed in the front yard. Ginny supervised the move with her customary efficiency. He could picture her now, standing on the colonnaded porch in her lumber jacket, brown hair pulled into a ponytail, glasses slipping down her nose as she consulted a clipboard. She kept yelling at Jordan to stop distracting the movers. "The campaign's over. You won. Remember?" In the evening friends dropped by for beer and chili dogs and a tour of the house. Spilling over with excitement, Jordan and Ginny shared their vision of a new kind of political life. As well as introducing reform programs, they planned to revolutionize the usual governor's lifestyle of stiff, hierarchical functions with barbecues and Little League games and swings on the lawn. Jordan unearthed the stereo and played all eight albums of Motown Chartbusters, turning the evening into an impromptu party. Everyone felt the same. The dream was happening. A new generation was on its way to creating a new society.

After their friends had gone home, Jordan and Ginny stayed up. This day had a special, private meaning for them. Alone, they walked hand in hand through their new home, allocating rooms: the den here, a study for Ginny there, and at the top bedrooms for the family they now planned to have. At least two children, thought Ginny. Four, Jordan insisted, thinking of his solitary childhood, dreaming of all the things he would do and be as a father. He had steered her toward the bedroom, eager to begin right away. He could still remember the way their laughter had echoed round the huge, half-furnished house as they invented ever more outlandish names for their children.

But of course there had been no children.

Ginny suddenly opened her eyes, as if sensitive to Jordan's thoughts even in her sleep, and caught his wistful look. She reached for him across the aisle. "Something the matter?"

He caught her hand and stroked his thumb across her fingers, feeling the hard metal of her wedding ring. "You look tired," was all he said.

Ginny gaped at him. "No kidding. I've heard the earth is round too."

Jordan laughed. "Dumb comment," he agreed. "I was just thinking of this tour of yours. Will you be all right by yourself? It's a hell of a schedule."

It had been decided that Ginny would split off at Denver for another minicampaign of her own, something she had done more and more as they neared election day.

Ginny pulled her hand free. "Of course I'll be all right."

"It isn't the way I wanted things to be," Jordan persisted. "We're a team, you and I. But the guys thought it was better for you to, you know—"

"—stay in the background looking pretty? Keep a low profile on my own little circuit of schools and mothers' groups and welfare clinics? We've been over this, Jordan."

"It will be different in the White House, I promise—if I make it."

"Yeah." Ginny smiled wearily.

The plane was bustling. There were people perched on the edge of seats and draped over the backs—talking, arguing, laughing. Jordan hated not knowing what was going on. He got up and pushed past the coatrack that offered him and Ginny some measure of privacy at the back of the plane. On the other side of it the Secret Service boys were playing poker. Some nights, when Jordan was too wound up to sleep, he'd invite them to his hotel suite for a few rounds of hearts—better for his image than poker. Individually they were good guys, but as a breed they made him nervous. Their muscle-bound physiques and ticktock eyes reminded him of Arnold Schwarzenegger—and everyone knew where *he* stood politically.

Every day the plane got more cluttered. Miniature Stars and Stripes hung above the seats along each side. Between them, taped to the luggage lockers, were signed celebrity photographs, favorite cartoons, good luck cards from Secret Service agents who'd completed their duty tours, campaign slogans, random memorabilia. Every spare inch of floor space was covered with cardboard boxes crammed with campaign buttons, banners, posters, pennants, photographs. Sometimes Jordan got off the plane and wondered, Who is this guy Hope? He would look at his own name repeated a hundred, a thousand times, and it wasn't a word he even recognized.

Jordan felt a hand on his elbow. It was one of his speechwriters, wanting him to approve a couple of new paragraphs he'd added to the Denver speech, rebutting the latest attack on Jordan's defense policy. Jordan skimmed the material. Suddenly his eyebrows snapped together. He hit the paper with the back of his hand.

"What's this war-record crap?" he growled. "Did you clear that with Rick?"

"Actually, no. It just sort of came to me."

"Well, take it the fuck out!" Jordan exploded. "Don't you read the goddamn signs around here?" He put his hand on the speechwriter's head and forced it around to face the slogan that read: A CLEAN FIGHT! "That's what it says, and that's what it means." Jordan tossed the speech into the man's lap. "The rest is okay." He patted his shoulder. "Thanks."

The first galley doubled as a kind of technical control center. Dozens of mobile phones, each with a name tag, hung from a makeshift row of hooks. There was a printer, a fax machine that doubled as a photocopier, some spare laptops. Two guys were fiddling with tape machines. Jordan got a sudden blast of an old Fleetwood Mac song that he used to like.

"This for tonight?"

"No, sir. Denver's done. This is for Chicago."

Chicago. It was racing toward him full tilt, and he still didn't know what to do. His mouth felt dry with anxiety. Collecting his notes on Rapid City, he headed for the next galley to get himself a ginger ale. He found Bonnie there, among the piles of cardboard lunch boxes and crates of soft drinks, munching a cupcake. She eyed him critically.

"Uh-oh. Emergency repair time. What exactly is it you do to your hair?"

"I don't know." Jordan grinned, automatically ruffling it up from the back.

"We're landing in fifteen minutes." Calmly she brushed the crumbs from her fingers. "How about we make it look like you traveled *inside* the plane?"

Bonnie was one of the assistants in charge of Jordan's personal appearance, and his favorite. Short and plump, with a smile like Bugs Bunny, she had magic hands and a fund of lurid stories about her extended Italian-American family. She settled Jordan down on a stool and wedged a mirror into position—a makeshift arrangement they had perfected. She started massaging Jordan's neck and shoulders. He shuffled the pages of his notes but found his thoughts drifting back to Ginny.

It had taken them three years of trying before Jordan had agreed to visit a fertility specialist. He dreaded the possibility that the fault might lie with him. In fact it was Ginny who could not conceive normally. They had tried temperature charts, fertility drugs, surgery, even a faith healer. Nothing had worked. Eventually Jordan was prepared to settle for adoption. Ginny refused. She said it must be God's will.

Jordan had reacted badly. Cheated out of the dream of fatherhood that he had nursed since childhood, he blamed Ginny for the cruelest disappointment of his life. The realization that they were not to be part of a family, just two striving individuals yoked together, made him a little crazy. The future seemed empty. Recklessly Jordan set out to fill the void. Without consulting Ginny, he started gambling their money on speculative business schemes. He became obsessed by sex and started affairs with a string of women, the dumber the better. He didn't even feel guilty. Ginny complained, threatened, cried. Jordan heard, but he wouldn't listen.

One day, quietly, over the lamb chops, Ginny told him she

wanted a divorce. She had packed her bags for a visit with her parents. Jordan had two weeks to clean up his act; otherwise she was leaving him for good. Jordan had raged through the empty house, knowing he didn't really have a choice. He visualized gossip and scandal spreading like a stain across his record. Deep down, it hurt him that he had lost Ginny's good opinion.

That all seemed a long time ago now. It had been a slow road back to a new kind of partnership, but the dream of the presidency had brought them together and driven them on. They had worked together like one perfectly oiled machine until the nomination—at which point Jordan's "two for the price of one" slogan had backfired disastrously. Ginny wasn't cute. She wasn't a beauty. She wasn't a housewife or a mother. Middle America didn't know what to make of her but feared that it was she who might be wearing the pants in the White House. Hence the softening of Ginny's image, the separate tours, the insistence that Jordan mention her as little as possible. The situation made him squirm. It was as if he had an unmentionable social disease. He longed to find a means of making people understand her quality without alienating them. He wished he could explain just why she wasn't a mother. But Ginny wouldn't let him.

It was one of the few secrets they had kept from the American people. Not even Rick or Shelby knew. "Let them call me pushy and tough," Ginny had insisted. "Let them say I'm too selfish to have a baby or too feminist. Just let me keep my dignity." And what if it became known that Jordan had fathered a son by someone else? What would that do to her dignity?

Annie and Ginny: They were so different, one exotic and unexplored, the other everyday and familiar. Whenever he pictured Annie, it was out of doors, against trees and grass and soft summer skies. Ginny belonged in a room—at a podium or a conference table, managing things.

"Tell me I'm a genius." Bonnie slapped down her comb and peered over Jordan's shoulder at his reflection. "You sit down looking like a cockatoo, and you leave looking like Richard Gere."

For a wild moment Jordan wondered if Bonnie could help get him into Annie's hotel. Everyone said she had a crush on him. He met her guileless gaze in the mirror and felt ashamed. He stood up and gave her a sudden hug.

"Thanks, kiddo. You're a doll."

Head bent, Bonnie helped him into his jacket and whisked him furiously with a clothes brush.

Jordan made his way back to his seat. That dumb song was still buzzing in his head. *Yesterday's gone, yesterday's gone.* He could feel the plane bank as it began its descent into Rapid City. Another crowd, another speech, another milestone toward the magic 270—the number of electoral votes he needed to win. His skin prickled with anticipation. He could almost feel the hot blaze of lights, see the clouds of campaign balloons, hear the screams and brassy oom-pah-pah renditions of "Happy Days Are Here Again." Out of the corner of his eye he saw swift hands gathering up the poker cards and felt as if a lightbulb had been switched on in his head. Suddenly he knew exactly how he could escape to meet Annie.

It would be madness to risk being caught in a hotel room with a strange woman. He had everything to lose—his wife, his career, his future. But reason melted to nothing in the heat of his desire to see Annie again and to find out about his son. After all those barren years—*a son.* Jordan's heart speeded. He knew he had to go.

25

In the Midnight Hour

After four rings, the answering machine kicked in with its terse announcement. *Rose Cassidy. Leave me a message.* Tom put down the receiver and looked about him in rising desperation. Gum wrappers, cigarette butts, and old bus tickets littered the floor. A drunk lay passed out on one of the benches. The telephone booths were sprayed with graffiti. A man in a hooded tracksuit patrolled one end of the waiting area, pacing off his territory with precise, ritualistic steps, talking to himself and snapping his fingers. This was New York's Port Authority Bus Terminal. Tom didn't like it one bit.

Outside didn't look much better, the streets dark and ominously empty. This menacing, midnight city was not the New York Tom remembered. Two years ago, at May half-term, his mother had brought him with her on one of her business trips. They had stayed in a suite with a minibar and a television *each*. Tom remembered how he used to get up late and order pancakes or eggs Benedict from room service. During the day, while his mother went to meetings, he wandered around the Village and hung out in Washington Square Park, watching the RollerBladers. That's where he had met some students from NYU who had told him to check out the range of music at Tower Records. One incredible afternoon he had taken an elevator ride to the top of the Empire State Building. In the evenings his mother took him to movies and to restaurants that served enormous steaks and amazing ice cream. Afterward, while she slept or worked next door, he sprawled on his king-size bed, blissfully channel surfing.

It was different being alone. First of all, he had landed at a strange airport called Newark, which turned out to be in New Jersey. The immigration officer was huge and unfriendly.

"Business or pleasure?" he had asked curtly, scrutinizing Tom's passport.

When Tom, with a weak grin, said he wasn't quite sure, the officer had expanded his massive chest and growled, "Which is it, pal?"

The bus had taken him through unfamiliar territory, along a superhighway. Tom had pressed his forehead against the dirty windows, desperate to recognize a landmark in this alien wasteland, seeing only the reflection of his own anxious face. Once the bus had traveled through a long tunnel and out again, it deposited its passengers at the Port Authority. The biggest disaster of all was finding that Rose wasn't at home. She was crucial to his plans. He had always known that she would be surprised to see him—in fact, he had felt unexpectedly awkward just dialing her number. But it had never occurred to him that she wouldn't be there when he wanted her.

Tom looked at the big clock on the wall. It was one in the morning. Perhaps Rose had gone to bed and switched on her machine so that she wouldn't be disturbed. The more Tom thought about it, the more likely this explanation seemed. If he turned up at her apartment she might be rather cross, but that was preferable to walking the streets all night. He couldn't afford a hotel. In the long hours he had spent at Gatwick waiting for his standby ticket, Tom had changed all his remaining pounds into dollars—fifty dollars to be precise. It had seemed a princely sum, but nearly ten had gone already on the bus fare and phone calls. He would have to be careful with the rest.

Not liking the look of anyone inside the terminal, Tom went back out to where the buses were parked and asked a driver how to get to Central Park West. Amazingly, he was already on the right street, except it was called Eighth Avenue here. He learned that about twenty blocks north it would turn into Central Park West. The bus driver told him to take a bus or the subway, but twenty blocks didn't sound too bad. Tom went back through the terminal and out into the street, standing for a moment in the brisk crosstown wind while he got his bearings. From the shadows he heard a low, aggressive voice.

"Hey, you buying, man?"

"Sorry?" Automatically Tom moved toward the voice. A tall figure stepped from a doorway tossing something casually in his hand. Tom could see a big, bulbous hat and eyes glittering above a scarf wound tight. The thing in his hand was a tiny plastic bag. Christ, a drug dealer!

"No thanks," Tom said politely, backing off. He turned up his palms and added cunningly, "No money, I'm afraid."

The man let out a derisive giggle and turned back to the doorway. Two more men lurched into the streetlight, punching one another with exaggerated hilarity. "Neo money, I'm afride," they mimicked. The three of them moved toward Tom in a jostling, menacing group. Tom turned and ran. He could hear them shouting, but they didn't bother to chase him. Too stoned, probably.

Tom walked purposefully uptown, giving a wide berth to the figures who scrabbled in trash cans or swayed at street corners. Gradually the neighborhood improved, though the blocks were much longer than he remembered. Taxis bounced past, but Tom refused even to turn his head to check if their roof lights were on. He was determined to make it alone. At length the glittering, black canyon opened out into the lower end of Central Park. There were still a couple of carriages waiting for lovers or insomniac tourists. The horses slept between the shafts, each with one back hoof cocked restfully. Tom was daunted to see that the numbers on the buildings started again at one. How much farther could it be?

He was waiting for the lights to turn at the next cross street when he saw a woman in shorts and a jersey jogging toward him. Perhaps she would know. He stepped forward to intercept her with a polite "Excuse me."

"Outta my way, creep!" she yelled, putting a hand to her waist. "I've got a knife."

Tom leaped out of her path, his heart hammering. The woman ran on, skinny arms pumping, ponytail swinging.

Tom began to hug the buildings, hurrying from one pool of light to the next, aware of figures across the street skulking in and out of the park. Finally, on the corner of Seventy-second Street, he reached number 120. It was an extraordinary building, like a giant's castle out of *Grimm's Fairy Tales*. There were iron railings outside, decorated with gods and dragons, and a guard in the sentry box.

"May I help you, sir?"

"I'm looking for Rose Cassidy."

"Out of town."

"Are you sure?"

"A hundred and ten percent."

"Do you know when she's coming back?"

"It's against house rules to say. She expecting you?"

Tom explained who he was. He tried to imply that Rose would be thrilled to see him and shocked to hear that he had been turned away from her door.

"I've known her all my life. I'm sure she wouldn't mind if I slept on her floor—just for one night," he pleaded.

The doorman's eyebrows beetled down to nose level. "You English?"

"Yes, as a matter of fact."

"How about that?" The man's face cleared. "My wife's crazy about *Upstairs, Downstairs*. Watches all the reruns. Drives me nuts telling me about Sir James this and Lady that. I say to her, 'Edna, don't bother me with that stuff.' " He shrugged. "Women."

Tom nodded politely.

"I'm sorry, son, but I can't let you into Miss Cassidy's apartment without her say-so. Why don't you just check into a hotel?" His eyes skimmed Tom's jeans and football jacket. "Or a hostel. I think there's one a few blocks away. Wait here and I'll check."

Armed with an address and a sketched map, Tom trudged back the way he had come. He must have walked over forty blocks now. His feet were stinging. When he reached the cross street where the hostel was supposed to be, he turned into it cautiously. This was where he had met the jogger. He had gone only a few steps when he saw a figure straightening from a crouch. Tom froze. Then he saw that it was an elegantly dressed man with a poodle on a leash, who had been bending down to scrape its steaming droppings into a plastic bag. The two of them minced past Tom. The poodle's hair had been clipped into pom-poms around each paw and at the tip of its tail. The man swung his little trophy bag like an Elizabethan courtier with his pomander. Suddenly Tom wanted to laugh. This was a seriously weird town.

The hostel was a brownstone, guarded by a taciturn Pole with more creases in his face than W. H. Auden. The price of the cheapest room, sharing with five others, was nineteen dollars, and Tom had to pay another nineteen dollars for a youth-hostel card. They didn't take credit cards. Tom counted the bills onto the desk, one by one, as fatalistic as a gambler placing his last stake in the pot. He now had precisely four dollars and fifty cents left.

The man unlocked a closet and wordlessly piled two blankets and a towel into Tom's arms. He escorted him up the stairs and swung open a door. The light from the corridor showed a dormitory-style room with six beds, the bedclothes humped over five of them. There were backpacks spilled open on the floor and a strong smell of socks.

"Swedes." The man jerked a thumb. "From Sweden."

Tom crept to his bed among the sleeping strangers. He stripped to his underwear in the dark and slid under the covers. After a few seconds he jumped out again, retrieved his wallet from his jeans pocket, and put it under the thin pillow. He lay tensely on the iron bedstead, his brain jumbled with questions. The night porter at Rose's building had given him a meaningful look at the last moment and told him to try again the next evening. Was that a hint? What if Rose didn't return? Would anyone accept his British credit card? Did they serve breakfast in this place? What was he doing here anyway?

With difficulty Tom brought his thoughts under control. It was really very simple. Problem one: He needed money. Problem two: He needed to find out where Jordan Hope was. Both could be solved with one visit to a newspaper office. The *New York Times* was supposed to be a decent paper. He didn't even need Rose.

One of the Swedes was snoring like a pig. Tom pulled up the blankets and held them over his ears. Gradually his muscles relaxed and his eyes closed. The man at Rose's apartment building had been quite nice in the end, he thought, stretching his feet down to a cool part of the sheet. Just before his mind finally drifted free, it snagged on one tiny, puzzling detail. What on earth, he wondered, was *Upstairs, Downstairs*?

26

Let It Be

HOPE FOR PRESIDENT—PRESIDENT FOR HOPE. Jordan's face was the first thing Annie saw at O'Hare Airport, smiling out at her from an election poster ten feet high. Coming closer, she saw that somebody had crossed out the hs and substituted ds. Exhausted as she was, she couldn't help smiling. The ruckus about whether Jordan had, or had not, smoked pot at Oxford was absurd—as if every institution on both sides of the Atlantic wasn't stuffed with respectable fortysomethings who had gotten high in their youth. Annie could have told anyone who asked that the stuff made him sick.

She took a taxi into Chicago, dazed by the headlights speeding around huge, looping highways. Her body told her it was way past bedtime, but here it was only ten-thirty on a busy Friday night. The traffic thickened as they neared the heart of the city. Outside movie theaters and jazz clubs people stood in line on the sidewalks, loosing trickles of cloudy breath into the cold air. Everywhere she looked there were flags and banners and election posters.

"Have you decided who you're voting for?" Annie asked her taxi driver.

He pressed his beefy shoulders against the seat and turned his head to shout through the grille. "Listen, lady, you know what Jordan Hope did last time he was in Chicago? After his speeches and stuff he went out to the stadium to watch the Bears play. He was eating popcorn and cheering like one of the guys. So what if he's fooled around—who wouldn't with that uptight wife of his? Sure, he gets my vote.

"He's going to be in town tomorrow for some big shindig at the Hilton. That's right by your hotel. Look out your window. You might get to see his motorcade."

"Really," Annie said faintly. She subsided in her seat, feeling her stomach knot. Don't think about it, she told herself. First things first.

There were no messages at her hotel, which meant no news of Tom. It was the fifth day. Hiding her anxiety, Annie followed the bellhop to her room. It was large and old-fashioned, with big windows looking across Grant Park to Lake Michigan. Annie thought of Jordan, sure that he too would remember this park as the scene of a notorious riot between police and anti-Vietnam protesters during another Democratic convention, in 1968. On one of the side tables was a huge display of flowers, which she at first assumed was courtesy of the hotel. Then she saw the card: *Welcome to Chicago —Lee Spago.*

He sounded like a nice man. They had spoken several times on the telephone to arrange Annie's visit. She had felt churlish resisting his repeated offers of invitations to stay at his home, but of course it was out of the question. Instead he was picking her up at the hospital at noon tomorrow and taking her to lunch. Annie was curious to see her mother's second choice of marriage partner. She imagined someone dashing and slightly shady. This was Al Capone's hometown, after all.

After she had unpacked, Annie undressed and took a long shower. She was so tired her legs trembled. The last few days she had worked feverishly in the office trying to clear her desk, then gone home and stayed up late, toiling over her own secret plans. It was a kind of therapy: She was too worried about Tom to sleep much anyway. Each night, when she finally crept into bed, her mind was like a boiling sea that took a long time to subside. Each morning, she would wake early and steal out to the bathroom to listen to the radio, counting the minutes until the news came on, waiting for a matter-of-fact voice to announce: "Democratic candidate Jordan Hope's chances of the U.S. presidency look slim today, following rumors of an illegitimate son fathered when he was a Rhodes scholar at Oxford. . . ." It hadn't happened yet. Meanwhile, she tried to present a normal front to the girls, to whom she and Edward had decided to say nothing about Tom's disappearance. It was fortunate that there was no creature so self-absorbed as a teenage girl.

Emma and Cassie remained as dreamy, unreasonable, and casually charming as always.

Annie dried her skin and hair slowly, savoring her privacy, profligate with the thick hotel towels. Then she tied her robe around her waist and returned to the bedroom. She longed for sleep, but there was one more job to finish. At Heathrow she had managed to buy a cheap photo album of the sort used for holiday pictures. She tore off its plastic wrapping, then tipped the contents of a large brown envelope onto the bed. Photographs cascaded out: babies, birthday parties, holidays, her wedding—twenty years' worth of simple, domestic memories. It had been Edward's idea to raid the family albums and present Annie's mother with a record of their lives. At the time, safely in London, Annie had agreed that it would be a generous gesture. Now, as she began to sort the pictures, her good intentions faltered. She lingered over one photo of Tom as a beaming six-month-old, spherical and featureless as an egg, that made her want to laugh out loud with love. Instead, her face tightened as an old, resentful fury flamed through her. If she had followed her mother's advice, Tom would never have existed.

Annie slumped on the bed and closed her eyes, wondering whether she had the courage to face her mother tomorrow. Was there anything to be said between them? For her part, there was no way of forgetting a single detail of their last meeting or of forgiving the careless cruelty of her mother's words: "You'll have to have yourself seen to"—as if she were a tomcat.

It had taken a long time for Annie to discover that she was pregnant. After the climactic events of what was to prove her last term at Oxford she was in an unsettled, reckless state. As planned, she had joined a group of friends who were backpacking across Europe. When the group split up, Annie stayed on in the Greek islands, sleeping on beaches, waitressing in bars and taverns. She put her loss of appetite down to the heat and a monotonous diet of kebabs. In early September she had returned to London, driven home by the relentless, seasonal wind that was said to incite murder and madness. Aunt Betty had taken one look at her and insisted on a medical checkup. The doctor had asked her a few questions, given her a brief examination, and pronounced her ten weeks pregnant. At first Annie had felt literally nothing, not even surprise. It was as if the world had dissolved under her feet. Wandering through the London streets, she remembered the television images of last summer's moonwalkers. She too felt like an eerie, faceless blob drifting in slow motion through space. Then a horrible panic gripped her. Rose was still in America. Not knowing where else to turn, Annie had gone to her mother.

Her mother was in Kent, staying with a legendary family figure known as "my friend Gloria," an old schoolmate who had married well. Annie had arrived at the rose-covered house on a hot September afternoon. Gloria's daughter Camilla was to be married the next day, and the hall was full of wedding clutter. The talk was all of lace-edged pillow cases and buttonholes and reception lines. Skinny and sickly, still wearing the Greek sandals that wound halfway up her calves, Annie had felt like a ghost at the feast. While the others took tea on the terrace, she managed to get her mother alone in the drawing room. It was cool out of the sun. Annie remembered how she had shivered among the brocaded sofas and expensive knick-knacks while she waited for her mother to settle herself in an armchair.

There were no histrionics when Annie blurted out the bald, still unbelievable fact of her pregnancy. Her mother's face had simply closed down into its harsh, discontented lines. When at last she spoke, it was with a familiar, wounding undercurrent of sarcasm.

"Am I to assume that there is no young man prepared to make an honest woman of you?"

Annie thought of Jordan in his faraway American town; of Edward, whom she had treated so badly. She couldn't admit that she didn't even know which man was the father.

"No. I mean, yes, there's nobody I would want to ask."

"Well, then, you'll just have to have yourself seen to. Believe me, Annie, I know what I'm talking about. You see"—she paused delicately—"I was once in the same position."

Her mother rose and walked over to the mantelpiece. She had started smoking again since Annie's father had died. Annie watched, mesmerized, as she picked a cigarette out of a silver box and clicked her lighter.

"I've never told you this before because your father insisted that I didn't, but I think the time has come. It might stop you making a stupid mistake that could ruin your life."

Annie could hardly breathe. "What?"

Her mother pulled hard on her cigarette, head tilted back, one arm along the mantelpiece, then released the smoke in a fretful burst.

"The truth is, darling, that when I married your father I was already pregnant."

Through the open window Annie could hear wood pigeons and the sound of workmen hammering in pegs for the tent.

"With me?" she ventured.

"Of course with you. What do you take me for? I'll have you know that your father was the first man I ever went to bed with—and only then after we were engaged. Unfortunately, he scored a direct hit first time. Rather uncharacteristic, wouldn't you say?"

Annie just stared.

"In those days, one simply got married. There was no question of having an illegitimate baby. Abortion was a nasty backstreet affair. And of course," she added, "your father and I were in love."

Annie sat on the sofa as still as stone.

"Darling, you have no idea what it's like to have a baby. They may look rather sweet as they gurgle past in their prams, but when you have to look after them day in, day out, night after sleepless night, it's a very different affair. They don't even look you in the eye for weeks, just scream and shit and demand to be fed. The whole thing's so *boring*. I was already feeling ghastly at our wedding—though I didn't show," she added proudly. "The next thing I knew I was knee-deep in nappies. It wasn't the way to begin a marriage, and it certainly isn't the way for you to start your life."

"Is that what you felt like, having me? Boredom? Disgust? Regret that you couldn't go out on the town every night?" Annie's voice trembled.

"It's only like that at the beginning. Don't be cross, darling. Of course it was more fun when you got older. One could dress you up and take you about. You were much prettier than most people's children, you know."

"And then, as soon as you could, you sent me off to school."

Her mother stubbed out her cigarette. "Annie, I do find this holier-than-thou attitude rather tiresome. It doesn't suit you—especially in your present situation. It is not my idea of fun to have you turning up like this the day before Camilla's wedding. I'm sorry that you've got yourself into a pickle. But I'm telling you, you are not ready to be a mother." She looked unselfconsciously into the mirror over the mantelpiece and smoothed back a sickle of blond hair. "And I am far too young to be a grandmother. Tell you what." She spun round girlishly. "I'll pay for the operation, and afterward we'll go away somewhere nice for a couple of weeks. I could do with a little holiday."

Annie stood up. "I hate you," she shouted, backing away. Tears spouted from her eyes. "You must be the worst mother in the whole world."

"Keep your voice down." Her mother eyed the door. "Think what you must. I am only trying to help you."

"Bullshit! The only person you've ever wanted to help is yourself. You couldn't even be bothered with Daddy. I think he *died* of disappointment. Don't worry, you needn't bother about me anymore either."

"Annie!"

Annie saw, with an ignoble thrill, that she had shaken her mother. Power surged through her. "I never want to see you again. I hope you have a horrible, lonely life."

"Wait! Where are you going?"

"Away. Anywhere." Annie fumbled for the door handle. Tears spilled over her mouth and ran into her neck.

Her mother's angry hiss followed her into the hall. "What shall I tell Gloria?"

Annie found herself shaking at the memory. She stood up abruptly and crossed her hotel room to the minibar. She pulled open the door and stared at the bottles. Whiskey—that's what she needed. Picking out a miniature, she wrestled off the cap, slopped some liquid into a glass, and then drank the whole lot neat, her eyes watering. Her mother had been vile, unforgivable. It was no excuse that Annie had been born too soon for her liking—or born at all. Life dealt you the cards and you bloody well played them.

Annie poured the rest of the bottle into her glass and this time topped it off with water and ice. She returned to the bed and sipped slowly, spreading the photographs across the bed. Here was Emma, dwarfed by her first school uniform; Cassie playing the innkeeper with a tea towel on her head in the Christmas play; Edward in a panama hat on the Spanish Steps. This was *her* family, *her* life. She owned none of it—not a single possession, not a second's thrill of achievement, not one jot of happiness—to her mother. Annie's mouth set in a harsh line. What Edward had intended as a gift might easily be twisted into a punishment.

Annie put down her glass and began to slot the pictures into the plastic envelopes, scribbling brief captions underneath. Yes, she thought vengefully, let the old horror see what she had missed. Her hands moved swiftly, mechanically, the way forward clear. She had almost finished when a recent photo of Tom, snapped in a mock-macho pose with his hair ruffled, caught her attention. She paused, then withdrew it from the album and popped it into the drawer of her bedside table. In a few minutes she had completed her task and laid out the album ready for tomorrow. At last she climbed between the stiff, clean sheets, switched off the light, and fell instantly asleep.

27

Rescue Me

In Times Square the giant Calvin Klein girl posed in her underpants above a swirl of people and cars. Steam rose from the subway grates into the night sky. Horns blared. Music thumped. Neon signs in a dozen different colors winked and flashed and glittered on rain puddles. Then the lights changed, and the car sped uptown between looming towers to Columbus Circle. Huddled below the statue of the great explorer slept one of New York's homeless, wrapped in what looked like sheets of bubble paper that flapped in the vicious wind. Couples in evening dress swept into the circle from Lincoln Center, clutching their minks and cashmere coats about them, desperate for a cab.

Rose watched this familiar Friday night spectacle through the window of her car and let out a deep sigh of happiness. If there was one thing even better than escaping the city, it was returning to its brutish charms. Though she was supposed to have stayed through the weekend, twenty-four hours in the country had been enough for her, and she had caught a train home, pleading pressure of work. No one could question the lavishness of Blaine and Dexter's hospitality. Their position in New York society was such that their invitation to see their refurbished mansion on the Hudson could absolutely not be ignored. But admiring curtain fabrics and chandeliers and imported French stoves was not Rose's idea of entertainment. At lunch she had been pinned to her seat by their new steeplechaser's trainer, a bore of the first water. She never wanted to hear another word about bloodlines or bone chips or linseed poultices. All that way out into the sticks, and all the way back to Penn Station. Was it worth it, just so she could get first rights to publish the photographs of Blaine's baby, due on New Year's Day?

You bet. The Blaine-Dexter romance was a real-life soap opera, of which the American public showed no sign of tiring. Did Blaine get pregnant on purpose? Would Dexter marry her? Would she sign a prenuptial agreement? A gooey picture *à trois* on the front of *The Magazine* would boost sales by twenty thousand minimum.

Rose's car whispered to the curb, precisely level with the entrance to her apartment block. The doorman hurried to open her door.

"Good trip, Miss Cassidy?"

"Fabulous. Can you get the bags out of the trunk?"

"Brad says a young man came asking for you last night."

"How exciting. Who was it?"

"I don't know. He said he'd left you a phone message."

Probably that photographer who kept bugging her, Rose thought, a pushy amateur who thought he was the new Herb Ritts. Any more harassment, and she would set the cops on him. She let the doorman bring her bags up in the elevator and deposit them in the hall of her apartment. Shutting the door behind him, she hung up her coat and slid off the phony riding boots that had been slowly strangling her feet. If anyone needed a linseed poultice, it was her. There was a pile of mail waiting. Rose limped through to her study, shuffling the usual mix of bills and invitations. She zapped the "play" button of her answering machine and stretched out on the couch with her letter opener in hand.

Beep, click.

Hi, this is Cindy. I thought you'd like to know that some great new pictures of Ginny Hope just came in. They're from an old schoolfriend who's quarreled with her. You'll just die when you see Ginny in her senior prom dress. I've put them in an envelope on your desk in case you want to come in and look at them over the weekend. See you Monday.

Hurray. That meant she hadn't lied when she told Blaine that she couldn't stay for the weekend after all. Rose laid aside her florist's bill, her credit card bill, and a circular from the Bodleian Library.

Beep, click.

Hello, Rose. Rick Goodman. We need to talk. Call me.

Rose shivered. Not for nothing had one of the scandal sheets dubbed him Jordan Hope's *Gauleiter.* She was going to have to handle Rick very carefully indeed. Rose slit open her phone bill.

Beep, click.

Rose, this is Tom . . .

Rose leaped up so quickly she stabbed her thigh with the letter opener. Hopping across the floor, she turned up the volume on her machine.

. . . I'm at the airport. I know it's rather short notice, but I was hoping I might be able to stay with you for a night or two. Er . . . Tom Hamilton, your godson. I suppose you must be out. I'll try you again when I get into New York.

Beep, click.

Sorry, it's me again. Don't tell Mum I'm here. I'll explain later. Good-bye.

Rose fast-forwarded through the remaining messages. Altogether there were six from Tom, unfolding like a radio drama. He was at such and such a hostel. He had left the hostel. He was at a phone booth downtown. He was in a coffeeshop. He was in a music store. He was running out of money, but she wasn't to worry. The silly boy never told her the time he was calling, but fortunately her machine did. He had made the last call half an hour before from an eating spot in the East Village, shouting above the clash of plates. Rose grabbed a pencil and wrote down the name, gloating with excitement.

Walk into my parlor, said the spider to the fly. Tom Hamilton, the boy who thought Jordan Hope might be his father; the boy who could turn the election upside down; the boy whom every single journalist in the world would kill to interview. Everyone was looking for Tom Hamilton. And he had come to *her.* Why exactly, she didn't know. But she intended to find out. Rose called down to the lobby for a cab, then ran to her bedroom for some comfortable shoes, grabbed her wallet and a coat, and raced out of the apartment.

The cabdriver didn't know where he was going, which made two of them. "Just off St. Mark's Place," Tom had said. "I think." They cruised the blocks until Rose finally shouted to the driver to pull up outside a lowlife eaterie with RIBS! scrolled on its facade in blinking lights. There was a row of motorcycles outside. Through the glass Rose could see that the joint was jumping. She climbed out of the car, cutting short the driver's protests.

"If you want to get paid—wait here," she ordered.

A blast of salsa music and the smell of greasy meat hit her in the stomach as soon as she opened the restaurant door. Rose picked her way through the rabble like a princess in a pigsty. She saw Tom before he saw her. *He's grown up,* she thought. Far from the forlorn figure she had expected, he was sitting at a table crowded with beer bottles, apparently at ease, holding forth to a trio of highly unprepossessing characters. Then he looked up and caught sight of her. Rose read relief on his young face. But he kept his cool.

"Hello, Rose," he said smoothly, kissing her cheek. "Let me introduce you: Mickey, Ramon, and Buck."

"Hi, boys." Rose nodded, keeping her hands in her pockets. Needless to say, Buck was the leering giant in the sleeveless leather vest with a tiger's head tattooed on his biceps.

"Would you like a drink?" Tom asked politely. "I'm afraid you'd have to pay for it yourself, though—I've run out of cash. Or some barbecued ribs?"

At that moment a sweating waiter pushed past Rose with a giant platter, bearing what looked to her like an entire cow's carcass lying in its own blood.

"That's very sweet of you, Tom, but I think we should get back. Can I settle up here?"

As she went to pull out her wallet, an arm gripped hers. Rose looked down into a pair of hot, dark eyes. This must be Ramon, a skinny street kid with a baseball cap on backward.

"We got a deal here, lady. We buy him one beer. When we come to London he's gonna take us to some fancy place for tea and scones—hey, Tom?"

"Absolutely." Tom flashed a grin at Rose. "I've been telling them about London."

"So I see." Rose raised her eyebrows. Some charm, she thought, to make these guys turn down hard cash. "Tom, shouldn't you have some luggage somewhere?"

"This is it." Tom held up a loathsome object of shiny nylon to Rose's wondering gaze. She had taken three suitcases to the country. Tom's backpack wasn't even full.

She shepherded him out to the taxi and directed the driver back to the apartment. Side by side with Tom in the backseat, Rose could feel his awkwardness gather as the obvious question loomed between them. What was Tom doing in New York? She made herself relax against the seat and gave him a teasing smile.

"Of all the joints in all the towns in all the world, you have to walk into this one. Good grief, Tom, I've never seen such a creepy bunch of hoods."

"*Casablanca.*" Tom smiled delightedly. "Ace film. Oh, they were all right. Except that they kept telling me where I could buy crack, when what I really wanted was something to eat. I'm starving. I've only had two of those bagel-things off a street cart all day."

"Oh." Rose was disconcerted. No one in her world ever admitted to being hungry. "Well, we'll have to see what we can find for you."

"You mustn't go to any trouble. Just an omelette or something would be fine."

Rose made small talk for the rest of the journey, pointing out landmarks. Under his polite public schoolboy veneer Tom seemed keyed up. Rose's instincts told her to go slow. She would find out everything in time.

It had been a long while since Rose had had a houseguest, as opposed to a bed partner. She felt almost shy as she let Tom in and showed him around. He could sleep on the foldout living-room couch, she decided. She would need her study, officially the second bedroom, to work in. But first she suggested that he might like to take a shower, while she prepared a little supper for him. He seemed to have only the clothes he stood up in. Rose had the distinct impression that he had been wearing them far longer than was strictly desirable. She led him to the guest bathroom and was amused to see his reaction to the array of shaving equipment and other male toiletries. There was nothing worse than bringing home a lover for the night and then finding that he'd borrowed her leg razor and left a tide mark of stubble in her basin.

The moment she heard the bathroom door lock, Rose raced to the telephone. Then she paused. Was it really a good idea to let Annie know where Tom was? Emotionally, she was in a critical state: If she did her hysterical mother bit on Tom, he would probably walk straight out and into the arms of some drug dealer or pederast or—ghastly thought!—tabloid reporter. It would be much better to calm him down, ascertain how much he knew and what he was up to. If Annie insisted on flying to New York to talk to Tom, she might miss her secret rendezvous with Jordan—the dazzling pinnacle of Rose's whole brilliant master plan. It was unthinkable. Anyway, Tom had specifically asked her not to tell his mother. Her conscience clear, Rose gave the telephone a dismissive little pat and went into the kitchen. The poor boy was starving.

She pulled open the door of the refrigerator and took a rapid inventory of its contents. One bottle of vitamin pills, three lemons, two rolls of fast film, eight bottles of mineral water, two half-bottles of pink champagne, and an eye pack. Didn't you need eggs to make an omelette?

Rose considered. She could always get Sfuzzi to deliver something yummy, but Tom was obviously used to his mother rustling up a little supper for him. If Annie could manage it, so could she. Rose started opening cupboards and drawers she hadn't touched in months. The only edible things seemed to be teeny jars of luxury items flounced with ribbon. In one drawer she found an apron. What a good idea. She put it on and got to work. She was still surveying her efforts critically when Tom reappeared, looking faintly sheepish in a terry-cloth robe, wet hair slicked back.

"Gosh, this looks fantastic."

Rose smiled like a sphinx. She had laid a small table for two by the window overlooking the park. Candlelight flickered on silver dishes of macadamia nuts and California olives. There was a cut-glass bowl of caviar flanked by lemon wedges and a fan-shaped arrangement of crackers—the limp remnants of some forgotten diet that she had crisped up in the oven. Both bottles of champagne stood chilling in an ice bucket. Rose had even found time to change into black velvet leggings and a cream sweater loosely belted with a gold chain. On her feet were little gold ballet slippers to match. She eased out the champagne cork and poured pink bubbles into two antique glass flutes. Handing one to Tom, she held the other aloft.

"Welcome to New York."

Tom clinked her glass. "Cheers."

They sat down opposite each other in the glow of candlelight. Rose sipped her champagne for a while, watching Tom make short work of the nuts and olives. Then she put down her glass. She leaned her elbows on the table, chin propped on her hands, eyes alight.

"So. Do tell, Tom. I'm dying of curiosity. Have you run away?"

Tom frowned. "Sort of. I'm—I'm on a quest."

"How thrilling. And you want me to help you?"

Rose slid the caviar toward him. Tom piled a mound onto a

cracker and took a bite. Rose waited while he chewed noisily and swallowed. He looked up.

"You know Jordan Hope, don't you?"

Son of a bitch. He was on the right track after all. Rose stretched her eyes wide.

"Jordan Hope! Well, I used to. Our paths have somewhat diverged in recent years."

"I want to meet him," Tom said doggedly. "I want you to arrange it. Mum always says you know everyone and can fix anything."

"Everyone has their limitations." Rose's eyebrows curved ironically. "Why on earth do you want to meet him?"

Tom reached for another cracker. "That's my business."

"Tom," Rose purred reproachfully. "You know I'd do anything for you. But how can I help if I don't know what's going on?"

There was a *ping* from the kitchen. Rose excused herself and reappeared shortly with the crab supreme she had found at the back of the freezer. Transferred from its tinfoil container to a grand Wedgwood platter, it looked surprisingly impressive. Rose placed it temptingly in front of Tom, refilled his glass, and sat down again, waiting.

"Something funny is going on," Tom began.

Gradually she coaxed the story out of him. It was much as Annie had feared—the photograph, Tom's search for his birth certificate, his growing anxiety that his real father might not be the man who had brought him up, but some strange American whom his mother professed not even to know. Rose murmured sympathetically, making no judgments. She could see that Tom was genuinely troubled. At the same time, she had the impression that he had driven himself into a corner and didn't know how to get out.

"I even got as far as looking up the address of the *New York Times*," he admitted, too self-absorbed to notice Rose choking on her champagne. "But I lost my nerve. I don't really know anything for certain."

"What does Annie say?" Rose asked.

"She's too busy with her work," he said witheringly. "She won't even listen to me."

"And she thinks you're in Oxford, does she?"

"I suppose so." Tom shrugged it aside. "The thing is, I know now that Mum and Dad weren't married when I was born. But I'm not sure they were even living together." He lifted his chin challengingly at Rose. "Well, were they?"

"Goodness, it's all so long ago. To tell you the truth, I lost touch with Annie for a bit when she left Oxford. She was certainly going out with Edward then. The next I knew, they were married with a baby."

Tom banged his knife onto the plate with a clank. "You know that's not true," he attacked hotly, blue eyes wide. "Why does everyone lie to me? *I* know it isn't true because I've seen my birth certificate. The person who registered my birth is you. 'Rose Cassidy, Lady Margaret Hall, Oxford. Occupation: student. Relationship: friend.' I've got a copy in my backpack. Do you want to see it?"

This time Rose was truly shaken. "I'd forgotten," she said softly. Suddenly she remembered Annie in the hospital among the neat rows of mothers, with nurses starchily ferrying babies back and forth according to some mysterious timetable. Neither she nor Annie had a clue what to do with a baby.

"What is it you're all protecting me from?" Tom asked. "No one will tell me the truth. Mum won't. You won't. I can't ask . . . 'Dad.' " His face twisted. "Maybe Jordan Hope will."

"Hmm. Tom, you don't think it would be a bit awkward to confront Jordan with this four days before the election?"

"I don't give a damn if it's awkward. What do you think it's like for me, not even knowing who my father is?" Tom's voice broke embarrassingly. He looked terribly young and serious. His hair had dried and stood up in back, where he kept ruffling it, like a woodpecker's crest.

"I'm sorry," Rose said contritely. "You're quite right, of course. Ice cream?"

"What? Oh, yes, please."

Rose brought him a large bowl of loganberry sorbet. It was crystallized with age, but Tom seemed too absorbed with his own thoughts to notice. When he had finished, he set down his spoon. His shoulders sagged.

"No, I'm not right," he said heavily. "I've made a mess of everything. I've made everyone hate me. I've spent all my money. They'll probably expel me from Oxford." He looked beseechingly across at Rose. "What do you think? Honestly."

Rose reached over and squeezed his arm. "I think you've had an absolutely beastly time," she said solemnly. "And I think you've been incredibly brave and resourceful, if perhaps a little . . . confused? What I honestly think is that you should go to bed right now and get a good night's sleep. And don't worry." She smiled bewitchingly. "I have a plan."

28

Have Mercy

*I*n the morning Annie dressed carefully, choosing one of the power suits she had brought for her business in New York the following week. She put up her hair in the severe style she adopted when she wanted to look especially competent—what Edward disparagingly called her "Fräulein" look. There was to be no mistake that she was now an adult in full command of her life. She looked approvingly in the mirror at her unsmiling, immaculate self. Only as she entered the hospital and caught that telltale smell of sickness and hygiene did she remember Edward's last words to her on the subject of her mother: "Be generous."

In the event she had no need of his reminder. When the nurse showed her to the glass cubicle labeled "Marie Spago," Annie's heart flooded with dismay. A woman lay flat on her back, so thin that she scarcely rippled the bedclothes. She seemed to be sleeping. Her hair had been cut short and clung to her head in yellowish gray clumps, the same color as her skin. Her arms had been neatly arranged outside the sheet, stiff and pale as a doll's. They were taped with tubes carrying the drugs and nourishment that kept her just this side of death. Annie stood watching for a long moment. Last night's raging fire of resentment went out like a snuffed candle. This was not the monster who cruised her dreams, just an old woman in pain.

She pushed open the door and sat down quietly in the chair by her mother's head. Suddenly she felt strong.

"Mummy?" she said gently. "It's Annie."

The woman's eyes opened. Very slowly she turned her head on the pillow, and now, for the first time, Annie could recognize the outlines of her mother's face, like the strokes of a half-erased drawing. Her lips moved. As Annie bent forward to catch the words, she could see a pale crust of dried saliva on her mouth.

"I look a fright," her mother said.

It was so honest that Annie's heart went out to her.

"Never mind. Lee wrote to me. He sounds very nice."

Her mother just gazed, her eyes traveling slowly over Annie's face and hair and clothes.

"He said you might like to know about my life—what I've been doing—my children."

Annie saw a slow fire kindle deep in her eyes. "Tell me."

So Annie told her. About Edward and Tom, about Cassie and Emma, about the house they lived in and the lives they led. As she listened to herself, she realized how lucky she had been. She talked for a long time. Often her mother's eyes closed. Once or twice Annie lifted her carefully to take tiny sips of water. Her body felt like a huddle of twigs. After she stopped talking, there was a long silence. Annie could hear her mother's breath move painfully in and out of her body.

"I'd like to have seen your children."

The admission turned a knife in Annie's heart. She held up the album, trying to smile. "I've brought some pictures. You can look at them when you feel stronger."

"Ohhh." It was a sigh of pure joy.

Annie put the album on the bedside table. When she turned back she found her mother staring.

"You look very important," she said with a trace of her old waspishness.

"I know. I'm sorry. It was a mistake."

Her mother closed her eyes. Her fingers twitched. "I was a lousy mother."

Annie's eyes filled with tears. "Yes, you were," she said truthfully. "But I'm not," she added, struck by a new thought. "I've had fun with my children. You didn't spoil it for me. Perhaps you were better than we both remember."

"Lee has improved me . . . I think. Kind man . . . Hate to leave him alone."

"Oh, Mummy . . ." Annie leaned forward and touched the stiff hair. "I'll stay in touch, if that would help. Perhaps Lee would like to come and visit us in London."

Her mother moved her head in approval. Annie could see she was past speech.

"You should rest now. I'll come again tomorrow." She stroked her mother softly on the hand. The skin of her wrists was like old cloth stretched between two pegs of bone. "I'm glad I came. Good-bye."

Annie went out into the hall and stood for a moment, fighting for control of her emotions.

"Annie?"

She looked up blankly. In front of her was a thickset man of about seventy, with a face like a boxer's and a slick of improbably black hair. Annie saw that his navy blazer was too tight, the cloth straining at bright anchor-stamped buttons. He didn't look like a doctor. He touched her gently on the elbow, as if waking a sleepwalker.

"I'm Lee," he said.

Lee took her to lunch in a skyscraper restaurant famed for its panorama of Chicago, apologizing for the fog that had rolled in overnight from the lake, eclipsing the view. He was desperate to talk, so Annie let him. He told her how he had met "Marie" on a cruise. It was the first vacation he had ever taken, a celebration of the sale of his bathroom fixture business, which he had started from scratch—the first of many successes, Annie deduced.

"She was the classiest woman I'd ever met. All the men were after her—and all their wives were mad as hell." He chuckled. "My advantage was, I didn't have a wife. Never had time."

As if he could hear Annie's private thoughts, he added, "I guess it didn't hurt that I had plenty of money, but we clicked just like that. Boy, did she know how to have fun. She made everything an adventure. My whole life had been work, work, work. I guess I overdid it. My father blew his brains out in the Depression, did you know that? When I was a kid I promised myself I was never, ever going to kowtow to somebody else for a job. So, Marie and me, we were kind of like Beauty and the Beast. When the cruise was over, I flew back with her to England, packed up her stuff, and brought her home. We got married a week later."

It had clearly been a very happy marriage. For some years after Lee retired, they had owned a house in Florida, joining the "snowbirds" who flocked there every winter. They played golf and swam. In Chicago they went to the opera and the theater. They belonged to some kind of country club and drove out there every Sunday for lunch. Marie had become interested in historic houses and took guided tours round the old mansions. She took *cordon bleu* lessons and gave dinner parties. Annie listened intently, waiting for some trace of the discontented, selfish person she remembered. When Lee asked if she'd like to see their apartment, Annie said yes, hoping to find some key to the mystery. They lived in a lavish block over-looking the lake, some twenty minutes' drive out of the city. Annie had been in dozens of American apartments like it: pale carpets, dark reproduction furniture, neat to the point of anonymity. It told her nothing.

Lee gave her coffee, fussing with silver spoons. Finally he got to the point.

"So what happened between you and your mom? She never even told me she'd been married and had a kid, until a couple of years ago, when she saw that article about you. That's about the time she knew she was starting to get sick."

Annie hesitated. "What did she tell you?"

"Just that her husband had died and her daughter didn't like her. I couldn't get any more out of her. She'd kind of laugh it off, saying, 'Think of me as a woman of mystery.' "

Annie looked into his baffled, tough-guy face, seeing the dread in his eyes. He didn't want to know the whole truth.

"I got pregnant when I was very young. I wasn't married, and Mummy was terribly shocked. I was . . . rather pigheaded. We both were, I suppose."

"I see," Lee said doubtfully.

"It was my fault," Annie added quickly. "I sort of ran away. I didn't tell her where I was. It came at a very bad time for her. My father had died recently. He was an army doctor, so when she lost him she lost her home as well. I don't think she was emotionally capable of any more demands. She needed to be free to find her feet as a woman on her own. Which she seems to have done—very suc-cessfully and happily."

Lee nodded slowly. "I just couldn't understand why Marie would turn her back on her own daughter. Or how anyone wouldn't love Marie. You sounded okay on the phone but, well, I wondered if you were going to turn out to be some kind of monster."

"I thought you might be a gangster," Annie confessed.

Lee laughed delightedly. "That's my nose. If you grow up on the South Side you learn to be a pretty good streetfighter."

It was time to go. At Annie's insistence, Lee called a cab to take her back to the hotel. As they waited for the elevator to take them down to the lobby, Lee gripped her hand.

"I can't tell you how much I appreciate your coming—and not just for Marie. For me too. It's been like going back twenty years."

Annie was puzzled. "In what way?"

"Well, you know, the way you look just like Marie. Same eyes, same skin, same great legs—if I may say so."

Annie felt the hair rise on her neck. Her mouth opened, but no words came out.

"Wait here," Lee commanded, turning back toward the apartment.

Annie waited, watching the empty elevator come and go. She couldn't have moved if she had wanted to. She heard the apartment door slam. Lee hurried back with a photograph in his hand.

"That's Marie on the cruise ship in 1974. Now," he challenged, "tell me that isn't where you got your looks. You two could be sisters."

Annie stared at the picture in astonishment. It was true. She grabbed the photo and held it close, tracing familiar features.

"Could I keep this?" she asked.

Lee hesitated for a second, then pressed it into her hands. "She'll be happy to know you wanted it."

Annie traveled back to her hotel along the shrouded lake road, oblivious to anything but her own thoughts. *She looked like her mother.* People had told her that when she was a girl. How could she have forgotten? Her appearance had sometimes pleased her, more often disappointed her, but she had always thought of it as *hers*. She felt suddenly awed by the potency of genetic inheritance. How precise it was and how utterly impersonal. Human beings were always so eager to read messages into coincidence or accident. It was hard to accept that physical resemblance had nothing to do with love and everything to do with the random encounter of this particular egg and that particular sperm. Annie thought of the way Lee had looked at the photograph one last time, clenching his teeth against any show of emotion. She had seen how much he would miss this elusive woman who Annie had never dreamed existed. She had missed her mother all her life. Now it was too late.

For the first time it occurred to Annie that her father, for all his qualities, had simply not been the right man for her mother. Perhaps nothing else marked one's life so strongly as one's choice of marriage partner—not parents, not schools, not even love affairs. Marriage was never the simple sum of one plus one. It had the potential to enhance or to diminish out of all recognition the individuals it bound so tightly together.

As soon as she was back in her room, Annie called home. She could have cried when she heard the click of the answering machine and Edward's remote, recorded voice. She started to dial Rose's number, then remembered that she was away in the country for the weekend. Instead, she ordered tea from room service and huddled in an armchair by the window, staring out at the fog that held her blindly in midair. But the hot drink could not warm her. At length she unpinned her hair and took off her ridiculous suit. She climbed into bed in her underwear and lay there shivering, longing for someone to hold her close.

29

Jumping Jack Flash

The lobby of the Savoy Hotel was thronged with Japanese tourists. Jack Robertson waited for his wife from the shelter of a palm frond, his tongue furtively probing his back teeth to dislodge a nugget of wedding cake. He was feeling disgruntled.

It was bad enough to be dragged away from the golf course to waste his precious Saturday at a wedding reception. He never enjoyed these occasions—all ridiculous hats and chitchat and Jane digging him in the ribs to be polite to people he didn't recognize. Worse, in this case he had never even met the parties involved. He had been invited only because Jane edited the schlockbusters of the bride's mother, a terrifying harridan spiked with teeth and false eyelashes. Knowing no one, Jack had been in the humiliating position of wandering around in his wife's wake. Consequently, he had drunk too much champagne, and his head hurt. Worse still, halfway through the reception he realized that on Friday evening he had forgotten to bring home the advance copies of Molly McFiddick's latest Inspector Giles mystery. He would have to go past the office now to pick them up. Jane would not be pleased.

Jack transferred the weight of his wife's fake leopard-skin coat to the other arm with a gingerly air, as if it might bite him. He would simply have to insist. He needed those books to get him out of an awkward hole. First thing on Monday morning he was driving to Molly's cottage in some godforsaken corner of Norfolk. There had been a certain unpleasantness about Smith & Robertson's failure to forward royalties from her publishers. It was intensely irritating that she should find fault with the firm that had handled her books for thirty years and made her a fortune—"made a fortune out of me, more like," she had cackled rudely. Nevertheless, Jack had eventually agreed to visit the old bat in person. He had been dreading it for days. When copies of her new book had arrived at the office yesterday, providing the peace offering he needed, it had seemed like a miracle. Then he had forgotten the damned things.

At last Jane emerged from the ladies' room. Jack watched her bustle toward him, fresh lipstick gleaming. It was difficult to believe that she once had the reputation of a vamp in publishing circles. Though never exactly pretty, there had been something inexplicably arousing about her plump-breasted, schoolgirl looks that Jack was by no means the first man to notice. He had felt rather honored when Jane had swiveled her guns on him. Her ambition was as voracious as her other appetites, and she had swiftly soared—no one quite knew how—from copy editing drone to queen bee of commercial fiction. But three children and a regime of publishing lunches had left a trail of fat from jawline to hip. If Jack did not, on the whole, regret his graceful surrender six years ago, he had to acknowledge that the figure now advancing on him was unequivocally matronly.

Jane smiled approvingly as he helped her into her coat. "Wasn't that fun?" she chirped over her shoulder. "Famous faces practically wall to wall. Did you see the photographers? We might get our pictures in *Harper's!*"

Jack grunted.

"It's good publicity," she urged. " 'Jack Robertson of Smith & Robertson, accompanied by his successful wife and mega-successful author, et cetera.' Wake up, Jack. You could do with some new clients."

Jack cleared his throat. "Speaking of clients . . ." he began.

Jane's lecture on modern managerial principles lasted all the way up the Strand. She illustrated it with several examples of her husband's shortcomings that she had at her fingertips. After a while Jack tuned out. His wife's advice was always horribly sensible, but the truth was that he didn't like running a company. Every day since his father's death he had felt less like the beneficiary of his inheritance and more like its victim. Of course clients were disappointed in him; he would never be his father. No matter how often Jane pumped him up with ambition, he deflated of his own accord. He would have been quite happy trundling along as a dependable, middle-ranking editor publishing rather nice, rather old-fashioned books on golf and gardening and natural history. But such figures were redundant these days. Sometimes he felt like the Prince Charles of the publishing world.

This glimmer of self-knowledge did nothing to improve Jack's temper. He swore at the door locks and thumped up the stairs to stand glowering in the empty, echoing offices. Where had his damn secretary put those bloody books?

While Jack searched the outer office, Jane unashamedly riffled through his in tray, picking up papers and opening folders, her spirits restored. She adored poking around other people's offices.

"What's this?" he heard her say from next door.

"What's what? I wish you'd leave my things alone."

Thank God, there were the books, neatly labeled. Jack picked up the package and hurried back. His wife was sitting at his desk, hefting a thick envelope.

"I smell trouble," she said, tossing it over to him.

Jack recognized the writing at once. "It's from Annie," he said in surprise.

He put down his package and picked up the envelope. His wife was right. There was something ominous about its weight and the firm underlining of the word PERSONAL. As he searched for his letter opener and slit open the envelope, Jack felt a nudge of conscience. Perhaps he had been a little hard on Annie recently, but he had his reasons. Besides, it was essential that she appreciate the new management structure. Jane had told him so.

Jack unfolded the thick sheaf and began to read. At first he couldn't make sense of it—some apologetic waffle about loyalty and his father. Eventually its message bit into his brain.

"The bitch!" he shouted.

"What is it?" Jane rushed around the desk to read over his shoulder.

Together they skimmed the paragraphs over which Annie had agonized. She was sorry to end her long partnership with Smith & Robertson in this abrupt way—"partnership," snorted Jane—but circumstances had forced her to act quickly. Believing that there was no future for her at the agency, she had decided to set up her own company. Sebastian Winter wanted to come with her and had asked her to conclude the American deal on his behalf. That's what she would be doing in New York early next week. Details were enclosed. Naturally, Annie went on, Smith & Robertson would retain its share of revenue from their contract for the first book. She had carefully documented all recent business and would consider herself available for consultation for one month. Meanwhile, she hoped that by the time Jack read this letter she would have concluded a deal for Sebastian Winter that would be extremely profitable for all parties.

"She knew I was going to spend Monday in Norfolk." Jack's voice was shrill with injury. "She was banking on the fact that I wouldn't find her letter until Tuesday. The devious little two-faced bitch."

Jack slunk about the room, his eyes narrowed menacingly. "By God, there's going to be a hell of a stink when she gets back from New York."

"Don't be stupid, Jack." Jane snatched the letter from his hand. "We're not going to wait for her to come back."

She stalked into the secretary's office and sat down at the computer, leopard-skin folds trailing onto the floor. "How do I get into your files?"

"I don't know. What are you doing?"

"*You don't know?* Aren't you networked?"

When Jack was a boy, his father had delighted in reading P. G. Wodehouse stories aloud on family holidays. Jack's memory flashed up the image of Lord Emsworth frozen in the headlamps of Aunt Agatha's imperious gaze. "Er . . ." he floundered.

But Jane had already switched on the machine and was tapping away with an authoritative hand. "You'd better ring home and tell Nanny she's got to look after the kids until we get back. And can't you at least make some tea? It's freezing in here."

Jack hovered. "What are you going to do?"

"*You* are going to fax all the American publishers and warn them what Annie is up to. You are also going to send a press release to all the trade magazines. Snotty bitch—she never even offered me Sebastian Winter; she said it was too 'up-market' for my list. We can't stop her leaving, but we can damn well ruin her career before it's even started."

Jack's heart swelled with gratitude for that "we." His wife was a remarkable woman. He watched her read through the enclosures in Annie's letter, frowning as if something puzzled her.

"I always said Annie must have had an affair with your father,"

she mused. "It's a jolly good way of making yourself indispensable."
Jane gave a secret smile.

For a moment Jack said nothing. He was remembering the affectionate letters he had found between his father and Annie and their
baffling references to a baby. It was hard to believe that there had
been an affair, but what was he to make of that outburst in the
office the other day, when Annie's son had been shouting about his
father? There was definitely something odd about the boy's birth.
Jack had worked out that when Annie had rejected his advances at
that drunken party, years ago, she must have been an unmarried
mother. And she had acted like the Virgin Mary!

"It can't have been brains that gave her such a key position in
this agency," Jane went on.

"Why do you say that?"

Jane clicked her tongue impatiently. "Just look at all this stuff."

Jack looked. Annie had included a copy of her submission letter
to all the American publishers and a list of the editors included in
the auction. As far as he could see, everything was immaculately
detailed—telephone numbers, bidding rules, marketing expectations. Secretly Jack was impressed. He couldn't accuse Annie of not
playing fair.

Jane's scathing voice slashed across his thoughts. "God, what a
ninny," she said. "She's handed you her head on a plate."

30

Downtown

*T*om drifted slowly up from sleep. The room he was in glowed with strong sunshine filtered through heavy curtains. He felt a tingle of expectation, as if this were the first day of the summer holidays at Grandpa's house, with the sea and the beach waiting. Idly he watched stripes of light shimmer on a geometric painting that reminded him of a stained-glass window—or was it a butterfly? Tom sat up suddenly. His grandparents didn't have paintings like this. And their house had low ceilings, with beams. Where was he?

His eyes swept the room, taking in the curving furniture, the sofa bed he was lying in, his backpack on the floor. Of course—Rose's apartment. The events of the past few days rushed back: Oxford, his mother, Rebecca, Jordan Hope. Suddenly he was wide awake, a familiar anxiety knotting his stomach. He threw back the bedcovers and walked across the soft carpet to open the curtains. Christ! What had looked, last night, like the glitter of a thousand stars turned out to be a line of magnificent buildings, windows glinting, flags flying, drawn up on the other side of the park like an invading army. Below him were a sparkling lake dotted with boats and the canopies of trees in brilliant fairground colors. He could hear the howl of sirens and car horns honking impatiently. Wake up, they urged, time to get going.

He looked around for his watch and saw that it had been used as a paperweight, to secure an envelope laid prominently in the middle of the floor. He opened the flap and pulled out a sheet of thick writing paper. *Tom—I've gone to the office for a couple of hours.*

Grab a cab and meet me for lunch at one o'clock. Coffee and rolls etc. in kitchen. Please double-lock door. Love, Rose. P.S. Phone is switched on to machine—no need to answer. She had written down her office telephone number for him and the address of the restaurant. Enclosed in the envelope, along with a set of keys, was a wad of folded dollar bills. Tom counted them out: five crisp twenties— a hundred dollars! He slid them reverently into his thin wallet. Rose had never done things by halves. He thought of the presents she used to send him on his birthday—a Superman outfit, a skateboard, an Instamatic camera, an American football helmet—when she remembered. Her visits to London were like brief but spectacular volcanic eruptions. Sometimes she had been too busy to do more than zoom in and out of the house, leaving a vapor trail of distinctive perfume. When there had been time for treats, they had always been on an extravagant scale. He would never forget going with her to the Men's Final at Wimbledon, the year Boris Becker won for the first time. Once she had managed to get them tickets to a Michael Jackson concert that had sold out months beforehand. He would rather have died than gone with his mother; somehow Rose was different. But recently Tom had seen less of her. The last gift had been a check, on his eighteenth birthday. It was as if she didn't quite know what to do with him now he was no longer a boy.

Tom strapped on his watch: half-past eleven. He put on the terry-cloth robe and wandered barefoot into the kitchen, where everything had been neatly laid out on the counter. He made coffee, piled his breakfast onto a tray, and carried it back to the table by the window where they had eaten last night. Spotting a pile of newspapers on a side table, he hauled over the *New York Times*. On the front page was a photograph of Jordan Hope, caught in midsashay across a spotlit stage. HOPE PROMISES A FAIRER DEAL read the caption. Tom peered close. Behind Hope, he could see television cameras and banners and row upon row of upturned, rapturous faces. They looked more like fans than voters.

He read the article as he ate, showering the paper with flakes of croissant. Hope was on the last lap of the most punishing campaign tour in election history. It struck Tom that, even if Jordan Hope wanted to see him, he might be too busy.

Nevertheless, Tom clung doggedly to his belief that Rose could fix a meeting for him if she wanted. More than anything else, he was curious. What kind of man was this Hope? Would he be pleased or horrified to know he had an unknown son? Was Tom the sort of son he would like? The problem was like an itch he had to scratch, knowing it might bleed.

Tom dumped his dishes in the sink and went into the bathroom to wash. He stared at himself for a long time in the mirror, wondering, *Who are you?* Did he want to find out? Would it make any difference? Hope was hardly going to adopt him. Finally Tom turned away, impatient with himself, and went to put on yesterday's clothes. As he passed the open door of Rose's study, he peeked in curiously. Like the rest of the apartment, it was immaculate and stylish, with an array of high-tech office machinery and an extraordinary red sofa in the shape of lips. Tom went to take a closer look. The phone on the desk next to him began to ring. Despite what Rose had said about the machine, it seemed churlish not to answer it. He picked up the receiver.

"Hello?"

There was a surprised pause and then a man's voice asked, "Is this Rose Cassidy's apartment?"

"Yes, it is, but I'm afraid she's out at the moment. She's at her office, actually, if you have the number."

"Thanks." The man didn't ask for the number. Tom had the odd impression that he was making some rapid calculations. There was the tiniest hesitation before he asked his next question.

"Tell me, is . . . Annie there?"

Tom felt a flutter of surprise. "My mother, do you mean?" Immediately he could have bitten his tongue. Of course the man could not mean her.

"I'm sorry, I don't seem to have her last name," the voice said smoothly. "I understood that a friend of Rose's called Annie might be staying with her. I need to talk to her."

"Well, she's not here," Tom said, beginning to feel frightened. "I mean, no one's here but me."

"I see. Thank you for being so helpful . . . Who am I talking to, by the way?"

"Tom—" At the last moment, Tom bit back his surname. He had heard that burglars sometimes called places they had their eye on, casing the place—not that he really believed that this man was a burglar. He sounded like one of those smoothie American lawyer types that Michael Douglas played in films. A cunning idea occurred to Tom.

"When I see Rose, who shall I say phoned?" he asked.

"She'll know," the voice said coolly. "Good-bye, Tom, it's been nice talking to you." He hung up.

Tom put the receiver down, feeling unsettled. Then he shrugged. Perhaps Rose would be able to make sense of it.

On his way out of the apartment he caught sight of his reflection in the long hall mirror and paused. He was definitely the least stylish object in this whole apartment. He tried zipping his jacket up to the neck to hide his grubby T-shirt. Now he looked like a mugger. Tom returned the zipper to its half-staff position, hoping that the restaurant—an Italian-sounding place—wasn't fancy.

But of course it was. Tom could tell he was in deep Trendsville by the offhand charm of the waiters and the way heads swiveled to check out each new arrival. Rose was already there, looking dead cool in sunglasses. She poured him a glass of white wine and smiled conspiratorially across the table.

"Guess what I've been doing this morning? Choosing pictures of Jordan Hope's wife for a feature in the magazine. It's going to be sensational."

His wife! Here was yet another element that Tom had not fully taken into account. In his fantasized meetings with Jordan Hope, he had never envisaged the presence of a third person.

"Is she interesting?" Tom asked.

Rose considered. "People's reactions to her are. She's exactly the sort of role model women are always clamoring for—smart, successful, in charge of her own life, good marriage, blah-de-blah. But now they've got her, women say she's cold and calculating. It's as if she represents some kind of threat to their femininity." Rose cocked her head, thinking aloud. "I suppose one could say she has put a new spin on the old story. Bedroom or boardroom? Kitchen and kids—or limos and lovers? Do 'real' women run families or companies? Or the presidency, for that matter?"

Suddenly Rose took off her sunglasses and sank back in her chair with a gurgle of laughter. "For God's sake, Tom, tell me to shut up. Tell me I'm not just a walking repository of crass copy lines."

"No, it's fascinating," Tom insisted, half-truthfully. There was something he wanted to know. "Do they have children, Hope and his wife?"

"No!" Rose said emphatically. "People who don't like Ginny say that she was so busy with her career, and helping Jordan with his, that she couldn't face the hassle." Rose sipped her wine. "I don't know though . . ."

"What?" Tom prompted.

"Well, there are couples who can't have children. There could be a physical problem with her," Rose paused delicately. "Or with him. Shall we order?"

Tom looked at his menu. *Bruschetta*, arugula, angel-hair pasta— the unfamiliar words blurred as his mind veered off on a new tack. If Jordan Hope couldn't have children, then he couldn't be Tom's father. Or perhaps the fact that Hope didn't have children meant he didn't want children. In which case . . . Caught in the confusion of his thoughts, Tom heard the waiter acting out the day's specials and Rose explaining precisely how she wanted something cooked. There was an expectant pause.

"I'll have the same," Tom said, handing back his menu.

The food was delicious. While he ate, Rose told him one scandalous story after another about the private lives of Hollywood film stars. Tom forgot all about Jordan Hope. Rose persuaded Tom to have a dessert, then recklessly ordered one for herself. Afterward they had some kind of fiery liqueur that you were supposed to drink while holding a coffee bean between your teeth. By the time they managed to empty the small glasses, they were both helpless with laughter.

"Tom, thank you," Rose said, dabbing her eyes with her napkin. "You don't know how much fun this is for me. Usually I get to eat lunch with fat men or pencil-thin women who shriek if they spy a blob of dressing on their lettuce leaf." She shook her hair into place and sighed happily. "I've probably gained five pounds—and I feel marvelous."

Tom was feeling pretty marvelous himself as he stepped out onto the sunny sidewalk. They had not gone more than a few paces before Rose stopped at the entrance to some kind of clothing store. She slid her sunglasses up her forehead.

"Oh, look," she said wonderingly, as if the building had been set down overnight by Martians. "Barneys. Let's go in."

Tom followed slowly, stopping to admire a pair of opaque black Ray Bans with gold rims. When he saw the price, he nearly dropped them on the counter in fright. Rose beckoned him over. There was something about her small, imperious figure, looking dashing in high-heeled ankle boots and a sleek leather jacket, that made him smile. She was frowning at the floor-by-floor list of the store's contents.

"What do you think, Tom? Kenzo? No, too gimmicky. Armani? Calvin?"

"Don't ask me." Tom laughed. "I don't know anything about women's clothes."

"Ah, but we're not talking about women's clothes." Rose tapped him playfully on the chest, "We're talking about *you*."

One hour later Tom was gazing at a vision: himself. At his feet knelt a salesman, reverently adjusting the length of Tom's new trousers. Behind him he could hear Rose quizzing another salesman about the cotton weights of shirts. Her hand rested proprietorially on a pile of jackets, trousers, sweaters, and a rainbow selection of shirts and T-shirts—all his. Inwardly exulting, Tom gave himself an implacable Clint Eastwood stare in the mirror. Good-bye, grungy student. Hello, film star. He wished Rebecca could see him.

Tom had always loathed shopping, especially for clothes. To wake up one morning and set out deliberately to make yourself as tired and as cross as possible, and pay for the privilege, had always struck him as an exquisite torture. This was different. There had been none of that aimless trailing from shop to shop; no hopeless sorting through racks of identically dreary suits; no frustrated searching for your size in teetering piles of shirts that cascaded to the floor; no lining up for a sweaty changing room so small that when you bent down to take off your shoes you banged your ass. All Tom had been required to do was to sit in a potentate's chair while Rose commanded things to be shown him. Those that he liked he tried on. Those that he tried on looked wonderful. For there was something different about the clothes too. Tom didn't quite know what it was, but they felt and looked nicer than any he had ever owned. He wondered if it could have anything to do with money.

The best thing of all was the speed with which everything was accomplished. Before he had tired of this new game of make-believe, Rose was snapping a card onto the sales desk. "Okay, I want these things sent over to this address this afternoon. The usual discount, naturally."

"And what shall we do with these?" someone asked.

A salesman was emerging from the changing room, holding Tom's old clothes at arm's length. His disdainful tone made Tom feel like a schoolboy.

"Pack them up with the other things, of course," Rose shot back without batting an eye. Tom could have kissed her.

"Now." Rose rapped on the counter. "Where can I get my friend a tux?"

"What on earth's a 'tux'?" Wandering over to her, Tom smiled at the unfamiliar word.

"Tuxedo. Dinner jacket." Rose's eyes widened teasingly. "They won't let you into the party without one, you know."

"What party?"

Rose waggled her eyebrows. "Wait and see."

31

Tired of Waiting

It was already dark when Annie woke. She lay still for several tranquil moments, as warm and lazy as a cat in the sun, assembling her thoughts. Something mysterious had happened while she slept. The emotional turbulence of this morning's meeting with her mother and the memories it provoked had been magically soothed away, and with it the lump of resentment Annie had carried for half her life. She had regained a part of herself, some wellspring of confidence that her mother's opinion no longer had the power to block. There was something else too, a distant fluttering that was both alarming and pleasurable. What was it? Annie sat bolt upright in bed. Jordan!

She switched on the light and blinked at her watch. Eight o'clock. Her heartbeat slowed. There was plenty of time. Jordan had told her on the telephone that he could not possibly make it until late, probably the middle of the night—possibly not at all. Annie sank back on the pillows, admitting to herself how bitterly disappointed she would be if he didn't come. Jordan had streaked through her private emotional universe like a shooting star, blazing one moment, gone the next. Over the years she had held hundreds of imaginary conversations with him. She had fantasized scores of improbable meetings. Even though he could not possibly know her married name, she had daydreamed about him opening a book by one of her authors and reading: "Last but not least, my thanks to my heroically patient agent, Annie Hamilton, without whom . . ."

She liked to think that Jordan had not forgotten her. She could never have forgotten him, even if every detail of his life had not been ferreted out by the media. Annie had read far more than she wanted about his wife, haircuts, and girlfriends; his devotion to jogging and his fondness for playing pool. Through countless pictures and yards of film footage she had witnessed his transformation into a public figure, handsomely packaged in slick suits. But she wanted to see him for herself. In the flesh. Was this disloyal to Edward? Annie didn't want to think about that. Squirming down into the warm nest of bedclothes, she tried to hold on to that floating sense of well-being with which she had awoken. Soon enough she would get up. The practicalities of her life, its urgent demands, would resume. But for a little while longer she held them at bay, allowing herself to drift back to the very last time she had seen Jordan, remembering how it was.

On that bright midsummer morning twenty-two years and four months ago, Jordan had punted her back to the boatyard under Magdalen Bridge. Annie could see him now, trousers rolled up over bare feet, water glistening on his forearms, smiling down at her. She had lain among the cushions, thinking, *He's leaving today. I'll never see him again.*

He had taken her to breakfast at George's in the covered market. She remembered the smell of freshly roasted coffee wafting out of Cardew's and the solid feel of Jordan's body next to hers as he steered her through the warren of cool, dimly lit alleys. There had been cherries and strawberries piled high on the fruit stalls, silver salmon laid out on slabs of ice, hams and salamis hanging outside Palm's Delicatessen. Annie had been conscious of her crumpled ball dress and tangled hair, but no one took much notice. It was always the same at the end of the summer term. Students were students. Soon they would be gone.

George's was an Oxford institution, a workingman's café accustomed to reviving the occasional hungover undergraduate with milky tea and a fry-up. Jordan couldn't believe that she had never been inside before. He ate there practically every day. They had climbed narrow wooden stairs to a crowded room where the windows ran with steam. Jordan had led her from table to table, greeting delivery men and construction workers like old friends.

Too lovesick to eat, Annie had leaned her elbows on the Formica tabletop and watched dreamily as Jordan worked his way through a plateful of eggs, bacon, tomatoes, mushrooms, sausages, and fried bread. She followed the movements of his hands as he cut up his food in that odd American way, laying down his knife and switching over his fork at every mouthful. Faint hollows appeared under his cheekbones as he chewed. She saw how his hair curled over his collar and ears, how his eyelids curved to give him that perpetual lazy smile she found so seductive. Every few seconds he forgot his food and looked up at her. Underneath the table his legs had clasped hers tight.

They had driven back to LMH with the top down. Oxford had never looked more beautiful. Some kind of academic ceremony delayed them in Broad Street. They had waited in traffic to allow a procession of dons and dignitaries to cross to the Sheldonian Theatre, splendid in their velvets and silks and ermine-edged hoods. Annie remembered how Jordan had jumped out of the car to get his camera from the trunk, while she slid down out of sight, feigning embarrassment at his crass American behavior. As he stood on the driver's seat to take pictures—still in his dinner jacket, bow tie dangling from his pocket, the sun on his hair—he had looked quite glorious, a golden boy among the golden towers.

In Parks Road the acacias were in flower. Speeding under their cool canopy, Jordan banged the steering wheel angrily.

"Why did you have to wait until now? We could have done so much together. Everything would have been different."

"Not everything," she replied. "You'd still be going home."

As soon as they reached her room, she burst into tears. Jordan held her in his arms. "It's okay, baby. Don't cry."

She had left the room to wash her eyes. When she returned, Rose was sitting in her armchair, talking to Jordan like an old friend. A terrible thought had struck her. Surely Jordan couldn't be Rose's American—not the 120-guinea abortion man?

"You know each other?"

"Sure." Jordan grinned easily. "We've had some gritty sessions in the Union bar."

"Oh, *politics*." Annie breathed again.

Jordan asked Rose to take a picture of him with Annie in the garden. The two of them sat on a slope of bright-green lawn where pink rambler roses climbed up to Annie's window.

"Don't look so tragic," Rose had shouted, and Annie had leaned into Jordan's shoulder and laughed.

Jordan had promised to send her the picture in care of LMH. Annie's last memory was of standing by his car under the big lime tree, mute with misery. She was rubbing her finger back and forth over the red upholstery, summoning the courage to say good-bye, when Jordan reached into his pocket.

"So what do you think of my little car?"

"I love it."

"Good."

He had taken her hand and folded her fingers over the key. "You keep it."

He laid his jacket and camera on the dusty hood and kissed her until she could hardly stand. Finally they pulled apart. He smoothed her hair tenderly over each shoulder and smiled into her face.

"Two-times girl," he had murmured, almost to himself.

Then he had slung his jacket over his shoulder and walked out of her life.

Annie shivered with nostalgia. Was there anything on earth as exciting as the beginning of a romance, when one was nothing but a bundle of emotions and nerve endings? No wonder people had affairs. She wondered what Jordan would remember—*if* he would remember. Their lives were so different. For all these years she had carried him around in her heart like a secret. But for Jordan it might have been no more than a one-night stand in a faraway country that he had never, as far as she knew, revisited. Perhaps the idea that he might have fathered a son would fill him with revulsion. Or would it excite him?

Feeling restless, Annie jumped out of bed and stepped to the window. She drew back the heavy drapes and caught her breath. The fog had cleared. The city glittered before her, an urban fairyland full of promise. Suddenly she felt capable of anything.

She decided to celebrate her new self by dining in the hotel. Like most women she knew, she usually hated eating alone in formal restaurants. Men always seemed to feel honor bound to inquire after her cotelettes d'agneau or to send over a glass of champagne and toast her exaggeratedly, drawing every eye in the room to her solitary female plight. Normally it was preferable to sneak out to some anonymous coffeeshop to eat tuna salad behind a propped-up book. But just occasionally, maybe once every five years, there was nothing more sublime than striding alone into a grand dining room and eating a full three-course meal entirely on her own, with no need to make conversation or consult others. Tonight, Annie decided, was one of those nights.

First she showered, taking time afterward to smooth cream into her body. She slipped on her underwear and carefully drew on sheer black stockings, fastening them high on her thighs. Then she put on her makeup—not too much. Stepping into black high-heeled shoes, she sucked in her stomach and cheeks and studied the effect in the full-length mirror. Not bad. She turned her attention to the contents of her closet. She wanted to look marvelous for Jordan without appearing to have made any particular effort.

Twenty minutes later she was still scowling at herself in the full-length mirror. No, no, no. The black slacks and cream silk shirt were all wrong. Just when she wanted to present an image of mysterious, unfathomable experience, here she was looking exactly like Mary Tyler Moore. Annie turned away from her dispiriting image and stripped again to her underwear, adding the latest discards to a growing pile on the bed. Her secondhand Armani suit was heaven but too formal. The leggings she always wore on planes were too sloppy. Her pink Chanel copy made her feel as if she were about to conduct an interview. So what was left? It would have to be her slinky black, a knee-length dress in fluid jersey that crossed over her breasts and fastened at the waist with two diamante buttons. It was a little dressy, but the minute she put it on she felt better. She put her hair up and took it down again, pinned it back from her forehead and unpinned it. Eventually she brushed it until it gleamed and let it fall where it would. A generous dab of perfume in all the key places, and she was ready.

She went down to dinner, daring the maître d' to seat her invisibly by the kitchen doors. He didn't. The dining room was a homage to turn-of-the-century ostentation, an extravaganza of marble columns and chandeliers, gilt mirrors, tropical plants, and white linen. A pianist in the corner tinkled out Gershwin tunes. "You like potayto and I like potahto. . . ." Thoroughly enjoying the tender attentions of a dark-eyed waiter young enough to be her son, Annie took her time. She ordered an expensive Beaujolais and, somewhat to her surprise, an hour or so later found that she had drunk the entire bottle.

After coffee she got her coat and took a walk around the block, relishing the sting of chilly air on her flushed cheeks. She saw the banks of police cars and limousines outside the Hilton and imagined Jordan inside, doing his stuff. It struck her that there were an extraordinary number of people out on the streets. Surely they couldn't all be Democrats. It was only when a party of teenagers in devil masks came shrieking around a corner that the truth dawned on her. Of course! It was Halloween. That explained the festive atmosphere in her hotel. When she returned to the lobby she could still hear the piano: "Thanks for the memory. . . ." Annie lingered, browsing through the little shop that sold magazines, toiletries, and cheap souvenirs. As she looked to see whether there was anything to take home for the girls, she hummed along with the music. There was nothing suitable for Cassie or Emma. Nevertheless, she made one small purchase.

By the time she returned upstairs, it was almost midnight. But she still had time to kill. She turned her attention to the room itself, closing the bathroom door and tidying away her clothes and makeup bottles. Then she dragged the two armchairs across the carpet to make a kind of conversation group with the huge Empire-style sofa under the window. She switched off the overhead light and moved a table lamp over to the sofa. This hotel had been built on a grand scale, at the height of Chicago's prosperity. Though now slightly fusty, the high ceilings and heavy mahogany doors with gilt fixtures gave her room the air of a fin de siècle salon. She might have been an Edith Wharton heroine awaiting an illicit beau. What else? Jordan might be thirsty after all that speechifying. She checked that the minibar was fully stocked: It had everything. She brushed her hair smooth and touched up her makeup. Now she was ready for him. The question was, would he come?

32

Mama Told Me Not to Come

The Temple of Dendur was on the first floor of the Metropolitan Museum, a short drive across the park from Rose's apartment. It was early evening when Rose's limousine drew up in front of an imposing turn-of-the-century building supported by massive columns and flanked by spotlit fountains. Tom peered out at the people streaming up the vast flight of steps and fingered his bow tie self-consciously. Never had he been to such a classy party. The men were dressed as he was. The women glittered with jewels.

"Do people really do this every week?" he asked Rose as he helped her out of the car.

She laughed, smoothing down the short black coat that stood out around her knees like a ballerina's skirt. "Every week? Some people do this practically every *night*." She caught Tom's bemused expression and shook her head. "You still don't get it, do you? Look, Manhattan is a tiny island with some very rich people and thousands more people who would like to be very rich. These parties are all about connections, society, money. Who's in, who's out. Who's together, who's not. Remember, everyone lives in tiny apartments. American television is terrible. What else is there to do?" She took his arm. "It may not be Ascot, but these affairs do raise a lot of money for good causes, and you can make them fun." She lifted her chin at him. "Actually, that is my speciality."

They moved across the grand hall and through to a lofty gallery. Tables had been set for dinner around a stunning, subtly lit Egyptian temple, but no one was sitting down yet. A few conscientious guests peered perfunctorily at the exhibits, but most stood in chattering groups with their backs to the pictures, hoping to be photographed by the paparazzi. Waiters circulated with trays of champagne and mineral water. Tom chose champagne. He sipped it appreciatively as he cruised the room with Rose, head bent to her running commentary.

"See the one with the amazing boobs?" Tom saw, all right. "Seventy-five percent silicone. They say she went from a 32A to a 36D overnight. The redhead she's talking to is the latest weather girl: Where she needs an implant is in her brain . . . See the man with the ponytail and the earring? He makes sculptures out of chocolate. People are being very nice to him at the moment because Milton Vanderpump bought one of his pieces. Plus he's Mexican, and that makes everybody feel better about exploiting their Hispanic maids. . . . Darling, how are you?" Rose proffered her cheek to a pretty woman with huge, dark eyes, who kept fingering her necklace nervously. "She's rather sweet," said Rose, after they had moved on. "She just gave a million dollars to the Met, hoping to crack Manhattan society. But her husband made his money in something embarrassing like manhole covers or funeral parlors, and they're both Jewish. People are waiting to see."

Tom was scandalized. "Surely no one cares about people being Jewish anymore. I thought there were supposed to be more Jews in New York than in Israel—or is it Tel Aviv?"

Rose gave him a sardonic look. "Check out some of the exclusive country-club registers. I can tell you now you're not going to find too many Goldbergs or Rabinowitzes. Look, over there, the bimbette with the hair next to the tubby old man with the suntan— she's his fifth wife. The rumor is that she once posed for a *Playboy* centerfold, but no one's been able to track down the pictures yet."

They circled the room slowly. Rose pointed out publishers, playboys, currency traders, heiresses, politicians, journalists, interior decorators, even a hairdresser. She seemed to know most of them. Each time she introduced Tom as her godson. He got some funny looks.

"I had no idea it would be so exciting coming with you," Rose whispered in amusement. "Everyone's wondering who you are. Let's keep them guessing. And stop fiddling with your tie. You look great . . . Uh-oh." Her hand tightened warningly on his arm. "Here she comes, Muffin Grondquist, the grande dame of the benefit circuit. Her parents must have thought 'Muffin' was a cute nickname back in nineteen-o-something. Don't worry if she doesn't smile at you. She's had so many face-lifts she can't."

A silver-haired woman in a long black dress glided toward them as smoothly as if she were on castors. Her face was a collection of bones glued together with makeup. Tom watched as the two women leaned toward each other and kissed the air.

"And who is this lovely young man?" The woman swiveled her body toward Tom.

"This is Tom Hamilton." Rose's eyes sparkled with mischief. "My godson."

"Ohhh." It was a swooping note of innuendo, as if *godson* were a code word for some new kind of sexual relationship, probably deviant.

The dinner began. Rose had warned that the people at their table were her guests and that she would have to leave Tom to his own devices while she gave them her full attention. She seated him opposite her, next to a sculptress with short, streaked hair, called Sidney. Tom quickly learned that Sidney was a Sagittarius, never touched meat, and was very concerned with the issue of Tibetan independence. She was extremely attractive, but it took Tom a little time to hit on a subject they could both talk about. Eventually they discovered that she had exhibited her work in Berlin. While they ate, Tom told her about his months in Eastern Europe. She watched him raptly, in fact so unblinkingly that he began to wonder if her eyes were glazing over in boredom. But when he broke off, she laid an insistent hand on his arm.

"Don't stop," she breathed. "I love listening to your voice. It's just like *Masterpiece Theater*."

Tom was enjoying himself. Everyone was being very nice to him, and he realized that this was because of his special status as Rose's partner. He had not appreciated how famous she was. He glanced across the table, tuning in to her provocative announcement that Oliver North would be elected president in '96. Tom caught her expression of satisfaction as a chorus of disagreement broke out around her. She was wearing a dress in some kind of shiny sea-green material with crisscross straps over her bare back. A slim necklace sparkled at her throat. Matching earrings peeped from her glossy hair. Her lipstick was scarlet. She possessed an aura of power that was not just to do with looking glamorous. There was something about the way she sat, straight-backed and poised, that gave her distinction. She never fidgeted, he realized, never simpered or fiddled with her hair. She looked utterly concentrated, controlling her guests as expertly as, earlier, she had tied his bow tie for him. *Formidable*: That was the word. Suddenly Rose looked across the table and caught him staring at her. She gave him a secret smile.

Sidney must have been following his gaze. "Isn't Rose Cassidy a little old for you?" She smiled insinuatingly.

Tom looked at her pearly little teeth. "I don't think so," he said shortly.

During coffee there was some kind of award presentation, accompanied by fulsome speeches and applause. Afterward people got up to leave or table-hop. Rose disappeared. A man at their table launched into an involved story of a leveraged buyout, of which he was evidently the hero. Tom began to feel bored. Sidney was just asking in a meaningful way if Tom was interested in primitive sculpture, when Rose reappeared at his side.

"I'm frightfully sorry, Sidney," she said smoothly. "I'm afraid we have to leave early tonight."

Tom made his good-byes and accompanied Rose downstairs.

"This is so wicked," she moaned as they emerged out onto the steps of the museum. "I never behave like this. But I thought it was time to get you away from Sidney. She would have eaten you for breakfast."

Tom shook his head in innocent wonder. "And she told me she was a vegetarian."

"Ha-ha. Get into the car. There's someplace I want to show you."

They rode downtown, gossiping about the party.

"You certainly seem to know a lot of people," Tom commented.

Rose flipped off her spiky-heeled shoes and exercised her toes. "That's one way of putting it."

"You mean, they all want to know you?"

"Attaboy. I'm glad they still go for brains at Oxford."

Oxford. Rose had a trick of bringing him back to earth with a bump. Remembering that he had never told her about the curious telephone call at her apartment this morning, he did so now. Rose quizzed him sharply but offered no explanation. She swore she had told no one where he was. The car dropped them off at the glitzy entrance to a skyscraper. An elevator shot them up to the sixty-fifth floor. RAINBOW ROOM read the control panel. When the doors opened, Tom stepped out and exclaimed in wonder at a dizzying, wraparound view of the whole city.

Looking smug, Rose took him on a tour of the floor. It was divided into different sections—a restaurant, bars, and a revolving dance floor where couples swayed to old-fashioned music. Tom and Rose walked slowly around the periphery of the room and then found a dimly lit table on the south side, looking downtown. Rose ordered them both something called a Perfect Manhattan. The drink was delicious and very strong, clinking with ice.

"God, I love this view," Rose burst out passionately. "It always makes me feel as if I'm king of the castle and a nobody, both at the same time."

They stared at the winking panorama in silence. Then Tom put down his glass and turned to Rose. "It's wonderful. So were the clothes and the lunch and the party. Why do I get the feeling that you've planned all this to distract me from thinking about Jordan Hope?"

Rose let out her breath as if she had been expecting this. "Because I have," she said seriously. She set her elbows on the table and leaned toward him intently. "Listen to me, Tom. It's time you dropped this whole Jordan Hope thing. One, it's impractical. You know it's out of the question for you to meet Jordan right now. Two, if you go around saying Jordan is your father—without a shred of evidence, remember—you'll make trouble for yourself and everyone else. The man you talked to this morning is a very smart and very powerful slimeball called Rick Goodman. He's been helping Jordan Hope run his campaign, and if Jordan wins Rick will expect to be rewarded with a key government position. Before the election he would do literally anything to shut you up. Afterward he wouldn't hesitate to use you as a threat to dangle over Jordan's head. I can deal with him, because that's the world I move in. But it's not your world and it's not Annie's."

"Yes, but—"

"Three," Rose continued, "there's your family to think about—a nice, happy family where everyone cares about one another."

Tom made a face.

"Yes, it sounds schmaltzy, but it's not common. I know." Rose took a sip of her drink. "My parents never really cared about us at all, though it took me years to figure it out. They always seemed so proud of the great Cassidy tribe: 'All for one and one for all.' " Rose gave a brittle laugh. "They think what I do is terribly trivial and rather amusing. They pride themselves on never having had the time, or the frivolity, to look at a single issue of *The Magazine*." Rose stared out the window, holding herself stiffly. Then she shook back her hair and turned to Tom. "Your parents will always love you, whatever you do. But you can wound them irretrievably. You can make them sad. Why? Don't do it."

"But there *is* something about Jordan Hope," Tom persisted. "Otherwise why would Mum be so cagey about it? Why would this Goodman person be interested in me?"

Rose looked at him thoughtfully, as if making a decision. "Tom," she began portentously, "promise you'll never tell Annie I told you this, but I think she may have had a one-night stand with Jordan. They met at a demo when they were students. Something happened, though she was always very secretive about it."

"A demo?"

"Demonstration. Protest. You know, Vietnam and all that." She put a hand to her forehead and groaned softly. "God, I suppose you don't know. Anyway, it was one of the violent ones—riot shields and charging police horses and so on."

"Mum?"

"Yes, 'Mum.' I know this will come as a terrible shock to you, Tom, but she was once even younger than you are now. Anyway, there was some trouble, and Jordan rescued her—just like a knight on a white charger. I don't think she's ever quite got over it."

Tom's mind clicked slowly. "And when was that?" he asked casually. "Roughly."

Rose looked at the ceiling. "Let's see, that must have been about . . . October 1969."

Tom worked it out. He couldn't have been conceived then.

"Look." Rose smiled persuasively. "You're a mature adult. If Annie has some adolescent fixation about Hope, you're just going to have to forgive her. Everyone has a streak of silliness. It's not as if she and Edward aren't happy together. Even back in Oxford, everyone could see that they were made for each other."

"Then why did they wait so long to get married?"

"I don't know. But the responsible thing to do would be to go home and ask them. Get the story straight before you blow Hope's chance of the presidency and make yourself and your family miserable." Rose sat back and slapped her hands lightly on the table. "Okay. End of lecture." She stood up. "I'm going to the ladies' room."

While she was gone, Tom stared out across the alien city. Everything Rose had said made sense. He wished his mother spoke to him like this, as an equal. He tried to imagine his mother, "younger than you are now," fighting the police and falling for a handsome American called Jordan Hope. Deep down Tom had always known that it would be difficult to meet Hope. Coming to America had been an act of defiance, to make everyone aware that he was upset. But if anything, his curiosity was intensified. He vowed that one day they would meet. And in the meantime, he had enjoyed his stolen weekend in New York. Turning from the window, Tom looked across the glamorous room. He watched Rose approach with her quick step, flashing him a smile, and saw how people turned their heads as she passed, then checked to see who her partner was. Tom felt a surge of pride.

Rose settled back in her chair, waiting for him to speak.

"I've been thinking," he began hesitantly. "I've had a great time being with you, and I'd love to stay on. But I've decided that tomorrow morning I should go out to Newark and see if I can get a standby flight to London."

Rose eyed him consideringly. He couldn't tell if she was pleased or not. She reached for something in her bag and placed it before him: an airline ticket.

"I've ordered the car for 7 A.M. tomorrow," she said calmly. "Your plane leaves at nine."

Tom opened his mouth. He didn't know whether to protest or to thank her. The expression on Rose's face, half smiling, half defiant, touched him unexpectedly. Before he could say anything, Rose stretched out her hand and pressed two fingers gently to his lips. Tom felt his face flush scarlet. More as a distraction than anything else, he heard himself say, "Do you want to dance?"

Tom didn't really know how to dance, but Rose seemed happy to be steered around the floor under the giant chandelier. She felt surprisingly fragile under his hands. Her skin was warm and smooth. Tom's spirits rose. Now that he had made his decision, he was determined to wring the last drop of pleasure from his New York escapade. Rose seemed to have relaxed too. When the number ended, she held on to him lightly, waiting for the music to begin again. "I haven't done this in years." She laughed. Tom became bolder, trying a couple of twirls. When they eventually left the dance floor, she gave a little pirouette. The sash of her dress flew out beguilingly. Her cheeks glowed.

"Tell me," she asked, "am I smashed, or am I having a good time?"

Tom looked her over carefully, from her gleaming cap of hair to her foot-fetishist shoes. "Smashed," he pronounced.

"Tom!"

They left soon afterward. Alone with Rose in the elevator, Tom experienced a piercing moment of nostalgia and traced its source to Rose's perfume, the same one she'd worn ever since he could remember. He shut his eyes for a second, inhaling the familiar fragrance. When he opened them again he found Rose looking at him intently. He stared back.

"What?" She laughed, sounding embarrassed. "Tom, you're staring."

"You've got green eyes," Tom said wonderingly, bending close. "Really and truly green."

"But they've always been this color."

Tom's gaze slipped lower. Her coat had fallen open. He could see the swell of her breasts. "Perhaps." He stepped back. "I've never noticed before."

Outside, they waited in silence for Rose's car to draw up. The heater was on in the car. It was very warm. Tom sank into the cushioned seat next to Rose, feeling suddenly awkward. Here he was in the most glamorous city in the world—in a limo, wearing a tuxedo, with a beautiful woman—and he couldn't think of a thing to say. To tell the truth, his body was behaving rather disturbingly. The thoughts in his mind were not the sort you were supposed to have about your godmother.

He was struggling to construct some remark about New York traffic when he felt Rose place her hand unambiguously on his thigh. His body contracted with shock.

"To-om?" she asked, stroking absentmindedly.

Tom summoned his entire store of oxygen. "Yes?" he answered. The pitch was a little high, but it would do.

"What do you think?" Rose looked up at him, eyes glinting in that mischievous way she had, as if everything were a game. Her head barely came up to his shoulder. "Is it incest if a woman goes to bed with her godson?"

Tom laughed out loud, too loud. He raised his arm and pulled her close. There was nothing to her. Suddenly he felt supremely confident. "Definitely not."

Rose slid her hand upward. "Hallelujah," she breathed.

33

You Can't Always Get What You Want

A nnie sat down in the armchair, then sprang up again. It was too quiet. She tensed every time she heard the rumble of the elevator doors. She turned on the television and quickly switched it off. Then she noticed a radio built into the wall by her bed. After some experimentation she tuned into a golden-oldies music station: an inexplicable string of initials that sounded like the last line of an eye chart. But the music was good. Annie opened her briefcase and laid out her papers on the desk, making herself look busy. There was a business plan to prepare for her bank manager. Annie stared at her cash-flow chart, pencil poised, pretending to concentrate.

It was just after two when she heard a soft knock on her door. She leaped up to turn off the radio with fumbling fingers and then peered through the spyhole. All she could make out was a figure in a dark overcoat, head lowered. She unlocked the door.

"Jordan?"

The door swung open. A tall man in a hurry stepped inside. It was him.

"Annie, hi. It's wonderful to see you again."

Jordan reached for her hand and shook it, clasping his other hand warmly to her elbow.

"You look terrific," he said huskily, though his eyes skipped quickly over her to scan the dim room.

He unbuttoned his coat and raked a hand through his hair. "I'm sorry it's so late, but it was tricky to get away."

Annie took his coat for him and laid it on a chair. She felt as stiff as a marionette.

"What's wrong with your voice?" she asked.

"Too many speeches, I guess. You got anything to drink here?"

Annie silently poured him a beer and decided to make a whiskey for herself. He hadn't even looked at her properly. She watched him roaming about the room, glass in hand, circling the ornate furniture, twitching back the curtain, peering at the gloomy reproductions on the wall. He was so wired up she thought he might strike sparks. His face was squarer than she remembered, and his body had filled out. The rich chestnut of his hair had faded. But it was still thick and wavy. The streaks of gray suited him.

"So"—he turned—"tell me what's going on."

"Why don't you sit down." Annie waved at the sofa.

Jordan sat down on the extreme edge, leaning his elbows on his knees. He was wearing dark trousers and a blue shirt that matched his eyes. Light from the table lamp glinted on the fair hairs on the back of his hands.

Annie remained standing. Holding on to the back of a chair, she began the speech she had rehearsed.

"First of all, I want to say that I'm really sorry to make trouble for you. I hope it wasn't a terrible shock when I telephoned. I wanted to warn you but also to explain."

Jordan nodded. "Okay. Shoot."

"I, er, got pregnant at the end of my second year at Oxford— the summer of 1970. At the time I was going out with someone, but we broke up that term. Anyway, I had the baby—he's called Tom —and eventually I met up again with my old boyfriend and we got married. As far as we're all concerned, Tom is Edward's—my husband's—son. But just recently Tom has taken it into his head that Edward isn't his real father and that—well, that you might be."

Jordan jiggled his glass, swirling the beer. "How come?"

Annie felt that she was talking to a wall. She took a sip of whiskey and sat down in the armchair opposite Jordan.

"Do you remember a photograph you sent me? You and I on the lawn at LMH the day after—the day you left Oxford?"

Jordan blinked. Then, for the first time, he looked her in the eye. She thought his expression softened, but he was holding himself on a very tight rein.

"You still have it?" he asked.

"Tom has it."

"Jesus."

"He found it in my old trunk. It seems to have affected him very powerfully. He thinks that you might be his father. I tried to tell him it wasn't true, but I didn't do it very well. We quarreled. He's been missing for nearly a week now. Nobody knows where he's gone. I just thought I should tell you. Tom hasn't got a sophisticated bone in his body. He could blurt out his worries to anyone. A rumor might get into the papers. Something he said made me think that he might even try to get in touch with you."

Jordan was frowning. "Is that it? Is that the evidence? Some kid finds an old photograph of his mother with a guy he doesn't recognize and decides the man must be his father?"

Annie's lips tightened. How could he be so cold about this? "No, that isn't the 'evidence,' as you call it. I obviously haven't made myself clear about this meeting. This isn't a scam, Jordan. This isn't blackmail. It isn't some ludicrous attempt to stop you being elected president. I am trying to help you."

Jordan bowed his head. "I'm sorry. Right now I'm living in a crazy world. There's no one I can talk to about this." He smiled in a way that transformed his face. "Forgive me."

"Don't mention it." Annie straightened herself in her chair and crossed her legs.

"No," she continued, "the 'evidence,' such as it is, is that Tom decided to look up his birth certificate and discovered that Edward and I weren't married when he was born. Naturally, he was upset and confused. Plus the fact—" Annie hesitated. "Well, I think somebody must have said to him that he looked like you. Like you used to look. Like you looked in that picture."

For a long moment Jordan sat utterly still.

"Your son looks like me?" he said slowly, looking up at Annie from under his eyebrows. Something inside her jumped. His eyes, she thought, those lazy-lidded smiling eyes were exactly as she had remembered.

"Actually, most people say Tom looks like me."

Jordan shook his head in confusion. "Annie, let me get this straight. Are you telling me this isn't just some cockamamie idea of your son's? You mean he really could be mine? When was he born?"

Was it her imagination, or did he actually looked pleased by the idea? More than pleased—triumphant?

"We all consider him to be Edward's," Annie said stiffly. "Tom is a lovely, uncomplicated boy. I'd like him to stay that way. I also have two other children to consider and my husband. You have your wife and your position. All I want to do is find him and straighten him out. Then we can all get on with our lives." She smoothed her dress over her thigh, adding quickly, "He was born on March seventeenth, 1971."

"I see." Jordan was silent for a moment. Anne could practically hear him counting out the months in his head. Changing tack, he asked, "How did you know where to call me?"

"Don't worry. I was very discreet. I got my friend Rose to help me. You must remember—"

"Rose Cassidy?" Jordan interrupted, horrified. "Queen of the Schmooze? Motormouth of the magazines? Jesus, Annie, why didn't you just go on *Larry King Live* and get it over with?"

"Rose would never say anything," Annie protested. "She's my best friend."

"Hmm. And does she know why you wanted to get in touch with me?"

"Of course not," Annie lied.

"How did she know how to reach me?"

"She didn't. She asked one of your henchmen."

"My *henchmen*?" Jordan's mouth quivered just the way it used to when he was amused by some ridiculous English phrase.

"Your campaign people"—Annie waved her hand—"whatever you call them. Rick somebody. She knew him at Oxford."

"*Rick Goodman?*" Jordan's eyebrows snapped together.

"I think so. Is something wrong?"

Jordan didn't answer. She glimpsed an expression of intense calculation, quickly smoothed away. He leaned forward.

"Tell me about Tom."

Annie tried to sketch Tom's character without sounding too much like a proud mother. She told Jordan about Tom's determination to go to Oxford—how he had failed the entrance examinations once and had the grit to wait a year and try again. Jordan prompted her with typically male questions that made her smile inwardly. Was Tom good at sports? Did he have a girlfriend? What had he thought of the former Soviet bloc? Jordan seemed fascinated by her answers. Annie remembered the speculation that he and his wife had been unable to have children, and wondered.

"He sounds like a great kid." Jordan sighed wistfully. "But, Jesus, Annie, pregnant at nineteen! I wish I could have done something."

"Well, you did, you know." She smiled. "I admit it wasn't all that easy at the beginning. I had no money, a tiny baby, and a grim little flat—just a couple of rooms, really, with a stove on the landing and a shared bathroom two flights down. I was working in the day and studying at night to *try* to complete my degree at London University. But I had one marvelous, liberating luxury." She cocked her head at Jordan. "Your car. Remember?"

Jordan nodded slowly. The memory of their parting outside LMH rose between them. For a moment, Annie forgot what she was saying. Then she continued.

"Every Sunday I used to put his baby bed in the backseat and drive out to Richmond Park or into the country. I'd park Tom on a blanket and lie in the grass reading the Sunday papers. I can't tell you what it meant to me. It was the best part of my week. Even now, when I look at the car, I often remember those times."

"You mean you still have it?"

"Tom has it. I gave it to him as a present to take to Oxford."

"No kidding!" Jordan laughed incredulously, shaking his head. He leaned back against the sofa, visibly relaxing. "It's so peaceful here," he said, clasping his hands behind his head and stretching out his legs with the easy physical charm that seemed the birthright of every American male. "I don't know when I was last away from people and telephones and newspapers."

"How did you get away tonight?"

"I went to play cards with the Secret Service men. I do that sometimes, when I need to wind down. Usually they come to my suite, but tonight they were having a Halloween party. I played a few hands and then said I was going to bed. Then I kind of snuck out. They were having too good a time to notice much. I stole one of their masks and pulled a hat over my head. Even my mother wouldn't have recognized me."

"What's it like, campaigning? I can't imagine it."

Jordan tilted back his head and laughed. "Like riding the Coney Island Cyclone. Unpredictable. Exhilarating. Scary. Funny too sometimes."

"Why funny?"

"Oh . . . people—what they want, the things they say. The other day I was in New Jersey someplace, taking questions from the floor, and this elderly woman asks me about health care. She's kind of specific and this is a speech, so I just answer in general terms. But I say, why doesn't she come up and talk to me afterward? So up she comes, a nice little old lady all dressed up, with her friend egging her on. 'Go on, go on. He won't bite.' Anyway, I listen to her problems and I try to answer her concerns; then I have to shake her hand and leave. But just as I'm going, I hear her turn to her friend. 'What a mensch,' she says. 'He shows more interest than my son. Are you sure he isn't Jewish?' "

Annie laughed with him. "You love it, don't you?"

"I guess I do. Sometimes it's like winning the Super Bowl and opening on Broadway and having sex all at the same time."

He turned his head to look at her. "But you know something about that. It's not so different from acting." His warm gaze slid over her. "I remember you in that play in the garden, wearing those great boots."

Annie shifted. "That was a long time ago."

"Was it?" Jordan's eyes lingered. "You look the same. I'm glad you kept your hair long. I've thought about you so many times."

"Me too," Annie said softly.

The silence lengthened as they stared into each other's eyes.

Jordan put out his hand to her. "Annie," he said gently, "tell me the truth. Tom is my son, isn't he?"

"I don't know." Annie could feel her face betray her.

Jordan sat up. "But you think he's mine." He leaned toward her, searching her face.

Annie suddenly felt breathless. She stood up and moved toward the minibar. "Do you want another drink?"

Jordan followed her.

"You think he's mine," he repeated exultantly. He grabbed her hand and pulled her around to face him. "Don't you?"

Annie had forgotten how big he was. Her mouth was level with the triangle of flesh at his open shirt collar. She could see the rise and fall of his chest as he breathed. She looked away.

"Maybe." Annie tugged her hand free. "I've said all I know for certain. Tom could be your son. He could be Edward's. If . . . if I've sometimes thought he was yours, it's only because we were so— because it was so—" She cleared her throat. "I mean, you may not remember—"

"Remember?" Jordan clutched her shoulders. "Are you kiddling?" he asked hoarsely. "The river and the willow trees? And your face when we said good-bye? You never even wrote back to me!"

"I couldn't! I wasn't even at Oxford anymore. The college only had a temporary address that summer; afterward they didn't know where I was." Annie twisted away, pushing back the hair from her face. "Anyway, what would have been the point? What could I have said? 'I'm having your baby'?"

The silence vibrated between them. Jordan's face softened into a slow, intimate smile that made Annie's heart turn over.

"Maybe, huh?" he said teasingly, his eyes flickering up and down her body. "Maybe you and I made a baby." He took a step toward her. "Is that a definite maybe? . . . Or a maybe maybe?" Another step. "Or an 'I hope so' maybe?"

Annie backed away. She could feel herself flushing. She shouldn't have drunk that whiskey. She couldn't think properly. She wished she'd left more lights on. Suddenly the wall was at her back. Jordan stepped close. Slowly, seductively, he rested his hands on the wall on either side of her head, imprisoning her. He leaned over her, rocking gently, smiling his lazy smile. His breath was warm on her cheeks. Annie could smell his sweat.

"Stop it, Jordan," she said.

"You stop it," he whispered, and bent his head to kiss her.

Annie opened her mouth to protest and instead drew his warm tongue inside her. Sensation detonated through her body, leaping from one nerve ending to the next. Every thought evaporated except how good he felt—his thighs hard against hers, the breadth of his back warm under her hands, his tongue sliding and tugging and coiling, heating her up like a furnace. Jordan swept back her hair with both hands, tilting her head, pulling her to him. He kissed her eyes, her cheeks. He licked the corners of her mouth and ran his tongue wantonly around and around her lips until she had to reach up and plunge her fingers into his hair to draw him back to her.

You shouldn't be doing this, nagged a distant voice. But her hunger for him left no room for pretense or withdrawal. *Just once,* she pleaded. She slid her hands around to the back of Jordan's neck, feeling his warm, soft skin and the taut muscles beneath. She pulled out the tail of his shirt from his trousers so that she could slip her hands up his bare back and over his ribs. When she let him step away, it was only so that he could lay her down on the bed.

His weight came down on her. Annie closed her eyes, stretching herself out for his pleasure. He was kissing her throat, her ears, the tender spots behind her earlobes. She could feel his hair brush across her cheek. His breath on her neck spread ripples of excitement down her body. Jordan drew back his head, his expression dreamy and absorbed. Their eyes locked as he undid her dress and spread it open. His hand slid down to her breast. Her skin was damp with sweat. She felt him scoop the fullness of her breast into his palm and roll the ball of his thumb over her nipple.

There were too many clothes, Annie raged, craving the feeling of his flesh against hers. All these hooks and buttons and belts. She clawed at Jordan's collar and forced his shirt off one shoulder so that she could rub her teeth across his skin. Jordan lowered his head and lazily ran his tongue down the groove of her rib cage. Annie arched her back and moaned. She felt him licking her navel until it was too tantalizing to bear. Reaching down, she flipped the tongue of his belt out of the buckle.

When the telephone rang, they both yelled with fury, then fell into a panic-stricken silence. They could hear themselves panting. Jordan bowed his head agonizingly onto Annie's breasts. His eyes squeezed tight with frustration.

"*Shit.*"

The telephone went on ringing. Annie suddenly remembered who they were and where they were and all the reasons she must— *must!*—answer it. She rolled Jordan aside and clambered over him, trailing her dress from one bare arm. Her hand nudged the bedside table and set it rocking. She could hear the thump of her handbag falling to the floor and the rattle of its contents spilling across the carpet. Trying to concentrate, she huddled on the edge of the bed with her back to Jordan and steadied her feet on the carpet. She picked up the receiver and took a deep, calming breath.

"Annie Hamilton. Hello?"

"Annie, my darling girl, what grand news!" boomed a voice. "You should have taken the plunge years ago, didn't I always say so? Of course you must represent my work. You wouldn't leave me with Harry Robertson's mimsy milksop of a son, would you now?"

Annie breathed out a shiver of silent laughter. Trelawny Grey, sounding more faux-Irish than ever. How utterly typical of him to have no concept of transatlantic time changes! It was one of his famous eccentricities that he never ventured beyond the borders of civilized Europe. She pictured him in his half-paneled Georgian study, slippered feet to the fire and a cat on his knee. It would be breakfast time in County Tipperary.

"I had your letter yesterday," Trelawny was saying, "but I've been up to Naas for the November Handicap. I knew it was a sign when Robertson's Lad was pulled up at the five-furlong post."

While she listened to him rattle on, Annie fished behind her for the other sleeve of her dress. She felt Jordan slide it over her shoulder, then the brief pressure of his hand laid gently on the back of her head. The mattress bounced as he got off the bed. She could hear him putting things back into her bag. She did not look around.

While she drew her dress around her, the significance of Trelawny's phone call trickled into her brain. He had gotten her letter. He wanted her to be his literary agent.

"I'm honored, Trelawny—and very grateful. I intend to make a great deal of money for you. But I should warn you, Jack may take it hard."

Trelawny Grey made a rude noise down the phone. "One tiny fart out of that pipsqueak, and I'll put him in my book. I've got as far as '36, the year his father and I went up to Univ together. Harry Robertson nearly got sent down, you know, for painting a fig leaf on the Shelley Memorial."

Annie struggled to make sense of this. "Do you mean to say that you're actually writing your memoirs at last?"

"Most enjoyable thing I've ever done, my dear. It's funny the things you remember. Did I ever tell you the story of Willie Maugham and the oysters, the time he took a fancy to a waiter on the Blue Train?"

"No, Trelawny," Annie said slowly, fastening her buttons. "I don't think you ever did."

By the time he had regaled her with several more anecdotes and was winding up to his last round of good-byes, several things had become clear to Annie. First, Trelawny Grey's book would need the best libel reading that money could buy. Second, it was going to sell faster than any cakes, hot or otherwise, in the history of the world. Third, her percentage of the advance, as Trelawny's agent, would keep her new business going for at least a year. Fourth and last, she was not going to make love with Jordan.

While she laughed aloud at Trelawny's stories, even while she coolly assessed the likelihood of his book being ready for publication next Christmas, Annie remained acutely aware of Jordan's presence in the room, of his eyes on her back. After Trelawny had hung up, she held the receiver to her ear for a few more moments, taking time to collect herself. Then she replaced the receiver carefully and stood up, adjusting her dress to cover her stockinged legs. She turned to face Jordan. He was sitting on the couch, shirt tucked in, hair smoothed, watching her.

She managed a shaky laugh. " 'Fate keeps on happening.' Isn't that what the girl says in *Gentlemen Prefer Blondes*?" She located her shoes and stepped into them. "Honestly, Jordan, we must be mad. What came over us?"

Jordan waggled his eyebrows. "Sex?" he hazarded.

Annie saw that he had her bag next to him. He took something out and held it up like Exhibit A. With anguished embarrassment Annie recognized the package of condoms she had bought in the hotel lobby. Jordan was smiling wickedly, holding her gaze. He put the condoms down on the couch, then drew something out of his trouser pocket. "Snap!" he said, placing an identical package on top of hers.

Their eyes met in a long, rueful look. Then Jordan swept up the incriminating evidence and patted the seat beside him.

"Come over here, superwoman, and tell me about this scheme you're cooking up. Was that really *the* Trelawny Grey you were talking to?"

Annie sat down—not too close—and told him how she had decided to start her own agency. She allowed Jordan to draw her out on the details of the business—copyright, subagents, percentages. They both knew that what they were really trying to do was to turn down the heat that still simmered between them. And it worked. Annie's mind started racing ahead to the big auction that awaited her in New York. Jordan slipped into his professional role as listener.

"Go for it," he said with that infectious American enthusiasm. "I believe you can do anything you set your heart on."

Annie shook her head, recalling his own, infinitely grander ambitions. "It all sounds so trivial compared to your job."

"If I win."

"Oh, you'll win. You have winner written all over you. I think that's what confused me back in Oxford. Everyone likes a winner, but not necessarily to live with all the time. Just in the last couple of days I've realized something about myself. *I* like to win too sometimes."

"You sound just like Ginny." Jordan sighed and rubbed a hand over his face as if trying to soothe an ache. "She's helped me so much to get this far. We both know I'd never have gotten close without her. But right at the most important moment I have to cut her out of the limelight. I'm not even supposed to mention her anymore in case it loses me votes. I feel bad about that."

"So you should," Annie said tartly. "Advisors aren't always right, you know. If you're going to be a good president, you'll have to follow your own instincts sometimes, no matter what anybody else says. Don't you think you owe it to her to acknowledge her help?"

"But how?" Jordan looked troubled. "Every time I say how much I depend on her intelligence and her moral judgment, people think I'm going to let her run the country."

Annie clicked her tongue in exasperation. "Well, no wonder they're worried. They don't want to rely on her moral judgment. It's not her they're electing. The point is what *you* think of her."

Jordan considered this. "But what could I say?"

"Speak from your heart. Just say you love her, that you're proud of her. There's no need to go into detail."

" 'Never apologize, never explain'?"

"Exactly."

"Speak from the heart," Jordan repeated thoughtfully. "Yeah, I like that." He nodded. "I can do that." He leaned back against the arm of the couch and gave her a look that made her toes tingle. "You know, you really are something."

Annie smiled into his eyes. "I know."

She saw his face tighten hungrily. It was time to break the spell.

"Jordan, shouldn't you be getting back?"

Jordan looked at his watch. "Jesus, five o'clock!" He leaped to his feet. "The morning editions will be out. I want to catch the news on TV."

Annie followed as he crossed the room to pick up his coat. Thrusting one arm into the sleeve, Jordan looked down and fingered his shirt. He shot Annie a sly look. "Uh-oh, I've lost a button. Now how in the world did that happen?"

Annie blushed.

"What do you think of my disguise?" he asked, pulling a Halloween mask from his pocket.

Seeing what it was, Annie burst out laughing.

"Yeah, yeah, I know." Jordan grinned. "Let me tell you, Annie, Secret Service men are not subtle people. This is their idea of a joke—a Halloween party where everyone comes dressed as a president."

"You might at least have chosen Abraham Lincoln or Franklin Roosevelt." Annie put the mask to her face, intoning, " 'There can be no whitewash at the White House.' "

"Hey, give me that." Jordan snatched it back and looped the elastic over his wrist. "I just picked up the first one that came to hand. At least it got me here. Let's hope it works for the return trip. And don't worry, I'll put it on in the hall."

He stooped over the desk to scribble something on a piece of hotel stationery. "Here's where you can reach me if Tom shows up. If you don't get me, leave a message—something like 'Annie says everything's okay.' If he contacts me, of course I'll let you know. Meanwhile, let's try not to worry," he said, catching her anxious look. "He sounds like a smart boy."

Suddenly Annie remembered something. "Wait!"

She went over to the bedside table and drew out the photograph of Tom that she had saved for Jordan. She had picked it out at random, she imagined. Now she admitted to herself that she had chosen it because in this particular photograph, above all others, Tom looked like Jordan. Holding the photograph so Jordan couldn't see it, she lifted the flap of his coat pocket and slid it in.

"What—?"

"A present. A good-luck charm. Look at it later, when you're by yourself."

Jordan pressed his hand tenderly to his pocket, speculation leaping in his eyes.

"I'd like to meet him one day," he said seriously. "Of course I'd never say anything to him. I have too much to lose. But it would mean a lot to me." Jordan beat his fist against the other palm as if trying to express the depth of his feeling. "I sure would love to see him."

"I know. I'll think about it."

She watched him finish buttoning his coat. There was nothing to keep him now.

Jordan set his hands lightly on her shoulders. "Well, Annie, I guess this is it."

She nodded. She looked up into his face—his mouth, his eyes, the crisp wave of his hair above his ears, memorizing his features. His eyes told her all that she had longed to know for twenty-two years.

Jordan bent forward gravely.

"This is for my son." He kissed her cheek.

"And this is for you." He kissed the other cheek.

"And this is for me."

The touch of his lips on her mouth came without warning. Annie rocked back on her heels for an instant, feeling his grip tighten. Her eyelids flickered. Then Jordan released her and slipped into the corridor. The door clicked shut behind him.

Annie stood with her fingers held to her lips as if they burned. She couldn't even hear his footfall.

34

Sweet-talking Guy

"Rose? It's Rick. What the fuck is going on?"
    "You tell me."
    "Quit jerking me around! This is serious."
    "What exactly?"
    "At 5 A.M. this morning, the Secret Service guys called to tell me they'd 'lost' Jordan."
    "Careless."
    "He turned up. Said he'd been for a walk."
    "Hmm. Original."
    "Why do I get the feeling that this has to do with your friend 'Annie,' who wanted to talk to Jordan so badly?"
    "Pass."
    "And what about the English boy, Annie's son? He was in your apartment yesterday. What have you done with him?"
    "Darling, what an indelicate question!"
    "I thought you were on our side, Rose. I cannot have my candidate going AWOL. You want him to win. So what's going on? Who is Annie? I need to know."
    "Annie is my friend."
    "Oh, please. People like us, we have contacts, we pull strings, we do deals. We don't have friends."
    "Isn't Jordan your friend?"
    "Yes he is! And that's why I hope you're not about to run some scummy story. No one wants to hear any more scandal. I would really, really hate to see anyone as smart and talented as you just

pull the plug on your career. That's what would happen, believe me."

"So what's the deal?"

"I'm not asking you to betray any confidences. Just tell me Annie's last name. Whisper it. I can do the rest."

"How grateful would you be?"

"Very, very grateful. Humble. Positively prostrate."

"And what's in it for you? Your choice of desks at the White House?"

"Rose, you shock me."

"That's a first. Tell you what, I'll think about it."

"Think fast. We're running out of time. Two more days."

"You always were a bit of a Speedy Gonzalez, weren't you, darling? Personally, I like to take my time. Good-bye, Rick."

"Rose—?"

35

Good Vibrations

Annie's first inkling of disaster was an early telephone call to her room at the Algonquin Hotel. She had just returned from breakfast in the dining room downstairs, galvanized by the sight of immaculately dressed New Yorkers doing business at seven o'clock on a Monday morning. She had a good feeling about the Sebastian Winter auction. On her arrival from Chicago yesterday afternoon there had been a pile of faxes and messages waiting for her. Although the deadline wasn't until midday today, she already had notes from several publishers announcing their enthusiasm and their intention to bid. When the telephone rang, Annie picked up the receiver with a buoyant heart. "Annie Hamilton?"

"Well, hello, Annie Hamilton. And who's been a bad girl?" Annie immediately recognized the sardonic, Martini-rich voice of Peggy Rostoff, one of a dwindling breed of red-blooded female editors who still smoked and drank and knew the difference between "lie" and "lay." Peggy was also a world-class gossip.

Annie's heart went cold. This was it. The story of her romance with Jordan had finally broken. Someone had gotten hold of Tom. Her Chicago room had been bugged. She glanced wildly at the television, cursing herself for not having watched the morning news.

"Don't say that, Peggy," she pleaded. "I wouldn't call it exactly bad."

"Jack seems to think so."

"Jack?"

Peggy clicked her tongue reproachfully. "I know they say publishing is just a crazy game of musical chairs these days, but don't tell me you've forgotten your old boss already."

"No, of course not," Annie replied, flustered. "But what's Jack got to do with it?"

"Everything, I'd say, judging from this piece of toilet paper he sent me. He sounds pretty pissed at the way you've snatched Sebastian Winter from under his nose and given him the finger at the same time. Quoting at random from his fax: 'deep personal disappointment . . . irreconcilable conflict of interest . . . regrettable lapse of professional integrity.' Gee, I wonder which thesaurus he uses."

"His wife's probably," Annie muttered, her thoughts spinning. What had gone wrong? Jack was not supposed to have read her letter until tomorrow. And he would never have reacted in this aggressive way on his own initiative. Smothering panic, she forced her brain to work.

"Who else has received this fax, do you think?" she asked.

"Everyone who's considering the Winter books, I guess. You probably gave Jack a submission list, you upright little soul."

Annie groaned. "Peggy, I'm really sorry that you should have been troubled by this misunderstanding. Circumstances forced me to take a quick decision, and with Winter's books already under submission I just had to jump."

"Don't apologize to me, sweetie. I think it's great that you're setting up your own business. No one in this city gives a damn about Jack Robertson anyway. Right now all they care about is buying Sebastian Winter." She paused. "Winter really *is* your client, is he?"

"He most certainly is. If anyone doubts it they can phone him themselves. And he's by no means the only one," Annie added with bravado. Everyone in publishing respected Peggy. It would make a difference if she put out the word that Annie Hamilton was okay. "Several of the writers I've handled will be joining my new agency."

"Good for you . . . Such as?"

Annie played her ace. "Trelawny Grey, for starters. I'll be selling his autobiography next year."

"Nice work!" Peggy was impressed. "Listen, I'll get back to you with our bid, once I've had it signed in triplicate by the head honcho—you know how it is these days."

Annie put down the receiver with a shaky sigh. At once the phone trilled again under her hand. It was a reporter for *Publishers Weekly*. Would Annie care to comment on a press release received from

Smith & Robertson that morning? For a moment Annie was struck dumb.

"I'm in midauction at the moment," she rallied, summoning her most businesslike tone. "But I'd be happy to ring you back this afternoon and give you an interview about my new agency. You can have the scoop on who's bought Sebastian Winter too."

She hung up, feeling under siege. What had she done to deserve this torrent of nasty surprises? She had a mental picture of two devils propping up a bar in hell, beer cans in hand. "I'm bored," one was saying. "Me too," said the other. "Let's persecute Annie Hamilton."

She wondered where Tom was now. A week of silence: It seemed like months. This must be her punishment for seeing Jordan. Remembering the way she had practically flung herself into bed with him, Annie's cheeks flamed. She forced herself to banish the images that crowded her mind and to concentrate on the job in hand. She had failed as a mother, failed as a daughter, failed as a loyal wife. She could not allow herself to fail in her career too. Now, where was her daily planner?

The phone rang again. "Hello, it's me. How did the reunion go?"

Annie rolled her eyes. This was all she needed.

"Rose, do you mind if we talk later? My big auction has just blown up in my face, and I'm desperately trying to salvage the wreckage."

"Okay." Rose sounded hurt. "I just wanted to tell you—"

"Not now, Rose, please. I need to keep the line clear. I'll see you at lunch. Bye." Annie put down the phone, exasperated. How many times had Rose put Annie on hold or relayed a message through some secretary? Now that Annie was trying to launch her own career, all Rose was interested in was tittle-tattle. Sometimes Annie wondered whether Rose had a sensitive nerve in her body. Then she remembered the champagne that had been awaiting her at the Algonquin—without a card, but a typical Rose gesture—and felt a guilty pang.

She put Rose out of her mind, took a clean sheet of paper from the desk, and wrote herself a nice, neat list of things to do. First she telephoned Sebastian. He could not hide his disappointment that she had not already concluded a megadeal for him but rallied once she had explained the problem. As a former journalist, he adored emergencies. He promised to stand by for calls from doubting publishers, sounding positively excited by the prospect. Next she called every publisher on her list, reassuring them that Winter had now become her client and she was therefore empowered to act on his behalf, and apologizing for any confusion. The reaction was more curious than condemnatory; a couple of people even volunteered indiscreet anecdotes about Jack's judgment. Annie started to feel only 95 percent suicidal.

Now there was nothing to do but wait. Annie paced the small hotel room, biting her nails and staring out the window until she had memorized every rust spot on the water tank of the next-door building. She rechecked her notes on royalties and paperback splits and payment stages. Haunted by all the things that could go wrong, she prepared defensive strategies. At eleven o'clock she got her first serious call. The editor loved the book, he adored it, he would kill to have Winter on his list. But his paperback colleagues would not support his bid, the illiterate skunks. Regretfully, he was out. Annie commiserated and thanked him politely for his response, feeling the San Andreas Fault quiver beneath her brilliant career. The phone rang again: another publisher. The editor loved the book, he adored it, he would kill to have it—and he was offering $500,000. Annie leapt for her pen.

By the time the noon deadline expired, six more offers had come in and the bid had soared to three-quarters of a million. Annie called everyone back to tell them the figure they now had to beat, then phoned Sebastian to give him a progress report.

"Jesus!" His laugh was squeaky with hysteria.

"And that's only the first round. With so many publishers bidding, you'll probably be a millionaire by this afternoon."

There was a long ruminative pause. "I was looking at a sports car yesterday—you know, that new four-seater with the great big—"

"Buy it," Annie said crisply.

Interestingly, not a single publisher had called Sebastian. So far her reputation had carried the day. Annie thought she would have quite a lot to say to Jack when the time came. But now she deserved a treat: lunch.

The Royalton was staffed by the handsomest young men Annie had ever seen, coiffed to perfection. Loose, high-collared jackets gave them a look of Asian houseboys. Their smiles were pure Hollywood. "Hi, I'm Scott," said one, in such a friendly way that Annie felt bound to tell him her name too.

"I'm meeting a friend for lunch," she confided, "but she doesn't seem to be here yet."

Annie found herself expertly whisked into a quiet corner from which she could observe the power lunch in action. She had heard about the Royalton's transformation from poor-man's Algonquin to chic media hangout but had never ventured inside its almost masonically discreet entrance. Its waterfalls and Philippe Starck styling proclaimed a quiet, studied arrogance. At one table an Australian talk-show star was being interviewed on camera, winking his famous raisin-bun eyes. At another she recognized the diminutive media tycoon who owned the publishing house that had offered the highest bid for Sebastian. He was fiddling nervously with his glass of water, avoiding eye contact with his sober-suited lunch partner: not his banker, Annie hoped.

Ten minutes later she was beginning to get angry. She had told Rose that she wouldn't have much time. Rose herself had suggested this place because it was right across the street from the Algonquin. Annie walked over to Scott and asked if there had been any message. The second she mentioned Rose's name, the maître d' went into overdrive. Apologizing profusely, he swept Annie to a prominent table and begged for the privilege of bringing her a complimentary beverage. Torn between amusement and irritation at this charade, Annie agreed to a Virgin Mary. Now, of course, the whole restaurant was staring at her, wondering who she could be to command such deference. Annie lifted her chin and stared haughtily into the middle distance, trying to project the image of a fabulously exclusive literary agent accustomed to million-dollar deals. Oh, yes, sneered an inner voice, so exclusive that you have only two clients.

At last Rose breezed in, wearing a drop-dead gray silk suit with white facings. She waved gaily to Annie and came over, though not before pausing to share a little joke with Scott and then to shake hands with the minimogul. She pressed her cheek to Annie's, enveloping her in a cloud of perfume.

"Sorry to be late, I got stuck haggling with some unspeakable Hollywood agent over a cover photograph. Classic tinseltown machismo—don't you just hate it? How are you? You look divine."

"Fine." Annie smiled, feeling overwhelmed. It was always the same when they met after a long separation. "At least, I've had a horrible morning but I think I've salvaged the situation. You see, this auction—"

Rose held up a hand. "Sorry to interrupt, I'm dying to hear about your book thingie—and about everything else." She raised her eyebrows meaningfully. "But I have to tell you first: Tom is safe."

Annie stared. The words literally didn't make sense to her. She could think of no means by which Rose could possibly know this. "What do you mean?"

"What I say." Rose smiled triumphantly. "I was dying to tell you on the phone, but you didn't give me a chance. Tom's been here, in New York, staying at my apartment. He was very muddled, poor lamb, but I think I straightened him out. He's given up the, you know, wild goose chase, and I put him on a plane back to England yesterday."

Annie felt her face flush with rage. "Here?" she stammered. "In your . . . ? You knew where he was?" She half rose from her seat. Tears of relief and shock sprang to her eyes. "Why didn't you tell me?"

"I am telling you. Calm down, Annie. If you'd just listen, you'd understand that I've done you a favor."

"Favor! You call it a favor not to let me know that my son isn't lost or dead or—" Annie shook her head. Her throat was so tight she couldn't get out the words.

"Don't be upset," Rose said coaxingly. "Of course I realized how worried you were, but you didn't see what Tom was like when he turned up. Honestly, Annie, hand on heart, I know I made the right decision."

"Do you?" Annie flung her napkin onto the table. "You may be god in your own office, Rose, or in your precious magazine world, but you do not control my personal life. Tom is *my* son." She stabbed her chest with her finger. "If you want to play around with someone's family, get your own." Annie's voice rose aggressively. As she became aware of the eyes riveted to their table, her fury deepened. "And how could you possibly think it appropriate to tell me about Tom in this idiotic, self-regarding goldfish bowl, I don't know. It isn't the kind of news you just drop into the conversation over the beef *carpaccio*." Annie scraped her chair back and stood up. The sight of Rose's shuttered face made her say more calmly, "I'm sorry, but I'm too angry to stay. I'll call you later."

Annie strode out of the restaurant, stiff with emotion. One of the beautiful young men leaped to open the door. "Have a nice day," he chanted.

She ran across the street, oblivious to honking horns, avoiding the cars by instinct. When she reached her room, a winking light on the telephone indicated a message. Ignoring it, she dialed Edward, praying that he would be home from work. She almost burst into tears when she heard his voice, stumbling over her words as she told him the good news.

"Oh, good, you've seen Rose, then," he said in a matter-of-fact way. "Isn't it a relief? I slept properly last night for the first time in a week."

Annie gasped. "You mean you *knew*?"

"Rose phoned yesterday morning to say that Tom had turned up at her place. Darling, I was desperate to tell you, but Rose persuaded me to wait."

"But surely—"

"You know what I think about Rose's high-handed ways, but this time I think she is on the side of the angels. Apparently Tom has abandoned this Jordan Hope nonsense and is ready to go back to Oxford. We'll have to come clean with him about why we weren't married when he was born and all that—but it's high time, don't you think?"

Annie listened to his reasonable voice, wondering if she were on a different planet.

"It seemed the right decision to wait until Tom had left New York," he went on. "I thought you had enough to deal with, what with your mother and starting the new business and the book auction. Besides—" He hesitated.

"You didn't trust me!" Annie burst out. "You thought I'd throw a fit, act like a hysterical woman. Didn't you?"

"I hope we'll always trust each other," Edward answered after a cool pause. "And, yes, I thought it might be best to get Tom safely home, on familiar territory, before you two saw each other again. You've both been so wound up, I didn't want one of you to say something you didn't mean and spark the whole thing off again."

"Well, thanks for the vote of confidence," Annie spat sarcastically. She felt patronized beyond enduring. "Tom is *my* son, don't forget. I looked after him on my own for nearly three whole years before you even knew he existed."

The minute the words were out, Annie regretted them. But it was too late. Edward's voice came evenly down the line. "Tom is *our* son. You know that's the way I have always thought of him. And I always will. You're going to have to sort yourself out, Annie—decide what you want, and what you're going to tell Tom. I'll see you tomorrow."

There was a click, then the dial tone. He had hung up on her!

Annie was aghast. Edward had never done such a thing before. She had hurt him horribly. He had sounded so distant, as if her life were not bound inextricably and forever with his. It seemed that this whole trip—Rose's so-called master plan, which was supposed to straighten out her life—had only enmeshed her deeper in lies.

Annie tried to calm herself. At least Tom was safe. She must let Jordan know. Quickly Annie found her bag and drew out the piece of paper on which Jordan had written the phone number where he could be reached. She smoothed it out gently and dialed, telling herself that he could not possibly be available to answer it. Nevertheless, she was unreasonably disappointed when she had to leave her cryptic message. She would have liked to speak to him one more time, to wish him luck.

The light was still winking on the telephone. The message was to call back a publisher. Annie tapped in the number, her mind elsewhere. A gravelly voice growled in her ear. Suddenly her brain snapped into action. He was offering her a million dollars. After that, the phone hardly stopped ringing. No auction in her experience had ever gone at such a roller-coaster pace. Eventually it dawned on her that Jack's petulant attempt at sabotage had produced the opposite effect of what he intended. This was New York. "Buzz" was everything. The thrilling story of Annie's dramatic breakout from Smith & Robertson, Sebastian Winter's defection, and Jack's vengefulness constituted the perfect antidote to post-Frankfurt blues. By four-thirty the bidding had risen to $1.7 million and there were two bidders left, neither showing signs of slacking. Annie was in mid-phone call when she heard a knock at her door. She flung it open, expecting to shoo away an overzealous maid. There was Rose, offering an appeasing smile and a bottle of champagne.

Annie signaled her in. "I'm sorry, Elaine," she continued into the phone, "but if your offer is to be truly comparable with the others I have on the table, you're going to have to put more up front. Let's go through the payment stages again."

Rose tiptoed across the room and sat in a chair out of the way while Annie shuttled back and forth between the two remaining publishers, ratcheting up the advance each time. Annie maintained her icy control until one of them finally conceded. The deal was done.

Only then did Annie let out a whoop of triumph. "Two *million*!"

Rose came over and hugged her. "Well done. I had no idea you could be such a toughie. I'm impressed."

"Don't be impressed—open the champagne!" Annie shouted hysterically. She threw herself backward across the bed, arms outflung, beaming at the ceiling. Then she remembered. "Christ! I'd better tell the poor author."

Sebastian answered at the first ring. The news left him dazed. "I suppose I'll have to write that second book now," he said rather forlornly.

Next was Jack.

"Two million?"

"Don't worry. You'll get your fair share. You can get Julia to ring me about the contracts tomorrow." Annie paused. In the background she could hear the ten o'clock news. How could he just be watching TV, his conscience untroubled? "Why did you do it, Jack?"

"I—I thought you were behaving unprofessionally."

"No, *you* behaved unprofessionally, treating me as you did, forcing me to go behind your back. I hated it. Your father never—"

"My father's dead! I don't know what there was between you, or who is the father of your bastard son, but it's past history now. You have no claims on me or my business."

Annie caught her breath. So that's what it had all been about. Listening to his shrill, little-boy voice, she was surprised by sudden pity.

"Listen, Jack. Your father and I were friends—good friends. But I did not have an affair with him, and Tom is certainly not his son, if that's what you're worrying about. Tom was at least a year old when I came to work for him. And yes"—she gathered her strength to say the word—"Tom is illegitimate. He knows it. I don't see that it's anyone else's business."

Jack had the grace to sound ashamed. "I didn't really think—it's only, Janie said—" He stopped unhappily.

Annie's mouth tightened. Trust Jack's wife to judge other people by her own standards. She wondered if Jack knew that Jane had been nicknamed La Couchette after her practice of speeding to promotion on her back. Her spurt of sympathy subsided. She hung up the phone, thinking that the pair of them deserved each other.

Rose handed her a glass. "This is better than the movies," she said. "Who's next?"

Sprawled among the pillows, sipping champagne, Annie called back *Publishers Weekly* and gave them a string of hugely optimistic half-truths about her agency. They made her promise to messenger over a photograph of herself so that they could run a feature in the next issue. Annie put down the phone, extremely pleased with herself, and raised her glass to Rose.

"This is very nice of you. I haven't had a chance to drink the other one yet."

"What other one?"

"There was a bottle of champagne waiting when I arrived here. I assumed it was from you." A wild alternative seized her.

"Perhaps it was from Someone Else." Rose raised her eyebrows insinuatingly as she took off her suit jacket and hung it carefully over the back of a chair. Underneath she was wearing a skimpy silk top with spaghetti straps.

Annie frowned as she watched her climb onto the foot of the bed. "Why don't your arms wobble like mine?"

"Because I spend several hours a week and a fortune on a personal trainer to ensure they don't. You have a husband and a family; I have a perfectly toned body: the modern woman's dilemma in a nutshell. And stop changing the subject." Rose bounced gently on the bed, eyes sparkling. "I'm dying to know: Did Jordan make the meeting?"

Annie nodded. "He came to my hotel room."

"No!" Rose clasped her hands with excitement. "How did he manage it?"

"Oh . . . you know."

"No, I don't know, Annie. Come on, just a few teensy crumbs."

"Well, he came late, about two. We talked about Tom."

"Uh-huh." Rose nodded encouragingly.

"I told him I couldn't swear Tom was his, but he seemed to like the idea."

"Uh-huh."

"And he told me a bit about his wife."

"Uh-huh."

"And I told him about my job."

"Uh-huh."

"And, well, then he went back to his hotel."

"And what time was that?"

"Oh, fiveish." Annie shrugged.

Rose reached to the floor for the champagne bottle and filled Annie's glass, then her own. She gave Annie an appraising look. "Let me get this straight. You talked about Tom and Ginny and your job *for three hours?*"

"Yes. No. Sort of. It took a while to get used to each other again. I hadn't seen him for twenty-odd years. I thought he'd probably completely forgotten about me."

"But of course he hadn't."

"No," Annie said, remembering. She caught her friend's sly glance. "Oh, Rose, I know you always thought he was just a crude Yankee Doodle Dandy who wouldn't know the difference between a—a crouton and a futon. But, well, there's something about him." She started to smile, thinking of the feel of his big shoulders and that look he had, as if inviting the whole world to fall in love with him. Rose arched her eyebrows knowingly as Annie fumbled for the right words. "He is sort of attractive, in his way. I always . . . I mean, he always—" Annie hid her telltale face in her hands.

"Annie," whispered Rose in an awed voice. "You're not going to tell me that you actually fucked the next fucking president of the U.S. of A.?"

"Of course not!" Annie looked up and gave a little giggle. "Although we—" She sank back into the pillows and started to laugh. Egged on by Rose, her tongue loosened by champagne, Annie blushingly gave her an edited version of events leading up to the timely phone call from Trelawny Grey. By the time she had got to Trelawny's anecdote about the exceptionally hairy publishing grandee, whose nude sunbathing at Cap Ferrat had given rise to a local rumor of an escaped baboon, they were both rolling on the bed. Annie left out the bit about the condoms: best not to put too much temptation in Rose's way.

Rose wiped her eyes. "God, Annie, I have to hand it to you. Here I am thinking I'm the center of the bloody universe, when it's you that waltzes off into some loony escapade like this. I like to think

of you doing reassuring things like tidying the linen closet or entering the mothers' race on Sports Day."

It was an apology of sorts. Annie looked at her friend with affection. "I'm sorry about lunch," she offered. "Edward says you
made the right decision about Tom. It was just such a shock."

"Don't worry." Rose waved a hand. "I'll pay for my lapse of
tact. By tonight the news will be all over town that I've had a quarrel
with my hitherto unsuspected lesbian lover. Incidentally, when did
you say your plane left?"

Annie looked at her watch and shrieked. Rose reached for her
cellular phone. "You finish packing. I'll get my car to take you to
the airport. You can drop me on the way."

While they drove uptown, Annie interrogated Rose about Tom,
learning of his search for his birth certificate and his impulsive arrival in New York. He had shown surprising resourcefulness, she
thought, wondering how he had struck Rose.

"So what did you think of Tom?" she fished.

"Adorable—polite, handsome, good company. If I'd known children could turn out like that, I might have had one myself."

"Really?" Rose's long-ago abortion had always remained a taboo
subject between them. Having herself made such a different decision,
Annie had often wondered if Rose felt regrets.

"Sweetheart," Rose chided, "can you really see me with vomit
on my Chanel? Tom is different. He's grown up."

"Has he?" Annie asked dubiously.

"Yes, and at risk of having you jump out of the car, I suggest
that if you treat him like an adult, he'll respond like one."

"Oh," Annie said, surprised.

Everything seemed suddenly to be changing. If Tom was grown
up, what did that make her? With a shock she realized that when
her mother died, she would become the "older" generation. Annie
told Rose about her reconciliation with her mother, sharing her
thoughts.

"At least I don't have to worry about that," Rose said briskly.
"When I'm gone, nothing will remain except a tacky plaque in some
crematorium: 'Rose Cassidy, RIP. Not very nice, but a bloody good
magazine editor.' "

"Rubbish!"

"It's true. You were always the nice one."

"I don't feel very nice," Annie muttered. "I've neglected my mother until she's on her deathbed, gone behind Jack's back, lied to Tom and Edward. I'm not sure they're going to forgive me."

"We all make our choices," Rose said bracingly. "You're going back to a husband who adores you. Jordan and Ginny Hope are off to Washington, God help them. And I"—she gestured as the car drew up in front of her building—"have my fax machine to go home to."

Annie reached over to hug her. "Thanks for everything, Rose. It was a brilliant master plan. If there's anything I can do for you—"

"Well, actually, I was wondering about serial rights in Trelawny Grey's memoirs. They sound very juicy."

Annie laughed. "Don't you ever stop?"

"I hope not." Rose kissed her and climbed out of the car. She ducked her head back in. "Love to Edward." She looked Annie in the eye. "He's been a patient man, you know. Don't blow it."

With that she shut the door and the car took off. Annie twisted round. Through the rear window she could see Rose standing on the sidewalk, a small, solitary figure, watching her go.

Queasily she wondered what Rose had meant. It would be a cruel irony if, in the process of squaring things with Jordan, she had lost Edward.

36

Let's Work Together

*I*t was midnight when Tom drove up the hill toward Hampstead Heath and parked the Morris outside his home. He took his new suitcase of new clothes out of the trunk, locked the car, and stood for a minute breathing in the damp, bonfire-scented English air. It would be Guy Fawkes' Night on Thursday. Remembering that he had been invited to a fireworks party in Oxford, he felt a spark of anticipation.

As he set the suitcase down on the doorstep to search for his house keys, the door opened. His father drew him into the warm, lighted hall with a powerful hug.

"Tom—how marvelous!"

Tom patted his shoulder, feeling awkward. "Didn't Rose tell you I was coming?"

"Yes, but—I thought you'd be here earlier. I must have misunderstood."

This was exceptionally tactful, Tom thought. Usually it was the old line about punctuality being the politeness of kings. "I had to collect the car from Gatwick," he explained. "Seeing I was so near, I decided to drop in on Rebecca. Sorry, I probably should have phoned."

"Probably," his father agreed wryly. He picked up the suitcase and carried it to the foot of the stairs. "What can I get you? Tea, coffee, food? . . . Whiskey?"

"Thanks," Tom yawned, "but all I really want to do is sleep."

"Oh. Of course. Up you go, then." His father hesitated. "I've got to be off early tomorrow, so I probably won't see you. The girls are away for the night. But Annie should be back late tomorrow morning. She's been in New York, you know, and Chicago."

"New York?" Tom's drooping eyelids snapped open. Had his mother been following him? What if she had come to the apartment when he and Rose . . . ? His stomach curdled at the thought. "What's she been doing there?" he asked suspiciously.

"Selling a book. She'll tell you all about it—unless . . . I suppose you wouldn't like to come with me tomorrow? I'm driving up to Nottingham for another session with the UDM—the mineworkers. I'd have to go back to work afterward, but I could drop you at a tube station. You'd be home by mid-afternoon. We could chat in the car."

It was said lightly, but Tom detected an uncharacteristically diffident note. He glanced at his father's face. It looked strained and wary, as if he were uncertain of Tom. "No. You're tired," Edward concluded. He shook his head dismissively. "It's a stupid idea."

Tom gave him a slow smile. "Can I drive the BMW?"

His father's face cleared. "Within the speed limit, yes." He laughed. "And you'll need to wear a suit and tie."

Tom hefted his suitcase. "Suits, we got 'em. I'll tell you all about it tomorrow."

Tom went upstairs, pulled off his clothes, and got straight into his familiar bed without even turning the light on. The sheets felt soft and cool on his bare skin, reminding him of his very satisfactory reunion with Rebecca, to whom he had confessed everything. Well, nearly everything. He would never tell anyone about Rose, or not until he was an old man of forty or so, when life would be so dull that he might have to fall back on his memories. Tom settled his hands behind his head, grinning into the darkness. He had been to bed with two women in two countries in two days—and he didn't even feel guilty! He bet his Oxford roommate Brian had done nothing more exciting than go to the pub. For a while he watched the erratic flash of car headlights across the ceiling, remembering his adventures. Then his thoughts turned to tomorrow and the questions he wanted to ask. But it was late and he was tired. In a few minutes he was asleep.

The next morning it was raining hard. Driving up the crowded motorway was not as much fun as Tom had expected and required all his concentration. His father was still behaving oddly. He seemed reserved to the point of formality and had precluded conversation by studying his papers for the meeting. There had been no recriminations about Tom's disappearance from Oxford, no lecture on irresponsible behavior, no interrogation about what Tom had been doing and why. Tom had expected to have to defend himself; instead, his father had yielded him the ground without a fight. It was worrying.

"So what are we going to do in Nottingham—close down a coal mine?" Tom asked, trying to lighten the atmosphere.

"Hardly," his father answered dryly.

Tom learned that, on the contrary, it was the government that was planning to close several pits unless a private buyout could be negotiated. Tom's father was going up to advise them about their legal position. He talked to Tom about pensions, safety regulations, severance pay. Tom grunted in reply, thinking he was in for a dull morning.

In fact, it was a revelation. If Tom had half envisaged his father, the fancy London barrister, dispensing gobbledygook to a circle of coal-begrimed workers, he quickly discovered his error. For a start, the meeting was intensely emotional. The men were in shock—aggrieved, belligerent, frightened of the future. It was clear that they knew Edward well and looked to him for rescue. Equally clearly, his father felt passionately about their plight. During a coffee break, one man almost broke down as he spoke to Tom of his father's support over the years and how he had put in far more work than he ever charged for. There was no doubt that Edward held the meeting in control. As usual he was immaculate, dark hair swept back, charcoal suit spiced with an eccentric touch: today it was red socks, to match his tie. But he was receptive, sympathetic, anything but patronizing. Tom's concept of the legal profession as a dull, more or less cynical manipulation of statutes and precedents underwent a quiet revolution.

Afterward they lunched companionably in a pub. Over their halves of bitter and microwaved shepherd's pie, Tom began to tell his father about his experiences of Manhattan high life with Rose, making him laugh about her mesmerizing effect on the Barneys salesmen and her bizarre acquaintances at the benefit. They were both marking time, waiting to come to the point. Tom understood that he would have to take the plunge first.

"Did Rose tell you where I was before that—I mean, about going up to Southport to look at my birth certificate?"

"Yes." His father frowned into his beer, then drained the glass. "Come on, we'll talk about that in the car. I'll drive."

It wasn't until they were back on the motorway that he began to speak, with a quiet intensity that gripped Tom from his opening words.

"I loved your mother from the first moment I saw her," Edward began. "I know it's an old family story that we joke about, how I threw her into the river to get her attention. But before I even learned her name I thought: That is the woman for me. It does happen. At times it seemed more like a curse than a blessing. I was younger than you are now. I wanted to have a wild time, see the world, have adventures. I didn't want to settle down. But I wanted Annie.

"When you're young, you tend to grab at things. We'd been going out the whole of my last year at Oxford. When the time came for me to leave, I panicked. She still had another year to go. I was frightened of losing her. Unfortunately, I messed things up, rushing my fences. In fact, I made a fool of myself. I then made things even worse by writing her what I expect was a fearfully stiff-necked note saying I thought it would be better if we didn't see each other for a while. I didn't mean it, of course. It was just hurt pride."

His father broke off. "I'm sorry if this all seems a bit personal, but it is leading somewhere."

"No, go on."

"Well, that was the end of my last term at Oxford. June 1970." He glanced at Tom. "A date you may care to remember. Of course I missed her horribly all summer and wished I had never written that stupid letter. But I had no address for her. I simply had to wait until the new term started. I drove up to LMH the first weekend of the term, only to be told that she had abandoned her studies and left the college for good. I was stunned. I couldn't think what had happened. The college didn't have an address for her and couldn't give me any reason for her leaving."

"Didn't Rose know where she was?"

His father gave a harsh laugh. "She knew, all right, but she wouldn't tell me. Annie didn't want me to know, she said. Rose wouldn't even pass on a letter from me—not even a message. God, I hated her. I accused her of manipulating Annie, poisoning her mind with women's lib rubbish, hiding from me that Annie was ill or dying—everything I could think of. I simply could not believe that the Annie I knew could be so cruel. But you know Rose: She wouldn't budge."

His father fell silent. For a time there was nothing but the hissing of tires on the wet road and the faint squeak from the windshield wipers. Tom waited. At last, perhaps, all the missing links were coming together.

"Anyway," his father continued, "life carried on. I was accepted into chambers and managed to pass my bar exams. I even met some nice girls. But they weren't Annie. I looked for her everywhere—from the top decks of buses, in restaurants and shops, in the park. I used to run after total strangers in the street, thinking they were her. It was the mystery of the whole thing that drove me mad. I'm afraid the truth never crossed my mind."

Tom tried to picture his controlled, sophisticated father running after girls in the street. It was hard to imagine.

"One day at work, I answered the telephone and heard her voice. She had just started working at Smith & Robertson and was calling one of the partners for some advice on libel. It was like a miracle. I begged her to meet me, but she refused. I remember she said, 'My life has changed.' I couldn't think what she meant, but of course I was determined to find out. Now that I knew where she worked, it wasn't very difficult to invent some story and get hold of her address. The following Sunday I just turned up at her flat. She was living upstairs from a newsagent in a crummy old terrace in Battersea, with trucks roaring past and litter in the street. I parked the car and was just a few steps away when the front door opened and out came Annie, bumping a stroller down the steps. In the stroller was this funny little person in a pom-pommed hat." He smiled across at Tom. "You."

"What a horrible shock." Tom scowled, trying to disguise an unexpected flood of emotion.

"A wonderful surprise," his father corrected, "to find I had a son. I just knew the minute I saw you. It made sense of everything—Annie's disappearance, her peculiar reaction to me, Rose's hostility. It was all so typical of your mother—her bravery, that fierce pride of hers, that streak of secrecy she's always had. And I was so pleased. I felt an incredible elation that everything had at last come right.

"Of course it took a lot longer than that. Annie was very defensive. She had been through a bad time. We're all used to single mothers now, but in those days they were 'unmarried mothers' and much frowned upon. It was difficult to get a job or find anywhere to live. However, I'd learned my lesson by then. I took it slowly, inviting her out to a film or pushing you around Battersea Park, until eventually it seemed the right thing to get married. That's when we went to the registrar and got him to write out a new birth certificate, naming me as your father. Illegitimacy carried a stigma then, which we didn't want you to suffer. We thought we were doing our best for you. You were so young, we knew you'd never remember that I hadn't always been around."

Tom shook his head. "I don't remember. But I always knew there was something odd. Did I come to your wedding?"

"No. Annie said it wouldn't be right. But afterward we had an informal reception in the garden. It was summer. I had a flat in Islington then. We tried to make the party special for you. We had a huge chocolate concoction instead of the usual wedding cake, and that disgusting stripey ice cream you liked and—"

A vivid image of bright clouds falling out of the sky surged up from Tom's memory. "The balloons!" he burst out.

"Good Lord, you remember that? Yes, we let them go out of the top window, twenty or more. I can still remember the look on your face."

"And didn't I have some sort of scarf thing?" Tom frowned, in the grip now of some sweet, elusive recollection. "I remember I got it wet when I wasn't supposed to, but nobody told me off."

His father laughed aloud. "The tie of your sailor suit! Heavens, I'd forgotten. You got it covered in food and drink and grass and dirt until it looked like some horrible old kitchen rag. Though you did look very sweet."

His face grew sober. "We made sure you weren't in any pictures. We were covering our tracks already. It was the beginning of the lie. I see now that it was a foolish course. Too many people knew the truth. Someone was bound to make a slip one day. And I'm sorry, Tom. I apologize for not having trusted you with the truth and making you unhappy." He reached out to grip Tom's knee briefly. "I didn't mean to. Forgive me."

Tom had been only half listening. That distant memory had sparked off others: the birthday when his father had set up a children's climbing frame in the garden overnight that was the envy of his friends; the Christmas when they had gone shopping in Harrods to buy a present for Mum and eaten lunch at Wheeler's, sitting up at the marble-topped bar; the time his father had taken him night-fishing for shark in Cornwall. It was true that he could not remember a time without his father's presence.

"It's all right," Tom mumbled inadequately. "I mean, I wish you'd told me, but I suppose I can see why you didn't."

His father let out his breath. "Well, we'll try to do better in future. No more secrets. I'm afraid it's hard for parents to judge the moment when their children have grown up."

Tom nodded, warmed by the compliment.

"And you have to bear in mind that we were very young. Annie was only nineteen when she got pregnant."

Nineteen! Tom couldn't help remembering his boorish visit to Rebecca last week. If he had had his way, she could be pregnant now and himself a prospective father.

"I'm sorry you had to find out like this," his father went on. "It clearly made you unhappy." He hesitated. A note of puzzlement crept into his voice. "I can understand that discovering your birth certificate was a shock and made you start wondering if I really was your father, but what I still can't quite grasp is why you fixed on Jordan Hope."

Tom shifted in his seat, watching the sprawl of outer London flash past. "I found this old photo of him in Mum's trunk. My scout thought it was a picture of me, and quite honestly it did look a bit like me. I thought it was weird that Mum had kept it all this time, and when I asked her about it she told me all sorts of ridiculous lies."

"I see," his father said uncertainly. "At least—I know Hope was at Oxford at the same time as us, but so were thousands of people. I'm sure Annie never mentioned him at the time. I wasn't aware she even knew him until his name started appearing in the papers. She told me that Rose had known him slightly." He frowned. For the first time his fluency faltered. "I mean . . . who exactly was in this photo? Do you still have it?"

I think she may have had a one-night stand with Jordan. Rose's words flashed a sudden, electrifying warning in Tom's brain. Here was something he knew, or had reason to suspect, that his father didn't. It would be like Rebecca finding out he'd gone to bed with

Rose. The photograph was in his suitcase at home. Tom had pored over it so often that every detail was clear in his mind. He remembered its powerful aura of intimacy and happiness and the inscription: *For Annie, my two-times girl. Love always. J.*

Tom looked at his father, reading doubt and confusion in his face. He had to protect him.

"I think it must have been a party," he said casually. "There was Jordan Hope and Mum and a whole group of people in some garden. I had the photo in Southport with me, but one day I got so angry that I tore it up. I threw the pieces off Southport pier."

Tom looked his father innocently in the eye and shrugged. "Sorry, Dad."

37

All Right Now

As the taxi rumbled northward through the heavy morning traffic, the anxiety that had kept Annie awake all through the flight
renewed its grip on her imagination. What was she going to say to
Tom—and to Edward? She had a nightmare vision of the two of
them sitting at the kitchen table in judgment upon her, waiting for
her explanation. When the taxi drew up outside the house, she thrust
bills into the driver's hand, overtipping wildly, too impatient to wait
for her change. The front door was double-locked. Inside, the house
was silent. Annie picked up a piece of paper from the hall table.

*I've taken Tom to my meeting in Nottingham. He should be
back by midafternoon.—E.*

Annie's heart lurched at his chilly brevity. Why had he taken Tom
away? What were they telling each other? Edward didn't say when
he would be home. On impulse she ran down the hall to her study,
still wearing her coat, and tugged at the deep bottom drawer of her
desk. It was crammed with notes and cards from Edward—birthdays, anniversaries, valentines. There were no great love letters, just
a steady accumulation of small messages of love that she had popped
in this drawer, incapable of throwing them away. Annie picked one
out at random: a Cartier-Bresson photograph of a couple kissing
passionately. "Happy fifteenth anniversary—here's to the next
fifty." There were hundreds of them: foolish, funny, tender, self-
mocking—a twenty-year reiteration of love.

And what had she given in return? *Not enough* was the answer.
A corner of her heart, small but lovingly tended, she had reserved
for Jordan.

In a sudden revelation, Annie understood that it was not just for
Tom's sake that she had kept the circumstances of his birth secret.
She too had wanted to cling to the mystery of his conception, to the
memory of that magical, marvelous night under the willow trees. It
was shockingly unfair to Edward. No matter whose sperm had produced Tom, it was Edward who had taught him cricket, nursed him
through measles, showed up on Parents' Day. Edward was his real
father.

What were the two of them talking about, closeted in the car?
Remembering her last sight of Tom, distraught and angry, Annie
could imagine him disowning Edward and claiming Jordan as his
father. He would show Edward the photograph as proof. Edward
would recognize the dress she had worn to the ball and guess the
rest. He would never forgive her. The image of Edward hurling her
engagement ring into the river rose in her mind like an omen.

Annie slammed the drawer shut. There was nothing to do but
wait and see. She would unpack, change, buy something Edward
especially liked for dinner—and hope. Collecting her suitcase, she
heaved it up to her bedroom. Out of habit she switched on the radio,
just in time to catch the tail end of a news bulletin. *As the American
people awake to a day that will determine their future for the next
four years, we go to our Washington correspondent*—Annie turned
it off hastily. She would not allow herself to think about Jordan.
She absolutely forbade it. Nevertheless, as she hung up her clothes
and changed into slacks and a favorite old cashmere sweater, she
kept finding that she had unconsciously crossed her fingers.

By midafternoon, she had done her shopping, eaten a late lunch
of cheese on toast, and was peeling parsnips in the basement kitchen,
when she heard the front door slam and Tom's heavy tread in the
hall.

"I'm down here," she shouted.

There was a muffled reply, then the sound of him bounding upstairs. Annie's stomach tightened. For no very good reason, she
grabbed her hairbrush from her handbag and swept it vigorously
across her scalp. She heard him coming down again. Instinctively
she put on the kettle and rested her hands on the kitchen counter,
twisting her wedding ring, waiting.

Her first, irrelevant thought as her son appeared in the doorway was how handsome he looked. He was wearing a subtly colored gray suit and blue button-down shirt with a patterned tie in vibrant yellows that should have set a new standard in vulgarity but somehow looked supremely sophisticated. *I produced this,* she thought with a sudden thrill of wonder and pride—this handsome, six-foot, alien male. She felt faintly in awe of him.

"You look marvelous!" she exclaimed, then laughed to hear the surprise in her voice.

"Present from Rose." Tom ruffled his hair self-consciously. He lounged into the room. "Pretty cool, eh?"

"I should say." Annie felt a pang of something almost like jealousy. "You've always screamed blue murder when I wanted to buy you a suit."

"Mum," Tom reproved gently, "this is Armani."

Annie tried not to gape. Since when had Tom known the difference between Armani and army surplus? "Gosh," she said humbly.

Tom sat down at the kitchen table and reached casually for an apple from the fruit bowl. "Good trip?" he asked.

"Very successful, thanks. I gather we were both in New York at the same time." Annie's heart sank. This was sounding like a business dinner.

"Mmm." Tom nodded through a mouthful of apple, not volunteering more. Annie was trying to gauge his mood. If she wasn't certain that he must be very angry with her, she would have said he was relaxed, even happy.

"Tea?" she asked, giving herself time.

"Yeah, okay."

Annie poured it into mugs and carried them across to the table, seating herself opposite Tom. Treat him like an equal, not your son, Rose had advised. Well, she would try.

"It's lovely to have you back, darling. And before we go further, I'd like to apologize for not being straightforward with you about the circumstances of your birth and not taking proper account of your feelings when you discovered the truth. It was very wrong of me. It was only because I was frightened that it would make you unhappy. I'm sorry."

Tom was gazing at her in some astonishment, forgetting to chew his apple.

"It's all right," he said awkwardly.

"No, it's not all right. I can see that you feel there's a mystery that we've never explained, Edward and I, and it's time to put that right." Annie paused. She still hadn't decided what to tell Tom. She knew she owed him the truth. On the other hand, what was the truth? Did she have the right to make Tom and Edward unhappy by telling them about Jordan, when for all she knew Edward was Tom's true, biological father?

"It's all right, Mum," Tom repeated. "Dad's explained everything."

"He has?" Annie tried to hide her bewilderment. How could Edward explain what he didn't know? "Everything?" she asked.

Tom nodded. "All about how you two quarreled, and how you ran off and Dad couldn't find you—and then he did. You could have told me before, you know. It's not nearly as bad as some of the things I've been imagining. I've already told Rebecca about being illegitimate. She thinks it's romantic."

Tom grinned, taking Annie's breath away. Then he sobered. "Except Dad made me see it wasn't very romantic from your point of view—I mean having a baby on your own when you were so young, without anyone to help."

Annie felt a lump form in her throat. "That was my fault," she said. "I didn't want Edward to feel that he had to look after you."

"But he wanted to, he said." Tom frowned. "Didn't he?"

"Oh, he did." Annie was quick to reassure him. "He was thrilled when he found out about you. But I couldn't guess that he would react that way. Besides"—she sipped her tea—"there was something else."

Even from the other side of the table she felt Tom tense. "What?" he asked warily.

Annie began to describe the day long ago when she had gone to tell her mother that she was pregnant, only to learn that she herself had been conceived out of wedlock.

"I don't think my mother wanted a baby—not at all. She couldn't understand why I wanted to keep you." Annie leaned urgently toward Tom. "That's what I want you to understand: It was my choice to have you and to keep you. That's another reason I kept the truth from you. I never wanted you to think that you had just been a—an annoying accident I had to put up with. It wasn't true. *I wanted you.*"

"Oh." Tom was silent for a long time, staring into his tea. When at last he looked up, there was a gleam of amusement in his eyes. "So does that mean you're sort of illegitimate too?"

Annie couldn't resist running around the table to hug him. He took it quite well, patting her shoulder as if she were a nice old horse.

"And is that why you never talked about your mother?"

"Partly." Annie told Tom about seeing her mother and meeting Lee, trying to convey her feelings of sorrow and joy and disappointment. "That's another reason I wanted to protect you, to make you feel just like any other boy. I didn't have much of a family life, and I missed it. I know it can be claustrophobic, but sometimes it's nice to have a family, if only as a sort of useful trampoline to bounce you back into the world."

Tom nodded slowly. "That's what Rose said."

"Really? I must say I've never seen Rose as a champion of family values."

"You were the one who chose her to be my moral guardian," Tom said teasingly. "Isn't that what a godmother is?" He fiddled with his mug. "She said some sensible things."

"Oh? Like what?"

Tom gave her a look she could not quite interpret. "Like telling me that I should forgive you your wild past."

"Ah." Annie felt herself blushing. What on earth had Rose said to him? As she fumbled for a sensible reply, she heard the door slam again—did no one in her family realize that it was possible to close doors gently?—and a familiar double thump as schoolbags hit the hall floor. The girls were home. She could hear them squabbling companionably as they scuffed down the stairs.

Tom jumped up and thrust something into her hand. "You'd better have this," he mumbled.

It was a plain white envelope. Annie pushed it into a pocket as her daughters burst into the room in their blue-and-yellow uniforms. Emma, as always, looked as if she had been put through the spin cycle of the washing machine, while Cassie was as stylishly disheveled as if each twist of her cardigan sleeves and each wantonly unfastened button had been arranged for the runway by a haute couture designer. To Annie's eyes, they both looked impossibly fresh and beautiful, two dark-haired, grave-eyed girls out of an early Italian painting.

"Tom!" Emma squeaked excitedly, rushing over to him. "What are you doing here? Don't you look lovely?"

"Hi, girls." Tom gave them a lordly wave. "My godmother just flew me to New York for a long weekend," he added, with stunning aplomb. "Didn't you know?"

Annie went over to her daughters and hugged them vigorously. "How wonderful to see you!" she exclaimed, her eyes moistening with emotion.

"Loosen up, Ma." Cassie rolled her eyes at Emma. "Anyone would think you'd been away a lifetime, not just a few days." She turned back to Tom. "That's a wicked suit. I suppose Rose bought it for you. It's not fair. When is she going to invite me to New York?"

Tom eyed her critically. "Don't call us. We'll call you."

Annie went back to her dinner preparations, chopping onions for the bread sauce, laying bacon over the pheasants, covering the vegetables with water, as she listened to her children chatter. Life was back to normal. She liked it that way. Soon the girls persuaded Tom upstairs to check out the rest of his new wardrobe; Annie was left alone. She began to assemble ingredients for a blackberry-and-apple pie and turned on the radio for company. This time, when the election report came on, she could not stop herself listening. According to the exit polls, Jordan was almost certain to carry most of the East Coast states, which had been the first to vote. Hurray! His opponent would probably win in Indiana, South Carolina, Virginia, Oklahoma—

"Oh, shut up!" Annie snapped at the radio, slicing apples viciously.

But the pundits gathered in the newsroom seemed to agree that a return of the Democrats to the White House after twelve years looked likely. That certainly was the verdict of Harry's Bar in Paris, where exiled Americans had traditionally conducted their own elections since 1924. In sixty-eight years they had been wrong only once.

Annie listened, wholly engrossed, while she laid the table and set out candles, until a time check alerted her to how late it was. Edward would be home soon, and she was sticky and bedraggled from cooking. She threw the pheasants into the oven, grabbed her handbag, and fled upstairs to run a bath. She had planned to be dressed up and immaculate when he returned. Instead, she was only just stepping into the water when she heard the front door bang. She nearly jumped out again, embarrassed as a schoolgirl, then forced herself to relax and wait. Edward had seen her naked before.

She heard his quick tread on the stairs, then the creak of the floorboards as he crossed the bedroom to the bathroom door. It swung open slowly. Edward stood in the doorway, hands in his coat pockets, looking at her across the room.

"You're back," he said with that impassive look she knew so well.

"Of course I'm back." Even to her own ears, Annie sounded horribly sprightly. "Can't you smell the pheasant?"

"Are we celebrating?"

"I hope so." Annie smiled tentatively, sinking deeper into the water under his stern gaze. "You've still got your coat on."

"Have I?" Edward took it off and ducked out of sight for a moment to hang it up. Annie waited for him to reappear.

"Tom seems in a very good mood," she offered. "I don't know what you said to him, but he seems different—calm, sure of himself."

"Good." Edward sat down in the wicker chair at the foot of the bath.

"So what did you tell him?" Annie persisted.

He eyed her mildly. "The truth, of course."

Annie hesitated, then summoned her courage. "Edward, I'm sorry we quarreled on the phone. I'm sorry for what I said. It was unfair and unforgivable. You've been the best possible father to Tom. I realize now how cruel I was to cheat you out of the early years. I never thought so before. I thought I was being noble."

"You're wrong." He paused ominously. "It isn't unforgivable," Edward went on, "because I forgive you. And I understand why you did it, and so does Tom now. The truth is, I don't mind what you do, as long as you love me."

He gave her such a warm, sad smile that Annie could hardly bear it. She sat up in the bath, clasping her knees. "Edward," she began, "there's something I should explain."

"No!" Edward sprang from the chair, making an odd gesture with his hand as if warding off a blow. He paced to the other end of the room and turned back to her, gripping the towel rail. "No more words. I don't want to hear anything I won't be able to forget." He took a breath and said more calmly, "It's enough that you're back and that there are no more secrets in the family, and that we're truly together." Edward plucked at the bath towel under his hand and came over to her, holding it up.

"Come on, you beautiful mermaid. I'm starving."

Annie stood up, water running down her body, and stepped into the warm embrace of the towel. Edward wound it about her, pulling her possessively close. She rested there a moment, eyes closed, ear to his heartbeat. This was how their love affair had begun, on a chilly night in Oxford when Edward had stepped from the shadows and enfolded her in his cloak. She had always known that he was the man for her. She could feel the depth of his anxiety and his passion. Tonight she would find a way to obliterate the last of his doubts.

While Edward went down to see to the wine, Annie put on her clothes, dressing up her slacks with a shimmery silk blouse and earrings, and spent extra time on her makeup and hair—enough to make her children whistle at her as she came down the stairs into the kitchen.

"I basted the pheasants," Emma announced with a pink face. "Was that right?"

"Absolutely inspired." Annie hugged her.

When everyone was ready and the candles had been lit, Annie carried the platter of pheasants to the table. Edward produced a bottle of champagne, eased out the cork with a gentle pop, and poured everyone a glass.

"What's this for?" Emma asked, putting her finger in the bubbles and licking it.

"A toast," Edward said solemnly, "to your mother—"

"*Me?*" Annie looked at him in surprise.

"—who, Rose tells me, has pulled off a two-million-dollar book deal."

There was silence for a millisecond before Cassie asked, "Are we rich? Can I go to New York and buy Armani clothes?"

"When you're as wise and mature as your brother perhaps," Annie answered, smiling into Tom's blue eyes.

He held her gaze. "Can we watch the election on TV after dinner?"

When the last piece of pie had been consumed, Annie urged everyone upstairs to the living room while she cleared away and made coffee. Now that the moment had come, she felt too nervous to watch the election. She didn't think she could bear to see Jordan's face it he lost. And if he won, she wasn't sure she wanted anyone to see hers. When she could delay no longer, she carried up the coffee tray. Edward and Tom were on the sofa, the girls sprawled on the floor in front of a coal fire. Nothing much seemed to be happening, just a screenful of talking heads.

"Why do they keep talking about a 'young' generation taking over?" Cassie was complaining. "Jordan Hope is forty-six. He's got gray hair!"

"Only round the edges," Emma pointed out fairly. "I think he's rather dishy. And he's miles younger than the other one, who fought in the First World War."

"Second, birdbrain." Tom walloped her over the head with a cushion.

When the squabble had died down, Annie concentrated on the television. Gradually it dawned on her that everyone was acting as if Jordan had already won.

"Yeah!" Tom bounced on the sofa. "He's got another state. He's bound to win now."

"You're for Hope, then, are you?" Edward asked. "Why?"

"He's so energetic, so alive. He really wants to help people—like you, Dad." Tom sipped his coffee and then added, "Besides, he wears great suits."

"I suppose Rose will be very well positioned if he wins," Edward commented.

Annie looked at him. "In what way?"

"Well, isn't she a friend of his?"

"Yes, but—" Annie fell silent. "I mean, it was very long ago." Edward was right, though, she realized. It had not occurred to her before that Rose might have a personal stake in all this. Could Rose have been playing a double game all along? Friend or ambitious editor: Which would come first?

Cassie uncurled herself elegantly from the floor. "If the drama's over, I'm going to bed," she announced with a yawn.

"Me too." Emma scrambled after her.

Annie waved them good night, her eyes fixed to the screen, which was flashing up scenes of jubilation across the country. Two more states fell to Jordan. They were talking of a landslide. A statistician came on, standing in front of a bank of giant bar charts. Tom drained his coffee and said it was time to hit the pillow. He wanted to set off for Oxford early the next day. Edward thought he had seen enough too, but when Annie rose to follow, he shook his head at her.

"No, you watch if you want to. I need to have a shower first. I'll see you upstairs."

Annie reached her hand over the back of the sofa. "I won't be long—promise. You won't go to bed without me?"

Edward took her hand and rubbed it gently. "I'll come and carry you up if I have to."

He was at the door, when something clicked in Annie's head. "Edward . . . it was you who sent me champagne at the Algonquin, wasn't it?"

"Who else?" The door shut behind him.

When Annie turned back to the screen, it was showing pictures of a little American town, the crowded streets hung with flags. The camera panned across stone and clapboard houses, with deep porches and scraps of front lawn. Even before the reporter said the words "Indian Bluffs" Annie knew that this was Jordan's hometown. She leaned forward, transfixed. There it was, just as he had described, the old schoolhouse with the bell on top, the white Baptist chapel, the grocery store shaded by a maple with astonishing bright leaves. And there was Jordan's childhood house, small and ordinary-looking, and a view of the Mississippi River, so vast it took her breath away. The Cherwell must have seemed like a ditch in comparison.

Before she had taken it all in, the scene changed. Another reporter was shouting into the microphone against the baying of an ecstatic crowd. This was a clip from Jordan's airport reception at Jefferson City, where he had returned to the governor's mansion that morning. Drum majorettes in high white boots and very little else twirled batons with red, white, and blue streamers. There were men in cowboy hats with HOPE rosettes in the hatband, women in shorts, and T-shirts that proclaimed: I LOVE HOPE. And suddenly there he was, dressed in jeans and a tan suede jacket, smiling like an Oscar winner and shaking the hands stretched out to him. Annie pressed her fingers to her mouth, gazing at his face. Then he moved aside, and Annie saw his wife. She peered closer, trying to read the character of this neat, smiling woman, looking smaller and more vulnerable than Annie had expected.

When the telephone rang, Annie reached impatiently for it next to the sofa, then realized that it was her work line ringing. Immediately she thought of Sebastian. Had something gone wrong with the American deal? Dragging her eyes from the screen, she ran into the small back room and picked up the receiver. It sounded like a party. There was a roar of conversation and muffled squeals of excitement.

"Sebastian?" she asked doubtfully, when no one spoke.

The noise receded, as if a door had been closed. "Are you alone?" a voice asked.

"Jordan!" Annie gave an incredulous laugh. "I've just been watching you on television. You were getting off a plane. I've seen your house and your little town and the river." She tugged at her hair, to stop herself babbling. ". . . Is anything wrong?"

"Nothing's wrong. I just called to say thank you."

"For what?"

"For telling me about Tom," he said, his voice low. "It was kind of a turning point for me. Last week I was almost beginning to lose faith in myself—wondering if I was just a smiling dummy with nothing inside, begging the world to love me. I'd even started writing my speech conceding victory. You changed that. You can't imagine what it was like seeing you again, remembering the old days, and knowing I had a son."

"We don't *know* that," Annie said gently. "We'll never know for sure."

She heard Jordan sigh. "Maybe it isn't the biological truth, but for me it's a kind of moral truth. It feels right. It makes sense of all that doubt and turmoil at Oxford. It makes up for not having kids with Ginny. When I saw that picture of Tom, I suddenly felt as if I had a personal stake in the next generation. I was darned if I was going to let the other guy win. I think that knowing about Tom will make me a better president."

"You'll be a brilliant president," Annie said. Hot tears stung her eyes.

"It means that what we felt for each other all those years ago was real. It wasn't true what I said in Chicago, in that funny old hotel room. It wasn't just sex, was it?"

"No," she whispered.

"Well, not *just* sex, anyway," Jordan teased, trying to make her laugh. "By the way, who's Sebastian?"

"One of my lovers, of course," Annie said lightly. With a wave of anguish she realized that she would never see him again. This would be the last time they spoke. She swallowed hard, determined not to cry.

"Annie, I wish—" But she would never know what he wished. There was another burst of celebratory noise at Jordan's end, and a woman's voice yelling "Come *on!*"

"I have to go," Jordan said urgently. "I'm sorry. Thanks for everything. I won't forget."

"Good luck!" Annie called as the line went dead. She wondered if he had heard.

For a long moment she stood quietly in her study, staring into the garden. Then she took a tissue from her desk drawer, blew her nose firmly, and went back into the living room. She switched off the television. She had seen all she needed to. Jordan had won. Tom had not stopped him. It seemed, in fact, that he had helped him. And she had made the right decision, all those years ago. She was glad not to be the wife standing in the shadows. She was herself, Annie Hamilton. A new career awaited her and, upstairs, Edward's warm, familiar presence.

The fire was still burning brightly. Annie squatted down to scatter the coals and felt something jab her thigh. She reached into her pocket and drew out the envelope Tom had given her earlier. She had forgotten all about it. Her heart jumped when she saw what was inside: the photograph that Rose had taken of her and Jordan the morning after the Magdalen Ball. Annie knelt on the floor and peered closely at the faded image in the firelight. It was years since she had seen it. A flood of nostalgia washed over her. She couldn't help smiling. There was Jordan, young and carefree and irresistible, with his shirt unbuttoned and his laughing eyes creased against the sun. She rubbed a finger gently over his face and sighed, then turned the photograph over. Her heart melted at the sight of his sloping American handwriting. The old song ran through her head. *Love me two times, girl.* "Oh, I did," she whispered. "I did."

She looked again at the image of the two of them, at Jordan's bare forearm clasping her tight, at the intimate curve of her body into his. Tom's instincts had been impeccable. She was filled with amazement and gratitude. Giving her back the photograph was a gesture of tact and grace worthy of Edward. On the other hand, the eyes that looked out at her from the faded old picture—those eyes, surely, were also the eyes of her son.

Annie roused herself. The picture had caused enough trouble. Her final glance was at herself—at the glowing face and tumbling hair of the girl she once was, that she was no longer. With a resolute gesture, she held the picture to the fire. The shiny surface blistered and blackened and spurted into flame. She twisted it this way and that, then dropped the little square of burning paper into the grate and watched until the last corner was consumed.

EPILOGUE

*R*ose sat at the computer in her darkened study, still wearing the scarlet dress that had caused such a sensation at her election party. It was four in the morning, but sleep was out of the question. Entering the list of files, she brought down the highlighter bar to 'SPECIAL.REL' and tapped the "Delete" key. Immediately the screen blinked at her: "Delete SPECIAL.REL? No/Yes?" Rose's hand hovered over the keyboard: One tap of her forefinger, and the whole thing would disappear.

Rose had promised herself that she would wipe the file if Jordan was elected president. She had no time for God, but she did have a shadowy concept of some giant ledger in the sky that balanced favors given with favors received. Jordan was on his way to the White House, where she wanted him; in return, she ought to consign the scandal of his illegitimate son to oblivion. But now that the moment had come, she hesitated.

She stood up and paced restlessly round the room, pausing at the window to raise the blind and look out at the city she had conquered. After tonight's spectacular success, there could be no doubt of that. It had been the kind of all-American party that only an English genius could have conceived and orchestrated. Rose had hired a huge loft space in Soho that perfectly combined Sixties casualness with the new Nineties disdain for ostentation. *Le tout* New York had crammed into the industrial iron-meshed elevator, decorated with red, white, and blue balloons, and pronounced it *fun*: senators and anchorwomen, millionaires and rock stars; society women in Versace and diamonds, who had hardly ever been farther downtown than Lord & Taylor; busty arrivistes in leather miniskirts and peroxide crops who had only ever gone uptown to neck in Central Park. The photographers and gossip columnists were in seventh heaven. In one corner the latest supermodel wilted anorectically before a famous American writer in his trademark white suit. In another, the latest Oscar winner flashed her horsy teeth at a handsome young Kennedy. On the dot of midnight, that new English novelist with a face like a bloodhound, who was covering the party up for *Harper's*, had passed out dramatically in the arms of a famously camp painter.

Music from Jordan Hope's baby-boomer generation had played all night—the Supremes, the Rolling Stones, Joni Mitchell, Bob Dylan, the Doors. Rose had raided the model agencies for the prettiest boys and girls in town to act as waiters. Dressed in jeans and white T-shirts, they had served minihamburgers, oysters, Cajun delicacies, and the special brand of corn chips Jordan was known to favor. To drink, there was champagne, American beer in cans, and Ozark Mountain Spring Water. All evening giant television screens relayed the election drama as it unfolded. After Jordan's acceptance speech, the waiters had poured more champagne and handed round slices of Mississippi mud pie.

The event had been original and hugely enjoyable. It would not be forgotten. The society pages would be plastered with photographs and reports. Rose's status would soar, transforming her from trivial magazine queen to an opinion-former, a broker between the worlds of politics and the media. Her network of friends and contacts included the man who was now president. Rose intended to be a frequent guest at the White House over the next four years. She would make sure that Jordan knew how much he owed her. Not only had she averted the scandal of Tom; she had neutralized someone much closer to home.

Rose had enjoyed her game of cat and mouse with Rick. He had been smart enough to guess at some scandal threatening Jordan, but without names he was nowhere. Rick was a control freak. He hated anyone knowing something he didn't. If she played him right, she might be able to keep him interested right through the presidency.

Rose had not forgotten the humiliation and pain she had endured in that Harley Street clinic twenty-two years ago. Yes, Rick had paid for the damned thing, but that had been the limit of his involvement.

He had never shown the slightest sympathy, never asked afterward if she was all right, never apologized. Now she could yank his leash. Rose sighed with satisfaction. She had eaten her cake, and had it too. She had helped Annie, as she had promised. She had distracted Tom from his dangerous quest—that had been more fun than she expected. In return she had a foothold in the White House. She could persuade Rick to give her profiles when she wanted them, and she had a link to the president himself. One day she would find an opportunity to lure Jordan to a quiet corner of the Rose Garden and tell him, oh so regretfully, the truth about Rick Goodman. She was looking forward to it.

Rose had begun recording the story of Jordan, Annie, and Tom as a form of insurance. It was not impossible that some reporter could have got on to Tom and leaked the scandal; Rose couldn't endure the notion that someone else might get the jump on her. Now the danger had passed; it would be foolhardy to preserve the evidence.

Still she hesitated. It was such a great story: the illegitimate son searching for his father, the ambitious politician; the pretty, sympathetic girl who falls from grace; even the scheming, go-between editrix, always calculating the angles, figuring the pitch. She could just see the movie—with Anjelica Huston playing her part. At last she could be tall! With legs!

Rose turned back into the room eerily lit from the blue screen. That bloody cursor was still winking at her: "Delete SPECIAL.REL? No/Yes." Rose could not help feeling that it would be a terrible shame to waste it. One day, when her stock had peaked and some young whippersnapper threatened to cut her off at the knees, as she had done to many a rival, she might need a good story. Reelection time was not that far away: Who knew what skeletons might have popped out of Jordan and Ginny Hope's cupboard by then? Rose wouldn't want to forgo the chance to play her trump card.

Rose waggled her head in a way that her close colleagues would recognize as the sign of a deliciously intriguing, slightly naughty, hugely salable idea scorching its path through her brain. She shook back her bangles with a defiant flourish and with an immaculately buffed fingernail tapped: "No."

· A NOTE ON THE TYPE ·

The typeface used in this book is a version of Sabon, originally designed in the 1960s by Jan Tschichold (1902–1974) at the behest of a consortium of manufacturers of metal type. As one who began as an outspoken design revolutionary—calling for the elimination of serifs, scorning revivals of historic typefaces—Tschichold seemed an odd choice, but he met the challenge brilliantly: The typeface was to be based on the fonts of the sixteenth-century French typefounder Claude Garamond but five percent narrower; it had to be identical for three different processes, working around the quirks of each, such as linotype's inability to "kern" (allow one character into the space of another, the way the top of a lowercase f overhangs other letters). Aside from Sabon, named for a sixteenth-century French punch cutter to avoid problems of attribution to Garamond, Tschichold is best remembered as the designer of the Penguin paperbacks of the late 1940s.